A collection of contemporary and classic stories

D1346664

The Dedalus Book of
*F*EMMES
*F*ATALES

Edited by Brian Stableford

DEDALUS

EASTERN *Arts*

SUPPORTED BY THE EASTERN ARTS ASSOCIATION

Published in the UK by Dedalus Limited,
Langford Lodge, St Judith's Lane, Sawtry, Cambs, PE17 5XE

ISBN 0 946626 77 4

First published in 1992
Compilation copyright © Brian Stableford 1992
Introductory essay copyright © Brian Stableford 1992
All the contemporary stories are copyright © their respective authors 1992
Translations of 'The Metamorphoses of the Vampire' and 'Arachne'
copyright © Francis Amery 1992

Printed in England by Clays Ltd, St Ives plc

A C.I.P. listing for this title is available on request

Dedalus would like to express its gratitude to Aysha Rafaele for her assistance
in the preparation of this book.

Dedalus would like to thank Eastern Arts for their generous support in
producing this book, with especial thanks to Don Watson and
Alison Blair-Underwood.

CONTENTS

ILLUSTRATIONS

THE SIREN SONG OF SEXUALITY

The sirens, half-bird and half-woman, lived on the island of Anthemöessa. Opinions differ as to whether they numbered two or three, or whether their songs were accompanied by musical instruments, but there is unanimity as to the nature of their song: it drove men mad, causing them to lose their memories of wives and children, hearth and home. Deprived of their will to resist, the luckless sailors who heard the sirens sing would plunge into the water and swim towards the isle; many never reached it, and those who did lay listless upon the shore, utterly bewitched, until they wasted away. The shores of Anthemöessa shone white in the sunlight, littered as they were with bleached bones.

Such is the myth of the *femme fatale* in its elementary form. She is irresistibly attractive; the intoxication of her presence overrides all other loves, all dutiful obligations and every instinct of self-preservation. Those who follow her lure are lost, and are usually doomed to ignominious extinction.

Two heroes, having been forewarned by rumour, did contrive to avoid destruction by the sirens. The *Argo* steered past their isle because Orpheus fought fire with fire, drowning out their song with the equally powerful music of his lyre. Odysseus was even cleverer, and also more ambitious; he stopped the ears of his crewmen with wax, so that they could not hear the song, and had himself securely bound to the mast of his ship, so that he would be able to hear it without being able to respond. Ironically enough, this ruse was suggested to him by another *femme fatale* of his acquaintance, the sorceress Circe. He had escaped her clutches quite easily, exerting a greater attractive force upon her than she could exert upon him.

Circe forsook her own power to captivate men when she fell in love with Odysseus; such a reversal of fortune is the prescribed path by which *femmes fatales* may seek and sometimes find redemption. The irredeemable tend to find a different destiny, exemplified by the fate of the sirens. They, following their failure to entrap Odysseus, were bound by an ancient curse to fling themselves into the sea and drown. Temptresses who cannot resign themselves to become dull wives only thrive until that fateful moment comes when they lose their glamour.

The *femme fatale* is one of the most ancient mythical motifs, but she is sometimes hidden away, banished to the borderlands of folklore in order that socially-sanctioned images of woman-as-wife and woman-as-mother may take centre stage. Official morality necessarily disapproves of the power which women have to infatuate men, because that power is a threat to the marriage-contract which is one of the fundamental pillars of social order.

Official morality in all cultural traditions must come to terms with the untameability of erotic attraction one way or another; the Judaeo-Christian tradition which produced modern Western values took the path of forthright opposition. The principal weapons deployed in this war were vilification and taboo, and the guiding strategy was demonization. That is how the power of female sexuality became imaginatively incarnate in the figure of the *femme fatale*: a creature to be feared and avoided because the mere sight or sound of her is enough to obliterate other loyalties and obligations. The *femme fatale* is frequently represented as a witch or a vampire: as a mistress of black magic or a frankly supernatural being. Either way, her sexual magnetism is held to be unnatural, and her embrace injurious.

The acute discomfort which the official myth-makers of our own cultural tradition felt when confronted with the "problem" of female sexuality is nowhere more evident than in the history of Adam's lost wife, Lilith. *Genesis*, chapter 1, verse 27 describes the creation of man, observing that "male and female created he them", and yet chapter 2 finds Adam alone for some considerable time before God takes pity on his loneliness and forges Eve out of one of his ribs. Apocryphal legend reconciles the two passages by explaining that Adam's first consort was Lilith, who rebelled against the role allotted to her by the Creator and fled from Eden, borne aloft by wings which she had conjured up by magic.

Lilith's rebellion cost her dear; angels sent to bring her back warned her that if she would not accept subordination she would be accursed, and that all her children would die in infancy. Still she refused, and became instead the consort of the demon Samael, but she was deeply embittered by her treatment. Her fury and frustration made her the relentless enemy of all the newborn children of her successor, who frequently needed charms to ward her off.

Lilith's obliteration from the orthodox faith of Christianity was completed in the Authorised Version when the sole remaining citation of her name (in *Isaiah 34:14*) was dismissively translated as "screech-owl". (The Latin Vulgate uses "Lamia", a generic term for female demons which is usually used nowadays – thanks to the popularising activities of Philostratus, Robert Burton and John Keats – to refer to vampiric shape-shifting spirits which can manifest themselves as beautiful women or snakes). She survived nevertheless in oral tradition, and made a triumphant reappearance in Medieval Christian mythology, by which time she had been elevated by some writers to the status of Satan's mistress and Queen of Hell. She was rumoured to be the presiding genius of the succubi, female demons sent to earth to wring semen from righteous men by visiting them in lurid dreams, and she was given a key role in the Faust legend, as the seductress whose charms compounded and corrupted the doctor's idealistic quest for knowledge with unholy lust.

The replacement of the carnal and unsubmissive Lilith by the modest and acquiescent Eve – of mistress by wife – represents the domestication of the sexual impulse by society. But that victory could never be complete; it is not only the subsequent history of Lilith which testifies to the fact, but also the fate of Eve. The harmonious relationship which Adam and Eve initially share lasts only as long as it takes for sex to rear its ugly head. Eve is cast in the role of corrupter; she it is who is tempted by the phallic serpent to taste the fruit of the tree of knowledge of good and evil, and she in turn tempts Adam. Having accepted her subordinate position within their relationship, she is forced also to take the blame for their fall from grace. In order that she be able to play the part of dutiful wife and mother, there must of necessity be a little of the glamour of Lilith in her, for which she and all her female descendants are required to feel eternally guilty. Such is the logic of ideological warfare.

The stories of Lilith and Eve demonstrate that the social contract underlying the Western cultural tradition is awkwardly loaded; buried somewhere in the fine print is a clause which says that no matter what they do, women cannot win. The reason that they cannot win, of course, is that the demands which the contract makes of them are contradictory: *femmes fatales* are damned for not being wifely enough, wives for not being sufficiently *fatale*.

All the kinds of social order that have so far manifested themselves within the Judaeo-Christian tradition (and perhaps all other kinds of social order) are founded in the marriage tie, which determines patterns of responsibility and patterns of inheritance, and that tie must somehow be made secure. Adulterous desires pose a significant threat to social order, and if they cannot be accommodated by everyday mores they must be subject to stringent prohibition. Christianity – like the other bargain basement religions, which set out to win converts by promising salvation in return for rigorous virtue and Hell as the wages of sin – went for stringent prohibition. But it is one thing to legislate against an act; it is quite another to legislate against an emotion.

Sexual arousal is not entirely subject to the authority of conscious control. It is something which can happen whether a human being wills it or not. Moreover, in the male of the species arousal is clearly stigmatised; it cannot be denied. Despite the immensely useful invention of clothing, which helps to conceal the fact of arousal from witnesses, males cannot deny the experience of sexual arousal, and cannot help but know how feebly their desire is constrained by the bounds of marital legitimacy. The male of the species, continually embarrassed by the taboo-breaking inclinations of his unruly member, is inevitably tempted to shift the blame – and the stronger the taboos which confront him are, the stronger that temptation will become. If he has been reared in the Judaeo-Christian tradition, the temptation is likely to be overwhelming, and the strategy of blame-shifting is openly sanctioned by the holy scriptures.

"I couldn't help it," he will say. "It was *her* fault; *she tempted me.*"

This is, of course, a stupid and hypocritical excuse. It is dishonest and it is cowardly. But males of the species generally have the power to make such slanders stick, if the incentive is strong enough.

Females suffer from wayward sexual arousal too, but their situation is different even at the physical level. Arousal in females is more easily concealed, and hence more easily denied. It is easier for females to pretend – perhaps even to themselves – that they are not really carnal by nature. Anyway, women generally do not have the power to attribute blame where none really belongs; hypocrisy and dishonesty can only become blatant when backed by the kind of authority which defies contradiction.

The idea of the *femme fatale* is one of the products of this blame-shifting facility. In our cultural tradition the woman who tempts the man to forget his contractually-bound social responsibilities is not often permitted merely to be the hapless victim of his overactive hormones; she is frequently charged instead with being a demon or a witch exerting some evil supernatural force upon him. This too is an imaginative move which smacks of self-justificatory exaggeration. (Surely it could not have been the widow who lives over the hill who seduced True Thomas away from his vocation for seven long years, which flew by so quickly that they seemed but a single night? No, of course not – it must have been the Queen of the Fairies!)

In some instances the object of desire is let off this hook because the blame is shifted again, in whole or in part, to the wife of the "victim", whose own powers of attraction are adjudged to be fading, and who might, therefore have trapped him in the first place by means of some temporary charm or spell whose moral propriety must now be doubted. In either case, though, the situation is grim and the prognosis pessimistic. Somebody –

perhaps everybody – is going to suffer.

Such is the legacy of the men – they *must* have been men – who invented the story of Adam and Eve, and exiled Lilith (with extreme prejudice) from the official record.

Given all this, it is hardly surprising that when we consult the literary record of our culture we discover that it features two distinct kinds of ideal love.

The first is the social ideal. This is the kind of love which exists, or is supposed to exist, within marriage; it is essentially dutiful, and usually calm. There is no great sexual tension in married love simply because sexual intercourse is fully integrated into the relationship; lust can normally be assuaged as soon as it is aroused.

This kind of ideal love is intrinsically undramatic, and rarely recommends itself to literary celebration except as a goal to be won at last; the vast majority of run-of-the-mill love stories come to an end when a commitment to this kind of relationship has been made, all the dramatic potential created by the initial arousal thus being released. Tolstoy, in the first line of *Anna Karenina*, writes off this kind of love with the casual observation that "all happy marriages are alike" before instantly turning his lascivious contemplation to the heartache which can spring from marriages which fail to meet the standard, every single one of which he holds to be uniquely interesting.

The other kind of ideal love is essentially anti-social. This is the grand passion, born of and based in *frustrated* arousal; it is essentially spontaneous, and powerfully intoxicating. Sexual tension is intrinsic to this kind of love, which is for that very reason difficult to sustain indefinitely. In order for grand passion to endure, the pressure of lust must either be permanently unrelieved or obsessively renewed. For this reason, this second kind of ideal love may easily be reckoned a delusionary snare – a purely hypothetical ideal imaginatively extrapolated from the feelings associated with arousal – or a kind of mental aberration, a neurotic *ideé fixe*.

It is entirely natural that in spite of its evident disadvantages, men should retain a profound respect for the second kind of ideal love, and deem it in some ways more precious than the first; it is, after all, hopelessly impractical. (Whatever is practically attainable is easily taken for granted, even by those who never quite contrive to attain it; whatever is imaginable but forever out of reach always retains its power to fascinate.)

Tranquil contemplation of the second kind of ideal love may easily inspire a certain bitterness, after the celebrated pattern noted by Aesop's fable of the fox and the grapes, but it can also nurture a warm and lachrymose sentimentality. The simple fact that men continue to be capable of spontaneous arousal in spite of every ideological move they make to constrain, or explain, or shift the blame for it, ensures that many of them cannot help but retain their passionate regard for their *femmes fatales* while whatever passionate regard they once had for their wives is patiently eroded by time and familiarity. This occasions in some men a particular kind of melancholy which is uniquely bitter-sweet.

The idea of grand passion as a form of unfortunate folly verging on outright madness is, of course, familiar to us by courtesy of the mythology and the literature of the Greeks, which the Western World inherited along with all the other detritus of the Alexandrian and Roman Empires. The attitudes of the Greeks to sexual matters were somewhat different to those enshrined in the Judaeo-Christian tradition, their myth-makers having followed the strategy of accommodation rather than that of opposition. The continued influence of Classical ideas upon scholarly men has helped to increase the confusion and ambivalence which is frequently seen in literary treatments of the *femme fatale*; Circe and the sirens are far less demonic than Lilith, and can become interestingly ambiguous when seen from a viewpoint which partakes of both Classical and Christian attitudes.

Ironically, but perhaps inevitably, it was the Christian world which eventually produced a version of grand passion which sought to excuse it from being reckoned either foolish or insane, seeking to defuse its disruptive power by representing it as something potentially noble and sacred. The myth of courtly love first popularised by the troubadours of the twelfth and thirteenth centuries argued that a grand passion, indefinitely sustained by virtue of its careful non-consummation, might – if properly handled – become a fountainhead of virtuous inspiration. The idea was widely touted that a knight's love for his liege-lord's wife, provided always that it remained a chaste and unspoken adoration from a discreet distance, might increase his devotion to the lord and to his knightly duties. This attempted accommodation of the notion of grand passion within the ideology of chivalry was to cast a literary shadow every bit as confused as that cast by Classical representations.

That grand passion has and always has had relatively little effect on the conduct of real life is easily demonstrated by consulting the works of serious historians, who very rarely need to refer to it in order to explain the actions of men of the past. The situation in literature is very different, because literature's primary concern is the dramatic and the routines of social order are inherently undramatic; any sensible definition or explanation of what we mean by the word "dramatic" is forced to refer to the threatened or actual breakdown of social order. For this reason, there is nothing more dramatic than grand passion. As has already been noted, it is Anna Karenina's adulterous passion which makes her a fit subject for literary consideration; had she been happily married there would have been nothing to attract the interest of Tolstoy or anyone else. Similarly, it is the fact that Tristan's love for Isolde, and Lancelot's for Guinevere, tried so very hard hard to pass, *but ultimately failed*, the test of chaste containment which fits them for the role of tragic heroes in literature.

In the real world, *femmes fatales* are rare, and whenever a candidate for that status emerges she is quickly shifted from the realm of history to the realm of legend. The reality is immediately obscured, and soon completely obliterated, by the glamour of the myth. There *was* a real Cleopatra, but she has been comprehensively eclipsed by the mythical Cleopatra; nor is it simply her antiquity which has allowed this to happen. Even in the modern world, attempts by historians to rescue the actual, tawdry, ineffectual Mata Hari from the cloak of mystique with which the forces of rumour and anecdote instantly draped her were always doomed to fail.

The gulf between reality and supernatural literature is, of course, even more exaggerated than that between reality and mundane fiction. It is in literary fantasy that the delusory aspect of grand passion really comes into its own, because the imaginative extrapolation of hypothetical ideals to their logical (or illogical) limit is there permissible. In fantastic fiction the force of grand passion can be given literal supernatural force and sexual arousal can be literally magical. Passion can easily be credited with the power to defy the bounds of everyday reality.

In mundane fiction, grand passion can have only two outcomes: it can be domesticated, decaying into mere married love; or it can lead inexorably to stark tragedy. (The latter is, of course, the preferred outcome in purely aesthetic terms, although there do exist readers so addicted to happy endings that they would rather have seen Romeo and Juliet married than dead.) Fantastic fiction, by contrast, offers the opportunity to discover more exotic escape-routes from this dilemma, as well as the opportunity to remake – and perhaps correct – the myths and legends which embody our attitudes to sexuality. In fantastic literature, the vaguely supernatural quality with which the mundane *femme fatale* is uneasily imbued can be brought into sharp and explicit focus, and completely unfettered. It is through the medium of supernatural fiction that literary men can attempt to come to terms with the essence and the archetype of the *femme fatale*.

The modern literary history of the *femme fatale* begins with the Romantic Movement. The Romantics – diehard champions of the emotions against the intellect – took it upon themselves to undertake a sceptical re-evaluation of received ideas of evil, and their sympathy for grand passion inevitably produced numerous accounts of *femmes fatales* which interrogated all aspects of the idea. Even before the advent of the Romantics some such reappraisal had begun in France, as exemplified by Jacques Cazotte's remarkable short novel *Le Diable Amoureux* (1772; tr. as *The Devil in Love*), where the demonic seductress Biondetta evidently fascinates the author as much as the hero, and is far from being a spirit of pure malevolence.

In the horror stories, whose production the Romantic Movement greatly encouraged, the *femme fatale* often does appear as a straightforward force of evil. The seductress Matilda in Matthew Gregory Lewis's *The Monk* (1796) is a cardinal example, as is the central character of Goethe's necrophiliac ballad *Die Braut von Korinth* (1798; tr. as *The Bride of Korinth*) and the eponymous vampiric succubus in Charles Nodier's *Smarra; ou, Les Démons de la nuit* (1820). The image is much more ambiguous, however, in the phantasmagoric and quasi-allegorical horror stories of Ernst Hoffmann, including "Der Goldene Topf" (1813; tr. as "The Golden Flower-Pot") and "Der Sandmann" (1816; tr. as "The Sandman") and John Keats' poems "La Belle Dame Sans Merci" and "Lamia" (both 1820). The *femme fatale* became a viewpoint character, treated entirely sympathetically – as an unfortunate victim of the waywardness of male passion – in the Baron de la Motte Fouqué's popular and influential *Undine* (1811). Throughout the nineteenth century the motif was to remain problematic, encouraging writers to strike dozens of new – and sometimes very uncomfortable – poses in the hope of getting a clearer and more controllable view of it.

Of all the Romantics, the one most fervently fascinated by the idea of the *femme fatale* was Théophile Gautier, who wrote a series of stories in which idealistic young men are beguiled by supernatural lovers. The stories explore a whole spectrum of possible attitudes and evaluations, ranging from the light comedy of "Omphale" (1834) through the feverish melodrama of "La Morte amoureuse" (1836; tr. as "Clarimonde") and the piquant tragedy of "Arria Marcella" (1852) to the whole-heartedly sentimental *Spirite* (1866). Gautier undertook a much more elaborate and much more self-indulgent exploration of sexuality in *Mademoiselle de Maupin* (1835), where the *femme fatale* motif is deployed in a broader context, but his most intensely-focused and lushly stylish *femme fatale* story is the non-supernatural "Une Nuit de Cléopâtre" (1838; tr. as "One of Cleopatra's Nights"), which introduces an element of masochism into the grand passion far more striking than that in "Clarimonde", whose hero is not altogether delighted to be rescued from his vampire lover.

The calculated and luxurious exoticism of Gautier's *femmes fatales* is frequently echoed in French literature, and sometimes – as for instance in the work of Gerard de Nerval – vividly amplified. It is hardly surprising, given the delicious notoriety of the (forbidden) works of the so-called Divine Marquis, that their incipient sadistic streak should also be echoed and similarly magnified. Charles Baudelaire, the forefather of the Decadents, was perfectly fascinated by exotic *femmes fatales*, and wrote numerous hymns of praise of them, most notably "Les Metamorphoses du Vampire".

Partly in consequence of this chain of influential exemplars, French literature in the latter half of the century is quite saturated by *femmes fatales*. The motif is displayed with particular extravagance in a remarkable series of highly-coloured historical romances: Gustave Flaubert's *Salammbô* (1862), Anatole France's *Thaïs* (1890), Pierre Louÿs' *Aphrodite* (1896) and Alfred Jarry's *Messaline* (1900). It also features to notable effect in cynical exercises in misogyny like Barbey D'Aurevilly's *Les Diaboliques* (1874; tr. as *The She-Devils*) and Villiers de l'Isle Adam's *L'Ève Future* (1890; tr. as *The Future Eve*) and in conscientiously Decadent works like Remy de Gourmont's *Lilith* (1892), Rachilde's *La Marquise de Sade* (1887), and Octave Mirbeau's *Le jardin de supplices* (1899; tr. as *Torture Garden*). The most obsessive painter of *femmes fatales*, Gustav Moreau, belonged to the same cultural *milieu*, and we can also see the power of the motif in less likely places, notably *La Sorcière* (1862; tr. as *Satanism and Witchcraft*) by Jules Michelet, a remarkable exercise in historical apologetics which sets out to redeem the supposedly worthy tradition of female magic from the allegedly slanderous abuse heaped upon it by Religion and Science. Many of the notable deployments of the *femme fatale* motif outside France can also be attributed to the specific influence of French writers and fashions. The most obvious example is the early, conscientiously Decadent, work of the Italian writer Gabriele d'Annunzio, especially *Il Trionfo della Morte* (1894; tr. as *The Triumph of Death*); another is provided by Franz Wedekind, a German writer raised in Switzerland, in *Der Erdgeist* (1895; tr. as *Earth-Spirit*) and its sequel *Die Büsche der Pandora* (1904; tr. as *Pandora's Box*).

The reasons for this astonishing profusion of images are complex. France was a Catholic country, where the propriety of seeking redemption by confessing one's sins was acknowledged, and where a salacious appetite for especially lurid and horrific confessions had been cultivated and lavishly fed for hundreds of years, since the days of Gilles de Rais and Urbain Grandier. France was also the birthplace of Jean-Jacques Rousseau, who had laid down a stern challenge to official morality in proclaiming the virtue of natural affections and the tyrannical perversity of cultural regulation. It was Rousseau who became the philosophical guiding light of French Romanticism and the petty Satan of the Decadents, provoking a war of ideas between adherents of Nature and Artifice in which literary investigations of the role of female glamour in provoking male arousal became a curious battleground. On a less elevated plane, it is also worth noting that syphilis was rife in nineteenth century Paris, and that several of the notable writers who were fascinated by the fatal consequences of seduction had contracted it. Other European capitals undoubtedly had their fair share of poxy whores, but were much more inclined to deny steadfastly that decent people ever associated with them. France was the most liberal of nineteenth century nations in terms of what could be publicly admitted, and hence in terms of what writers could produce without worrying overmuch about censorship. In Britain, Germany and America, all of which produced memorable images of the *femme fatale* during the heyday of Romanticism, further developments were somewhat inhibited, or forced into eccentricity in order to avoid collision with moral strictures.

In English fiction, the supernatural *femme fatale* is far more often deployed as a straightforward figure of menace. She is a lesbian vampire in "Carmilla" (1872), a daughter of Pan in "The Great God Pan" (1890) by Arthur Machen, a hagwife with occult powers of attraction in Arthur Conan Doyle's *The*

Parasite (1894), an ice-cool shapeshifter in Clemence Housman's *The Werewolf* (1896) – and all of these stories end with her destruction, so that the course of ordinary life can be resumed with a deep sigh of relief. Two of the very best English ghost stories are studies of men driven horribly mad by demanding and indestructible admirers from beyond the grave: "How Love Came to Professor Guildea" (1900) by Robert Hichens and "The Beckoning Fair One" (1911) by Oliver Onions.

English stories which take a more tolerant and understanding view of the attraction which the male characters feel when faced by supernatural temptresses often compensate by making their *femmes fatales* sociopathically amoral – a pattern found in *Marahuna* (1888) by H. C. Marriott-Watsdon, *The Witch of Prague* (1891) by F. Marion Crawford and *The Sea Lady* (1902) by H. G. Wells. George MacDonald's attempt to get to grips with the archetypal Christian *femme fatale* myth, *Lilith* (1895), is far too coy about sex to accomplish much, and dissolves into confusion, while W. H. Hudson's *Green Mansions* (1904), which is quite exceptional in its exaggeratedly sentimental and sympathetic portrayal of the nature-spirit Rima, over-humanises her to the extent of equipping her with moral views which enable the author to avoid coming to terms with her sexuality.

The most sustained and respectful celebration by an English prose writer of the attractive and destructive power of the *femme fatale* is to be found, ironically enough, in the work of the lesbian Vernon Lee, in "Amour Dure" and "Dionea" from *Hauntings* (1890) and "Prince Alberic and the Snake Lady" in *Pope Jacynth and Other Fantastic Tales* (1904). England also produced the first great homosexual fantasy in which the *femme fatale* role is played by a young male: *The Picture of Dorian Gray* (1891) by Oscar Wilde. Both writers were forced into exile. Poets, however, were granted greater licence, and a wholehearted and emotionally feverish adoration of the *femme fatale* is elaborately displayed in the nakedly masochistic works of Algernon Swinburne, especially "Dolores" and "Faustine" (both 1866). Dante Gabriel Rossetti's most memorable *femmes fatales* are to be found in his paintings, but they crop up occasionally in his poems too, notably in "Sister Helen" (1870). A more satirical view of the *femme fatale*, sometimes verging on black comedy, can be found in Arthur W. O'Shaughnessy's *An Epic of Women* (1870).

Far more in tune with the English temper was the uneasy and awe-stricken contemplation of imperious but ultimately impotent female sexuality contained in the work of H. Rider Haggard, particularly in *She* (1887) and its sequels but also in such works as *The World's Desire* (1890, co-authored with Andrew Lang). *She* was much-imitated, having revealed a formula by which powerful and extraordinarily sexy women could be accommodated within plots which never had to come into conflict with contemporary morality, and there is a certain eccentric propriety in the fact that so many English literary *femmes fatales* were displaced into tiny enclaves where "lost races" survived in the remote corners of vast trackless wildernesses. It is hardly surprising that it was an Englishman who was eventually to produce the most sarcastic *reductio ad absurdum* of the *femme fatale* motif: Max Beerbohm's *Zuleika Dobson* (1911).

In America, the early precedents set by Edgar Allan Poe had far less influence than they had in France, where such stories as "Berenice" (1833), "Morella" (1835) and "Ligeia" (1838) were all translated by Baudelaire. The American *femme fatale* was rapidly retired to such studied moral fables as Nathaniel Hawthorne's "Rappaccini's Daughter" (1844) and Oliver Wendell Holmes's *Elsie Venner* (1859), although an intriguing supernatural female is contemplated from afar (with no hope that the gulf which separates her from her observer could possibly be crossed) in Fitz-James O'Brien's "The Diamond Lens" (1858).

Even by comparison with England, the *femme fatale* is conspicuous by her absence from late nineteenth century American fiction. It is also notable that when pulp fiction writers in the early years of the twentieth century began to send heroic adventurers into imaginary worlds far more peculiar than any imagined before, the women they met there – however exotically glamorous they might be – showed a remarkable willingness to become submissive wives. It mattered not whether they were egg-laying Martian princesses, as in Edgar Rice Burroughs' *A Princess of Mars* (1912), or inhabitants of an atomic microcosm, as in Ray Cummings' "The Girl in the Golden Atom" (1919), or fairy-like creatures with butterfly wings, as in Ralph Milne Farley's *The Radio Man* (1924); the principles of literary respectability demanded that they must fall in love by the book and marry before any serious thought of hanky-panky could be permitted to cross their minds. These stories follow a pattern initially laid down by Robert W. Chambers in "The Maker of Moons" (1896), which represented a decisive step towards careful conventionality by comparison with his much more intense French-influenced timeslip romance "The Demoiselle d'Ys" (1896). Only A. Merritt, author of the most exotic of early pulp magazine odysseys in exotica, dared to allow one of his heroes briefly to lament the fact that he had ended up with the nice girl instead of the far sexier witch-woman who had been her rival, and that was not until 1932, in *Dwellers in the Mirage*.

This situation was sufficiently absurd to attract the attention of several notable satirists, who provided scathingly sarcastic commentaries on the prudish refusal of American fiction to acknowledge female sexuality or the potential sexiness of fabulous females. The most notable of these satirists was James Branch Cabell, who mocked American attitudes to sex in a series of flirtatious comedies beginning with *The Cream of the Jest* (1917). This and many other works by Cabell offer significant, if sometimes fleeting, glimpses of an idealised exotic female named Ettarre, who is explicitly represented as a paradoxical archetype of male sexual desire, but is never *threatening* in the way that true *femmes fatales* are. She features most prominently in two melancholy short stories, "The Music from Behind the Moon" (1926) and "The Way of Ecben" (1927). A more slickly cynical kind of satire can be found in the sarcastic allegories of John Erskine, most notably *The Private Life of Helen of Troy* (1925) and *Adam and Eve* (1927), the latter of which exhibits considerable sympathy for Lilith but maintains its misogynistic credentials by putting the boot into Eve in no uncertain terms. This was to become a favourite tactic of American satirists, who often presented sexy women as misunderstood hedonists whose lack of hypocrisy makes them morally superior to wives. This attitude can be seen in the works of the mildly salacious humorist Thorne Smith, and it is rather ironic that the only real *femme fatale* in his canon was foisted on him by a posthumous collaborator, Norman Matson, in *The Passionate Witch* (1941). Even she was to be carefully domesticated in the film version of the story, *I Married a Witch,* and the subsequent TV series *Bewitched*, as was the witch in John van Druten's play (also successfully filmed), *Bell, Book and Candle* (1951).

American pulp fiction did eventually find room for *femmes fatales* in the pages of the horror story pulp *Weird Tales*, which featured conventionally nasty glamorous female vampires and werewolves in some profusion. *Weird Tales* briefly played host to the one American writer who was significantly and deeply affected by French Romanticism and Decadence, Clark Ashton Smith, whose several *femme fatale* stories include two – "The Witchcraft of Ulua" (1934) and "Mother of Toads" (1937) – which warranted recent re-issue in unexpurgated versions. Curiously enough, it was in the borderlands where pulp weird fiction overlapped the nascent science fiction genre that the *femme fatale* obtained a new lease of life. Science fantasy, as the hybrid genre has sometimes been called, set out to combine the lurid exoticism of Burroughsian interplanetary fantasy with the harder logical edge and more fertile teratological imagination of science fiction. An important early example is C. L. Moore's story of a Martian Medusa, "Shambleau" (1933), and Moore went on to produce other stories in the same vein, including "Black Thirst" (1934), "Julhi" (1935) and "Yvala" (1936). Jack Williamson played sciencefictional tricks with time in order that the hero of *The Legion of Time* (1938) could have the *femme fatale* and the nice girl rolled into one, but achieved a more significant subversion of convention in *Darker Than You Think* (1940), in which the hero is given leave to throw in his lot with the lycanthropic sorceress who has beguiled him. Later writers working on this fringe were to produce some of the most interesting modern stories of *femmes fatales*. These include Fritz Leiber's "The Girl with the Hungry Eyes" (1949), Robert F.

Young's "To Fell a Tree" (1959) and Theodore Sturgeon's "Bianca's Hands" (1960). Also notable as a writer of science fantasy is the British writer J. G. Ballard, who wrote a number of *femme fatale* stories, including several of the items in his collection *Vermilion Sands* (1971).

Although it emerged from rather different nineteenth century roots, the eventual development of the American situation mirrors the fate of the *femme fatale* in twentieth century Europe. Once her heyday in *fin de siècle* France was over she became a rather enfeebled creature, thoroughly de-mystified even though she was never quite completely or convincingly explained by the theories of Freud and his successors. Once the libido was brought into the arena of clinical study it became a chimera of a rather different stripe, and the occult power of the *femme fatale* was reduced to something much more ordinary. She became a mere cliché, or – even worse – a figure of fun. She became understandable, a deserving recipient of civilized tolerance more to be pitied than condemned.

The cinema, which gave the *femme fatale* a new visual image in characters memorably played by Theda Bara and Marlene Dietrich, also played a major part in reducing her ruthlessly to merely human dimensions. As in pulp fiction, convention demanded that – in Hollywood, at least – all *femmes fatales* should either accept domestication or die. Even this humiliation was not the end; dissatisfaction with the female stereotypes contained in the media was a significant aspect of the feminist movement, and some of the feminist writers who attempted to redress the cultural balance were prepared to re-appraise the psychological implications of *femme fatale* figures. Their work has provided a new dimension of satirical irony for the subversion and mockery of the motif, which is clearly evident in such novels as Angela Carter's *The Passion of New Eve* (1977).

But this relative decline in the power of the image does not mean that the problematic conflict of ideas which spawned the image has been solved. Sexuality still sings the same old siren song, and the old taboos – albeit weaker and more flexible – are still in place. The discipline of official morality is no longer as

27

strict or severe as it once was, and that softening is reflected in the character of modern *femmes fatales*, who are far more often victims than villains, but as feminists constantly point out and lament, female sexuality has not yet been liberated from its straitjacket, and the demands which men make of their lovers and wives remain paradoxical as well as oppressive. Shifting the blame for infidelity is as popular as it ever was – and just as stupidly dishonest and hypocritical. It is still written into the fine print of the social contract that women cannot win.

While this situation endures, the *femme fatale* can never entirely lose her glamour or her dramatic potential. A shadow of her former self she may be, but there is an undeniable aesthetic appeal in the enigmatic character of shadows. The modern *femme fatale* story is inevitably more analytical and more subtly ironic than its nineteenth-century ancestors; it is often apologetically urbane or flippantly witty – and yet it cannot entirely hide or set aside the anxiety which underlies it. And we must remember that the conquest of venereal disease by antibiotics has proved in the end to be temporary; the whores who function as an extra-marital outlet for the more exotic desires of so many men are once again becoming carriers of a sinister plague. The story is not over; a new chapter has already begun.

LA BELLE DAME SANS MERCI
by
John Keats

I

O, WHAT can ail thee, knight at arms,
Alone and palely loitering;
The sedge is wither'd from the lake,
And no birds sing.

II

O, what can ail thee, knight at arms,
So haggard and so woe-begone?
The squirrel's granary is full,
And the harvest's done.

III

I see a lilly on thy brow,
With anguish moist and fever dew;
And on thy cheek a fading rose
Fast withereth too.

IV

I met a lady in the meads
Full beautiful, a faery's child;
Her hair was long, her foot was light,
And her eyes were wild.

V

I made a garland for her head,
And bracelets too, and fragrant zone;
She look'd at me as she did love,
And made sweet moan,

VI

I set her on my pacing steed,
And nothing else saw all day long;

For sideways would she lean, and sing
A faery's song.

VII

She found me roots of relish sweet,
And honey wild, and manna dew;
And sure in language strange she said,
I love thee true.

VIII

She took me to her elfin grot,
And there she gaz'd and sighed full sore,
And there I shut her wild wild eyes
With kisses four.

IX

And there she lulled me asleep,
And there I dream'd, ah woe betide,
The latest dream I ever dream'd
On the cold hill side.

X

I saw pale kings, and princes too,
Pale warriors, death-pale were they all;
They cry'd – "La belle Dame sans merci
Hath thee in thrall!"

XI

I saw their starv'd lips in the gloam
With horrid warning gapèd wide,
And I awoke, and found me here
On the cold hill side.

XII

And this is why I sojourn here
Alone and palely loitering,
Though the sedge is wither'd from the lake,
And no birds sing.

ONE OF CLEOPATRA'S NIGHTS
by
Théophile Gautier
Translated by Lafcadio Hearn

CHAPTER 1

Nineteen hundred years ago from the date of this writing, a magnificently gilded and painted cangia was descending the Nile as rapidly as fifty long, flat, oars, which seemed to crawl over the furrowed water like the legs of a gigantic scarabaeus, could impel it.

This cangia was narrow, long, elevated at both ends in the form of a new moon, elegantly proportioned, and admirably built for speed; the figure of a ram's head, surmounted by a golden globe, armed the point of the prow, showing that the vessel belonged to some personage of royal blood.

In the centre of the vessel arose a flat-roofed cabin – a sort of *naos*, or tent of honour – coloured and gilded, ornamented with palm-leaf mouldings, and lighted by four little square windows.

Two chambers, both decorated with hieroglyphic paintings, occupied the horns of the crescent. One of them, the larger, had a second story of lesser height built upon it, like the *chateaux gaillards* of those fantastic galleys of the sixteenth century drawn by Della-Bella; the other and smaller chamber, which also served as a pilot-house, was surmounted with a triangular pediment.

In lieu of a rudder, two immense oars, adjusted upon stakes decorated with stripes of paint, which served in place of our modern row-locks, extended into the water in rear of the vessel like the webbed feet of a swan; heads crowned with *pshents*, and bearing the allegorical horn upon their chins, were sculptured upon the handles of these huge oars, which were manoeuvred by the pilot as he stood upon the deck of the cabin above.

He was a swarthy man, tawny as new bronze, with bluish surface gleams playing over his dark skin; long oblique eyes, hair deeply black and all plaited into little cords, full lips, high cheek-bones, ears standing out from the skull – the Egyptian type in all its purity. A narrow strip of cotton about his loins, together with five or six strings of glass beads and a few amulets, comprised his whole costume.

He appeared to be the only one on board the cangia; for the rowers bending over their oars, and concealed from view by the gunwales, made their presence known only through the symmetrical movements of the oars themselves, which spread open alternately on either side of the vessel, like the ribs of a fan, and fell regularly back into the water after a short pause.

Not a breath of air was stirring; and the great triangular sail of the cangia, tied up and bound to the lowered mast with a silken cord, testified that all hope of the wind rising had been abandoned.

The noonday sun shot his arrows perpendicularly from above; the ashen-hued slime of the river banks reflected the fiery glow; a raw light, glaring and blinding in its intensity, poured down in torrents of flame; the azure of the sky whitened in the heat as a metal whitens in the furnace; an ardent and lurid fog smoked in the horizon. Not a cloud appeared in the sky – a sky mournful and changeless as Eternity.

The water of the Nile, sluggish and wan, seemed to slumber in its course, and slowly extend itself in sheets of molten tin. No breath of air wrinkled its surface, or bowed down upon their stalks the cups of the lotus-flowers, as rigidly motionless as though sculptured; at long intervals the leap of a bechir or fabaka expanding its belly scarcely caused a silvery gleam upon the current; and the oars of the cangia seemed with difficulty to tear their way through the fuliginous film of that curdled water. The banks were desolate, a solemn and mighty sadness weighed upon this land, which was never aught else than a vast tomb, and in which the living appeared to be solely occupied in the work of burying the dead. It was an arid sadness, dry as pumice stone, without melancholy, without reverie, without one pearly gray cloud to follow toward the horizon, one secret spring wherein to lave one's dusty feet; the sadness of a sphinx weary of eternally gazing upon the desert, and unable to detach herself from the granite socle upon which she has sharpened her claws for twenty centuries.

So profound was the silence that it seemed as though the world had become dumb, or that the air had lost all power of conveying sound. The only noises which could be heard at intervals were the whisperings and stifled "chuckling" of the crocodiles, which, enfeebled by the heat, were wallowing among the bulrushes by the river banks; or the sound made by some ibis, which, tired of standing with one leg doubled up against its stomach, and its head sunk between its shoulders, suddenly abandoned its motionless attitude, and, brusquely whipping the blue air with its white wings, flew off to perch upon an obelisk or a palm-tree.

The cangia flew like an arrow over the smooth river-water, leaving behind it a silvery wake which soon disappeared; and only a few foam-bubbles rising to break at the surface of the stream bore testimony to the passage of the vessel, then already out of sight.

The ochre-hued or salmon-coloured banks unrolled themselves rapidly, like scrolls of papyrus, between the double azure of water and sky so similar in tint that the slender tongue of earth which separated them seemed like a causeway stretching over an immense lake, and that it would have been difficult to determine whether the Nile reflected the sky, or whether the sky reflected the Nile.

The scene continually changed. At one moment were visible gigantic propylaea, whose sloping walls, painted with large panels of fantastic figures, were mirrored in the river; pylons with broad-bulging capitals; stairways guarded by huge crouching sphinxes, wearing caps with lappets of many folds, and crossing their paws of black basalt below their sharply projecting breasts; palaces, immeasurably vast, projecting against the horizon the severe horizontal lines of their entablatures, where the emblematic globe unfolded its mysterious wings like an eagle's vast-extending pinions; temples with enormous columns thick as towers, on which were limned processions of hieroglyphic figures against a background of brilliant white – all the monstrosities of that Titanic architecture. Again the eye beheld only landscapes of desolate aridity – hills formed of stony fragments from excavations and building works, crumbs of that gigantic debauch of granite which lasted for more than thirty centuries; mountains exfoliated by heat, and mangled and striped with black lines which seemed like the cauterizations of a conflagration; hillocks humped and deformed, squatting like the criocephalus of the tombs, and projecting the outlines of their misshapen attitude against the sky-line; expanses of greenish clay, reddle, flour-white tufa; and from time to time some steep cliff of dry, rose-coloured granite, where yawned the black mouths of the stone quarries.

This aridity was wholly unrelieved; no oasis of foliage refreshed the eye; green seemed to be a colour unknown to that nature; only some meagre palm-tree, like a vegetable crab, appeared from time to time in the horizon; or a thorny fig-tree brandished its tempered leaves like sword blades of bronze; or a carthamus-plant, which had found a little moisture to live upon in the shadow of some fragment of a broken column, relieved the general uniformity with a speck of crimson.

After this rapid glance at the aspect of the landscape, let us return to the cangia with its fifty rowers, and without announcing ourselves, enter boldly into the *naos* of honour.

The interior was painted white with green arabesques, bands of vermilion, and gilt flowers fantastically shaped; an exceedingly fine rush matting covered the floor; at the further end stood a little bed, supported upon griffin's feet, having a back resembling that of a modern lounge or sofa; a stool with four steps to enable one to climb into bed; and (rather an odd luxury according to our ideas of comfort) a sort of hemicycle of cedar wood, supported on a single leg, and designed to fit the nape of the neck so as to support the head of the person reclining.

Upon this strange pillow reposed a most charming head, one look of which once caused the loss of half a world; an adorable, a divine head; the head of the most perfect woman that ever lived; the most womanly and most queenly of all women; an admirable type of beauty which the imagination of poets could never invest with any new grace, and which dreamers will find forever in the depths of their dreams – it is not necessary to name Cleopatra.

Beside her stood her favourite slave Charmion, waving a

large fan of ibis feathers; and a young girl was moistening with scented water the little reed blinds attached to the windows of the *naos*, so that the air might only enter impregnated with fresh odours.

Near the bed of repose, in a striped vase of alabaster with a slender neck and a peculiarly elegant, tapering shape, vaguely recalling the form of a heron, was placed a bouquet of lotus-flowers, some of a celestial blue, others of a tender rose-colour, like the finger-tips of Isis the great goddess.

Either from caprice or policy, Cleopatra did not wear the Greek dress that day. She had just attended a panegyris, and was returning to her summer palace still clad in the Egyptian costume she had worn at the festival.

Perhaps our fair readers will feel curious to know how Queen Cleopatra was attired on her return from the Mammisi of Hermonthis whereat were worshipped the holy triad of the god Mandou, the goddess Ritho, and their son, Harphra; luckily we are able to satisfy them in this regard.

For headdress Queen Cleopatra wore a kind of very light helmet of beaten gold, fashioned in the form of the body and wings of the sacred partridge. The wings, opening downward like fans, covered the temples, and extending below, almost to the neck, left exposed on either side, through a small aperture, an ear rosier and more delicately curled than the shell whence arose that Venus whom the Egyptians named Athor; the tail of the bird occupied that place where our women wear their chignons; its body, covered with imbricated feathers, and painted in variegated enamel, concealed the upper part of the head; and its neck, gracefully curving forward over the forehead of the wearer, formed together with its little head a kind of horn-shaped ornament, all sparkling with precious stones; a symbolic crest, designed like a tower, completed this odd but elegant headdress. Hair dark as a starless night flowed from beneath this helmet, and streamed in long tresses over the fair shoulders whereof the commencement only, alas! was left exposed by a collarette, or gorget, adorned with many rows of serpentine stones, azodrachs, and chrysoberyls; a linen robe diagonally cut – a mist of material, of woven air, *ventus textilis* as Petronius says, undulated in vapoury whiteness about a lovely body whose outlines it scarcely shaded with the softest shading. This robe had half-sleeves, tight at the shoulder, but widening toward the elbows like our *manches-à-sabot*, and permitting a glimpse of an adorable arm and a perfect hand, the arm being clasped by six golden bracelets, and the hand adorned with a ring representing the sacred scarabaeus. A girdle, whose knotted ends hung down in front, confined this free-floating tunic at the waist; a short cloak adorned with fringing completed the costume; and, if a few barbarous words will not frighten Parisian ears, we might add that the robe was called *schenti*, and the short cloak, *calisiris*.

Finally, we may observe that Queen Cleopatra wore very thin, light sandals, turned up at the toes, and fastened over the instep, like the *souliers-à-la-poulaine* of the mediaeval *chatelaines*.

But Queen Cleopatra did not wear that air of satisfaction which becomes a woman conscious of being perfectly beautiful and perfectly well dressed. She tossed and turned in her little bed, and her sudden movements momentarily disarranged the folds of her gauzy *conopeum*, which Charmion as often rearranged with inexhaustible patience, and without ceasing to wave her fan.

"This room is stifling," said Cleopatra; "even if Pthah the God of Fire established his forges in here, he could not make it hotter; the air is like the breath of a furnace!" And she moistened her lips with the tip of her little tongue, and stretched out her hand like a feverish patient seeking an absent cup.

Charmion, ever attentive, at once clapped her hands. A black slave clothed in a short tunic hanging in folds like an Albanian petticoat, and a panther-skin thrown over his shoulders, entered with the suddenness of an apparition; with his left hand balancing a tray laden with cups, and slices of watermelon, and carrying in his right a long vase with a spout like a modern teapot.

The slave filled one of these cups, pouring the liquor into it from a considerable height with marvellous dexterity, and placed it before the queen. Cleopatra merely touched the beverage with her lips, laid the cup down beside her, and turning upon Charmion her beautiful liquid black eyes, lustrous with living light, exclaimed: "O Charmion, I am weary unto death!"

CHAPTER II

Charmion, at once anticipating a confidence, assumed a look of pained sympathy, and drew nearer to her mistress.

"I am horribly weary!" continued Cleopatra, letting her arms fall like one utterly discouraged. "This Egypt crushes, annihilates me; this sky with its implacable azure is sadder than the deep night of Erebus; never a cloud, never a shadow, and always that red, sanguine sun, which glares down upon you like the eye of a Cyclops. Ah, Charmion, I would give a pearl for one drop of rain! From the inflamed pupil of that sky of bronze no tear has ever yet fallen upon the desolation of this land; it is only a vast covering for a tomb – the dome of a necropolis; a sky dead and dried up like the mummies it hangs over; it weighs upon my shoulders like an over-heavy mantle; it constrains and terrifies me; it seems to me that I could not stand up erect without striking my forehead against it. And, moreover, this land is truly an awful land; all things in it are gloomy, enigmatic, incomprehensible. Imagination has produced in it only monstrous chimeras and monuments immeasurable; this architecture and this art fill me with fear; those colossi, whose stone-entangled limbs compel them to remain eternally sitting with their hands upon their knees, weary me with their stupid immobility; they trouble my eyes and my horizon. When, indeed, shall the giant come who is to take them by the hand and relieve them from their long watch of twenty centuries? For even granite itself must grow weary at last! Of what master, then, do they await the coming, to leave the mountain-seats and rise in token of respect? Of what invisible flock are those huge sphinxes the guardians, crouching like dogs on the watch, that they never close their eyelids, and forever extend their claws in readiness to seize? Why are their stony eyes so obstinately fixed upon eternity and infinity? What weird secret do their firmly locked lips retain within their breasts? On the right hand, on the left, withersoever one turns, only frightful monsters are visible – dogs with the heads of men; men with the heads of dogs; chimeras begotten of hideous couplings in the shadowy depths of the labyrinths; figures of Anubis, Typhon, Osiris; partridges with great yellow eyes that seem to pierce through you with their inquisitorial gaze, and see beyond and behind you things which one dare not speak of – a family of animals and horrible gods with scaly wings, hooked beaks, trenchant claws, ever ready to seize and devour you should you venture to cross the threshold of the temple, or lift a corner of the veil.

"Upon the walls, upon the columns, on the ceilings, on the floors, upon palaces and temples, in the long passages and the deepest pits of the necropoli, even within the bowels of the earth where light never comes, and where the flames of the torches die for want of air, forever and everywhere are sculptured and painted interminable hieroglyphics, telling in language unintelligible of things which are no longer known, and which belong, doubtless, to the vanished creations of the past – prodigious buried works wherein a whole nation was sacrificed to write the epitaph of one king! Mystery and granite – this is Egypt! Truly a fair land for a young woman, and a young queen.

"Menacing and funereal symbols alone meet the eye – the emblems of the *pedum*, the *tau*, allegorical globes, coiling serpents, and the scales in which souls are weighed – the Unknown, death, nothingness. In the place of any vegetation only *stelae* limned with weird characters; instead of avenues of trees, avenues of granite obelisks; in lieu of soil, vast pavements of granite for which whole mountains could each furnish but one slab; in place of a sky, ceilings of granite – eternity made palpable, a bitter and everlasting sarcasm upon the frailty and brevity of life – stairways built only for the limbs of Titans, which the human foot cannot ascend save by the aid of ladders; columns that a hundred arms cannot encircle; labyrinths in which one might travel for years without discovering the termination – the vertigo of enormity, the drunkenness of the gigantic, the reckless efforts of that pride which would at any cost engrave its name deeply upon the face of the world.

"And, moreover, Charmion, I tell you a thought haunts me which terrifies me. In other lands of the earth, corpses are burned, and their ashes soon mingle with the soil. Here, it is said that the living have no other occupation than that of preserving the dead. Potent balms save them from destruction; the remains endure after the soul has evaporated. Beneath this people lie twenty peoples; each city stands upon twenty layers of necropoli; each generation which passes away leaves a population of mummies to a shadowy city. Beneath the father you find the grandfather and the great-grandfather in their gilded and painted boxes, even as they were during life; and should you dig down forever, forever you would still find the underlying dead.

"When I think upon those bandage-swathed myriads – those multitudes of parched spectres who fill the sepulchral pits, and who have been there for two thousand years face to face in their own silence, which nothing ever breaks, not even the noise which the graveworms make in crawling, and who will be found intact after yet another two thousand years, with their crocodiles, their cats, their ibises, and all things that lived in their lifetime – then terrors seize me, and I feel my flesh creep. What do they mutter to each other? For they still have lips, and every ghost would find its body in the same state as when it quitted it, if they should all take the fancy to return.

"Ah, truly is Egypt a sinister kingdom and little suited to me, the laughter-loving and merry one. Everything in it encloses a mummy; that is the heart and the kernel of all things. After a thousand turns you must always end there; the Pyramids themselves hide sarcophagi. What nothingness and madness is this! Disembowel the sky with gigantic triangles of stone – you cannot thereby lengthen your corpse an inch. How can one rejoice and live in a land like this, where the only perfume you can respire is the acrid odour of the naphtha and bitumen which boil in the caldrons of the embalmers, where the very flooring of your chamber sounds hollow because the corridors of the hypogea and the mortuary pits extend even under your alcove? To be the queen of mummies, to have none to converse with but statues in constrained and rigid attitudes – this is, in truth, a cheerful lot. Again, if I only had some heartfelt passion to relieve this melancholy, some interest in life; if I could but love somebody or something; if I were even loved; but I am not.

"This is why I am weary, Charmion. With love, this grim and arid Egypt would seem to me fairer than even Greece with her ivory gods, her temples of snowy marble, her groves of laurel, and fountains of living water. There I should never dream of the weird face of Anubis and the ghastly terrors of the cities underground."

Charmion smiled incredulously. "That ought not, surely, to be a source of much grief to you, O queen; for every glance of your eyes transpierces hearts, like the golden arrows of Eros himself."

"Can a queen," answered Cleopatra, "ever know whether it is her face or her diadem that is loved? The rays of her starry crown dazzle the eyes and the heart. Were I to descend from the height of my throne, would I even have the celebrity or the popularity of Bacchis or Archianassa, of the first courtesan from Athens or Miletus? A queen is something so far removed from men, so elevated, so widely separated from them, so impossible for them to reach! What presumption dare flatter itself in such an enterprise? It is not simply a woman, it is an august and sacred being that has no sex, and that is worshipped kneeling without being loved. Who was ever really enamoured of Hera the snowy-armed or Pallas of the sea-green eyes? Who ever sought to kiss the silver feet of Thetis or the rosy fingers of Aurora? What lover of the divine beauties ever took unto himself wings that he might soar to the golden palaces of heaven? Respect and fear chill hearts in our presence, and in order to obtain the love of our equals, one must descend into those necropoli of which I have just been speaking."

Although she offered no further objection to the arguments of her mistress, a vague smile which played about the lips of the handsome Greek slave showed that she had little faith in the inviolability of the royal person.

"Ah," continued Cleopatra, "I wish that something would happen to me, some strange, unexpected adventure. The songs of the poets; the dances of the Syrian slaves; the banquets, rose garlanded, and prolonged into the dawn; the nocturnal races; the Laconian dogs; the tame lions; the humpbacked dwarfs; the brotherhood of the Inimitables; the combats of the arena; the new dresses; the byssus robes; the clusters of pearls; the perfumes from Asia; the most exquisite of luxuries; the wildest of splendours – nothing any longer gives me pleasure. Everything has become indifferent to me, everything is insupportable to me."

"It is easily to be seen," muttered Charmion to herself, "that the queen has not had a lover nor had anyone killed for a whole month."

Fatigued with so lengthy a tirade, Cleopatra once more took the cup placed beside her, moistened her lips with it, and putting her head beneath her arm, like a dove putting its head under its wing, composed herself for slumber as best she could. Charmion unfastened her sandals and commenced to gently tickle the soles of her feet with a peacock's feather, and Sleep soon sprinkled his golden dust upon the beautiful eyes of Ptolemy's sister.

While Cleopatra sleeps, let us ascend upon deck and enjoy the glorious sunset view. A broad band of violet colour, warmed deeply with ruddy tints towards the west, occupies all the lower portion of the sky; encountering the zone of azure above, the violet shade melts into a clear lilac, and fades off through half-rosy tints into the blue beyond; afar, where the sun, red as a buckler fallen from the furnace of Vulcan, casts his burning reflection, the deeper shades turn to pale citron hues, and glow with turquoise tints. The water, rippling under an oblique beam of light, shines with the dull gleam of the quicksilvered side of a mirror, or like a damascened blade. The sinuosities of the bank, the reeds, and all objects along the shore are brought out in sharp black relief against the bright glow. By the aid of this crepuscular light you may perceive afar off, like a grain of dust floating upon quicksilver, a little brown speck trembling in the network of luminous ripples. Is it a teal diving, a tortoise lazily drifting with the current, a crocodile raising the tip of his scaly snout above the water to breathe the cooler air of evening, the belly of a hippopotamus gleaming amidstream, or perhaps a rock left bare by the falling of the river? For the ancient Opi-Mou, Father of Waters, sadly needs to replenish his dry urn from the solstitial rains of the Mountains of the Moon.

It is none of these. By the atoms of Osiris so deftly resewn together, it is a man, who seems to walk, to skate, upon the water! Now the frail bark which sustains him becomes visible, a very nutshell of a boat, a hollow fish; three strips of bark fitted together (one for the bottom and two for the sides), and strongly fastened at either end by cord well smeared with bitumen. The man stands erect, with one foot on either side of this fragile vessel, which he impels with a single oar that also serves the purpose of a rudder; and although the royal cangia moves rapidly under the efforts of the fifty rowers, the little black bark visibly gains upon it.

Cleopatra desired some strange adventure, something wholly unexpected. This little bark which moves so mysteriously seems to us to be conveying an adventure, or, at least, an adventurer. Perhaps it contains the hero of our story; the thing is not impossible.

At any rate he was a handsome youth of twenty, with hair so black that it seemed to own a tinge of blue, a skin blonde as gold, and a form so perfectly proportioned that he might have been taken for a bronze statue by Lysippus. Although he had been rowing for a very long time he betrayed no sign of fatigue, and not a single drop of sweat bedewed his forehead.

The sun half sank below the horizon, and against his broken disk figured the dark silhouette of a far distant city, which the eye could not have distinguished but for this accidental effect of light. His radiance soon faded altogether away, and the stars, fair night-flowers of heaven, opened their chalices of gold in the azure of the firmament. The royal cangia, closely followed by the little bark, stopped before a huge marble stairway, whereof each step supported one of those sphinxes that Cleopatra so much detested. This was the landing-place of the summer palace.

Cleopatra, leaning upon Charmion, passed swiftly, like a gleaming vision, between a double line of lantern-bearing slaves.

The youth took from the bottom of his little boat a great lion-skin, threw it across his shoulders, drew the tiny shell upon the beach, and wended his way towards the palace.

CHAPTER III

Who is this young man, balancing himself upon a fragment of bark, who dares follow the royal cangia, and is able to contend in a race of speed against fifty strong rowers from the land of Kush, all naked to the waist, and anointed with palm-oil? What secret motive urges him to this swift pursuit? That, indeed, is one of the many things we are obliged to know in our character of the intuition-gifted poet, for whose benefit all men, and even all women (a much more difficult matter), must have in their breasts that little window which Momus of old demanded.

It is not a very easy thing to find out precisely what a young man from the land of Kemi, who followed the barge of Cleopatra, queen and goddess Evergetes, on her return from the Mammisi of Hermonthis two thousand years ago, was then thinking of. But we shall make the effort notwithstanding.

Meïamoun, son of Mandouschopsh, was a youth of strange character; nothing by which ordinary minds are affected made any impression upon him. He seemed to belong to some loftier race, and might well have been regarded as the offspring of some divine adultery. His glance had the steady brilliancy of a falcon's gaze, and a serene majesty sat on his brow as upon a pedestal of marble; a noble pride curled his upper lip, and expanded his nostrils like those of a fiery horse. Although owning a grace of form almost maidenly in its delicacy, and though the bosom of the fair and effeminate god Dionysos was not more softly rounded or smoother than his, yet beneath this soft exterior were hidden sinews of steel and the strength of Hercules – a strange privilege of certain antique natures to unite in themselves the beauty of woman with the strength of man.

As for his complexion, we must acknowledge that it was of a tawny orange colour, a hue little in accordance with our white-and-rose ideas of beauty; but which did not prevent him from being a very charming young man, much sought after by all kinds of women – yellow, red, copper-coloured, sooty-black, or golden skinned, and even by one fair, white Greek.

Do not suppose from this that Meïamoun's lot was altogether enviable. The ashes of aged Priam, the very snows of Hippolytus, were not more insensible or more frigid; the young white-robed neophyte preparing for the initiation into the mysteries of Isis led no chaster life; the young maiden benumbed by the icy shadow of her mother was not more shyly pure.

Nevertheless, for so coy a youth, the pleasures of Meïamoun were certainly of a singular nature. He would go forth quietly some morning with his little buckler of hippopotamus hide, his *harpe* or curved sword, a triangular bow, and a snake-skin quiver filled with barbed arrows; then he would ride at a gallop far into the desert, upon his slender-limbed, small-headed, wild-maned mare, until he could find some lion-tracks. He especially delighted in taking the little lion-cubs from underneath the belly of their mother. In all things he loved the perilous or the unachievable. He preferred to walk where it seemed impossible for any human being to obtain a foothold, or to swim in a raging torrent, and he had accordingly chosen the neighbourhood of the cataracts for his bathing place in the Nile. The Abyss called him!

Such was Meïamoun, son of Mandouschopsh.

For some time his humours had been growing more savage than ever. During whole months he buried himself in the Ocean of Sands, returning only at long intervals. Vainly would his uneasy mother lean from her terrace and gaze anxiously down the long road with tireless eyes. At last, after weary waiting, a little whirling cloud of dust would become visible in the horizon, and finally the cloud would open to allow a full view of Meïamoun, all covered with dust, riding upon a mare gaunt as a wolf, with red and bloodshot eyes, nostrils trembling, and huge scars along her flanks – scars which certainly were not made by spurs.

After having hung up in his room some hyena or lion skins, he would start off again.

And yet no one might have been happier than Meïamoun. He was beloved by Nephthe, daughter of the priest Afomouthis, and the loveliest woman of the Nome Arsinoïtes. Only such a being as Meïamoun could have failed to see that Nephthe had the most charmingly oblique and indescribably voluptuous eyes, a mouth sweetly illuminated by ruddy smiles, little teeth of wondrous whiteness and transparency, arms exquisitely round, and feet more perfect than the jasper feet of the statue of Isis. Assuredly there was not a smaller hand nor longer hair than hers in all Egypt. The charms of Nephthe could have been eclipsed only by those of Cleopatra. But who could dare to dream of loving Cleopatra? Ixion, enamoured of Juno, strained only a cloud to his bosom, and must forever roll the wheel of his punishment in hell.

It was Cleopatra whom Meïamoun loved.

He had at first striven to tame this wild passion; he had wrestled fiercely with it; but love cannot be strangled even as a lion is strangled, and the strong skill of the mightiest athlete avails nothing in such a contest. The arrow had remained in the wound, and he carried it with him everywhere. The radiant and splendid image of Cleopatra, with her golden-pointed diadem and her imperial purple, standing above a nation on their knees, illuminated his nightly dreams and his waking thoughts. Like some imprudent man who has dared to look at the sun and forever thereafter beholds an impalpable blot floating before his eyes, so Meïamoun ever beheld Cleopatra. Eagles may gaze undazzled at the sun, but what diamond eye can with impunity fix itself upon a beautiful woman, a beautiful queen?

He commenced at last to spend his life in wandering about the neighbourhood of the royal dwelling, that he might at least breathe the same air as Cleopatra, that he might sometimes kiss the almost imperceptible print of her foot upon the sand (a happiness, alas! rare indeed). He attended the sacred festivals and *panegyreis*, striving to obtain one beaming glance of her eyes, to catch in passing one stealthy glimpse of her loveliness in some of its thousand varied aspects. At other moments, filled with sudden shame of this mad life, he gave himself up to the chase with redoubled ardour, and sought by fatigue to tame the ardour of his blood and the impetuosity of his desires.

He had gone to the panegyris of Hermonthis, and, in the vague hope of beholding the queen again for an instant as she disembarked at the summer palace, had followed her cangia in his boat – little heeding the sharp stings of the sun – through a heat intense enough to make the panting sphinxes melt in lava-sweat upon their reddened pedestals.

And then he felt that the supreme moment was nigh, that the decisive instant of his life was at hand, and that he could not die with his secret in his breast.

It is a strange situation truly to find oneself enamoured of a queen. It is as though one loved a star; yet she, the star, comes forth nightly to sparkle in her place in heaven. It is a kind of mysterious rendezvous. You may find her again, you may see her; she is not offended at your gaze. Oh, misery! to be poor, unknown, obscure, seated at the very foot of the ladder, and to feel one's heart breaking with love for something glittering, solemn and magnificent – for a woman whose meanest female attendant would scorn you! – to gaze fixedly and fatefully upon one who never sees you, who never will see you; one to whom you are no more than a ripple on the sea of humanity, in nowise differing from the other ripples, and who might a hundred times encounter you without once recognizing you; to have no reason to offer should an opportunity for addressing her present itself in excuse for such mad audacity – neither poetical talent, nor great genius, nor any superhuman qualification – nothing but love; and to be able to offer in exchange for beauty, nobility, power, and all imaginable splendour only one's passion and one's youth – rare offerings, forsooth!

Such were the thoughts which overwhelmed Meïamoun. Lying upon the sand, supporting his chin on his palms, he permitted himself to be lifted and borne away by the inexhaustible current of reverie; he sketched out a thousand projects, each madder than the last. He felt convinced that he was seeking after the unattainable, but he lacked the courage to frankly renounce his undertaking, and a perfidious hope came to whisper some lying promises in his ear.

"Athor, mighty goddess," he murmured in a deep voice, "what evil have I done against thee that I should be made thus miserable? Art thou avenging thyself for my disdain of Nephthe, daughter of the priest Afomouthis? Hast thou afflicted me thus for having rejected the love of Lamia, the Athenian hetaira, or of Flora, the Roman courtesan? Is it my fault that my heart should be sensible only to the matchless beauty of thy rival, Cleopatra? Why hast thou wounded my soul with the envenomed arrow of unattainable love? What sacrifice, what offerings dost thou desire? Must I erect to thee a chapel of the rosy marble of Syene with columns crowned by gilded capitals, a ceiling all of one block, and hieroglyphics deeply sculptured by the best workmen of Memphis and Thebes? Answer me."

Like all gods or goddesses thus invoked, Athor answered not a word, and Meïamoun resolved upon a desperate expedient.

Cleopatra, on her part, likewise invoked the goddess Athor. She prayed for a new pleasure, for some fresh sensation. As she languidly reclined upon the couch she thought to herself that the number of the senses was sadly limited, that the most exquisite refinements of delight soon yielded to satiety, and that it was really no small task for a queen to find means of occupying her time. To test new poisons upon slaves; to make men fight with tigers, or gladiators with each other; to drink pearls dissolved; to swallow the wealth of a whole province – all these things had become commonplace and insipid.

Charmion was fairly at her wit's end, and knew not what to do for her mistress.

Suddenly a whistling sound was heard, and an arrow buried itself, quivering, in the cedar wainscoting of the wall.

Cleopatra well-nigh fainted with terror. Charmion ran to the window, leaned out, and beheld only a flake of foam on the surface of the river. A scroll of papyrus encircled the wood of the arrow. It bore only these words, written in Phoenician characters, "I love you!"

CHAPTER IV

"I love you," repeated Cleopatra, making the serpent-coiling strip of papyrus writhe between her delicate white fingers. "Those are the words I longed for. What intelligent spirit, what invisible genius has thus so fully comprehended my desire?"

And thoroughly aroused from her languid torpor, she sprang out of bed with the agility of a cat which has scented a mouse, placed her little ivory feet in her embroidered *tatbebs*, threw a byssus tunic over her shoulders, and ran to the window from which Charmion was still gazing.

The night was clear and calm. The risen moon outlined with huge angles of light and shadow the architectural masses of the palace, which stood out in strong relief against a background of bluish transparency; and the waters of the river, wherein her reflection lengthened into a shining column, were frosted with silvery ripples. A gentle breeze, such as might have been mistaken for the respiration of the slumbering sphinxes, quivered among the reeds and shook the azure bells of the lotus flowers; the cables of the vessels moored to the Nile's banks groaned feebly, and the rippling tide moaned upon the shore like a dove lamenting for its mate. A vague perfume of vegetation, sweeter than that of the aromatics burned in the *anschir* of the priests of Anubis, floated into the chamber. It was one of those enchanted nights of the Orient, which are more splendid than our fairest days; for our sun can ill compare with that Oriental moon.

"Do you not see far over there, almost in the middle of the river, the head of a man swimming? See, he crosses that track of light, and passes into the shadow beyond! He is already out of sight!" And, supporting herself upon Charmion's shoulder, she leaned out, with half of her fair body beyond the sill of the window, in the effort to catch another glimpse of the mysterious swimmer; but a grove of Nile acacias, dhoum-palms, and sayals flung its deep shadow upon the river in that direction, and protected the flight of the daring fugitive. If Meïamoun had but had the courtesy to look back, he might have beheld Cleopatra, the sidereal queen, eagerly seeking him through the night gloom – he, the poor obscure Egyptian, the miserable lion-hunter.

"Charmion, Charmion, send hither Phrehipephbour, the chief of the rowers, and have two boats despatched in pursuit of that man!" cried Cleopatra, whose curiosity was excited to the highest pitch.

Phrehipephbour appeared, a man of the race of Nahasi, with large hands and muscular arms, wearing a red cap not unlike a Phrygian helmet in form, and clad only in a pair of narrow drawers diagonally striped with white and blue. His huge torso, entirely nude, black and polished like a globe of jet, shone under the lamplight. He received the commands of the queen and instantly retired to execute them.

Two long, narrow boats, so light that the least inattention to equilibrium would capsize them, were soon cleaving the waters of the Nile with hissing rapidity under the efforts of the twenty vigorous rowers, but the pursuit was all in vain. After searching the river banks in every direction, and carefully exploring every patch of reeds, Phrehipephbour returned to the palace, having only succeeded in putting to flight some solitary heron which had been sleeping on one leg, or in troubling the digestion of some terrified crocodile.

So intense was the vexation of Cleopatra at being thus foiled, that she felt a strong inclination to condemn Phrehipephbour either to the wild beasts or to the hardest labour at the grindstone. Happily, Charmion interceded for the trembling unfortunate, who turned pale with fear, despite his black skin. It was the first time in Cleopatra's life that one of her desires had not been gratified as soon as expressed, and she experienced, in consequence, a kind of uneasy surprise; a first doubt, as it were, of her own omnipotence.

She, Cleopatra, wife and sister of Ptolemy – she who had been proclaimed goddess Evergetes, living queen of the regions Above and Below, Eye of Light, Chosen of the Sun (as may still be read within the cartouches sculptured on the walls of the temples) – she to find an obstacle in her path, to have wished aught that failed of accomplishment, to have spoken and not been obeyed! As well be the wife of some wretched Paraschistes, some corpse-cutter, and melt natron in a caldron! It was monstrous, preposterous! And none but the most gentle and clement of queens could have refrained from crucifying that miserable Phrehipephbour.

You wished for some adventure, something strange and unexpected. Your wish has been gratified. You find that your kingdom is not so dead as you deemed it. It was not the stony arm of a statue which shot that arrow; it was not from a mummy's heart that came those three words which have moved even you – you who smilingly watched your poisoned slaves dashing their heads and beating their feet upon your beautiful mosaic and porphyry pavements in the convulsions of death-agony; you who even applauded the tiger which boldly buried its muzzle in the flank of some vanquished gladiator.

You could obtain all else you might wish for – chariots of silver, starred with emeralds; griffin-quadrigerae; tunics of purple thrice-dyed; mirrors of molten steel, so clear that you might find the charms of your loveliness faithfully copied in them; robes from the land of Serica, so fine and subtly light that they could be drawn through the ring worn upon your little finger; Orient pearls of wondrous colour; cups wrought by Myron or Lysippus; Indian paroquets that speak like poets – all things else you could obtain, even should you ask for the Cestus of Venus or the *pshent* of Isis, but most certainly you cannot this night capture the man who shot the arrow which still quivers in the cedar wood of your couch.

The task of the slaves who must dress you to-morrow will not be a grateful one. They will hardly escape with blows. The bosom of the unskilful waiting-maid will be apt to prove a cushion for the golden pins of the toilette, and the poor hair-dresser will run great risk of being suspended by her feet from the ceiling.

"Who could have had the audacity to send me this avowal upon the shaft of an arrow? Could it have been the Nomarch Amoun-Ra who fancies himself handsomer than the Apollo of the Greeks? What think you, Charmion? Or perhaps Cheâpsiro, commander of Hermothybia, who is so boastful of his conquests in the land of Kush? Or is it not more likely to have been young Sextus, that Roman debauchee who paints his face, lisps in speaking, and wears sleeves in the fashion of the Persians?"

"Queen, it was none of those. Though you are indeed the fairest of women, those men only flatter you; they do not love you. The Nomarch Amoun-Ra has chosen himself an idol to which he will be forever faithful, and that is his own person. The warrior Cheâpsiro thinks of nothing save the pleasure of recounting his victories. As for Sextus, he is so seriously occupied with the preparation of a new cosmetic that he cannot dream of anything else. Besides, he has just purchased some Laconian dresses, a number of yellow tunics embroidered with gold, and some Asiatic children which absorb all his time. Not one of those fine lords would risk his head in so daring and dangerous an undertaking; they do not love you well enough for that.

"Yesterday, in your cangia, you said that men dared not fix their dazzled eyes upon you; that they knew only how to turn pale in your presence, to fall at your feet and supplicate your mercy; and that your sole remaining resource would be to awake some ancient, bitumen-perfumed Pharaoh from his gilded coffin. Now here is an ardent and youthful heart that loves you. What will you do with it?"

Cleopatra that night sought slumber in vain. She tossed feverishly upon her couch, and long and vainly invoked Morpheus, the brother of Death. She incessantly repeated that she was the most unhappy of queens, that every one sought to persecute her, and that her life had become insupportable; woeful lamentations which had little effect upon Charmion, although she pretended to sympathize with them.

Let us for a while leave Cleopatra to seek fugitive sleep, and direct her suspicions successively upon each noble of the court. Let us return to Meïamoun, and as we are much more sagacious than Phrehipephbour, chief of the rowers, we shall have no difficulty in finding him.

Terrified at his own hardihood, Meïamoun had thrown himself into the Nile, and had succeeded in swimming the current and gaining the little grove of dhoum-palms before Phrehipephbour had even launched the two boats in pursuit of him.

When he had recovered breath, and brushed back his long black locks, all damp with river foam, behind his ears, he began

54

to feel more at ease, more inwardly calm. Cleopatra possessed something which had come from him; some sort of communication was now established between them. Cleopatra was thinking of him, Meïamoun. Perhaps that thought might be one of wrath; but then he had at least been able to awake some feeling within her, whether of fear, anger, or pity. He had forced her to the consciousness of his existence. It was true that he had forgotten to inscribe his name upon the papyrus scroll, but what more of him could the queen have learned from the inscription, *Meïamoun, Son of Mandouschopsh?* In her eyes the slave and the monarch were equal. A goddess in choosing a peasant for her lover stoops no lower than in choosing a patrician or a king. The Immortals from a height so lofty can behold only love in the man of their choice.

The thought which had weighed upon his breast like the knee of a colossus of brass had at last departed. It had traversed the air; it had even reached the queen herself, the apex of the triangle, the inaccessible summit. It had aroused curiosity in that impassive heart; a prodigious advance, truly, toward success.

Meïamoun, indeed, never suspected that he had so thoroughly succeeded in this wise, but he felt more tranquil; for he had sworn unto himself by that mystic Bari who guides the souls of the dead to Amenthi, by the sacred birds Bermou and Ghenghen, by Typhon and by Osiris, and by all things awful in Egyptian mythology, that he should be the accepted lover of Cleopatra, though it were but for a single night, though for only a single hour, though it should cost him his life and even his very soul.

If we must explain how he had fallen so deeply in love with a woman whom he had beheld only from afar off, and to whom he had hardly dared to raise his eyes – even he who was wont to gaze fearlessly into the yellow eyes of the lion – or how the tiny seed of love, chance-fallen upon his heart, had grown there so rapidly and extended its roots so deeply, we can answer only that it is a mystery which we are unable to explain. We have already said of Meïamoun, – The Abyss called him.

Once assured that Phrehipephbour had returned with his rowers, he again threw himself into the current and once more swam toward the palace of Cleopatra, whose lamp still shone through the window curtains like a painted star. Never did Leander swim with more courage and vigour toward the tower of Sestos; yet for Meïamoun no Hero was waiting, ready to pour vials of perfume upon his head to dissipate the briny odours of the sea and banish the sharp kisses of the storm.

A strong blow from some keen lance or *harpe* was certainly the worst he had to fear, and in truth he had but little fear of such things.

He swam close under the walls of the palace, which bathed its marble feet in the river's depths, and paused an instant before a submerged archway into which the water rushed downward in eddying whirls. Twice, thrice he plunged into the vortex unsuccessfully. At last, with better luck, he found the opening and disappeared.

This archway was the opening to a vaulted canal which conducted the waters of the Nile into the baths of Cleopatra.

CHAPTER V

Cleopatra found no rest until morning, at the hour when wandering dreams reënter the Ivory Gate. Amid the illusions of sleep she beheld all kinds of lovers swimming rivers and scaling walls in order to come to her, and, through the vague souvenirs of the night before, her dreams appeared fairly riddled with arrows bearing declarations of love. Starting nervously from time to time in her troubled slumbers, she struck her little feet unconsciously against the bosom of Charmion, who lay across the foot of the bed to serve her as a cushion.

When she awoke, a merry sunbeam was playing through the window curtain, whose woof it penetrated with a thousand tiny points of light, and thence came familiarly to the bed, flitting like a golden butterfly over her lovely shoulders, which it lightly touched in passing by with a luminous kiss. Happy sunbeam, which the gods might well have envied.

In a faint voice, like that of a sick child, Cleopatra asked to be lifted out of bed. Two of her women raised her in their arms and gently laid her on a tiger-skin stretched upon the floor, of which the eyes were formed of carbuncles and the claws of gold. Charmion wrapped her in a *calasiris* of linen whiter than milk, confined her hair in a net of woven silver threads, tied to her little feet cork *tatbebs* upon the soles of which were painted, in token of contempt, two grotesque figures, representing two men of the races of Nahasi and Nahmou, bound hand and foot, so that Cleopatra literally deserved the epithet, "Conculcatrix of Nations," which the royal cartouche inscriptions bestow upon her.

It was the hour for the bath. Cleopatra went to bathe, accompanied by her women.

The baths of Cleopatra were built in the midst of immense gardens filled with mimosas, aloes, carob-trees, citron-trees, and Persian apple-trees, whose luxuriant freshness afforded a delicious contrast to the arid appearance of the neighbouring vegetation. There, too, vast terraces uplifted masses of verdant foliage, and enabled flowers to climb almost to the very sky upon gigantic stairways of rose-coloured granite; vases of Pentelic marble bloomed at the end of each step like huge lily-flowers, and the plants they contained seemed only their pistils; chimeras caressed into form by the chisels of the most skilful Greek sculptors, and less stern of aspect than the Egyptian sphinxes, with their grim mien and moody attitudes, softly extended their limbs upon the flower-strewn turf, like shapely white leverettes upon a drawing-room carpet. These were charming feminine figures, with finely chiselled nostrils, smooth brows, small mouths, delicately dimpled arms, breasts, fair-rounded and daintily formed; wearing earrings, necklaces, and all the trinkets suggested by adorable caprice; whose bodies terminated in bifurcated fishes' tails, like the women described by Horace, or extended into birds' wings, or rounded into lions' haunches, or blended into volutes of foliage, according to the fancies of the artist or in conformity to the architectural position chosen. A double row of these delightful monsters lined the alley which led from the palace to the bathing halls.

At the end of this alley was a huge fountain-basin, approached by four porphyry stairways. Through the transparent depths of the diamond-clear water the steps could be seen descending to the bottom of the basin, which was strewn with gold-dust in lieu of sand. Here figures of women terminating in pedestals like Caryatides spurted from their breasts slender jets of perfumed water, which fell into the basin in silvery dew, pitting the clear watery mirror with wrinkle-creating drops. In addition to this task these Caryatides had likewise that of supporting upon their heads an entablature decorated with Nereids and Tritons in bas-relief, and furnished with rings of bronze to which the silken cords of a velarium might be attached. From the portico was visible an extending expanse of freshly humid, bluish-green verdure and cool shade, a fragment of the Vale of Tempe transported to Egypt. The famous gardens of Semiramis would not have borne comparison with these.

We will not pause to describe the seven or eight other halls of various temperature, with their hot and cold vapours, perfume boxes, cosmetics, oils, pumice stone, gloves of woven horsehair, and all the refinements of the antique balneatory art brought to the highest pitch of voluptuous perfection.

Hither came Cleopatra, leaning with one hand upon the shoulder of Charmion. She had taken at least thirty steps all by herself. Mighty effort, enormous fatigue! A tender tint of rose commenced to suffuse the transparent skin of her cheeks, refreshing their passionate pallor; a blue network of veins relieved the amber blondness of her temples; her marble forehead, low like the antique foreheads, but full and perfect in form, united by one faultless line with a straight nose, finely chiselled as a cameo, with rosy nostrils which the least emotion made palpitate like the nostrils of an amorous tigress; the lips of her small, rounded mouth slightly separated from the nose, wore a disdainful curve; but an unbridled voluptuousness, an indescribable vital warmth, glowed in the brilliant crimson and humid lustre of the under lip. Her eyes were shaded by level eyelids, and eyebrows slightly arched and delicately outlined. We cannot attempt by description to convey an idea of their brilliancy. It was a fire, a languor, a sparkling limpidity which might have made even the dog-headed Anubis giddy. Every glance of her eyes was in itself a poem richer than aught of Homer or Mimnermus. An imperial chin, replete with force and power to command, worthily completed this charming profile.

She stood erect upon the upper step of the basin, in an attitude full of proud grace; her figure slightly thrown back, and one foot in suspense, like a goddess about to leave her pedestal, whose eyes still linger on heaven. Her robe fell in two superb folds from the peaks of her bosom to her feet in unbroken lines. Had Cleomenes been her contemporary and enjoyed the happiness of beholding her thus, he would have broken his Venus in despair.

Before entering the water she bade Charmion, for a new caprice, to change her silver hair-net; she preferred to be crowned with reeds and lotos-flowers, like a water divinity. Charmion obeyed, and her liberated hair fell in black cascades over her shoulders, and shadowed her beautiful cheeks in rich bunches, like ripening grapes.

Then the linen tunic, which had been confined only by one golden clasp, glided down over her marble body, and fell in a white cloud at her feet, like the swan at the feet of Leda....

59

And Meïamoun, where was he?

Oh cruel lot, that so many insensible objects should enjoy the favours which would ravish a lover with delight! The wind which toys with a wealth of perfumed hair, or kisses beautiful lips with kisses which it is unable to appreciate; the water which envelopes an adorable beautiful body in one universal kiss, and is yet, notwithstanding, indifferent to that exquisite pleasure; the mirror which reflects so many charming images; the buskin or *tatbeb* which clasps a divine little foot – oh, what happiness lost!

Cleopatra dipped her pink heel in the water and descended a few steps. The quivering flood made a silver belt about her waist, and silver bracelets about her arms, and rolled in pearls like a broken necklace over her bosom and shoulders; her wealth of hair, lifted by the water, extended behind her like a royal mantle; even in the bath she was a queen. She swam to and fro, dived, and brought up handfuls of gold-dust with which she laughingly pelted some of her women. Again, she clung suspended to the balustrade of the basin, concealing or exposing her treasures of loveliness – now permitting only her lustrous and polished back to be seen, now showing her whole figure, like Venus Anadyomene, and incessantly varying the aspects of her beauty.

Suddenly she uttered a cry as shrill as that of Diana surprised by Actaeon. She had seen gleaming through the neighbouring foliage a burning eye, yellow and phosphoric as the eye of a crocodile or lion.

It was Meïamoun, who, crouching behind a tuft of leaves, and trembling like a fawn in a field of wheat, was intoxicating himself with the dangerous pleasure of beholding the queen in her bath. Though brave even to temerity, the cry of Cleopatra passed through his heart, coldly piercing as the blade of a sword. A death-like sweat covered his whole body; his arteries hissed through his temples with a sharp sound; the iron hand of anxious fear had seized him by the throat and was strangling him.

The eunuchs rushed forward, lance in hand. Cleopatra pointed out to them the group of trees, where they found Meïamoun crouching in concealment. Defence was out of the question. He attempted none, and suffered himself to be captured. They prepared to kill him with that cruel and stupid impassibility characteristic of eunuchs; but Cleopatra, who, in the interim, had covered herself with her *calasiris*, made signs to them to stop, and bring the prisoner before her.

Meïamoun could only fall upon his knees and stretch forth suppliant hands to her, as to the altars of the gods.

"Are you some assassin bribed by Rome, or for what purpose have you entered these sacred precincts from which all men are excluded?" demanded Cleopatra with an imperious gesture of interrogation.

"May my soul be found light in the balance of Amenti, and may Tmeï, daughter of the Sun and goddess of Truth, punish me if I have ever entertained a thought of evil against you, O queen!" answered Meïamoun, still upon his knees.

Sincerity and loyalty were written upon his countenance in characters so transparent that Cleopatra immediately banished her suspicions, and looked upon the young Egyptian with a look less stern and wrathful. She saw that he was beautiful.

"Then what motive could have prompted you to enter a place where you could only expect to meet death?"

"I love you!" murmured Meïamoun in a low, but distinct voice; for his courage had returned, as in every desperate situation when the odds against him could be no worse.

"Ah!" cried Cleopatra, bending toward him, and seizing his arm with a sudden brusque movement, "so, then, it was you who shot that arrow with the papyrus scroll! By Oms, the Dog of Hell, you are a very foolhardy wretch!... I now recognize you. I long observed you wandering like a complaining Shade about the places where I dwell.... You were at the Procession of Isis, at the Panegyris of Hermonthis. You followed the royal cangia. Ah! you must have a queen?... You have no mean ambitions. You expect, without doubt, to be well paid in return.... Assuredly I am going to love you.... Why not?"

"Queen," returned Meïamoun with a look of deep melancholy, "do not rail. I am mad, it is true. I have deserved death; that is also true. Be humane; bid them kill me."

"No; I have taken the whim to be clement to-day. I will give you your life."

"What would you that I should do with life? I love you!"

"Well, then, you shall be satisfied; you shall die," answered Cleopatra. "You have indulged yourself in wild and extravagant dreams; in fancy your desires have crossed an impassable threshold. You imagined yourself to be Caesar or Mark Antony. You loved the queen. In some moment of delirium you have been able to believe that, under some condition of things which takes place but once in a thousand years, Cleopatra might some day love you. Well, what you thought impossible is actually about to happen. I will transform your dream into a reality. It pleases me, for once, to secure the accomplishment of a mad hope. I am willing to inundate you with glories and splendours and lightnings. I intend that your good fortune shall be dazzling in its brilliancy. You were at the bottom of the ladder. I am about to lift you to the summit, abruptly, suddenly, without a transition. I take you out of nothingness, I make you the equal of a god, and I plunge you back again into nothingness; that is all. But do not presume to call me cruel or to invoke my pity; do not weaken when the hour comes. I am good to you. I lend myself to your folly. I have the right to order you to be killed at once; but since you tell me that you love me, I will have you killed tomorrow instead. Your life belongs to me for one night. I am generous. I will buy it from you; I could take it from you. But what are you doing on your knees at my feet? Rise, and give me your arm, that we may return to the palace."

CHAPTER VI

Our world of to-day is puny indeed beside the antique world. Our banquets are mean, niggardly, compared with the appalling sumptuousness of the Roman patricians and the princes of ancient Asia. Their ordinary repasts would in these days be regarded as frenzied orgies, and a whole modern city could subsist for eight days upon the leavings of one supper given by Lucullus to a few intimate friends. With our miserable habits we find it difficult to conceive of those enormous existences, realising everything vast, strange, and most monstrously impossible that imagination could devise. Our palaces are mere stables, in which Caligula would not quarter his horse. The retinue of our wealthiest constitutional king is as nothing compared with that of a petty satrap or a Roman proconsul. The radiant suns which once shone upon the earth are forever extinguished in the nothingness of uniformity. Above the dark swarm of men no longer tower those Titanic colossi who bestrode the world in three paces, like the steeds of Homer; no more towers of Lylacq; no giant Babel scaling the sky with its infinity of spirals; no temples immeasurable, builded with the fragments of quarried mountains; no kingly terraces for which successive ages and generations could each erect but one step, and from whence some dreamfully reclining prince might gaze on the face of the world as upon a map unfolded; no more of those extravagantly vast cities of cyclopaean edifices, inextricably piled upon one another, with their mighty circumvallations, their circuses roaring night and day, their reservoirs filled with ocean brine and peopled with whales and leviathans, their colossal stairways, their super-imposition of terraces, their tower-summits bathed in clouds, their giant palaces, their aqueducts, their multitude-vomiting gates, their shadowy necropoli. Alas! henceforth only plaster hives upon chessboard pavements.

One marvels that men did not revolt against such confiscation of all riches and all living forces for the benefit of a few privileged ones, and that such exorbitant fantasies should not have encountered any opposition on their bloody way. It was because those prodigious lives were the realizations by day of the dreams which haunted each man by night, the personifications of the common ideal which the nations beheld living symbolized under one of those meteoric names that flame inextinguishably through the night of ages. To-day, deprived of such dazzling spectacles of omnipotent will, of the lofty contemplation of some human mind whose least wish makes itself visible in actions unparalleled, in enormities of granite and brass, the world becomes irredeemably and hopelessly dull. Man is no longer represented in the realization of his imperial fancy.

The story which we are writing, and the great name of Cleopatra which appears in it, have promoted us to these reflections, so ill-sounding, doubtless, to modern ears. But the spectacle of the antique world is something so crushingly discouraging, even to those imaginations which deem themselves exhaustless, and those minds which fancy themselves to have conceived the utmost limits of fairy magnificence, that we cannot here forbear recording our regret and lamentation that we were not contemporaries of Sardanapalus; of Teglathphalazar; of Cleopatra, queen of Egypt; or even of Elagabalus, emperor of Rome and priest of the Sun.

It is our task to describe a supreme orgie – a banquet compared with which the splendours of Belshazzar's feast must pale – one of Cleopatra's nights. How can we picture forth in this French tongue, so chaste, so icily prudish, that unbounded transport of passions, that huge and mighty debauch which feared not to mingle the double purple of wine and blood, those furious outbursts of insatiate pleasure, madly leaping toward the Impossible with all the wild ardour of senses as yet untamed by the long fast of Christianity?

The promised night should well have been a splendid one, for all the joys and pleasures possible in a human lifetime were to be concentrated into the space of a few hours. It was necessary that the life of Meïamoun should be converted into a powerful elixir which he could imbibe at a single draught. Cleopatra desired to dazzle her voluntary victim, and plunge him into a whirlpool of dizzy pleasures; to intoxicate and madden him with the wine of orgie, so that death, though freely accepted, might come invisibly and unawares.

Let us transport our readers to the banquet-hall.

Our existing architecture offers few points for comparison with those vast edifices whose very ruins resemble the crumblings of mountains rather than the remains of buildings. It needed all the exaggeration of the antique life to animate and fill those prodigious palaces, whose halls were too lofty and vast to allow of any ceiling save the sky itself – a magnificent ceiling, and well worthy of such mighty architecture.

The banquet-hall was of enormous and Babylonian dimensions; the eye could not penetrate its immeasurable depth. Monstrous columns – short, thick, and solid enough to sustain the pole itself – heavily expanded their broad-swelling shafts upon socles variegated with hieroglyphics, and sustained upon their bulging capitals gigantic arcades of granite rising by successive tiers, like vast stairways reversed. Between each two pillars a colossal sphinx of basalt, crowned with the *pschent*, bent forward her oblique-eyed face and horned chin, and gazed into the hall with a fixed and mysterious look. The columns of the second tier, receding from the first, were more elegantly formed, and crowned in lieu of capitals with four female heads addorsed, wearing caps of many folds and all the intricacies of the Egyptian headdress. Instead of sphinxes, bull-headed idols – impassive spectators of nocturnal frenzy and the furies of orgie – were seated upon thrones of stone, like patient hosts awaiting the opening of the banquet.

A third story, constructed in a yet different style of architecture, with elephants of bronze spouting perfume from their trunks, crowned the edifice; above, the sky yawned like a blue gulf, and the curious stars leaned over the frieze.

Prodigious stairways of porphyry, so highly polished that they reflected the human body like a mirror, ascended and descended on every hand, and bound together these huge masses of architecture.

We can only make a very rapid sketch here, in order to convey some idea of this awful structure, proportioned out of all human measurements. It would require the pencil of Martin, the great painter of enormities passed away, and we can present only a weak pen-picture in lieu of the Apocalyptic depth of his gloomy style; but imagination may supply our deficiencies. Less fortunate than the painter and the musician, we can only present objects and ideas separately in slow succession. We have as yet spoken of the banquet-hall only, without referring to the guests, and yet we have but barely indicated its character. Cleopatra and Meïamoun are waiting for us. We see them drawing near....

Meïamoun was clad in a linen tunic constellated with stars, and a purple mantle, and wore a fillet about his locks, like an Oriental king. Cleopatra was apparelled in a robe of pale green, open at either side, and clasped with golden bees. Two bracelets of immense pearls gleamed around her naked arms; upon her head glimmered the golden-pointed diadem. Despite the smile on her lips, a slight cloud of preoccupation shadowed her fair forehead, and from time to time her brows became knitted in a feverish manner. What thoughts could trouble the great queen? As for Meïamoun, his face wore the ardent and luminous look of one in ecstasy or vision; light beamed and radiated from his brow and temples, surrounding his head with a golden nimbus, like one of the twelve great gods of Olympus.

A deep, heartfelt joy illumined his every feature. He had embraced his restless-winged chimera, and it had not flown from him; he had reached the goal of his life. Though he were to live to the age of Nestor or Priam, though he should behold his veined temples hoary with locks whiter than those of the high priest of Ammon, he could never know another new experience, never feel another new pleasure. His maddest hopes had been so much more than realised that there was nothing in the world left for him to desire.

Cleopatra seated him beside her upon a throne with golden griffins on either side, and clapped her little hands together.

Instantly lines of fire, bands of sparkling light, outlined all the projections of the architecture – the eyes of the sphinxes flamed with phosphoric lightnings; the bull-headed idols breathed flame; the elephants, in lieu of perfumed water, spouted aloft bright columns of crimson fire; arms of bronze, each bearing a torch, started from the walls and blazing aigrettes bloomed in the sculptured hearts of the lotos flowers.

Huge blue flames palpitated in tripods of brass; giant candelabras shook their dishevelled light in the midst of ardent vapours; everything sparkled, glittered, beamed. Prismatic irises crossed and shattered each other in the air. The facets of the cups, the angles of the marbles and jaspers, the chiselling of the vases – all caught a sparkle, a gleam or a flash as of lightning. Radiance streamed in torrents and leaped from step to step like a cascade, over the porphyry stairways. It seemed the reflection of a conflagration on some broad river. Had the Queen of Sheba ascended thither she would have caught up the folds of her robe, and believed herself walking in water, as when she stepped upon the crystal pavements of Solomon. Viewed through that burning haze, the monstrous figures of the colossi, the animals, the hieroglyphics, seemed to become animated and to live with a factitious life; the black marble rams bleated ironically, and clashed their gilded horns; the idols breathed harshly through their panting nostrils.

The orgie was at its height: the dishes of phenicopters' tongues, and the livers of scarus fish; the eels fattened upon human flesh, and cooked in brine; the dishes of peacock's brains; the boars stuffed with living birds; and all the marvels of the antique banquets were heaped upon the three table-surfaces of the gigantic triclinium. The wines of Crete, of Massicus, and of Falernus foamed up in cratera wreathed with roses, and filled by Asiatic pages whose beautiful flowing hair served the guests to wipe their hands upon. Musicians playing upon the sistrum, the tympanum, the sambuke, and the harp with one-and-twenty strings filled all the upper galleries, and mingled their harmonies with the tempest of sound that hovered over the feast. Even the deep-voiced thunder could not have made itself heard there.

Meïamoun, whose head was lying on Cleopatra's shoulder, felt as though his reason were leaving him. The banquet-hall whirled around him like a vast architectural nightmare; through the dizzy glare he beheld perspectives and colonnades without end; new zones of porticoes seemed to uprear themselves upon the real fabric, and bury their summits in heights of sky to which Babel never rose. Had he not felt within his hand the soft, cool hand of Cleopatra, he would have believed himself transported into an enchanted world by some witch of Thessaly or Magian of Persia.

Toward the close of the repast hump-backed dwarfs and mummers engaged in grotesque dances and combats; then young Egyptian and Greek maidens, representing the black and white Hours, danced with inimitable grace a voluptuous dance after the Ionian manner.

Cleopatra herself arose from her throne, threw aside her royal mantle, replaced her starry diadem with a garland of flowers, attached golden *crotali* to her alabaster hands, and began to dance before Meïamoun, who was ravished with delight. Her beautiful arms, rounded like the handles of an alabaster vase, shook out bunches of sparkling notes, and her *crotali* prattled with ever-increasing volubility. Poised on the pink tips of her little feet, she approached swiftly to graze the forehead of Meïamoun with a kiss; then she recommenced her wondrous art, and flitted around him, now backward-leaning, with head reversed, eyes half closed, arms lifelessly relaxed, locks uncurled and loose-hanging like a Bacchante of Mount Meanalus; now again, active, animated, laughing, fluttering, more tireless and capricious in her movements than the pilfering bee. Heart-consuming love, sensual pleasure, burning passion, youth inexhaustible and ever-fresh, the promise of bliss to come – she expressed all....

The modest stars had ceased to contemplate the scene; their

golden eyes could not endure such a spectacle; the heaven itself was blotted out, and a dome of flaming vapour covered the hall.

Cleopatra seated herself once more by Meïamoun. Night advanced; the last of the black Hours was about to take flight; a faint blue glow entered with bewildered aspect into the tumult of ruddy light as a moonbeam falls into the furnace; the upper arcades became suffused with pale azure tints – day was breaking.

Meïamoun took the horn vase which an Ethiopian slave of sinister countenance presented to him, and which contained a poison so violent that it would have caused any other vase to burst asunder. Flinging his whole life to his mistress in one last look, he lifted to his lips the fatal cup in which the envenomed liquor boiled up, hissing.

Cleopatra turned pale, and laid her hand on Meïamoun's arm to stay the act. His courage touched her. She was about to say, "Live to love me yet, I desire it!..." when the sound of a clarion was heard. Four heralds-at-arms entered the banquet-hall on horseback; they were officers of Mark Antony, and rode but a short distance in advance of their master. Cleopatra silently loosened the arm of Meïamoun. A long ray of sunlight suddenly played upon her forehead, as though trying to replace her absent diadem.

"You see the moment has come; it is daybreak, it is the hour when happy dreams take flight," said Meïamoun. Then he emptied the fatal vessel at a draught, and fell as though struck by lightning. Cleopatra bent her head, and one burning tear – the only one she had ever shed – fell into her cup to mingle with the molten pearl.

"By Hercules, my fair queen! I made all speed in vain. I see I have come too late," cried Mark Antony, entering the banquet-hall, "the supper is over. But what signifies this corpse upon the pavement?"

"Oh, nothing!" returned Cleopatra, with a smile; "only a poison I was testing with the idea of using it upon myself should Augustus take me prisoner. My dear Lord, will you not please

69

to take a seat beside me, and watch those Greek buffoons dance?"

THE METAMORPHOSES OF THE VAMPIRE
by
Charles Baudelaire
Translated by Francis Amery

Writhing like a serpent in the ashes of a fire,
Moulding her breasts upon her corset's wire
The woman from her luscious mouth lets spill
These words which musky perfumes fill:
"Mine are the moist lips, mine the cunning skill,
That in a bed can sap the force of conscientious will.
On my invigorating bosom all tears are dried,
And the grimace of the man becomes the smile of the child.
For he who sees me naked, unobscured by any veil,
I am the sun, the moon, the stars, the Holy Grail!
I am, dear scholar, so learned in voluptuous charms,
That once I smother a man with my awesome arms,
Or abandon my tender breasts to his hungry lust,
So timid yet licentious, fragile yet robust,
Even an angel would be powerless, damned for me,
Upon these very cushions, drowned by ecstasy."

When she had sucked the marrow from my every bone,
And I turned towards her, lumpen as a stone,
To bestow a loving kiss, I saw her thus:
As a slime-walled bladder full of oozing pus!
I closed my eyes, struck cold by fright,
And when I opened them again to vivid light,
Beside me, in place of the ardent mannequin
Which had drunk blood from veins beneath my skin,
Quivered in confusion a skeleton's wrack,
Creaking like a rusted weathercock,
Or a sign suspended from an iron ring
Made by the wind on a winter night to swing.

MORELLA
by
Edgar Allan Poe

With a feeling of deep yet most singular affection I regarded my friend Morella. Thrown by accident into her society many years ago, my soul, from our first meeting, burned with fires it had never before known; but the fires were not of Eros, and bitter and tormenting to my spirit was the gradual conviction that I could in no manner define their unusual meaning, or regulate their vague intensity. Yet we met; and fate bound us together at the altar; and I never spoke of passion, nor thought of love. She, however, shunned society, and, attaching herself to me alone, rendered me happy. It is a happiness to wonder; – it is a happiness to dream.

Morella's erudition was profound. As I hope to live, her talents were of no common order – her powers of mind were gigantic. I felt this, and, in many matters, became her pupil. I soon, however, found that, perhaps in account of her Pressburg education, she placed before me a number of those mystical writings which are usually considered the mere dross of the early German literature. These, for what reason I could not imagine, were her favourite and constant study – and that, in process of time they became my own, should be attributed to the simple but effectual influence of habit and example.

In all this, if I err not, my reason had little to do. My convictions, or I forget myself, were in no manner acted upon by the ideal, nor was any tincture of the mysticism which I read, to be discovered, unless I am greatly mistaken, either in my deeds or in my thoughts. Persuaded of this, I abandoned myself implicitly to the guidance of my wife, and entered with an unflinching heart into the intricacies of her studies. And then – then, when, poring over forbidden pages, I felt a forbidden spirit enkindling within me – would Morella place her cold hand upon my own, and rake up from the ashes of a dead philosophy some low, singular words, whose strange meaning burned themselves in upon my memory. And then, hour after hour would I linger by her side, and dwell upon the music of her voice – until, at length, its melody was tainted with terror – and there fell a shadow upon my soul – and I grew pale, and shuddered inwardly at those too unearthly tones. And thus, joy suddenly faded into horror, and the most beautiful became the most hideous, as Hinnôm became Gehenna.

It is unnecessary to state the exact character of those disquisitions which, growing out of the volumes I have mentioned, formed, for so long a time, almost the sole conversation of Morella and myself. By the learned in what might be termed theological morality they will be readily conceived, and by the unlearned they would, at all events, be little understood. The wild Pantheism of Fichte; the modified Παλιγγενεσια of Pythagoreans; and, above all, the doctrines of *Identity* as urged by Schelling, were generally the points of discussion presenting the most of beauty to the imaginative Morella. That identity which is termed personal, Mr. Locke, I think, truly defines to consist in the saneness of a rational being. And since by person we understand an intelligent essence having reason, and since there is a consciousness which always accompanies thinking, it is this which makes us all to be that which we call *ourselves* – thereby distinguishing us from other beings that think, and giving us our personal identity. But the *principium individuationis* – the notion of that identity *which at death is or is not lost for ever* – was to me, at all times, a consideration of intense interest; not more from the perplexing and exciting nature of its consequences, than from the marked and agitated manner in which Morella mentioned them.

But, indeed, the time had now arrived when the mystery of my wife's manner oppressed me as a spell. I could no longer bear the touch of her wan fingers, nor the low tone of her musical language, nor the lustre of her melancholy eyes. And she knew all this, but did not upbraid; she seemed conscious of my weakness or my folly, and, smiling, called it Fate. She seemed, also, conscious of a cause, to me unknown, for the gradual alienation of my regard; but she gave me no hint or token of its nature. Yet was she woman and pined away daily. In time, the crimson spot settled steadily upon the cheek, and the blue veins upon the pale forehead became prominent; and, one instant, my nature melted into pity, but, in the next, I met the glance of her meaning eyes, and then my soul sickened and became giddy with the giddiness of one who gazes downward into some dreary and unfathomable abyss.

Shall I then say that I longed with an earnest and consuming desire for the moment of Morella's decease? I did; but the fragile spirit clung to its tenement of clay for many days – for many weeks and irksome months – until my tortured nerves obtained the mastery over my mind, and I grew furious through delay, and with the heart of a fiend, cursed the days, and the hours, and the bitter moments, which seemed to lengthen and lengthen as her gentle life declined – like shadows in the dying of the day.

But one autumnal evening, when the winds lay still in heaven, Morella called me to her bedside. There was a dim mist over all the earth, and a warm glow upon the waters, and, amid the rich October leaves of the forest, a rainbow from the firmament had surely fallen.

"It is a day of days," she said, as I approached; "a day of all days either to live or die. It is a fair day for the sons of earth and life – ah, more fair for the daughters of heaven and death!"

I kissed her forehead, and she continued:

"I am dying, yet shall I live."

"Morella!"

"The days have never been when thou couldst love me – but her whom in life thou didst abhor, in death thou shalt adore."

"Morella!"

"I repeat that I am dying. But within me is a pledge of that affection – ah, how little! – which thou didst feel for me, Morella. And when my spirit departs shall the child live – thy child and mine, Morella's. But thy days shall be days of sorrow – that sorrow which is the most lasting of impressions, as the cypress is the most enduring of trees. For the hours of thy happiness are over; and joy is not gathered twice in a life, as the roses of Paestum twice in a year. Thou shalt no longer, then, play the Teian with time but, being ignorant of the myrtle and the vine, thou shalt bear about with thee thy shroud on the earth, as do the Moslemin at Mecca."

"Morella!" I cried, "Morella! how knowest thou this?" – but

74

she turned away her face upon the pillow, and, a slight tremor coming over her limbs, she thus died, and I heard her voice no more.

Yet, as she had foretold, her child – to which in dying she had given birth, which breathed not until the mother breathed no more – her child, a daughter, lived. And she grew strangely in stature and intellect, and was the perfect resemblance of her who had departed, and I loved her with a love more fervent than I had believed it possible to feel for any denizen of earth.

But, erelong, the heaven of this pure affection became darkened, and gloom, and horror and grief, swept over it in clouds. I said the child grew strangely in stature and intelligence. Strange, indeed, was her rapid increase in bodily size – but terrible, oh! terrible were the tumultuous thoughts which crowded upon me while watching the development of her mental being! Could it be otherwise, when I daily discovered in the conceptions of the child the adult powers and faculties of the woman? – when the lessons of experience fell from the lips of infancy? and when the wisdom or the passions of maturity I found hourly gleaming from its full and speculative eye? When, I say, all this became evident to my appalled senses – when I could no longer hide it from my soul, nor throw it off from those perceptions which trembled to receive it – is it to be wondered at that suspicions, of a nature fearful and exciting, crept in upon my spirit, or that my thoughts fell back aghast upon the wild tales and thrilling theories of the entombed Morella? I snatched from the scrutiny of the world a being whom destiny compelled me to adore, and in the rigorous seclusion of my home, watched with an agonizing anxiety over all which concerned the beloved.

And, as years rolled away, and I gazed, day after day, upon her holy, and mild and eloquent face, and poured over her maturing form, day after day did I discover new points of resemblance in the child to her mother, the melancholy and the dead. And, hourly, grew darker these shadows of similitude, and more full, and more definite, and more perplexing, and more hideously terrible in their aspect. For that her smile was like her mother's I could bear; but then I shuddered at its too perfect *identity* – that her eyes were like Morella's I could endure; but then they too often looked down into the depths of my soul with Morella's own intense and bewildering meaning. And in the contour of the high forehead, and in the ringlets of the silken hair, and in the wan fingers which buried themselves therein, and in the sad musical tones of her speech, and above all – oh! above all – in the phrases and expressions of the dead on the lips of the loved and the living, I found food for consuming thought and horror – for a worm that *would* not die.

Thus passed away two lustra of her life, and, as yet, my daughter remained nameless upon the earth. "My child," and "my love," were the designations usually prompted by a father's affection, and the rigid seclusion of her days precluded all other intercourse. Morella's name died with her at her death. Of the mother I had never spoken to the daughter; – it was impossible to speak. Indeed, during the brief period of her existence, the latter had received no impressions from the outer world, save such as might have been afforded by the narrow limits of her privacy. But at length the ceremony of baptism presented to my mind, in its unnerved and agitated condition, a present deliverance from the terrors of my destiny. And at the baptismal font I hesitated for a name. And many titles of the wise and beautiful, of old and modern times, of my own and foreign lands, came thronging to my lips, with many, many fair titles of the gentle, and the happy, and the good. What prompted me, then, to disturb the memory of the buried dead? What demon urged me to breathe that sound, which, in its very recollection, was wont to make ebb the purple blood in torrents from the temples to the heart? What fiend spoke from the recesses of my soul, when, amid those dim aisles, and in the silence of the night, I whispered within the ears of the holy man the syllables – Morella? What more than fiend convulsed the features of my child, and overspread them with hues of death, as starting to that scarcely audible sound, she turned her glassy eyes from the earth to heaven, and, falling prostrate on the black slabs of our ancestral vault, responded – "I am here!"

Distinct, coldly, calmly distinct, fell those few simple sounds within my ear, and thence like molten lead, rolled hissingly into my brain. Years – years may pass away, but the memory of

76

that epoch – never! Nor was I indeed ignorant of the flowers and the vine – but the hemlock and the cypress overshadowed me night and day. And I kept no reckoning of time or place, and the stars of my fate faded from heaven, and therefore the earth grew dark, and its figures passed by me, like flitting shadows, and among them all I beheld only – Morella. The winds of the firmament breathed but one sound within my ears, and the ripples upon the sea murmured evermore – Morella. But she died; and with my own hands I bore her to the tomb; and I laughed with a long and bitter laugh as I found no traces of the first, in the charnel where I laid the second, Morella.

DOLORES
(NOTRE-DAME DES SEPT DOULEURS)
by
Algernon Charles Swinburne

Cold eyelids that hide like a jewel
Hard eyes that grow soft for an hour;
The heavy white limbs, and the cruel
Red mouth like a venomous flower;
When these are gone by with their glories,
What shall rest of thee then, what remain,
O mystic and sombre Dolores,
Our Lady of Pain?

Seven sorrows the priests give their Virgin;
But thy sins, which are seventy times seven,
Seven ages would fail thee to purge in,
And then they would haunt thee in heaven:
Fierce midnights and famishing morrows,
And the loves that complete and control
All the joys of the flesh, all the sorrows
That wear out the soul.

O garment not golden but gilded,
O garden where all men may dwell,
O tower not of ivory, but builded
By hands that reach heaven from hell;
O mystical rose of the mire,
O house not of gold but of gain,
O house of unquenchable fire,
Our Lady of Pain!

O lips full of lust and laughter,
Curled snakes that are fed from my breast,
Bite hard, lest remembrance come after
And press with new lips where you pressed.
For my heart too springs up at the pressure,
Mine eyelids too moisten and burn;

Ah, feed me and fill me with pleasure,
Ere pain come in turn.

In yesterday's reach and to-morrow's,
Out of sight though they lie of to-day,
There have been and there yet shall be sorrows
That smite not and bite not in play.
The life and the love thou despisest,
These hurt us indeed, and in vain,
O wise among women, and wisest,
Our Lady of Pain.

Who gave thee thy wisdom? what stories
That stung thee, what visions that smote?
Wert thou pure and a maiden, Dolores,
When desire took thee first by the throat?
What bud was the shell of a blossom
That all men may smell too and pluck?
What milk fed thee first at what bosom?
What sins gave thee suck?

We shift and bedeck and bedrape us,
Thou art noble and nude and antique;
Libitina thy mother, Priapus
Thy father, a Tuscan and Greek.
We play with light loves in the portal,
And wince and relent and refrain;
Loves die, and we know thee immortal,
Our Lady of Pain.

Fruits fail and love dies and time ranges;
Thou art fed with perpetual breath,
And alive after infinite changes,
And fresh from the kisses of death;
Of languors rekindled and rallied,
Of barren delights and unclean,
Things monstrous and fruitless, a pallid
And poisonous queen.

Could you hurt me, sweet lips, though I hurt you?
Men touch them, and change in a trice
The lilies and languors of virtue
For the raptures and roses of vice;
Those lie where thy foot on the floor is,
These crown and caress thee and chain,
O splendid and sterile Dolores,
Our Lady of Pain.

There are sins it may be to discover,
There are deeds it may be to delight.
What new work wilt thou find for thy lover,
What new passions for daytime or night?
What spells that they know not a word of
Whose lives are as leaves overblown?
What tortures undreamt of, unheard of,
Unwritten, unknown?

A beautiful passionate body
That never has ached with a heart!
On thy mouth though the kisses are bloody,
Though they sting till it shudder and smart,
More kind than the love we adore is,
They hurt not the heart or the brain,
O bitter and tender Dolores,
Our Lady of Pain.

As our kisses relax and redouble,
From the lips and the foam and the fangs
Shall no new sin be born for men's trouble,
No dream of impossible pangs?
With the sweet of the sins of old ages
Wilt thou satiate thy soul as of yore?
Too sweet is the rind, say the sages,
Too bitter the core.

Hast thou told all thy secrets the last time,
And bared all thy beauties to one?

Ah, where shall we go then for pastime,
If the worst that can be has been done?
But sweet as the rind was the core is;
We are fain of thee still, we are fain,
O sanguine and subtle Dolores,
Our Lady of Pain.

By the hunger of change and emotion,
By the thirst of unbearable things,
By despair, the twin-born of devotion,
By the pleasure that winces and stings,
The delight that consumes the desire,
The desire that outruns the delight,
By the cruelty deaf as a fire
And blind as the night,

By the ravenous teeth that have smitten
Through the kisses that blossom and bud,
By the lips intertwisted and bitten
Till the foam has a savour of blood,
By the pulse as it rises and falters,
By the hands as they slacken and strain,
I adjure thee, respond from thine altars,
Our Lady of Pain.

Wilt thou smile as a woman disdaining
The light fire in the veins of a boy?
But he comes to thee sad, without feigning,
Who has wearied of sorrow and joy;
Less careful of labour and glory
Than the elders whose hair has uncurled;
And young, but with fancies as hoary
And grey as the world.

I have passed from the outermost portal
To the shrine where a sin is a prayer;
What care though the service be mortal?
O our Lady of Torture, what care?

All thine the last wine that I pour is,
The last in the chalice we drain,
O fierce and luxurious Dolores,
Our Lady of Pain.

All thine the new wine of desire,
The fruit of four lips as they clung
Till the hair and the eyelids took fire,
The foam of a serpentine tongue,
The froth of the serpents of pleasure.
More salt than the foam of the sea,
Now felt as a flame, now at leisure
As wine shed for me.

Ah thy people, thy children, thy chosen,
Marked cross from the womb and perverse!
They have found out the secret to cozen
The gods that constrain us and curse;
They alone, they are wise, and none other;
Give me place, even me, in their train,
O my sister, my spouse, and my mother,
Our Lady of Pain.

For the crown of our life as it closes
Is darkness, the fruit thereof dust;
No thorns go as deep as a rose's,
And love is more cruel than lust.
Time turns the old days to derision,
Our loves into corpses or wives;
And marriage and death and division
Make barren our lives.

And pale from the past we draw nigh thee,
And satiate with comfortless hours;
And we know thee, how all men belie thee,
And we gather the fruit of thy flowers;
The passion that slays and recovers,
The pangs and the kisses that rain

On the lips and the limbs of thy lovers,
Our Lady of Pain.

The desire of thy furious embraces
Is more than the wisdom of years,
On the blossom though blood lie in traces,
Though the foliage be sodden with tears.
For the lords in whose keeping the door is
That opens on all who draw breath
Gave the cypress to love, my Dolores,
The myrtle to death.

And they laughed, changing hands in the measure,
And they mixed and made peace after strife;
Pain melted in tears, and was pleasure;
Death tingled with blood, and was life.
Like lovers they melted and tingled,
In the dusk of thine innermost fane;
In the darkness they murmured and mingled,
Our Lady of Pain.

In a twilight where virtues are vices,
In thy chapels, unknown of the sun,
To a tune that enthralls and entices,
They were wed, and the twain were as one.
For the tune from thine altar hath sounded
Since God bade the world's work begin,
And the fume of thine incense abounded,
To sweeten the sin.

Love listens, and paler than ashes,
Through his curls as the crown on them slips,
Lifts languid wet eyelids and lashes,
And laughs with insatiable lips.
Thou shalt hush him with heavy caresses,
With music that scares the profane;
Thou shalt darken his eyes with thy tresses,
Our Lady of Pain.

Thou shalt blind his bright eyes though he wrestle,
Thou shalt chain his light limbs though he strive;
In his lips all thy serpents shall nestle,
In his hands all thy cruelties thrive.
In the daytime thy voice shall go through him,
In his dreams he shall feel thee and ache;
Thou shalt kindle by night and subdue him
Asleep and awake.

Thou shalt touch and make redder his roses
With juice not of fruit nor of bud;
When the sense in the spirit reposes,
Thou shalt quicken the soul through the blood.
Thine, thine the one grace we implore is,
Who would live and not languish or feign,
O sleepless and deadly Dolores,
Our Lady of Pain.

Dost thou dream, in a respite of slumber,
In a lull of the fires of thy life,
Of the days without name, without number,
When thy will stung the world into strife;
When, a goddess, the pulse of thy passion
Smote kings as they revelled in Rome;
And they hailed thee re-risen, O Thalassian,
Foam-white, from the foam?

When thy lips had such lovers to flatter;
When the city lay red from thy rods,
And thine hands were as arrows to scatter
The children of change and their gods;
When the blood of thy foemen made fervent
A sand never moist from the main,
As one smote them, their lord and thy servant,
Our Lady of Pain.

On sands by the storm never shaken,
Nor wet from the washing of tides;

Nor by foam of the waves overtaken,
Nor winds that the thunder bestrides;
But red from the print of thy paces,
Made smooth for the world and its lords,
Ringed round with a flame of fair faces,
And splendid with swords.

There the gladiator, pale for thy pleasure,
Drew bitter and perilous breath;
There torments laid hold on the treasure
Of limbs too delicious for death;
When thy gardens were lit with live torches;
When the world was a steed for thy rein;
When the nations lay prone in thy porches,
Our Lady of Pain.

When, with flame all around him aspirant,
Stood flushed, as a harp-player stands,
The implacable beautiful tyrant,
Rose-crowned, having death in his hands;
And a sound as the sound of loud water
Smote far through the flight of the fires,
And mixed with the lightning of slaughter
A thunder of lyres.

Dost thou dream of what was and no more is,
The old kingdoms of earth and the kings?
Dost thou hunger for these things, Dolores,
For these, in a world of new things?
But thy bosom no fasts could emaciate,
No hunger compel to complain
Those lips that no bloodshed could satiate,
Our Lady of Pain.

As of old when the world's heart was lighter,
Through thy garments the grace of thee glows,
The white wealth of thy body made whiter
By the blushes of amorous blows,

And seamed with sharp lips and fierce fingers,
And branded by kisses that bruise;
When all shall be gone that now lingers,
Ah, what shall we lose?

Thou wert fair in the fearless old fashion,
And thy limbs are as melodies yet,
And move to the music of passion
With lithe and lascivious regret.
What ailed us, O gods, to desert you
For creeds that refuse and restrain?
Come down and redeem us from virtue,
Our Lady of Pain.

All shrines that were Vestal are flameless,
But the flame has not fallen from this;
Though obscure be the god, and though nameless
The eyes and the hair that we kiss;
Low fires that love sits by and forges
Fresh heads for his arrows and thine;
Hair loosened and soiled in mid orgies
With kisses and wine.

Thy skin changes country and colour,
And shrivels or swells to a snake's.
Let it brighten and bloat and grow duller,
We know it, the flames and the flakes,
Red brands on it smitten and bitten,
Round skies where a star is a stain,
And the leaves with thy litanies written,
Our Lady of Pain.

On thy bosom though many a kiss be,
There are none such as knew it of old.
Was it Alciphron once or Arisbe,
Male ringlets or feminine gold,
That thy lips met with under the statue,
Whence a look shot out sharp after thieves

From the eyes of the garden-god at you
Across the fig-leaves?

Then still, through dry seasons and moister,
One god had a wreath to his shrine;
Then love was the pearl of his oyster,
And Venus rose red out of wine.
We have all done amiss, choosing rather
Such loves as the wise gods disdain;
Intercede for us thou with thy father,
Our Lady of Pain.

In spring he had crowns of his garden,
Red corn in the heat of the year,
Then hoary green olives that harden
When the grape-blossom freezes with fear;
And milk-budded myrtles with Venus
And vine-leaves with Bacchus he trod;
And ye said, "We have seen, he hath seen us,
A visible God."

What broke off the garlands that girt you?
What sundered you spirit and clay?
Weak sins yet alive are as virtue
To the strength of the sins of that day.
For dried is the blood of thy lover,
Ipsithilla, contracted the vein;
Cry aloud, "Will he rise and recover,
Our Lady of Pain?"

Cry aloud; for the old world is broken:
Cry out; for the Phrygian is priest,
And rears not the bountiful token
And spreads not the fatherly feast.
From the midmost of Ida, from shady
Recesses that murmur at morn,
They have brought and baptized her, Our Lady,
A goddess new-born.

And the chaplets of old are above us,
And the oyster-bed teems out of reach;
Old poets outsing and outlove us,
And Catullus makes mouths at our speech.
Who shall kiss, in thy father's own city.
With such lips as he sang with, again?
Intercede for us all of thy pity,
Our Lady of Pain.

Out of Dindymus heavily laden
Her lions draw bound and unfed
A mother, a mortal, a maiden,
A queen over death and the dead.
She is cold, and her habit is lowly,
Her temple of branches and sods;
Most fruitful and virginal, holy,
A mother of gods.

She hath wasted with fire thine high places,
She hath hidden and marred and made sad
The fair limbs of the Loves, the fair faces
Of gods that were goodly and glad.
She slays, and her hands are not bloody;
She moves as a moon in the wane,
White-robed, and thy raiment is ruddy,
Our Lady of Pain.

They shall pass and their places be taken,
The gods and the priests that are pure.
They shall pass, and shalt thou not be shaken?
They shall perish, and shalt thou endure?
Death laughs, breathing close and relentless
In the nostrils and eyelids of lust,
With a pinch in his fingers of scentless
And delicate dust.

But the worm shall revive thee with kisses;
Thou shalt change and transmute as a god,

As the rod to a serpent that hisses,
As the serpent again to a rod.
Thy life shall not cease though thou doff it;
Thou shalt live until evil be slain,
And good shall die first, said thy prophet,
Our Lady of Pain.

Did he lie? did he laugh? does he know it,
Now he lies out of reach, out of breath,
Thy prophet, thy preacher, thy poet,
Sin's child by incestuous Death?
Did he find out in fire at his waking,
Or discern as his eyelids lost light,
When the bands of the body were breaking
And all came in sight?

Who has known all the evil before us,
Or the tyrannous secrets of time?
Though we match not the dead men that bore us
At a song, at a kiss, at a crime –
Though the heathen outface and outlive us,
And our lives and our longings are twain –
Ah, forgive us our virtues, forgive us,
Our Lady of Pain.

Who are we that embalm and embrace thee
With spices and savours of song?
What is time, that his children should face thee?
What am I, that my lips do thee wrong?
I could hurt thee – but pain would delight thee;
Or caress thee – but love would repel;
And the lovers whose lips would excite thee
Are serpents in hell.

Who now shall content thee as they did,
Thy lovers, when temples were built
And the hair of the sacrifice braided
And the blood of the sacrifice spilt,

In Lampsacus fervent with faces,
In Aphaca red from thy reign,
Who embraced thee with awful embraces,
Our Lady of Pain?

Where are thy, Cotytto or Venus,
Astarte or Ashtaroth, where?
Do their hands as we touch come between us?
Is the breath of them hot in thy hair?
From their lips have thy lips taken fever,
With the blood of their bodies grown red?
Hast thou left upon earth a believer
If these men are dead?

They were purple of raiment and golden,
Filled full of thee, fiery with wine,
Thy lovers, in haunts unbeholden,
In marvellous chambers of thine.
They are fled, and their footprints escape us,
Who appraise thee, adore, and abstain,
O daughter of Death and Priapus,
Our Lady of Pain.

What ails us to fear overmeasure,
To praise thee with timorous breath,
O mistress and mother of pleasure,
The one thing as certain as death?
We shall change as the things that we cherish,
Shall fade as they faded before,
As foam upon water shall perish,
As sand upon shore.

We shall know what the darkness discovers,
If the grave-pit be shallow or deep;
And our fathers of old, and our lovers,
We shall know if they sleep not or sleep.
We shall see whether hell be not heaven,

Find out whether tares be not grain,
And the joys of thee seventy times seven,
Our Lady of Pain.

ARACHNE
by
Marcel Schwob
Translated by Francis Amery

You say that I am mad and you have locked me up, but I laugh at all your precautions and your pathetic attempts to scare me. On the day that I desire to be free, I shall escape along a thread of silk thrown to me by Arachne; I will flee from your guards and your prison bars to a place beyond your reach. The hour has not yet come, but you need not doubt that it is near; with every moment that passes my heart loses strength and my blood loses colour. You who now believe me to be mad will soon believe that I am dead, but I will be swinging away, borne by Arachne's thread to the wilderness beyond the stars.

If I really were mad, I would not be so distinctly aware of what has come to pass; I would not recall so precisely that which you have called my crime, nor the cunning arguments of your advocates, nor the sentence passed by your red-robed judge. I would not be able to laugh at the reports of your doctors, and I would not be able to see, even now, upon the ceiling of my cell the smooth features, the red frock-coat and the white cravat of that idiot who declared me irresponsible. No, I would not see any of that, because a madman does not have clear ideas in his mind, whereas I am reasoning with such logical lucidity and such extraordinary clarity that I astonish myself. And madmen suffer such terrible headaches! They believe, poor souls, that plumes of smoke are roiling within their brains, whereas my own head is so very light that it seems to me to be weightless. The novels I used to read, from which I once derived so much pleasure, I can now take in at a glance, instantly appraising their value; I can see every fault of composition – whereas the symmetry of my own inventions is so perfect that you would collapse if I were to expose them to you.

But I hold you in infinite contempt; you would never understand. I leave you these lines as a last testament and a parting jest, and in order that you might be confronted by your own insanity when you find my cell empty.

Ariane, the pale Ariane, beside whose body you seized me, was a seamstress. The one who actually caused her death is the one who will be my salvation. I loved her with an intense passion; she was petite, with a dark complexion and nimble fingers; her kisses were like the thrusts of a needle, her caresses were tremulous embroideries. The life of a seamstress is so unconsidered, and her caprices so fickle, that I soon wished that she could be made to give up her trade. But she would not consent to do that, and I was continually exasperated by the sight of the perfumed and gaudily dressed young men who would hang around the doorway of the shop where she worked. My irritation was so great that I tried to immerse myself again, even more deeply, in the studies which had formerly been my sole delight.

It was while I was thus engaged that I had occasion to take down the thirteenth volume of *Asiatic Researches*, published in Calcutta in 1820. Mechanically, I began to read an article on the Phansigars, or Stranglers of India, who were also known as the Thugs.

Captain Sleeman has had a good deal to say about this cult, and Colonel Meadows Taylor has uncovered the secrets of their organization. They were bound together by mysterious oaths, and some of them worked as domestic servants in the larger households of the country. In the evening, at supper, these would stupefy their masters with a concoction distilled from cannabis hemp. In the night their confederates would climb the walls, insinuate themselves by means of windows left open to the moonlight, and come silently to strangle the people of the house. Their strangling-cords were also made from hemp, with a large knot which could be positioned against the nape of the neck to hasten the kill.

Thus, by means of their revered hemp, the Thugs married sleep to death. The plant that provided the hashish which was the means by which the rich were stupefied, as though by alcohol or opium, served also for a means of vengeance. The idea then came to me that I might contrive to punish my seamstress Ariane with silk, and by such means attach her to me, unbreakably, in death. And that idea, so beautifully logical, became the sole focal point of my thoughts. I could not resist it for long.

And so, when Ariane next placed her bowed head upon my neck so that she might go to sleep, I carefully passed about her throat a thread of silk which I had taken from her sewing-basket; and I slowly drew it tight. I drank her last breath in her last kiss.

You found us thus, my mouth pressed against hers. You thought that I was mad, and that she was dead. What you do not know is that she is always with me, eternally faithful, because she is the nymph Arachne. Day after day, here in my white-washed cell, she reveals herself to me. She has done so since the time when I first glimpsed the petite, dark and nimble spider which wove its web above my bed.

On that first night she descended towards me upon a dangling thread. Suspended above me, she embroidered before my eyes a dark silken web with glistening reflections and luminous purple flowers. Then I felt the wiry and energetic body of Ariane beside me. She kissed me upon the breast, on the place which conceals the heart – and I was forced to cry out by the burning sensation. And we embraced one another, without saying any-thing, for a long time.

On the second night, she extended over me a phosphorescent veil, studded with green stars and yellow circles, traversed by gliding points of brilliant light which played amongst them-selves, expanding and diminishing and flickering in the dis-tance. While kneeling on my breast she closed my mouth with her hand and placed that same long kiss upon my heart. She bit into my flesh and sucked my blood, until she had brought me to the very brink of the void of oblivion.

On the third night, she bound my eyes with a blindfold of Madras silk, upon whose surface danced multicoloured spiders with scintillant eyes. Then she circled my throat with an endless thread of silk; and violently drew my heart towards her lips through the wound which her bite had made. That was when she slid into my arms, and murmured into my ear: "I am the nymph Arachne!"

Most certainly I am not mad; for I understood immediately that my seamstress Ariane was an avatar of a goddess, and that throughout eternity I had been the one who was destined to draw her, by her thread of silk, out of the labyrinth of humanity. And the nymph Arachne had recognised me as the one who would deliver her from her human chrysalis! With infinite care, she has bound up my heart – my poor heart! – with her sticky thread; she has entwined it in a thousand coils. Every night she tightens the meshes between which this human heart shrivels like the corpse of a captive fly. I had attached myself eternally to Ariane by embracing her throat with silk; now, Arachne has bound me eternally to her by means of the thread which chokes my very heart.

At midnight, I cross the mysterious bridge which permits me to visit the Realm of the Spiders, of which she is the queen. It is necessary to pass through that Hell in order that I may eventually be free to float amid the glittering host of the stars.

The spiders of the woodlands roam that realm with luminous ampullae mounted on their feet. The trapdoor spiders which bristle with hairs each have eight terrible, glowing eyes; they lie in wait for me wherever the roads curve. Beside the pools where water spiders quiveringly dance upon their great scythe-like legs, I am dragged vertiginously round and round by the dances of the Tarantulas. The garden spiders also lie in wait for me, each at the centre of its grey wheel traversed by spokes. They fix upon me the innumerable facets of their eyes, like sets of mirrors placed to trap birds, and they mesmerise me. As I pass through every copse, viscous webs tickle my face. Crouched in every thicket, hairy monsters with rapid feet await my passing.

Even Queen Mab herself is not so powerful as my Queen Arachne, for my queen has the power to take me up in her marvellous chariot, which runs along a silken thread. Its chassis is made from the hard shell of a gigantic trapdoor spider, bedecked with many-faceted gems cut from its eyes of black diamond. Its axles are the articulated feet of a giant harvest-spider. Transparent wings, patterned with veins like those of an insect, lift it up by striking the air with rhythmic beats. We soar aloft for hours; but then, all of a sudden, I become weak, enfeebled by the wound on my breast where Arachne probes incessantly with her sharp-edged lips.

In my nightmare I see an abdomen star-spangled with eyes looming above me, and I flee, pursued by rugose and hairy legs.

Now, I can distinctly feel the two limbs by which Arachne grasps my sides, and the gurgling of my blood as it rises towards her avid mouth. My heart will soon be sucked dry; then it will cease to beat, swathed in its prison of white threads – and my soul shall fly through the Realm of the Spiders, toward the glistening host of the stars.

Thus, by means of the silken cord which Arachne has hurled down to me, I shall escape with her. And I bequeath to you, poor fools, naught but a pale cadaver, with a tuft of blond hair stirring in that breeze which morning will surely bring.

THE DAUGHTER OF HERODIAS
by
Arthur W. O'Shaugnessy

My heart is heavy for each goodly man
Whom crownéd woman or sweet courtezan
Hath slain or brought to greater shames than death.
But now, O Daughter of Herodias!
I weep for him, of whom the story saith,
Thou didst procure his bitter fate: – Alas,
He seems so fair! – May thy curse never pass!

Where art thou writhing? Herod's palace-floor
Has fallen through: there shalt thou dance no more;
And Herod is a worm now. In thy place,
– Salome, Viper! – do thy coils yet keep
That woman's flesh they bore with such a grace?
Have thine eyes still the love-lure hidden deep,
The ornament of tears, they could not weep?

Thou wast quite perfect in the splendid guile
Of woman's beauty; thou hadst the whole smile
That can dishonour heroes, and recall
Fair saints prepared for heaven back to hell:
And He, whose unlived glory thou mad'st fall
All beautiful and spotless, at thy spell,
Was great and fit for thee by whom he fell.

O, is it now sufficing sweet to thee –
Through all the long uncounted years that see
The undistinguished lost ones waste away –
To twine thee, biting, on those locks that bleed,
As bled they through thy fingers on that day?
Or hast thou, all unhallowed, some fierce need
Thy soul on his anointed grace to feed?

Or hast thou, rather, for that serpent's task
Thou didst accomplish in thy woman-mask,

97

Some perfect inconceivable reward
Of serpent's slimy pleasure? – all the thing
Thou didst beseech thy master, who is Lord
Of those accursèd hosts that creep and sting,
To give thee for the spoil thou shouldest bring?

He was a goodly spoil for thee to win!
– Men's souls and lives were wholly dark with sin;
And so God's world was changed with wars and gold,
No part of it was holy; save, maybe,
The desert and the ocean as of old: –
But such a spotless way of life had he,
His soul was as the desert or the sea.

I think he had not heard of the far towns;
Nor of the deeds of men, nor of kings' crowns;
Before the thought of God took hold of him,
As he was sitting dreaming in the calm
Of one first noon, upon the desert's rim,
Beneath the tall fair shadows of the palm,
All overcome with some strange inward balm.

But then, so wonderful and lovely seemed
That thought, he straight became as though he dreamed
A vast thing false and fair, which day and night
Absorbed him in some rapture – very high
Above the common swayings of delight
And general yearnings, that quite occupy
Men's passions, and suffice them till they die:

Yea, soon as it had entered him – that thought
Of God – he felt that he was being wrought
All holy: more and more it filled his heart;
And seemed, indeed, a spirit of pure flame
Set burning in his soul's most inward part.
And from the Lord's great wilderness there came
A mighty voice calling on him by name.

He numbered not the changes of the year,
The days, the nights, and he forgot all fear
Of death: each day he thought there should have been
A shining ladder set for him to climb
Athwart some opening in the heavens, e'en
To God's eternity, and see, sublime –
His face whose shadow passing fills all time.

But he walked through the ancient wilderness.
O, there the prints of feet were numberless
And holy all about him! And quite plain
He saw each spot an angel silvershod
Had lit upon; where Jacob too had lain
The place seemed fresh, – and, bright and lately trod,
A long track showed where Enoch walked with God.

And often, while the sacred darkness trailed
Along the mountains smitten and unveiled
By rending lightnings, – over all the noise
Of thunders and the earth that quaked and bowed
From its foundations – he could hear the voice
Of great Elias prophesying loud
To Him whose face was covered by a cloud.

Already he was shown so perfectly
The awful mystic grace and sanctity
Of all the earth, there was no part his feet
With sandal covering might dare to tread;
Because that in it he was sure to meet
The fair sword-bearing angels, or some dread
Eternal prophet numbered with the dead.

So he believed that he should purify
His body, till the sin of it should die,
And the unfailing spirit and great word
Of One – who is too bright to be beheld,
And in his speech too fearful to be heard

By mortal man – should come down and be held
In him as in those holy ones of eld.

And to believe in this was rapture more
Than any that the thought of living bore
To tempt him: so the pleasant days of youth
Were but the days of striving and of prayer;
And all the beauty of those days, forsooth,
He counted as an evil or a snare,
And would have left it in the desert there.

Ah, spite of all the scourges that had bit
So fiercely his fair body, branding it
With many a painful over-written vow
Of perfect sanctity – what man shall say
How often, weak with groanings, he would bow
Before the angels of the place, and pray
That all his body might consume away?

For through whole bitter days it seemed in vain
That all the mighty desert had no stain
Of sin around him; that the burning breaths
Went forth from the eternal One, and rolled
For ever through it, filling it with deaths,
And plagues, and fires; that he did behold
The earthquakes and the wonders manifold:

It seemed in vain that all the place was bright
Ineffably with that unfading light
No man who worketh evil can abide;
That he could see too with his open eyes
Fair troops of deathless ones, and those that died
In martyrdoms, or went up to the skies
In fiery cars – walk there with no disguise; –

It seemed in vain that he was there alone
With no man's sin to tempt him but his own; –

Since in his body he did bear about
A seeming endless sin he could not quell
With the most sharp coercement, nor cast out
Through any might of prayer. O, who can tell –
Save God – how often in despair he fell?

The very stones seemed purer far than he;
And every naked rock and every tree
Looked great and calm, composed in one long thought
Of holiness; each bird and creeping thing
Rejoiced in bearing some bright sign that taught
The legend of an ancient minist'ring
To some fair saint of old there sojourning.

Yea, all the dumb things and the creatures there
Were grand, and some way sanctified; most fair
The very lions stood, and had no shame
Before the angels; and what time were poured
The floods of the Lord's anger forth, they came
Quite nigh the lightnings of the Mount and roared
Among the roaring thunders of the Lord:

Yet He – while in him day by day, divine,
The clear inspirèd thought went on to shine,
And heaven was opening every radiant door
Upon his spirit – He, in that fair dress
Of weak humanity his senses bore,
Did feel scarcely worthy to be there, and less
Than any dweller in the wilderness.

Wherefore his limbs were galled with many a stone;
And often he had wrestled all alone
With their fair beauty, conquering the pride
And various pleasure of them with some quick
And hard inflicted pain that might abide, –
Assailing all the sense with constant prick
Until the lust or pride fell faint and sick.

Natheless there grew and stayed upon his face
The wonderful unconquerable grace
Of a young man made beautiful with love;
Because the thought of God was wholly spread
Like love upon it; and still fair above
All crownèd heads of kings remained his head
Whereon the halo of the Lord was shed.

Ah, how long was it, since the first red rush
Of that surpassing thought made his cheek blush
With pleasure, as he sat – a tender child –
And wondered at the desert, and the long
Rough prickly paths that led out to the wild
Where all the men of God, holy and strong,
Had dwelt and purified themselves – how long? –

Before he rose up from his knees one day,
And felt that he was purified as they;
That he had trodden out the sin at last,
And that the light was filling him within?
How many of the months and years had past
Uncounted? – But the place he was born in
No longer knew him: no man was his kin.

O then it was a most sweet, holy will
That came upon him, making his soul thrill
With joy indeed, and with a perfect trust, –
For he soon thought of men and of the king
All tempted in the world, with gold and lust,
And women there, and every fatal thing,
And none to save their souls from perishing –

And so he vowed that he would go forth straight
From God there in the desert, with the great
Unearthliness upon him, and adjure
The nations of the whole world with his voice;
Until they should resist each pleasant lure

Of gold and woman, and make such a choice
As his, that they might evermore rejoice.

Thus beautiful and good was He, at length,
Who came before King Herod in his strength,
And shouted to him with a great command
To purify himself, and put away
That unclean woman set at his right hand;
And after all to bow himself and pray,
And be in terror of the Judgment Day!

He never had seen houses like to that
Fair-columned, cedar-builded one where sat
King Herod. Flawless cedar was each beam,
Wrought o'er with flaming brass: along the wall
Great brazen images of beasts did gleam,
With wondrous flower-works and palm trees tall;
And folded purples hung about it all.

He never had beheld so many thrones,
As those of ivory and precious stones
Whereon the noble company was raised
About the king: – he never had seen gems
So costly, nor so wonderful as blazed
Upon their many crowns and diadems,
And trailed upon their garments' trodden hems:

But he had seen in mighty Lebanon
The cedars no man's axe hath lit upon;
And he had often worshipped, falling down
In dazzling temples opened straight to him,
Where One who had great lightnings for His crown
Was suddenly made present, vast and dim
Through crowded pinions of the Cherubim!

Wherefore he had no fear to stand and shout
To all men in the place, and there to flout
Those fair and fearful women who were seen

Quite triumphing in that work of their smile
To shame a goodly king. And he cast, e'en
A sudden awe that undid for a while
The made-up shameless visages of guile.

And when Herodias – that many times
Polluted one, assured now in all crimes
Past fear or turning – when she, her fierce tongue
Thrice forked with indignation, hotly spoke
Quick wild beseeching words, wherewith she clung
To Herod, praying him by some death-stroke
To do her vengeance there before all folk –

Ah, spite of every urging that her hate
Did put into her lips, – so fair and great
Seemed that accuser standing weaponless,
Yet wholly terrible with his bright speech
As 'twere some sword of flaming holiness,
That no man dared to join her and beseech
His death; but dread came somehow upon each.

For he was surely terrible to see
So plainly sinless, so divinely free
To judge them; being in a perfect youth,
Yet walking like an angel in a man
Reproving all men with inspired truth.
And Herod himself spoke not, but began
To tremble: through his soul the warning ran.

– Then *that Salome* did put off the shame
Of her mere virgin girlhood, and became
A woman! Then she did at once essay
Her beauty's magic, and unfold the wings
Of her enchanted feet, – to have men say
She slew *him* – born indeed for wondrous things.
Her dance was fit to ruin saints or kings.

O, her new beauty was above all praise!
She came with dancing in shy devious ways,
And while she danced she sang.
The virgin bandlet of her forehead brake,
Her hair came round her like a shining snake;
To loving her men's hearts within them sprang
The while she danced and sang.

Her long black hair danced round her like a snake
Allured to each charmed movement she did make;
Her voice came strangely sweet;
She sang, "O, Herod, wilt thou look on me –
Have I no beauty thy heart cares to see?"
And what her voice did sing her dancing feet
Seemed ever to repeat.

She sang, "O, Herod, wilt thou look on me?
What sweet I have, I have it all for thee,"
And through the dance and song
She freed and floated on the air her arms
Above dim veils that hid her bosom's charms:
The passion of her singing was so strong
It drew all hearts along.

Her sweet arms were unfolded on the air,
They seemed like floating flowers the most fair –
White lilies the most choice;
And in the gradual bending of her hand
There lurked a grace that no man could withstand;
Yea, none knew whether hands, or feet, or voice,
Most made his heart rejoice.

The veils fell round her like thin coiling mists
Shot through by topaz suns, and amethysts,
And rubies she had on;
And out of them her jewelled body came,
And seemed to all quite like a slender flame

105

That curled and gilded, and that burnt and shone
Most fair to look upon.

Then she began, on that well-polished floor,
Whose stones seemed taking radiance more and more
From steps too bright to see,
A certain measure that was like some spell
Of winding magic, wherein heaven and hell
Were joined to lull men's souls eternally
In some mid ecstasy:

For it was so inexplicably wrought
Of soft alternate motions, that she taught
Each sweeping supple limb,
And in such intricate and wondrous ways
With bendings of her body, that the praise
Lost breath upon men's lips, and all grew dim
Save her so bright and slim.

And through the swift mesh'd serpents of her hair
That lash'd and leapt on each place white and fair
Of bosom or of arm,
And through the blazing of the numberless
And whirling jewelled fires of her dress,
Her perfect face no passion could disarm
Of its reposeful charm.

Her head oft drooped as in some languid death
Beneath brim tastes of joy, and her rich breath
Heaved faintly from her breast;
Her long eyes, opened fervently and wide,
Did seem with endless rapture to abide
In some fair trance through which the soul possest
Love, ecstasy, and rest.

But lo – while each man fixed his eyes on her,
And was himself quite fillèd with the stir

His heart did make within –
The place was full of devils everywhere:
They came in from the desert and the air;
They came from all the palaces of sin,
And each heart they were in:

They lurked beneath the purples, and did crawl
Or crouch in unseen corners of the hall,
Among the brass and gold,
They climbed the brazen pillars till they lined
The chamber fair; and one went up behind
The throne of Herod – fearful to behold –
The Serpent king of old.

Yea, too, before those blinded men there went
Some even to Salome; and they lent
Strange charms she did not shun.
She stretched her hand forth, and inclined her ear;
She knew those men would neither see nor hear:
A devil did support her head, and one
Her steps' light fabric spun.

O, then her voice with singing all unveiled,
In no trained timid accents, straight assailed
King Herod's open heart:
The amorous supplication wove and wound
Soft deadly sins about it; the words found
Fair traitor thoughts there, – singing snakes did dart
Their poison in each part.

She sang, "O look on me, and look on Love:
We three are here together, and above –
What heaven may there be?
None for thine heart without this spell of mine,
Yea, this my beauty, yea, these limbs that shine
And make thy senses shudder; and for me,
No heaven without thee!

"O, all the passion in me on this day
Rises into one song to sweep away
The breakers of Love's bond;
For is it not a pleasant bond indeed,
And made of all the flowers in life's mead?
And is not Love a master fair and fond?
And is not Death beyond?

"Oh, who are these that will adjure thee, King,
To put away this tender flower-thing,
This love that is thy bliss?
Dost thou think thou canst live indeed, and dare
The joyless remnant of pale days, the bare
Hard tomb, and feed through cold eternities
Thy heart without one kiss?

"Dost thou think empty prayers shall glad thy lips
Kept red and living with perpetual sips
Of Love's rich cup of wine?
That thy fair body shall not fall away,
And waste among the worms that bitter day
Thou hast no lover round thy neck to twine
Fond arms like these of mine?

"I say they are no prophets, – very deaths,
And plagues, and rottenness, do use their breaths
Who speak against delight;
Pale distant slayers of humanity
Have tainted them, and sent them forth to try
Weak lures to make man give up joyous right
Of days for empty night.

"I tell thee, in their wilderness shall be
No herbs enough for food for them and thee,
No rock to give thee drink;
I tell thee, all their heavens are a cheat,
Or but a mirage to betray thy feet,

And draw thee quicker to some grave's dread brink
Where thou shalt fall and sink.

"Turn rather unto me, and hear my voice
Against these desert howlings, and rejoice:
Now surely do I crave
To treble this my beauty, and embalm
My words with deathless thrill, singing the psalm
Of pleasure to thee, King, – so I may save
Thy fair days from this grave.

"Yea, now of all my beauty will I strive
With these mad prophesiers till I drive
Their ravings from thine ear:
Against their rudeness I will set my grace,
My softness, and the magic of my face;
And spite of all their curses thou shalt hear
And let my voice draw near:

"Against their loud revilings I will try
The long low-speaking pleadings of my sigh,
All my heart's tender way;
Against their deserts – here, before thine eyes
My love shall open thee a paradise,
Where, if thou comest, thou shalt surely stay
And seek no better way:

"And rather than these haters of thy joy
Should anyhow allure thee to destroy
Thy heart's prosperity, –
O, I will throw my woman's arms entwined
About thy body; ere thy lips can find
One word of yielding, I will kiss them dry:
– And failing, let me die!

"But look on me, for it is in my soul
To make the measure of thy glory whole –
With many goodly things

To crown thee, yea, with pleasure and with love,
Till there shall scarcely be a name above
King Herod's, in the mouth of one who sings
The fame of mighty kings:

"For see how great and fair a realm is this –
My untried love – the never conquered bliss
All hoarded in my breast;
My beauty and my love were jewels meet
To make the glory of a king complete,
And I, – O thou of kingship half-possest –
Can crown thee with the rest!

"I stand before thee – on my head the crown
Of all thou lackest yet in thy renown –
Ah, King, take this of me!
And in my hand I bear a brimming cup
That sparkles; to thine eyes I hold it up:
A royal draught of life-long pleasure – see,
The wine is fit for thee!

"Ah, wilt thou pass me? Wilt thou let me give
Thy fair life to some meaner man to live?
Nay, here – if I am sweet –
Thou shalt not. I will save thee with the sight
Of all my sweetness, save thee with the might
And charm of all my singing lips' deceit,
Or with my dancing feet.

"I have indeed some power. A lure lies
Within my tender lips – behind my eyes –
Concealed in all my way;
And while I seem entreating, I compel,
Yea, while I do but plead, I use a spell –
Ah secretly – but surely. Who are they
That ever turn away?

"Now, thou hast barely seen bright glittering
The gilded cup of pleasures that I swing
Before thy reeling gaze, –
The deep beginnings of sweet drunkenness
Are in thy heart already, more or less,
And on thy soul deliciously there preys
A thirst no joy allays.

"Dost thou not feel, each time my long hair sweeps
The glowing floor, how through thy being creeps
A vague yet sweet desire? –
How writhes in every sense a tiny snake
Of pleasure biting till it seems to wake
A fever of sharp lusts that never tire,
Unquenchable as fire?

"Is there not wrought a madness in thy brain
Each time my thin veils part and close again –
Each time their flying ring
Is seen a moment's space encircling me
With filmy changes – each time, rapidly
Rolled down, their cloud-like gauzes billowing
About my limbs they fling?

"Ah, seek not in this moment some cold will;
Attend to no false pratings that would kill
Thy heart, and make thee fall:
But now a little lean to me, and fear
My charming. Ah, thy fame to me is dear!
Some wound of mine, when me thou couldst not call,
Might slay thee after all.

"For even while I sing, the unseen grace
Of Love descending hath filled all this place
With most strong prevalence;
His miracle is raging in the breasts
Of all these men, and mightily he rests

On me and thee. His power is too intense,
No curse shall drive him hence.

"– O, Love, invisible, eternal God,
In whose delicious ways all men have trod,
This day Thou truly hast
My heart: thy inspiration fills my tongue
With great angelic madness; I have sung
Set words that in my bosom thou hast cast –
Thine am I to the last!

"My feet are like two liquid flames that leap
For joy at thee; I feel thy spirit sweep –
Yea, like a southern wind –
Through all the enchanted fibres of my soul;
I am a harp o'er which thy vast breaths roll,
And one day thou shalt break me: none shall find
A wreck of me behind.

"And now all palpitating, O I pray
Thy utmost passion while I cry – away
With all Love's enemies!
A man – borne up between the closing wings
Of two eternities of unknown things,
May catch this seraph charmer as he flies,
And hold him till he dies;

"And yet some bitter ones, whom coming night
Hath wholly entered, grudge man this small right
Of joy, and seek to fill
His rushing moment with the monstrous hiss
Of shapeless terrors, poisoning the bliss
Brief nestled in his bosom – merely till
Forced out by its death chill!

"What voice is this the envious wilderness
Hath sent among us foully to distress

112

And haunt our lives with fear?
What vulture, shrieking on the scent of death –
What yelping jackal – what insidious breath
Of pestilence hath ventured to draw near,
And enter even here?

"No kindred flesh of fair humanity
Yon fiend hath, seeking through lives doomed to die
Death's foretaste to infuse:
His body is but raised up from the slain
Unburied thousands that long years have lain
About the desert: Death himself doth choose
His pale disguise to use.

"But, even though he be from some new God,
He shall not turn us who love's ways have trod,
Nor make us break love's vow.
Nay, rather, if a single beauty dwells
In me, if in that beauty there be spells
To win my will of any man – O thou,
King Herod, hear me now! –

"Let *it* be for his ruin! Ah, let me,
With all in me thou countest fair to see,
Procure this and no more!
If yet, with tender prevalence, my voice
May ask a thing of thee – this is my choice,
Though thou wouldst buy my sweets with all thy store –
This all I sell them for.

"Yea, are there lures of softness in my eyes?
My eyes are – for his death. Is my heart's prize
A seeming fair reward?
My virgin heart is – for his blood here shed;
Its passion – for the falling of his head;
And on that man my kiss shall be outpoured
Who slays him with the sword!"

Invisible – in supernatural haze,
Of shapes that seem not shapes to human gaze –
The devils were half awed as they did stand
Around her; each one in his separate hell
All inwardly was forced to praise her well:
And every man was fain to lose his hand
Or do all that sweet woman might command.

There was a tumult. – Cloven foot and scale
Of fiend with iron heel and coat of mail
Were rolled and hustled in the rage to slay
That fair young Saviour: when they murdered him
And brought his head, still beautiful – though dim
And drenched with blood – the aureole did play
Above it, slowly vanishing away.

I weep to think of him and his fair light
So quenched – of him thrust into some long night
Of unaccomplishment so soon, alas!
And Thou, who on that ancient palace floor
Didst dance, where dost thou writhe now evermore –
Salome, Daughter of Herodias?
O woman-viper – may thy curse ne'er pass!

AMOUR DURE
by
Vernon Lee
Passages from the Diary of Spiridion Trepka

PART I

Urbania, August 20th, 1885. I had longed, these years and years, to be in Italy, to come face to face with the Past; and was this Italy, was this the Past? I could have cried, yes cried, for disappointment when I first wandered about Rome, with an invitation to dine at the German Embassy in my pocket, and three or four Berlin and Munich Vandals at my heels, telling me where the best beer and sauerkraut could be had, and what the last article by Grimm or Mommsen was about.

Is this folly? Is it falsehood? Am I not myself a product of modern, northern civilization; is not my coming to Italy due to this very modern scientific vandalism, which has given me a travelling scholarship because I have written a book like all those other atrocious books of erudition and art-criticism? Nay, am I not here at Urbania on the express understanding that, in a certain number of months, I shall produce just another such book? Dost thou imagine, thou miserable Spiridion, thou Pole grown into the semblance of a German pedant, doctor of philosophy, professor even, author of a prize essay on the despots of the fifteenth century, dost thou imagine that thou, with thy ministerial letters and proof sheets in thy black professional coat pocket, canst ever come in spirit into the presence of the Past?

Too true, alas! But let me forget it, at least, every now and then; as I forgot it this afternoon, while the white bullocks dragged my gig slowly winding along interminable valleys, crawling along interminable hillsides, with the invisible droning torrent far below, and only the bare grey and reddish peaks all around, up to this town of Urbania, forgotten of mankind, towered and battlemented on the high Apennine ridge. Sigillo, Penna, Fossombrone, Mercatello, Montemurlo – each single village name, as the driver pointed it out, brought to my mind the recollection of some battle or some great act of treachery of former days. And as the huge mountains shut out the setting sun, and the valleys filled with bluish shadow and mist, only a band of threatening smoke-red remaining behind the towers and cupolas of the city on its mountain-top, and the sound of church bells floated across the precipice from Urbania, I almost expected, at every turning of the road, that a troop of horsemen, with beaked helmets and clawed shoes, would emerge, with armour glittering and pennons waving in the sunset. And then, not two hours ago, entering the town at dusk, passing along the deserted streets, with only a smoky light here and there under a shrine or in front of a fruit stall, or a fire reddening the blackness of a smithy; passing beneath the battlements and turrets of the palace.... Ah, that was Italy, it was the Past!

August 21st. And this is the Present! Four letters of introduction to deliver, and an hour's polite conversation to endure with the Vice-Prefect, the Syndic, the Director of the Archives, and the good man to whom my friend Max had sent me for lodgings....

August 22nd-27th. Spent the greater part of the day in the Archives, and the greater part of my time there in being bored to extinction by the Director thereof, who to-day spouted Æneas Sylvius' Commentaries for three-quarters of an hour without taking breath. From this sort of martyrdom (what are the sensations of a former racehorse being driven in a cab? If you can conceive them, they are those of a Pole turned Prussian professor) I take refuge in long rambles through the town. This town is a handful of tall black houses huddled on to the top of an Alp, long narrow lanes trickling down its sides, like the slides we made on hillocks in our boyhood, and in the middle the superb red brick structure, turreted and battlemented, of Duke Ottobuono's palace, from whose windows you look down upon a sea, a kind of whirlpool, of melancholy grey mountains. Then there are the people, dark, bushy-bearded men, riding about like brigands, wrapped in green-lined cloaks upon their shaggy pack-mules; or loitering about, great, brawny, low-headed youngsters, like the parti-coloured bravos in Signorelli's frescoes; the beautiful boys, like so many young Raphaels, with eyes like the eyes of bullocks, and the huge women, Madonnas or St. Elizabeths, as the case may be, with their clogs firmly poised on their toes and their brass pitchers on their heads, as they go up and down the steep black alleys. I do not talk much to these people; I fear my illusions being dispelled. At the corner of a street, opposite Francesco di Giorgio's beautiful little portico, is a great blue and red advertisement, representing an angel descending to crown Elias Howe, on account of his sewing machines; and the clerks of the Vice-Prefecture, who dine at the place where I get my dinner, yell politics, Minghetti, Cairoli, Tunis, ironclads, etc., at each other, and sing snatches of *La Fille de Mme. Angot*, which I imagine they have been performing here recently.

No; talking to the natives is evidently a dangerous experiment. Except indeed, perhaps, to my good landlord, Signor Notaro Porri, who is just as learned, and takes considerably less snuff (or rather brushes it off his coat more often) than the Director of the Archives. I forgot to jot down (and I feel I must jot down, in the vain belief that some day these scraps will help, like a withered twig of olive or a three-wicked Tuscan lamp on my table, to bring to my mind, in that hateful Babylon of Berlin, these happy Italian days) – I forgot to record that I am lodging in the house of a dealer in antiquities. My window looks up the principal street to where the little column with Mercury on the top rises in the midst of the awnings and porticoes of the market-place. Bending over the chipped ewers and tubs full of sweet basil, clove pinks, and marigolds, I can just see a corner of the palace turret, and the vague ultramarine of the hills beyond. The house, whose back goes sharp down into the ravine, is a queer up-and-down black place, whitewashed rooms, hung with the Raphaels and Francias and Peruginos, whom mine host regularly carries to the chief inn whenever a stranger is expected; and surrounded by old carved chairs, sofas of the Empire, embossed and gilded wedding chests, and the cupboards which contain bits of old damask and embroidered altar cloths scenting the place with the smell of old incense and mustiness; all of which are presided over by Signor Porri's three maiden sisters – Sora

Serafina, Sora Lodovica, and Sora Adalgisa – the three Fates in person, even to the distaffs and their black cats.

Sor Asdrubale, as they call my landlord, is also a notary. He regrets the Pontifical Government, having had a cousin who was a Cardinal's trainbearer, and believes that if only you lay a table for two, light four candles made of dead men's fat, and perform certain rites about which he is not very precise, you can, on Christmas Eve and similar nights, summon up San Pasquale Baylon, who will write you the winning numbers of the lottery upon the smoked back of a plate, if you have previously slapped him on both cheeks and repeated three Ave Marias. The difficulty consists in obtaining the dead men's fat for the candles, and also in slapping the saint before he has time to vanish.

"If it were not for that," says Sor Asdrubale, "the Government would have had to suppress the lottery ages ago – eh!"

Sept. 9th. This history of Urbania is not without its romance, although that romance (as usual) has been overlooked by our Dryasdusts. Even before coming here I felt attracted by the strange figure of a woman, which appeared from out of the dry pages of Gualterio's and Padre de Sanctis' histories of this place. This woman is Medea, daughter of Galeazzo IV, Malatesta, Lord of Carpi, wife first of Pierluigi Orsini, Duke of Stimigliano, and subsequently of Guidalfonso II, Duke of Urbania, predecessor of the great Duke Robert II.

This woman's history and character remind one of that of Bianca Cappello, and at the same time of Lucrezia Borgia. Born in 1556, she was affianced at the age of twelve to a cousin, a Malatesta of the Rimini family. This family having greatly gone down in the world, her engagement was broken, and she was betrothed a year later to a member of the Pico family, and married to him by proxy at the age of fourteen. But this match not satisfying her own or her father's ambition, the marriage by proxy was, upon some pretext, declared null, and the suit encouraged of the Duke of Stimigliano, a great Umbrian feudatory of the Orsini family. But the bridegroom, Giovanfrancesco Pico, refused to submit, pleaded his case before the Pope, and tried to carry off by force his bride, with whom he was madly in love, as the lady was most lovely and of most cheerful and amiable manner, says an old anonymous chronicle. Pico waylaid her litter as she was going to a villa of her father's, and carried her to his castle near Mirandola, where he respectfully pressed his suit; insisting that he had a right to consider her as his wife. But the lady escaped by letting herself into the moat by a rope of sheets, and Giovanfrancesco Pico was discovered stabbed in the chest, by the hand of Madonna Medea da Carpi. He was a handsome youth only eighteen years old.

The Pico having been settled, and the marriage with him declared null by the Pope, Medea da Carpi was solemnly married to the Duke of Stimigliano, and went to live upon his domains near Rome.

Two years later, Pierluigi Orsini was stabbed by one of his grooms at his castle of Stimigliano, near Orvieto; and suspicion fell upon his widow, more especially as, immediately after the event, she caused the murderer to be cut down by two servants in her own chamber; but not before he had declared that she had induced him to assassinate his master by a promise of her love. Things became so hot for Medea da Carpi that she fled to Urbania and threw herself at the feet of Duke Guidalfonso II, declaring that she had caused the groom to be killed merely to avenge her good fame, which he had slandered, and that she was absolutely guiltless of the death of her husband. The marvellous beauty of the widowed Duchess of Stimigliano, who was only nineteen, entirely turned the head of the Duke of Urbania. He affected implicit belief in her innocence, refused to give her up to the Orsinis, kinsmen of her late husband, and assigned to her magnificent apartments in the left wing of the palace, among which was the room containing the famous fireplace ornamented with marble Cupids on a blue ground. Guidalfonso fell madly in love with his beautiful guest. Hitherto timid and domestic in character, he began publicly to neglect his wife, Maddalena Varano of Camerino, with whom, although childless, he had hitherto lived on excellent terms; he not only treated with contempt the admonitions of his advisers and of his suzerain the Pope, but went so far as to take measures to repudiate his wife, on the score of quite imaginary ill-conduct. The Duchess Maddalena, unable to bear this treatment, fled to the convent of the barefooted sisters at Pesaro, where she pined away, while Medea da Carpi reigned in her place at Urbania, embroiling Duke Guidalfonso in quarrels both with the powerful Orsinis, who continued to accuse her of Stimigliano's murder, and with the Varanos, kinsmen of the injured Duchess Maddalena; until at length, in the year 1576, the Duke of Urbania, having become suddenly, and not without suspicious circumstances, a widower, publicly married Medea de Carpi two days after the decease of his unhappy wife. No child was born of this marriage; but such was the infatuation of Duke Guidalfonso, that the new Duchess induced him to settle the inheritance of the Duchy (having, with great difficulty, obtained the consent of the Pope) on the boy Bartolommeo, her son by Stimigliano, but whom the Orsinis refused to acknowledge as such, declaring him to be the child of that Giovanfrancesco Pico to whom Medea had been married by proxy, and whom, in defence, as she had said, of her honour, she had assassinated; and this investiture of the Duchy of Urbania on to a stranger and a bastard was at the expense of the obvious rights of the Cardinal Robert, Guidalfonso's younger brother.

In May, 1579, Duke Guidalfonso died suddenly and mysteriously, Medea having forbidden all access to his chamber, lest, on his deathbed, he might repent and reinstate his brother in his rights. The Duchess immediately caused her son, Bartolommeo Orsini, to be proclaimed Duke of Urbania, and herself regent; and, with the help of two or three unscrupulous young men, particularly a certain Captain Oliverotto da Narni, who was rumoured to be her lover, seized the reins of government with extraordinary and terrible vigour, marching an army against the Varanos and Orsinis, who were defeated at Sigillo, and ruthlessly exterminating every person who dared question the lawfulness of the succession; while all the time, Cardinal Robert, who had flung aside his priest's garb and vows, went about in Rome, Tuscany, Venice – nay, even to the Emperor and the King of Spain, imploring help against the usurper. In a few months he had turned the tide of sympathy against the Duchess-Regent; the Pope solemnly declared the investiture of Bartolommeo Orsini worthless, and published the accession of

Robert II, Duke of Urbania and Count of Montemurlo; the Grand Duke of Tuscany and the Venetians secretly promised assistance, but only if Robert were able to assert his rights by main force. Little by little, one town after the other of the Duchy went over to Robert, and Medea da Carpi found herself surrounded in the mountain citadel of Urbania like a scorpion surrounded by flames. (This simile is not mine, but belongs to Raffaello Gualterio, historiographer to Robert II.) But, unlike the scorpion, Medea refused to commit suicide. It is perfectly marvellous how, without money or allies, she could so long keep her enemies at bay; and Gualterio attributes this to those fatal fascinations which had brought Pico and Stimigliano to their deaths, which had turned the once honest Guidalfonso into a villain, and which were such that, of all her lovers, not one but preferred dying for her, even after he had been treated with ingratitude and ousted by a rival; a faculty which Messer Raffaello Gualterio clearly attributed to hellish connivance.

At last the ex-Cardinal Robert succeeded, and triumphantly entered Urbania in November, 1579. His accession was marked by moderation and clemency. Not a man was put to death, save Oliverotto da Narni, who threw himself on the new Duke, tried to stab him as he alighted at the palace, and who was cut down by the Duke's men, crying, "Orsini, Orsini! Medea, Medea! Long live Duke Bartolommeo!" with his dying breath, although it is said that the Duchess had treated him with ignominy. The little Bartolommeo was sent to Rome to the Orsinis; the Duchess, respectfully confined in the left wing of the palace.

It is said that she haughtily requested to see the new Duke, but that he shook his head, and, in his priest's fashion, quoted a verse about Ulysses and the Sirens; and it is remarkable that he persistently refused to see her, abruptly leaving his chamber one day that she had entered it by stealth. After a few months a conspiracy was discovered to murder Duke Robert, which had obviously been set on foot by Medea. But the young man, one Marcantonio Frangipani of Rome, denied, even under the severest torture, any complicity of hers; so that Duke Robert, who wished to do nothing violent, merely transferred the Duchess from his villa at Sant' Elmo to the convent of the

Clarisse in town, where she was guarded and watched in the closest manner. It seemed impossible that Medea should intrigue any further, for she certainly saw and could be seen by no one. Yet she contrived to send a letter and her portrait to one Prinzivalle degli Ordelaffi, a youth, only nineteen years old, of noble Romagnole family, and who was betrothed to one of the most beautiful girls of Urbania. He immediately broke off his engagement, and shortly afterwards, attempted to shoot Duke Robert with a holster-pistol as he knelt at mass on the festival of Easter Day. This time Duke Robert was determined to obtain proofs against Medea. Prinzivalle degli Ordelaffi was kept some days without food, then submitted to the most violent torture, and finally condemned. When he was going to be flayed with red-hot pincers and quartered by horses, he was told that he might obtain the grace of immediate death by confessing the complicity of the Duchess; and the confessor and nuns of the convent, which stood in the place of execution outside Porta San Romano, pressed Medea to save the wretch, whose screams reached her, by confessing her own guilt. Medea asked permission to go to a balcony, where she could see Prinzivalle and be seen by him. She looked on coldly, then threw down her embroidered kerchief to the poor mangled creature. He asked the executioner to wipe his mouth with it, kissed it, and cried out that Medea was innocent. Then, after several hours of torments, he died. This was too much for the patience even of Duke Robert. Seeing that as long as Medea lived his life would be in perpetual danger, but unwilling to cause a scandal (somewhat of the priest-nature remaining), he had Medea strangled in the convent, and, what is remarkable, insisted that only women – two infanticides to whom he remitted their sentence – should be employed for the deed.

"This clement prince," writes Don Arcangelo Zappi in his life of him, published in 1725, "can be blamed only for one act of cruelty, the more odious as he had himself, until released from his vows by the Pope, been in holy orders. It is said that when he caused the death of the infamous Medea da Carpi, his fear lest her extraordinary charms should seduce any man was such, that he not only employed women as executioners, but refused to permit her a priest or monk, thus forcing her to die unshriven, and refusing her the benefit of any penitence that may have lurked in her adamantine heart."

Such is the story of Medea da Carpi, Duchess of Stimigliano Orsini, and then wife of Duke Guidalfonso II, of Urbania. She was put to death just two hundred and ninety-seven years ago, December 1582, at the age of barely seven-and-twenty, and having, in the course of her short life, brought to a violent end five of her lovers, from Giovanfrancesco Pico to Prinzivalle degli Ordelaffi.

Sept. 20*th.* A grand illumination of the town in honour of the taking of Rome fifteen years ago. Except Sor Asdrubale, my landlord, who shakes his head at the Piedmontese, as he calls them, the people here are all Italianissimi. The Popes kept them very much down since Urbania lapsed to the Holy See in 1645.

Sept. 28*th.* I have for some time been hunting for portraits of the Duchess Medea. Most of them, I imagine, must have been destroyed, perhaps by Duke Robert II's fear lest even after her death this terrible beauty should play him a trick. Three or four I have, however, been able to find – one a miniature in the Archives, said to be that which she sent to poor Prinzivalle degli Ordelaffi in order to turn his head; one a marble bust in the palace lumber room; one in a large composition, possibly by Baroccio, representing Cleopatra at the feet of Augustus. Augustus is the idealized portrait of Robert II, round cropped head, nose a little awry, clipped beard and scar as usual, but in Roman dress. Cleopatra seems to me, for all her Oriental dress, and although she wears a black wig, to be meant for Medea da Carpi; she is kneeling, baring her breast for the victor to strike, but in reality to captivate him, and he turns away with an awkward gesture of loathing. None of these portraits seem very good, save the miniature, but that is an exquisite work, and with it, and the suggestions of the bust, it is easy to reconstruct the beauty of this terrible being. The type is that most admired by the late Renaissance, and, in some measure, immortalized by Jean Goujon and the French. The face is a perfect oval, the forehead somewhat over-round, with minute curls, like a fleece, of bright auburn hair; the nose a trifle over-aquiline, and the cheekbones a trifle too low; the eyes grey, large, prominent, beneath exquisitely curved brows and lids just a little too tight at the corners; the mouth, also, brilliantly red and most delicately designed, is a little too tight, the lips strained a trifle over the teeth. Tight eyelids and tight lips give a strange refinement, and, at the same time, an air of mystery, a somewhat sinister seductiveness; they seem to take, but not to give. The mouth with a kind of childish pout, looks as if it could bite or suck like a leech. The complexion is dazzling fair, the perfect transparent roset lily of red-haired beauty; the head, with hair elaborately curled and plaited close to it, and adorned with pearls, sits like that of the antique Arethusa on a long, supple, swan-like neck. A curious, at first rather conventional, artificial-looking sort of beauty, voluptuous yet cold, which, the more it is contemplated, the more it troubles and haunts the mind. Round the lady's neck is a gold chain with little gold lozenges at intervals, on which is engraved the posy or pun (the fashion of French devices is common in these days), "Amour Dure – Dure Amour." The same posy is inscribed in the hollow of the bust, and, thanks to it, I have been able to identify the latter as Medea's portrait. I often examine these tragic portraits, wondering what this face, which led so many men to their death, may have been like when it spoke or smiled, what at the moment when Medea da Carpi fascinated her victims into love unto death – "Amour Dure – Dure Amour" as runs her device – love that lasts, cruel love – yes indeed, when one thinks of the fidelity and fate of her lovers.

Oct. 13th. I have literally not had time to write a line of my diary all these days. My whole mornings have gone in those Archives, my afternoons taking long walks in this lovely autumn weather (the highest hills are just tipped with snow). My evenings go in writing that confounded account of the Palace of Urbania which Government requires, merely to keep me at work at something useless. Of my history I have not yet been able to write a word.... By the way, I must note down a curious circumstance mentioned in an anonymous MS. Life of Duke Robert, which I fell upon to-day. When this prince had the equestrian statue of himself by Antonio Tassi, Gianbologna's pupil, erected in the square of the *Corte*, he secretly caused to be made, says my anonymous MS., a silver statuette of his familiar genius or angel – "familiaris ejus angelus seu genius, quod a vulgo dicitur *idolino*" – which statuette or idol (after having been consecrated by the astrologers – "ab astrologis quibusdam ritibus sacrato") was placed in the cavity of the chest of the effigy by Tassi, in order, says the MS., that his soul might rest until the general Resurrection. This passage is curious, and to me somewhat puzzling; how could the soul of Duke Robert await the general Resurrection, when, as a Catholic, he ought to have believed that it must, as soon as separated from his body, go to Purgatory? Or is there some semi-pagan superstition of the Renaissance (most strange, certainly, in a man who had been a Cardinal) connecting the soul with a guardian genius, who could be compelled, by magic rites ("ab astrologis sacrato," the MS. says of the little idol), to remain fixed to earth, so that the soul should sleep in the body until the Day of Judgement? I confess this story baffles me. I wonder whether such an idol ever existed, or exists nowadays, in the body of Tassi's bronze effigy?

Oct. 20th. I have been seeing a good deal of late of the Vice-Prefect's son: an amiable young man with a love-sick face and a languid interest in Urbanian history and archaeology, of which he is profoundly ignorant. This young man, who has lived at Siena and Lucca before his father was promoted here, wears extremely long and tight trousers, which almost preclude his bending his knees, a stick-up collar and an eyeglass, and a pair of fresh kid gloves stuck in the breast of his coat, speaks of Urbania as Ovid might have spoken of Pontus, and complains (as well he may) of the barbarism of the young men, the officials who dine at my inn and howl and sing like madmen, and the nobles who drive gigs, showing almost as much throat as a lady at a ball. This person frequently entertains me with his *amori*, past, present, and future; he evidently thinks me very odd for having none to entertain him with in return; he points out to me the pretty (or ugly) servant girls and dressmakers as we walk in the street, sighs deeply or sings in falsetto behind every tolerably young-looking woman, and has finally taken me to the house of the lady of his heart, a great black-moustached countess, with a voice like a fish-crier; here, he says, I shall meet all the best company in Urbania and some beautiful women – ah, too beautiful, alas! I find three huge half-furnished rooms, with bare brick floors, petroleum lamps, and horribly bad pictures on bright wash ball-blue and gamboge walls, and in the midst of it all, every evening, a dozen ladies and gentlemen seated in a circle, vociferating at each other the same news a year old; the younger ladies in bright yellows and greens, fanning themselves while my teeth chatter, and having sweet things whispered behind their fans by officers with hair brushed up like a hedgehog. And these are the women my friend expects me to fall in love with! I vainly wait for tea or supper which does not come, and rush home, determined to leave alone the Urbanian *beau monde*.

It is quite true that I have no *amori*, although my friend does not believe it. When I came to Italy first, I looked out for romance; I sighed, like Goethe in Rome, for a window to open and a wondrous creature to appear, "welch mich versengend erquickt." Perhaps it is because Goethe was a German, accustomed to German *Fraus*, and I am, after all, a Pole, accustomed to something very different from *Fraus;* but anyhow, for all my efforts, in Rome, Florence, and Siena, I never could find a woman to go mad about, either among the ladies, chattering bad French, or among the lower classes, as 'cute and cold as money-lenders; so I steer clear of Italian womankind, its shrill voice and gaudy toilettes. I am wedded to history, to the Past, to women like Lucrezia Borgia, Vittoria Accoramboni, or that Medea da Carpi, for the present; some day I shall perhaps find a grand passion, a woman to play the Don Quixote about, like the Pole that I am; a woman out of whose slipper to drink, and for whose pleasure to die; but not here! Few things strike me so much as the degeneracy of Italian women. What has become of the race of Faustinas, Marozias, Bianca Cappellos? Where discover nowadays (I confess she haunts me) another Medea da Carpi? Were it only possible to meet a woman of that extreme distinction of beauty, of that terribleness of nature, even if only potential, I do believe I could love her, even to the Day of Judgement, like any Oliverotto da Narni, or Frangipani or Prinzivalle.

Oct. 27th. Fine sentiments the above are for a professor, a learned man! I thought the young artists of Rome childish because they played practical jokes and yelled at night in the streets, returning from the Caffé Greco or the cellar in the Via Palombella; but am I not as childish to the full – I, melancholy wretch, whom they called Hamlet and the Knight of the Doleful Countenance?

Nov. 5th. I can't free myself from the thought of this Medea da Carpi. In my walks, my mornings in the Archives, my solitary evenings, I catch myself thinking over the woman. Am I turning novelist instead of historian? And still it seems to me that I understand her so well; so much better than my facts warrant. First, we must put aside all pedantic modern ideas of right and wrong. Right and wrong in a century of violence and treachery does not exist, least of all for creatures like Medea. Go preach right and wrong to a tigress, my dear sir! Yet is there in the world anything nobler than the huge creature, steel when she springs, velvet when she treads, as she stretches her supple body, or smooths her beautiful skin, or fastens her strong claws into her victim?

Yes; I can understand Medea. Fancy a woman of superlative beauty, of the highest courage and calmness, a woman of many resources, of genius, brought up by a petty princelet of a father, upon Tacitus and Sallust, and the tales of the great Malatestas, of Caesar Borgia and such-like! – a woman whose one passion is conquest and empire – fancy her, on the eve of being wedded to a man of the power of the Duke of Stimigliano, claimed, carried off by a small fry of a Pico, locked up in his hereditary brigand's castle, and having to receive the young fool's red-hot love as an honour and a necessity! The mere thought of any violence to such a nature is an abominable outrage; and if Pico chooses to embrace such a woman at the risk of meeting a sharp piece of steel in her arms, why, it is a fair bargain. Young hound – or, if you prefer, young hero – to think to treat a woman like this as if she were any village wench! Medea marries her Orsini. A marriage let it be noted, between an old soldier of fifty and a girl of sixteen. Reflect what that means: it means that this imperious woman is soon treated like a chattel, made roughly to understand that her business is to give the Duke an heir, not advice; that she must never ask "wherefore this or that?"; that she must show courtesy before the Duke's counsellors, his captains, his mistresses; that, at the least suspicion of rebelliousness, she is subject to his foul words and blows; at the least suspicion of infidelity, to be strangled or starved to death, or thrown down an oubliette. Suppose that she knows that her husband has taken it into his head that she has looked too hard at this man or that, that one of his lieutenants or one of his women have whispered that, after all, the boy Bartolommeo might as soon be a Pico as an Orsini. Suppose she knows that she must strike or be struck? Why, she strikes, gets someone to strike for her. At what price? A promise of love, of love to a groom, the son of a serf! Why, the dog must be mad or drunk to believe such a thing possible; his very belief in anything so monstrous makes him worthy of death. And then he dares to blab! This is much worse than Pico. Medea is bound to defend her honour a second time; if she could stab Pico, she can certainly stab this fellow, or have him stabbed.

Hounded by her husband's kinsmen, she takes refuge at Urbania. The Duke, like every other man, falls wildly in love with Medea, and neglects his wife; let us even go so far as to say, breaks his wife's heart. Is this Medea's fault? Is it her fault that every stone that comes beneath her chariot wheels is crushed? Certainly not. Do you suppose that a woman like Medea feels the smallest ill-will against a poor, craven Duchess Maddalena? Why, she ignores her very existence. To suppose Medea a cruel woman is as grotesque as to call her an immoral woman. Her fate is, sooner or later, to triumph over her enemies, at all events to make their victory almost a defeat: her magic faculty is to enslave all the men who come across her path; all those who see her, love her, become her slaves: and it is the destiny of all her slaves to perish. Her lovers, with the exception of Duke Guidalfonso, all come to an untimely end; and in this there is nothing unjust. The possession of a woman like Medea is a happiness too great for a mortal man; it would turn his head, make him forget even what he owed her; no man must survive long who conceives himself to have a right over her; it is a kind of sacrilege. And only death, the willingness to pay for such happiness by death, can at all make a man worthy of being her lover; he must be willing to love and suffer and die. This is the meaning of her device – "Amour Dure – Dure Amour." The love of Medea da Carpi cannot fade, but the lover can die; it is a constant and a cruel love.

Nov. 11th. I was right, quite right in my idea. I have found – Oh, joy! I treated the Vice-Prefect's son to a dinner of five courses at the Trattoria La Stella d'Italia out of sheer jubilation – I have found in the Archives, unknown, of course, to the Director, a heap of letters – letters of Duke Robert about Medea da Carpi, letters of Medea herself! Yes, Medea's own handwriting – a round, scholarly character, full of abbreviations, with a Greek look about it, as befits a learned princess who could read Plato as well as Petrarch. The letters are of little importance, mere drafts of business letters for her secretary to copy, during the time that she governed the poor weak Guidalfonso. But they are her letters, and I can imagine almost that there hangs about these mouldering pieces of paper a scent as of a woman's hair.

The letters of Duke Robert show him in a new light. A cunning, cold, but craven priest. He trembles at the bare thought of Medea – "la pessima Medea" – worse than her namesake of Colchis, as he calls her. His long clemency is a result of mere fear of laying violent hands upon her. He fears her as something almost supernatural; he would have enjoyed having had her burned as a witch. After letter on letter, telling his crony, Cardinal Sanseverino, at Rome his various precautions during her lifetime – how he wears a jacket of mail under his coat; how he drinks only milk from a cow which he has milked in his presence; how he tries his dog with morsels of his food, lest it be poisoned; how he suspects the wax candles because of their peculiar smell: how he fears riding out lest some one should frighten his horse and cause him to break his neck – after all this, and when Medea has been in her grave two years, he tells his correspondent of his fear of meeting the soul of Medea after his own death, and chuckles over the ingenious device (concocted by his astrologer and a certain Fra Gaudenzio, a Capuchin) by which he shall secure the absolute peace of his soul until that of the wicked Medea be finally "chained up in hell among the lakes of boiling pitch and the ice of Caina described by the immortal bard" – old pedant! Here, then, is the explanation of that silver image – *quod vulgo dicitur idolino* - which he caused to be soldered into his effigy by Tassi. As long as the image of his soul was attached to the image of his body, he should sleep awaiting the Day of Judgement, fully convinced that Medea's soul will then be properly tarred and feathered, while his – honest man! – will fly straight to Paradise. And to think that, two weeks ago, I believed this man to be a hero! Aha! my good Duke Robert, you shall be shown up in my history; and no amount of silver idolinos shall save you from being heartily laughed at!

Nov. 15th. Strange! That idiot of a Prefect's son, who has heard me talk a hundred times of Medea da Carpi, suddenly recollects that, when he was a child at Urbania, his nurse used to threaten him with a visit from Madonna Medea, who rode in the sky on a black he-goat. My Duchess Medea turned into a bogey for naughty little boys!

Nov. 20th. I have been going about with a Bavarian Professor of medieval history, showing him all over the country. Among other places we went to Rocco Sant' Elmo, to see the former villa of the Dukes of Urbania, the villa where Medea was confined between the accession of Duke Robert and the conspiracy of Marcantonio Frangipani, which caused her removal to the nunnery immediately outside the town. A long ride up the desolate Apennine valleys, bleak beyond words just now with their thin fringe of oak scrub turned russet, thin patches of grass seared by the frost, the last few yellow leaves of the poplars by the torrents shaking and fluttering about in the chill Tramontana; the mountain tops are wrapped in thick grey cloud; tomorrow, if the wind continues, we shall see them round masses of snow against the cold blue sky. Sant' Elmo is a wretched hamlet high on the Apennine ridge, where the Italian vegetation is already replaced by that of the North. You ride for miles through leafless chestnut woods, the scent of the soaking brown leaves filling the air, the roar of the torrent, turbid with autumn rains, rising from the precipice below; then suddenly the leafless chestnut woods are replaced, as at Vallombrosa, by a belt of black, dense fir plantations. Emerging from these, you come to an open space, frozen blasted meadows, the rocks of snow clad peak, the newly fallen snow, close above you; and in the midst, on a knoll, with a gnarled larch on either side, the ducal villa of Sant' Elmo, a big black stone box with a stone escutcheon, grated windows, and a double flight of steps in front. It is now let out to the proprietor of the neighbouring woods, who uses it for the storage of chestnuts, faggots, and charcoal from the neighbouring ovens. We tied our horses to the iron rings and entered: an old woman, with dishevelled hair, was alone in the house. The villa is a mere hunting lodge, built by Ottobuona IV, the father of Dukes Guidalfonso and Robert, about 1530. Some of the rooms have at one time been frescoed and panelled with oak carvings, but all this has disappeared. Only, in one of the big rooms, there remains a large marble fireplace, similar to those in the palace at Urbania, beautifully carved with Cupids on a blue ground; a charming naked boy sustains a jar on either side, one containing clove pinks, the other roses. The room was filled with stacks of faggots.

We returned home late, my companion in excessively bad humour at the fruitlessness of the expedition. We were caught in the skirt of a snowstorm as we got into the chestnut woods. The sight of the snow falling gently, of the earth and bushes whitened all round, made me feel back at Posen, once more a child. I sang and shouted, to my companion's horror. This will be a bad point against me if reported at Berlin. A historian of twenty-four who shouts and sings, and that when another historian is cursing at the snow and the bad roads! All night I lay awake watching the embers of my wood fire, and thinking of Medea da Carpi mewed up, in winter, in that solitude of Sant' Elmo, the firs groaning, the torrent roaring, the snow falling all round; miles and miles away from human creatures. I fancied I saw it all, and that I, somehow, was Marcantonio Frangipani come to liberate her – or was it Prinzivalle degli Ordelaffi? I suppose it was because of the long ride, the unaccustomed pricking feeling of the snow in the air; or perhaps the punch which my professor insisted on drinking after dinner.

Nov. 23rd. Thank goodness, that Bavarian professor has finally departed! Those days he spent here drove me nearly crazy.

Talking over my work, I told him one day my views on Medea da Carpi; whereupon he condescended to answer that those were the usual tales due to the mythopoeic (old idiot!) tendency of the Renaissance; that research would disprove the greater part of them, as it had disproved the stories current about the Borgias, etc.; that, moreover, such a woman as I made out was psychologically and physiologically impossible. Would that one could say as much of such professors as he and his fellows!

Nov. 24*th.* I cannot get over my pleasure in being rid of that imbecile; I felt as if I could have throttled him every time he spoke of the Lady of my thoughts – for such she has become – *Metea*, as the animal called her!

Nov. 30*th.* I feel quite shaken at what has just happened; I am beginning to fear that that old pedant was right in saying that it was bad for me to live all alone in a strange country, that it would make me morbid. It is ridiculous that I should be put into such a state of excitement merely by the chance discovery of a portrait of a woman dead these three hundred years. With the case of my uncle Ladislas, and other suspicions of insanity in my family, I ought really to guard against such foolish excitement.

Yet the incident was really dramatic, uncanny. I could have sworn that I knew every picture in the palace here; and particularly every picture of Her. Anyhow, this morning, as I was leaving the Archives, I passed through one of the many small rooms – irregular-shaped closets – which filled up the ins and outs of this curious palace, turreted like a French château. I must have passed through that closet before, for the view was so familiar out of its window; just the particular bit of round tower in front, the cypress on the other side of the ravine, the belfry beyond, and the piece of the line of Monte Sant' Agata and the Leonessa, covered with snow, against the sky. I suppose there must be twin rooms, and that I had got into the wrong one; or rather, perhaps some shutter had been opened or curtain withdrawn. As I was passing, my eye was caught by a very beautiful old mirror frame let into the brown and yellow inlaid wall. I approached, and looking at the frame, looked also, mechanically, into the glass, I gave a great start, and almost shrieked, I do believe (it's lucky the Munich professor is safe out of Urba-

132

nia!). Behind my own image stood another, a figure close to my shoulder, a face close to mine; and that figure, that face, hers! Medea da Carpi's! I turned sharp round, as white, I think, as the ghost I expected to see. On the wall opposite the mirror, just a pace or two behind where I had been standing, hung a portrait. And such a portrait! – Bronzino never painted a grander one. Against a background of harsh, dark blue, there stands out the figure of the Duchess (for it is Medea, the real Medea, a thousand times more real, individual, and powerful than in the other portraits), seated stiffly in a high-backed chair, sustained, as it were, almost rigid, by the stiff brocade of skirts and stomacher, stiffer for plaques of embroidered silver flowers and rows of seed pearl. The dress is, with its mixture of silver and pearl, of a strange dull red, a wicked poppy-juice colour, against which the flesh of the long, narrow hands with fringe-like fingers; of the long slender neck, and the face with bared forehead, looks white and hard, like alabaster. The face is the same as in the other portraits: the same rounded forehead, with the short fleece- like, yellowish-red curls; the same beautifully curved eyebrows, just barely marked: the same eyelids, a little tight across the eyes; the same lips, a little tight across the mouth; but with a purity of line, a dazzling splendour of skin, and intensity of look immeasurably superior to all the other portraits.

She looks out of the frame with a cold, level glance; yet the lips smile. One hand holds a dull-red rose; the other, long, narrow, tapering, plays with a thick rope of silk and gold and jewels hanging from the waist; round the throat, white as marble, partially confined in the tight dull-red bodice, hangs a gold collar, with the device on alternate enamelled medallions, "AMOUR DURE – DURE AMOUR."

On reflection, I see that I simply could never have been in that room or closet before; I must have mistaken the door. But, although the explanation is so simple, I still, after several hours, feel terribly shaken in all my being. If I grow so excitable I shall have to go to Rome at Christmas for a holiday. I feel as if some danger pursued me here (can it be fever?); and yet, and yet, I don't see how I shall ever tear myself away.

Dec. 10th. I have made an effort, and accepted the Vice-

Prefect's son's invitation to see the oil-making at a villa of theirs near the coast. The villa, or farm, is an old fortified, towered place, standing on a hillside among olive trees and little osier bushes, which look like a bright orange flame. The olives are squeezed in a tremendous black cellar, like a prison: you see, by the faint white daylight, and the smoky yellow flare of resin burning in pans, great white bullocks moving round a huge millstone; vague figures working at pulleys and handles: it looks, to my fancy, like some scene of the Inquisition. The Cavaliere regaled me with his best wine and rusks. I took some long walks by the seaside; I had left Urbania wrapped in snow clouds: down on the coast there was a bright sun; sunshine, the sea, the bustle of the little port on the Adriatic seemed to do me good. I came back to Urbania another man. Sor Asdrubale, my landlord, poking about in slippers among the gilded chests, the Empire sofas, the old cups and saucers and pictures which no one will buy, congratulated me upon the improvement in my looks. "You work too much," he says; "youth requires amuse-ment, theatres, promenades, *amori* – it is time enough to be serious when one is bald" – and he took off his greasy red cap. Yes, I am better! and, as a result, I take to my work with delight again. I will cut them out still, those wiseacres at Berlin!

Dec. 14*th*. I don't think I have ever felt so happy about my work. I see it all so well – that crafty, cowardly Duke Robert; that melancholy Duchess Maddalena; that weak, showy, would-be chivalrous Duke Guidalfonso; and above all, the splendid figure of Medea. I feel as if I were the greatest historian of the age; and, at the same time, as if I were a boy of twelve. It snowed yesterday for the first time in the city, for two good hours. When it had done, I actually went into the square and taught the ragamuffins to make a snow-man; no, a snow-woman; and I had the fancy to call her Medea. "La pessima Medea!" cried one of the boys – "the one who used to ride through the air on a goat?" "No, no," I said; "she was a beautiful lady, the Duchess of Urbania, the most beautiful woman that ever lived." I made her a crown of tinsel, and taught the boys to cry "Evviva, Medea!" But one of them said, "She is a witch! She must be burned!" At which they all rushed to fetch burning faggots and tow; in a minute the yelling demons had melted her down.

Dec. 15*th*. What a goose I am, and to think I am twenty-four, and known in literature! In my long walks I have composed to a tune (I don't know what it is) which all the people are singing and whistling in the street at present, a poem in frightful Italian, beginning "Medea mia dea," calling on her in the name of her various lovers. I go about humming between my teeth, "Why am I not Marcantonio? or Prinzivalle? or he of Narni? or the good Duke Alfonso? that I might be beloved by thee, Medea, mia dea," etc., etc. Awful rubbish? My landlord, I think, suspects that Medea must be some lady I met while I was staying by the seaside. I am sure Sora Serafina, Sora Lodovica, the Sora Adalgisa – the three Parcae or *Norns*, as I call them – have some such notion. This afternoon, at dusk, while tidying my room, Sora Lodovica said to me, "How beautifully the Signorino has taken to singing!" I was scarcely aware that I had been vociferating, "Vieni, Medea, mia dea," while the old lady bobbed about making up my fire. I stopped: a nice reputation I shall get! I thought, and all this will somehow get to Rome, and thence to Berlin. Sora Lodovica was leaning out of the window, pulling in the iron hook of the shrine-lamp which marks Sor Asdrubale's house. As she was trimming the lamp previous to swinging it out again, she said in her odd, prudish little way, "You are wrong to stop singing, my son" (she varies between calling me Signor Professore and such terms of affection as "Nino," "Viscere mie," etc.); "you are wrong to stop singing, for there is a young lady there in the street who has actually stopped to listen to you."

I ran to the window. A woman, wrapped in a black shawl, was standing in an archway, looking up to the window.

"Eh, eh! the Signor Professore has admirers," said Sora Lodovica.

"Medea, mia dea!" I burst out as loud as I could, with a boy's pleasure in disconcerting the inquisitive passer-by. She turned suddenly round to go away, waving her hand at me; at that moment Sora Lodovica swung the shrine-lamp back into its place. A stream of light fell across the street. I felt myself grow

135

quite cold; the face of the woman outside was that of Medea da Carpi!

What a fool I am, to be sure!

PART II

Dec. 17th. I fear that my craze about Medea da Carpi has become well known, thanks to my silly talk and idiotic songs. That Vice-Prefect's son – or the assistant at the Archives, or perhaps some of the company at the Contessa's, is trying to play me a trick! But take care, my good ladies and gentlemen, I shall pay you out in your own coin! Imagine my feelings when, this morning, I found on my desk a folded letter addressed to me in a curious handwriting which seemed strangely familiar to me, and which, after a moment, I recognized as that of the letters of Medea da Carpi at the Archives. It gave me a horrible shock. My next idea was that it must be a present from someone who knew my interest in Medea – a genuine letter of hers on which some idiot had written my address instead of putting it into an envelope. But it was addressed to me, written to me, no old letter; merely four lines, which ran as follows:-

"TO SPIRIDION. – A person who knows the interest you bear her will be at the Church of San Giovanni Decollato this evening at nine. Look out, in the left aisle, for a lady wearing a black mantle, and holding a rose."

By this time I understood that I was the object of a conspiracy, the victim of a hoax. I turned the letter round and round. It was written on paper such as was made in the sixteenth century, and in an extraordinary precise imitation of Medea da Carpi's characters. Who had written it? I thought over all the possible people. On the whole, it must be the Vice-Prefect's son, perhaps in combination with his lady-love, the Countess. They must have torn a blank page off some old letter; but that either of them should have had the ingenuity of inventing such a hoax, or the power of committing such a forgery, astounds me beyond measure. There is more in these people than I should have guessed. How pay them off? By taking no notice of the letter? Dignified, but dull. No, I will go; perhaps someone will be there, and I will mystify them in their turn. Or, if no one is there, how I shall crow over them for their imperfectly carried out plot! Perhaps this is some folly of the Cavaliere Muzio's to bring me into the presence of some lady whom he destines to be the flame of my future *amori*. That is likely enough. And it would be too idiotic and professorial to refuse such an invitation; the lady must be worth knowing who can forge sixteenth-century letters like this, for I am sure that languid swell Muzio never could. I will go! By Heaven! I'll pay them back in their own coin! It is now five – how long these days are!

Dec. 18*th*. Am I mad? Or are there really ghosts? That adventure of last night has shaken me to the very depth of my soul.

I went at nine, as the mysterious letter had bid me. It was bitterly cold, and the air full of fog and sleet; not a shop open, not a window unshuttered, not a creature visible; the narrow black streets, precipitous between their high walls and under their lofty archways, were only the blacker for the dull light of an oil lamp here and there, with its flickering yellow reflection on the wet flags. San Giovanni Decollato is a little church, or rather oratory, which I have always hitherto seen shut up (as so many churches here are shut up except on great festivals); and situate behind the ducal palace, on a sharp ascent, and forming the bifurcation of two steep paved lanes. I have passed by the place a hundred times, and scarcely noticed the little church, except for the marble high relief over the door, showing the grizzly head of the Baptist in the charger, and for the iron cage close by, in which were formerly exposed the heads of criminals; the decapitated, or, as they call him here, decollated, John the Baptist, being apparently the patron of axe and block.

A few strides took me from my lodgings to San Giovanni Decollato. I confess I was excited; one is not twenty-four and a Pole for nothing. On getting to the kind of little platform at the bifurcation of the two precipitous streets, I found, to my surprise, that the windows of the church or oratory were not lighted, and that the door was locked! So this was the precious joke that had been played upon me; to send me on a bitter cold, sleety night, to a church which was shut up and had perhaps been shut up for years! I don't know what I couldn't have done in that moment of rage; I felt inclined to break open the church door, or to go and pull the Vice-Prefect's son out of bed (for I felt sure that the joke was his). I determined upon the latter course; and was walking towards his door, along the black alley to the left of the church, when I was suddenly stopped by the sound as of an organ close by; an organ, yes, quite plainly, and the voice of choristers and the drone of a litany. So the church was not shut, after all! I retraced my steps to the top of the lane. All was dark and in complete silence. Suddenly there came again a faint gust of organ and voices. I listened; it clearly came from the other lane, the one on the right-hand side. Was there, perhaps, another door there? I passed beneath the archway, and descended a little way in the direction whence the sounds seemed to come. But no door, no light, only the black walls, the black wet flags, with their faint yellow reflections of flickering oil lamps; moreover, complete silence. I stopped a minute, and then the chant rose again; this time it seemed to me most certainly from the lane I had just left. I went back – nothing. Thus backwards and forwards, the sounds always beckoning, as it were, one way, only to beckon me back, vainly, to the other.

At last I lost patience; and I felt a sort of creeping terror, which only a violent action could dispel. If the mysterious sounds came neither from the street to the right, nor from the street to the left, they could come only from the church. Half-maddened, I rushed up the two or three steps, and prepared to wrench the door open with a tremendous effort. To my amazement, it opened with the greatest ease. I entered, and the sounds of the litany met me louder than before, as I paused a moment between the outer door and the heavy leathern curtain. I raised the latter and crept in. The altar was brilliantly illuminated with tapers and garlands of chandeliers; this was evidently some evening service connected with Christmas. The nave and aisles were comparatively dark, and about half-full. I elbowed my way along the right aisle towards the altar. When my eyes had got accustomed to the unexpected light, I began to look round me, and with a beating heart. The idea that all this was a hoax, that I should meet merely some acquaintance of my friend the Cavaliere's, had somehow departed: I looked about. The people were all wrapped up, the men in big cloaks, the women in woollen veils and mantles. The body of the church was comparatively dark, and I could not make out anything very clearly, but it seemed to me, somehow, as if, under the cloaks and veils, these people were dressed in a rather extraordinary fashion. The man in front of me, I remarked, showed yellow stockings beneath his cloak; a woman, hard by, a red bodice, laced behind with gold tags. Could these be peasants from some remote part come for the Christmas festivities, or did the inhabitants of Urbania don some old-fashioned garb in honour of Christmas?

As I was wondering, my eye suddenly caught that of a woman standing in the opposite aisle, close to the altar, and in the full blaze of its lights. She was wrapped in black, but held, in a very conspicuous way, a red rose, an unknown luxury at this time of the year in a place like Urbania. She evidently saw me, and turning even more fully into the light, she loosened her heavy black cloak, displaying a dress of deep red, with gleams of silver and gold embroideries; she turned her face towards me; the full blaze of the chandeliers and tapers fell upon it. It was the face of Medea da Carpi! I dashed across the nave, pushing people roughly aside, or rather, it seemed to me, passing through impalpable bodies. But the lady turned and walked rapidly down the aisle towards the door. I followed close upon her, but somehow I could not get up with her. Once, at the curtain, she turned round again. She was within a few paces of me. Yes, it was Medea. Medea herself, no mistake, no delusion, no sham; the oval face, the lips tightened over the mouth, the eyelids tight over the corner of the eyes, the exquisite alabaster complexion! She raised the curtain and glided out. I followed; the curtain alone separated me from her. I saw the wooden door swing to behind her. One step ahead of me! I tore open the door; she must be on the steps, within reach of my arm!

I stood outside the church. All was empty, merely the wet pavement and the yellow reflections in the pool: a sudden cold seized me; I could not go on. I tried to re-enter the church; it was shut. I rushed home, my hair standing on end, and trembling in all my limbs, and remained for an hour like a maniac. Is it a delusion? Am I too going mad? O God, God! am I going mad?

Dec. 19*th*. A brilliant, sunny day: all the black snowslush has disappeared out of the town, off the bushes and trees. The snow-clad mountains sparkle against the bright blue sky. A

Sunday, and Sunday weather; all the bells are ringing for the approach of Christmas. They are preparing for a kind of fair in the square with the colonnade, putting up booths filled with coloured cotton and woollen ware, bright shawls and kerchiefs, mirrors, ribbons, brilliant pewter lamps; the whole turn-out of the pedlar in "Winter's Tale." The pork shops are all garlanded with green and with paper flowers, the hams and cheeses stuck full of little flags and green twigs. I strolled out to see the cattle fair outside the gate; a forest of interlacing horns, an ocean of lowing and stamping: hundreds of immense white bullocks, with horns a yard long and red tassels, packed close together on the little piazza d'armi under the city walls. Bah! why do I write this trash? What's the use of it all? While I am forcing myself to write about bells, and Christmas festivities, and cattle fairs, one idea goes on like a bell within me: Medea, Medea! Have I really seen her, or am I mad?

Two hours later. That Church of San Giovanni Decollato – so my landlord informs me – has not been made use of within the memory of man. Could it have been all a hallucination or a dream – perhaps a dream dreamed that night? I have been out again to look at that church. There it is, at the bifurcation of the two steep lanes, with its bas-relief of the Baptist's head over the door. The door does look as if it had not been opened for years. I can see the cobwebs in the windowpanes; it does look as if, as Sor Asdrubale says, only rats and spiders congregated within it. And yet – and yet; I have so clear a remembrance, so distinct a consciousness of it all. There was a picture of the daughter of Herodias dancing, upon the altar; I remember her white turban with a scarlet tuft of feathers, and Herod's blue caftan; I remember the shape of the central chandelier; it swung round slowly, and one of the wax lights had got bent almost in two by the heat and draught.

Things, all these, which I may have seen elsewhere, stored unawares in my brain, and which may have come out, somewhere, in a dream; I have heard physiologists allude to such things. I will go again: if the church be shut, why then it must have been a dream, a vision, the result of over-excitement. I must leave at once for Rome and see doctors, for I am afraid of going mad. If, on the other hand – pshaw! there *is no other hand* in such a case. Yet if there were – why then, I should really have seen Medea; I might see her again; speak to her. The mere thought sets my blood in a whirl, not with horror, but with...I know not what to call it. The feeling terrifies me, but it is delicious. Idiot! There is some little coil of my brain, the twentieth of a hair's-breadth out of order – that's all!

Dec. 20th. I have been again; I have heard the music; I have been inside the church: I have seen Her! I can no longer doubt my senses. Why should I? Those pedants say that the dead are dead, the past is past. For them, yes; but why for me? – why for a man who loves, who is consumed with the love of a woman? – a woman who, indeed – yes, let me finish the sentence. Why should there not be ghosts to such as can see them? Why should she not return to the earth, if she knows that it contains a man who thinks of, desires, only her?

A hallucination? Why, I saw her, as I see this paper that I write upon; standing there, in the full blaze of the altar. Why, I heard the rustle of her skirts. I smelled the scent of her hair, I raised the curtain which was shaking from her touch. Again I missed her. But this time, as I rushed out into the empty moonlit street, I found upon the church steps a rose – the rose which I had seen in her hand the moment before – I felt it, smelled it; a rose, a real, living rose, dark red and only just plucked. I put it into water when I returned, after having kissed it, who knows how many times? I placed it on the top of the cupboard; I determined not to look at it for twenty-four hours lest it should be a delusion. But I must see it again; I must....Good Heavens! this is horrible, horrible; if I had found a skeleton it could not have been worse! The rose, which last night seemed freshly plucked, full of colour and perfume, is brown, dry – a thing kept for centuries between the leaves of a book – it has crumbled into dust between my fingers. Horrible, horrible! But why so, pray? Did I not know that I was in love with a woman dead three hundred years? If I wanted fresh roses which bloomed yesterday, the Countess Fiametta or any little seamstress in Urbania might have given them me. What if the rose has fallen to dust? If only I could hold Medea in my arms as I held it in my fingers, kiss her lips as I kissed its petals, should I not be satisfied if she too were to fall to dust the next moment, if I were to fall to dust myself?

Dec. 22nd, Eleven at night. I have seen her once more! – almost spoken to her. I have been promised her love! Ah, Spiridion! you were right when you felt that you were not made for any earthly *amori*. At the usual hour I betook myself this evening to San Giovanni Decollato. A bright winter night; the high houses and belfries standing out against a deep blue heaven luminous, shimmering like steel with myriads of stars; the moon has not yet risen. There was no light in the windows; but, after a little effort, the door opened and I entered the church, the altar, as usual, brilliantly illuminated. It struck me suddenly that this crowd of men and women standing all round, these priests chanting and moving about the altar, were dead – that they did not exist for any man save me. I touched, as if by accident, the hand of my neighbour; it was cold, like wet clay. He turned round, but did not seem to see me: his face was ashy, and his eyes staring, fixed, like those of a blind man or a corpse. I felt as if I must rush out. But at that moment my eye fell upon Her, standing as usual by the altar steps, wrapped in a black mantle, in the full blaze of the lights. She turned round; the light fell straight upon her face, the face with the delicate features, the eyelids and lips a little tight, the alabaster skin faintly tinged with pale pink. Our eyes met.

I pushed my way across the nave towards where she stood by the altar steps; she turned quickly down the aisle, and I after her. Once or twice she lingered, and I thought I should overtake her; but again, when, not a second after the door had closed upon her, I stepped out into the street, she had vanished. On the church step lay something white. It was not a flower this time, but a letter. I rushed back to the church to read it; but the church was fast shut, as if it had not been opened for years. I could not see by the flickering shrine-lamps – I rushed home, lit my lamp, pulled the letter from my breast. I have it before me. The handwriting is hers; the same as in the Archives, the same as in that first letter:–

"TO SPIRIDION. Let thy courage be equal to thy love, and thy love shall be rewarded. On the night preceding Christmas, take a hatchet and saw; cut boldly into the body of the bronze rider who stands in the Corte, on the left side, near the waist. Saw open the body, and within it thou wilt find the silver effigy of a winged genius. Take it out, hack it into a hundred pieces, and fling them in all directions, so that the winds may sweep them away. That night she whom thou lovest will come to reward thy fidelity."

On the brownish wax is the device –

"AMOUR DURE – DURE AMOUR."

Dec. 23rd. So it is true! I was reserved for something wonderful in this world. I have at last found that after which my soul has been straining. Ambition, love of art, love of Italy, these things which have occupied my spirit, and have yet left me continually unsatisfied, these were none of them my real destiny. I have sought for life, thirsting for it as a man in the desert thirsts for a well; but the life of the senses of other youths, the life of the intellect of other men, have never slaked that thirst. Shall life for me mean the love of a dead woman? We smile at what we choose to call the superstition of the past, forgetting that all our vaunted science of to-day may seem just another superstition to the men of the future; but why should the present be right and the past wrong? The men who painted the pictures and built the palaces of three hundred years ago were certainly of as delicate fibre, of as keen reason, as ourselves, who merely print calico and build locomotives. What makes me think this, is that I have been calculating my nativity by help of an old book belonging to Sor Asdrubale – and see, my horoscope tallies almost exactly with that of Medea da Carpi, as given by a chronicler. May this explain? No, no: all is explained by the fact that the first time I read of this woman's career, the first time I saw her portrait, I loved her, though I hid my love to myself in the garb of historical interest. Historical interest indeed!

I have got the hatchet and the saw. I bought the saw of a poor joiner, in a village some miles off; he did not understand at first what I meant, and I think he thought me mad; perhaps I am. But if madness means the happiness of one's life, what of it? The hatchet I saw lying in a timber yard, where they prepare the great trunks of the fir trees which grow high on the Apennines of Sant' Elmo. There was no one in the yard, and I could not resist the

144

temptation; I handled the thing, tried its edge, and stole it. This is the first time in my life that I have been a thief; why did I not go into a shop and buy a hatchet? I don't know: I seemed unable to resist the sight of the shining blade. What I am going to do is, I suppose, an act of vandalism: and certainly I have no right to spoil the property of this city of Urbania. But I wish no harm either to the statue or the city; if I could plaster up the bronze, I would do so willingly. But I must obey Her; I must avenge Her; I must get at that silver image which Robert of Montemurlo had made and consecrated in order that his cowardly soul might sleep in peace, and not encounter that of the being whom he dreaded most in the world. Aha! Duke Robert, you forced her to die unshriven, and you stuck the image of your soul into the image of your body, thinking thereby that, while she suffered the tortures of Hell, you would rest in peace, until your well-scoured little soul might fly straight up to Paradise – you were afraid of Her when both of you should be dead, and thought yourself very clever to have prepared for all emergencies! Not so, Serene Highness. You too shall taste what it is to wander after death, and to meet the dead whom one has injured.

What an interminable day! But I shall see her again tonight.

Eleven o'clock. No; the church was fast closed; the spell had ceased. Until tomorrow I shall not see her. But tomorrow! Ah, Medea! did any of thy lovers love thee as I do?

Twenty-four hours more till the moment of happiness – the moment for which I seem to have been waiting all my life. And after that, what next? Yes, I see it plainer every minute; after that, nothing more. All those who loved Medea da Carpi, who loved and who served her, died: Giovanfrancesco Pico, her first husband whom she left stabbed in the castle from which she fled; Stimigliano, who died of poison; the groom who gave him the poison, cut down by her orders; Oliverotto da Narni, Marcantonio Frangipani, and that poor boy of the Ordelaffi, who had never even looked upon her face, and whose only reward was that handkerchief with which the hangman wiped the sweat off his face, when he was one mass of broken limbs and torn flesh: all had to die, and I shall die also.

The love of such a woman is enough, and is fatal – "Amour

Dure," as her device says. I shall die also. But why not? Would it be possible to live in order to love another woman? Nay, would it be possible to drag on a life like this one after the happiness of tomorrow? Impossible; the others died, and I must die. I always felt that I should not live long; a gipsy in Poland told me once that I had in my hand the cut-line which signifies a violent death. I might have ended in a duel with some brother-student, or in a railway accident. No, no; my death will not be of that sort! Death – and is not she also dead! What strange vistas does such a thought not open! Then the others – Pico, the Groom, Stimigliano, Oliverotto, Frangipani, Prinzivalle degli Ordelaffi – will they all be *there*? But she shall love me best – me by whom she has been loved after she has been three hundred years in the grave!

Dec. 24*th.* I have made all my arrangements. Tonight at eleven I slip out; Sor Asdrubale and his sisters will be sound asleep. I have questioned them; their fear of rheumatism prevents their attending midnight mass. Luckily there are no churches between this and the Corte; whatever movements Christmas night may entail will be a good way off. The Vice-Prefect's rooms are on the other side of the palace; the rest of the square is taken up with state-rooms, archives, and empty stables and coach houses of the palace. Besides, I shall be quick at my work.

I have tried my saw on a stout bronze vase I bought off Sor Asdrubale; and the bronze of the statue, hollow and worn away by rust (I have even noticed holes), cannot resist very much, especially after a blow with the sharp hatchet. I have put my papers in order, for the benefit of the Government which has sent me hither. I am sorry to have defrauded them of their "History of Urbania." To pass the endless day and calm the fever of impatience, I have just taken a long walk. This is the coldest day we have had. The bright sun does not warm in the least, but seems only to increase the impression of cold, to make the snow on the mountains glitter, the blue air to sparkle like steel. The few people who are out are muffled to the nose, and carry earthenware braziers beneath their cloaks; long icicles hang from the fountain with the figure of Mercury upon it; one can imagine the wolves trooping down through the dry scrub and beleaguering this town. Somehow this cold makes me feel wonderfully calm – it seems to bring back to me my boyhood.

As I walked up the rough, steep, paved alleys, slippery with frost, and with their vista of snow mountains against the sky, and passed by the church steps strewn with box and laurel, with the faint smell of incense coming out, there returned to me – I know not why – the recollection, almost the sensation, of those Christmas Eves long ago at Posen and Breslau, when I walked as a child along the wide streets, peeping into the windows where they were beginning to light the tapers of the Christmas trees, and wondering whether I too, on returning home, should be let into a wonderful room all blazing with lights and gilded nuts and glass beads. They are hanging the last strings of those blue and red metallic beads, fastening on the last gilded and silvered walnuts on the trees out there at home in the North; they are lighting the blue and red tapers; the wax is beginning to run on to the beautiful spruce green branches; the children are waiting with beating hearts behind the door, to be told that the Christ-Child has been. And I, for what am I waiting? I don't know: all seems a dream; everything vague and unsubstantial about me, as if time had ceased, nothing could happen, my own desires and hopes were all dead, myself absorbed into I know not what passive dreamland. Do I long for tonight? Do I dread it? Will tonight ever come? Do I feel anything, does anything exist all round me? I sit and seem to see that street at Posen, the wide street with the windows illuminated by the Christmas lights, the green fir branches grazing the windowpanes.

Christmas Eve, Midnight. I have done it. I slipped out noiselessly. Sor Asdrubale and his sisters were fast asleep. I feared I had awakened them, for my hatchet fell as I was passing through the principal room where my landlord keeps his curiosities for sale; it struck against some old armour which he has been piecing. I heard him exclaim, half in his sleep; and blew out my light and hid in the stairs. He came out in his dressing-gown, but finding no one, went back to bed again. "Some cat, no doubt!" he said. I closed the house door softly behind me. The sky had become stormy since the afternoon, luminous with the full moon, but strewn with grey and buff-coloured vapours; every now and then the moon disappeared entirely. Not a creature abroad; the tall gaunt houses staring into the moonlight.

I know not why, I took a roundabout way to the Corte, past one or two church doors, whence issued the faint flicker of midnight mass. For a moment I felt a temptation to enter one of them; but something seemed to restrain me. I caught snatches of the Christmas hymn. I felt myself beginning to be unnerved, and hastened towards the Corte. As I passed under the portico at San Francesco I heard steps behind me; it seemed to me that I was followed. I stopped to let the other pass. As he approached his pace flagged; he passed close by me and murmured, "Do not go: I am Giovanfrancesco Pico." I turned round; he was gone. A coldness numbed me; but I hastened on.

Behind the cathedral apse, in a narrow lane, I saw a man leaning against a wall. The moonlight was full upon him: it seemed to me that his face, with a thin pointed beard, was streaming with blood. I quickened my pace: but as I grazed by him he whispered, "Do not obey her: return home: I am Marcantonio Frangipani." My teeth chattered, but I hurried along the narrow lane, with the moonlight blue upon the white walls.

At last I saw the Corte before me: the square was flooded with moonlight, the windows of the palace seemed brightly illuminated, and the statue of Duke Robert, shimmering green, seemed to advance towards me on its horse. I came into the shadow. I had to pass beneath an archway. There started a figure as if out of the wall, and barred my passage with his outstretched cloaked arm. I tried to pass. He seized me by the arm, and his grasp was like a weight of ice. "You shall not pass!" he cried, and, as the moon came out once more, I saw his face, ghastly white and bound with an embroidered kerchief; he seemed almost a child. "You shall not pass!" he cried, "you shall not have her! She is mine, and mine alone! I am Prinzivalle degli Ordelaffi." I felt his ice-cold clutch, but with my other arm I laid about me wildly with the hatchet which I carried beneath my cloak. The hatchet struck the wall and rang upon the stone. He had vanished.

I hurried on. I did it. I cut open the bronze; I sawed it into a wider gash. I tore out the silver image, and hacked it into in-

148

numerable pieces. As I scattered the last fragments about, the moon was suddenly veiled; a great wind arose, howling down the square; it seemed to me that the earth shook. I threw down the hatchet and the saw, and fled home. I felt pursued, as if by the tramp of hundreds of invisible horsemen.

Now I am calm. It is midnight; another moment and she will be here! Patience, my heart! I hear it beating loud. I trust that no one will accuse poor Sor Asdrubale. I will write a letter to the authorities to declare his innocence should anything happen.... One! the clock in the palace tower has just struck.... "I hereby certify that, should anything happen this night to me, Spiridion Trepka, no one but myself is to be held..." A step on the staircase! It is she! it is she! At last, Medea, Medea! Ah! AMOUR DURE – DURE AMOUR!

NOTE. – Here ends the diary of the late Spiridion Trepka. The chief newspapers of the province of Umbria informed the public that, on Christmas morning of the year 1885, the bronze equestrian statue of Robert II had been found grievously mutilated; and that Professor Spiridion Trepka of Posen, in the German Empire, had been discovered dead of a stab in the region of the heart, given by an unknown hand.

POISONING THE SEA
by
Storm Constantine

I have proved them all to be fools! Not that there was any doubt in my mind that my father, his scheming lackwit underlings and indeed all men on this world, were anything other than that to begin with, but this most recent victory has a delicious sweetness on my tongue.

I have just left him: once man, now animal. I left him fawning on my chamber floor. His name is Aertes. He was a poet. He is a dog, now.

Oh, beloved father, did you really think to pull my claws by expelling me into this isolation? I cannot believe that you underestimated my intelligence, but then, you are a man yourself and therefore lacking in wit of a sharper nature.

As I descend the cold, white stairs to the terrace, I can see, through the open shutters, that the sister ocean is choppy today. I will pour blood into her waves, as a blessing and in celebration of my triumph. There is little else to do upon this blasted rock. Then, I shall speak to my domestic, Baucis, and tell her to remove the beast from my rooms with a brief ritual; no doubt he will be whining there still among the curtains when I return from the sea.

Beyond the garden walls of my palace, there is a cluster of dwellings that hug the cliffs, inhabited by the rough folk who farm the waves beneath. These creatures, my royal father thought, would be my only companions until I learned humility. Imprisoning me upon this backward isle, secured by the prowling ships that haunt the horizon, he seeks to break my spirit, to imbue me with remorse for an act I can only regard as expedient. As I would have said to my dear sister, whom I miss intolerably, despite her limper nature: "It is beyond our beloved sire to penetrate the whims and desires of his female relatives, let alone their skills and caprices."

The path to the ocean is steep and winding, hemmed by stiff herbs of a thorny nature and shivering with green and turquoise lizards. The air is scented by a sharp, leafy reek that mingles with the smell of brine. The day is shaking to the sound of roaring waves and, from beneath my feet, I hear the brisk crunch of shells, which litter the path like little white flowers. I am wearing my favourite cloak of finely spun wool, dark in colour as befits my mood, and am accompanied by black Ishti, who is the largest and most splendid of my companion cats. Ishti, perhaps unusual among his kind, loves the sea. In fact, I took him half-drowned from the wreck of some vessel which had spewed lolling white corpses upon the beach some seasons back. Baucis maintains that he is not a cat at all, as he is rather too big to fit comfortably into that category, but to me, anything that purrs so divinely must surely be a scion of the tribe of the Egyptian Bast. I treat him as such, for which respect he repays me with touching loyalty.

We wind our way down through the black, damp rocks. At high tide, there is no beach at all on this side of the island and, when the sea draws back her foamy skirts, there are pleasing pools full of unusual, twisted shells and weed that streams like long switches of green hair. Sometimes, we find richer treasures, but I am not beachcombing today. Ishti has brought me a white cockerel from the village, which I drained into a bowl, ultimately transferring the blood to a stoppered vial. The villagers are afraid of my Ishti and never interfere with his excursions into their territory to bring me the things I need. They are also rather afraid of me, which effectively prevents them from taking the law into their own hands concerning Ishti. I give them things in return which my father has sent me – items of clothing, meaningless baubles, certain foods I dislike – so they cannot really complain.

Mad Helen is on the rocks today, an eerie figure amidst the foam. She is staring out across the grey waves, her pale hair blowing right over her face, standing still as a stone. She, of all the peasants, I find intriguing. Her people believe her to be simple-minded, yet I know she is merely stultified by the life she leads upon this rock, and would blossom away from it, if she could only find a place to exercise the skills with which I have

154

acquainted her. An eager student, Helen. When I am allowed to return home, I have a mind to take her with me. It would serve my father right.

"Good day to you my dear!" I announce. Helen does not move. She is thinking deeply. Sometimes I pinch her sharply to make her share her thoughts with me, because they can be so interesting. "I have some blood to cast!" That wakes her up a little. She turns her small pointed face in my direction, her narrow grey eyes screwed up against the wind.

"Have you, Mistress? May I watch?"

"Of course." I take the vial out of the pocket of my cloak and begin to wrestle with the stopper. The vials I use are quite old, but they are the only vessels suitable for this type of task that I can find among the rubbish of my equally old palace. I am always concerned they will spill their contents onto my clothes and consequently tend to stopper them too tightly.

"Allow me, Mistress," Helen says, and I hand the vial over to her clever fingers, surprisingly brutish and thick members on such a fragile body.

"There is talk that raised voices were heard coming from your windows last night, my lady Circe," she says.

"Indeed," I reply, as question or exclamation. Helen does not understand the difference, but she eyes the vial with greater interest.

"A cockerel," I say.

Together, smiling our different smiles, we turn towards the sea.

It was not a grey day when the *Persephone* came towards the island but, like this day, full of wind and clouds, I was standing on the rocks at the half tide, casting something – I have forgotten exactly what, perhaps an entrail or two – into the receding waters. Ishti was with me, as always, poking his long, stiff whiskers into the rock pools, sniffing for crablets and vulnerable fish spawn. Helen came sliding over the wet, weedy stones towards me from the direction of the village, her dripping skirts tucked up into her belt, her feet encased in sopping animal skin slippers tied at the ankle. She had her enhancing vitrine with her, something her grandmother – a woman of invention and devices – had fashioned. The ignorant people of the village believed Helen's grandmother to be a witch, but I know better and have used her inventions in many ways from time to time. The vitrine is a cleverly fashioned glass lens set in an embellished metal frame. Looking through it, things far from the eye appear close, and interesting details can be discerned. Helen, I am sure, has many clandestine uses for this device, (if she has not, she is no true disciple of mine!), but sometimes, on clear days, we take it in turns to squint through the vitrine at the distant waves. It is possible to distinguish the eyes painted on the hulls of my father's guardian ships on the horizon; a dull view, it is true, but I like to peer at the tiny figures of the men on board, wishing them various misfortunes, such as love and marriage.

Helen put the vitrine against her eye and described to me an elegant ship she perceived against the blue sky.

"Which direction is it taking, dearest?" I asked her.

She bared her teeth and said, "To the east, my lady, her sails are full of wind."

"So beyond the net of our influence," I said pensively, wrenching the vitrine from her hold. I was thinking about the number of vessels which sailed along the invisible ring-pass-not that surrounded my place of exile, all of them quite ignorant of the treasure that lay so close. Occasionally, I indulged in fantasies of ships bulging with creatures uneducated in my history, who might blunder in innocence towards the island. Unfortunately, my father – damn his seed – lavishes great care on advertising what he perceives to be my dangerous nature. He is superstitious and blind, but I cannot forgive him his childish misapprehensions. The murder I committed was necessary and just, in my eyes.

I adjusted the vitrine against my brow and peered into the blue. The ship was beautiful, a mere speck, like a model created by a craftsman, each detail precise and tiny. If only it would turn its slender prow towards the rocks. If only it would come to me. Who could tell what secrets it might spill among the weeds and shells? Rather wistfully, I handed the vitrine back to Helen.

"Perhaps, one day, we shall both sail away upon such a ship,"

I said. The girl liked to hear fabulous stories. We often invented new futures for ourselves, our words blown away by the sea winds, hopefully into the ears of some benign, indulgent deity.

"Perhaps we could sail away upon this one," she replied.

I laughed gently and laid a hand against her bony shoulder. "Perhaps, in dreams," I said.

"No, really," she replied, and I noticed a certain fervour in her tone.

Without words, I snatched the vitrine away from her eyes, causing her to yelp as her cheek caught a blow from the metal frame. It took only a moment to confirm my hope; the ship had turned towards the island. It took a further moment for me to control myself. With vile, girlish stupidity, I had allowed the prospect of visitors to excite me. This was the kind of weakness I would expect my sweet, simpering sister to display. Having recognised it, I stemmed it immediately, swiftly invoking a sense of weary nausea instead.

Owing to the fact that my father's navy patrols this stretch of water so assiduously, few vessels come to invade our privacy. Those that do are generally filled only with priests who come to pay visits to the lustreless shrines on top of the island. This rock was once the summer retreat of a noble family, who have since seen sense and built for themselves a grander retreat in more clement circumstances, but their ostentatious shrines still remain, though I suspect empty of divine presences. Occasionally, instead of priests, but only barely more tolerable, a shoal of slippery courtiers from my father's court might come to peer down their elegant noses at us, but these men are always decrepit and of little interest to me. Also, they carry lies back to my father, if they get the chance. I knew that whoever sailed towards us could only be further dregs of religious society or tell-tale buffoons. Still, it was possible I would have to receive one of them in my abode, which at least promised a minor diversion for the day, so I called Ishti from his explorations and, gathering up my skirts, hurried towards the cliff path.

I composed myself upon my terrace, had the tiles strewn with crushed blossom and pungent crushed fern, saw to it that Baucis and her crones had chilled the wine in spring snow, gathered from the higher slopes. I had dressed myself in a maidenly colour – pale saffron, I recall – and I reclined limpidly upon a couch; Ishti and his smaller companions were arranged around me on cushions and rugs and fleeces. I had tied back my hair – a style I loathe as it reveals the height and breadth of my forehead – and had donned some of the jewellery my father had sent me. Most of it, I throw into the sea or give away to the peasants, but I prudently keep a few choice items around me for occasions such as this. I never know who might come to me, with the express purpose of compiling an unflattering report of my mien and appearance to deliver to my father.

Baucis scuttled out onto the terrace. She is like a spider, having bent hairy limbs but an alarmingly quick gait. "Well, is it priest or sycophant this time?" I asked her, in a languid, bored voice, just in case there were ears pressed to the drapes beyond the terrace doors.

"Neither, mistress," Baucis lisped.

"Then what?"

"A man, mistress."

I sighed. "Naturally."

"A young man."

I raised an eyebrow. "Different!"

Baucis grinned. "An attractive young man."

"An occasion for grateful sacrifice! Is he gelded?"

My retainer grimaced. "Does not strike me as so," she said, "but perhaps it is difficult to tell."

I sat upright. "Well, I must confess to being intrigued as to why my beloved father should send such a creature to our island, but you must show him to me immediately."

Baucis hesitated. "Mistress, he does not claim to have come from the King."

I could not help gripping my own throat: excitement had leapt in it like a caged bird who spies the cage door open. No, no, I must not vault to conclusions that might lead to disappointment. "His name?" I asked.

Baucis bobbed a curtsey, still grinning. "Aertes of the house of Parmon," she said. "He is a poet of renown."

This man intrigued me from the start, but you must under-stand that the intrigue of a pretty face is commonplace. It is the deeper allure which manifests later that has the hardest hooks.

In appearance he was almost unkempt, his dark, gold-shot hair ungroomed and hanging nearly to his waist. He looked like some bedraggled satyr, although his cloak was spun of finest wool and edged with gold thread. The face was bare as if scoured by the salt sea. Indeed, I was reminded of bone; in shadow, he could resemble a skull, although he was undoubtedly attractive.

"My lady, Circe," he said, and swept a bow.

He had come to me seeking inspiration! Well, I was more than prepared to give him that.

Demurely, I allowed him a few minutes' audience while he extolled his own virtues in what he designed to be a modest manner. Smiling sweetly, I allowed him to exercise his vanities before dismissing him by claiming I had tasks to attend to, and that I would be unable to lavish more time on him until the following evening. This, he took in good part – disappointingly good part, I thought – but it did not matter. He had one foot in the web, at least, simply by virtue of being here.

Later, as Baucis brushed my hair before bedtime, in the low, captured sunset light of the lamps, within a veil of sweet, cedar incense, we made a small wager as to how long it would take me to ensnare him. "A day," I said, "all poets are romantics."

"No, he has a wolf's eyes," my faithful crone replied, skil-fully unknotting a persistent tangle. "I'll give it a week."

We were both in error.

I agreed to speak with Aertes at dusk, for that is my time, when I feel my strength most potent. Also, it becomes a woman to court the evening light. It is like a veil; you are seen through it only dimly.

From Baucis, I learned the poet had spent the day showing himself off in the village, escorted by a gambolling herd of coltish followers he had brought with him off the ship. Through Baucis, I had made it plain I would only interview him alone. Youths annoy me.

When I drifted out onto the terrace, Aertes was sitting on the stone wall that overlooked the sea.

"You like my palace?" I asked him, lifting back my veil and gliding over the marble. Baucis had permeated the whole building with overwhelming fumes, supposedly as a mark of welcome, although I suspected she harboured fears about disagreeable odours escaping from the kitchens. In truth, my eyes were stinging.

Aertes laughed softly, leaning forward, his forearms resting carelessly on his knees. I perceived a bloody scratch upon his bare shin. Perhaps he'd blundered through the thorns along the cliff-top. "The palace is graceful, but in a way, disappointing," he said.

"Oh, I am humbly shamed! Why so?" The answer was no great surprise.

"Well, I find no skulls, no blood upon the floor, no tortured statues suggesting men turned to stone and no animals wearing the tatters of human clothes."

"Perhaps you have not looked hard enough," I said, favouring him with a gentle smile. "I trust your day has been enjoyable, although I regret there is little upon this lump of rock to entertain."

"I visited the village," he said. "The people here are starved of culture."

"I have noticed this too," I said. "Perhaps you should perform for them."

He pulled a face at me, hoping to draw me into some intimate conspiracy. It struck me how similar he was to all the men I had known about my father's court; confident of his innate splendour and unafraid. He saw me as a simple woman; a mistake all men make when viewing the female form. They think of their poems, but not the reality. They cannot see into the dark.

"You are a legend," he said to me, gesturing abruptly with outstretched fingers. "Forgive my intrusion, but I was interested in finding you."

Clearly, he believed I would be delighted and grateful to have his company. It would not have surprised me to learn he had made wagers of his own concerning conquest and ravishment. "How brave you are to dodge my father's ships," I said.

He grinned, looking up at me with lowered head, expecting

me to see the face of a boy interested in wholesome games. What I saw instead – the truth of the matter – was the face of a dog; it was not so very far below the surface. "It was not difficult," he said. "I go where I please."

I sat down upon the stone shelf below him, and composed my body into a demure maidenly posture. Sometimes, I convince even myself I am what I pretend to be. "So, having found me, what do you want of me?" I asked him dulcetly, gazing at the floor.

"I would like to talk to you," he said, magnanimously.

"Then please do."

I watched him out of the corner of my eye as he rubbed his upper lip with a finger and picked up some parchment leaves he had beside him on the wall. "I will not waste time with foolish pleasantries," he said, "because I respect your station. I am interested in knowing the details of how you killed your husband." He had a charcoal stick poised above an empty page.

"Quite simply," I told him, staring him in the eye. "I fed him certain evils."

"How?" he asked, eagerly.

I curled my arms around my knees. "It is hardly an interesting story! My father had made me marry the man, after which I suffered his malodorous abuses for a week. Very soon, I became tired of his behaviour and, one evening, administered a bane mixed with his wine."

"Because he abused you?" Aertes' eyes had assumed a hero's glint.

I shrugged. "Yes, but I didn't like him anyway, and neither am I any man's property to barter. It was a lesson to my father. He will not sell me again."

"Yet you are here alone, imprisoned on this island."

"Unmarried," I reminded him.

Aertes made a flourish on his page with the charcoal. Black splinters flew everywhere. "Among the greater islands it's rumoured that you are an enchantress. It is said that you can turn men into beasts, and in fact took pleasure in doing so regularly about your father's court. Some say this was why your father was anxious to secure you in marriage to a man of strength. Is that true?"

I wriggled my shoulders. I could have told him then that all men are essentially beasts – some of them more personable than others – and that a clever female can easily draw out the feral element for display. There is no magic involved. However, I never divulge my knowledge to others and merely said, "If I was an enchantress, I would hardly be stuck here, would I?"

He smiled at me. "There are other legends," he said, "which present you in a less than kindly light."

"All princesses are the victims of other people's legends," I replied. "It is an inevitable consequence of being royal."

He nodded, grinning. "Of course, but if I may quote just one. It concerns how a certain young princess was approached by a woman of her father's court in order to dispense a gratuity upon this woman's sons. Apparently, the sons had recently performed some service for the King. The woman asked the princess to bestow upon her sons the greatest gift a man could have. It is said the princess agreed to do as much, and subsequently had the youths put to death in their sleep."

"It is a legend," I said, "perhaps a fable, the moral being that it is advisable to be precise when asking boons of those in power. I feel this is a lesson all should learn. The gods take the easiest path in granting wishes and it is the duty of their earthbound representatives to educate the people in this matter."

"A harsh judgment."

"Not at all."

"Then I am relieved you are not in the position to pass judgement on me!" He laughed loudly.

Fool.

Adopting the role of The Maiden was ineffective with Aertes. I felt as if a veil of ice was between us; either that, or he was made of ice himself. I extended all my subtle charms, gentle persuasions, movements of the body and the eyes, all designed to inflame his lust, but he did not respond. Obviously, I had chosen the wrong mask to wear that night. But there would be other nights. Sad that Baucis might have already won her wager though.

The following day, I worked upon another of my personae: the

162

Victim of Cruel Fate. This, a lady of more mature mien, was someone who had suffered upon life's path, yet whose bitterness was tinged by wry humour. The scenario in which this lady felt most comfortable was the long and shady hall that overlooked the hill behind the palace; a room I hardly used. Here, I had Baucis set out the supper; the fruits of the vine were frosted with sugar and all the tableware was white. Everything echoed around us.

I presented her to the cool Aertes at sundown. Again, I commanded the poet's presence alone and made sure that his company were fed in the kitchens. Having taken good care to make sure that Aertes would already be present in the shadowed, white hall, so that my entrance would take best effect upon his senses, I emerged between the columns, amid a cloud of incense more subtle and flowery than the previous night's dousing. I had dressed in black, and coiled my hair atop my head, allowing it to fall from this confinement in inky waves over my shoulders. The poet was again scribbling with a splintered stick of charcoal on one of his parchment leaves.

"This room: amazing!" he said, without looking up. "So full of atmosphere!" He paused then, and grinned at me. "Perhaps a hundred souls have met their unhappy end here, at your hands."

I was affronted because he clearly did not believe this was possible. "It is a joy to me you are finding much to stimulate your imagination in my home." I hoped to sound cold.

"I walked to the top of the island today," he said. "Tomorrow, I may walk with my company to the farthest shore. It shouldn't take more than a couple of days, should it?"

"How can I say?" I answered waspishly. "Generally, when wishing to make that particular trip, I anoint myself with the blood of virgin boys and fly there!"

He laughed, and I realised, with chagrin, that I had been careless enough to let my mask slip a little.

"I have already composed a few verses," he said.

"Oh, and are they about me?"

He grimaced. "Well, not exactly. I have been travelling

around collecting the stories of many infamous females. You are the last, but I already have a lot of material. I'm thinking of turning you all into a kind of composite; a goddess, I suppose, but a dark one."

"A goddess to whose powers you appear to be immune," I observed, smiling and helping myself to a frosted grape. Soon, Baucis would bring in the roast birds.

Aertes shrugged. "Perhaps I am too interested in the phenomenon to fall under its spell."

"What phenomenon?" I disliked the implication of being part of something common, or widespread.

"Well, it seems to me that women such as yourself are merely icons of men's fear of femalekind. In a way, you are created by the men that fear you: idols of perverse desire; malignant, destructive, frigid, yet ultimately fascinating."

"You flatter me!" I said.

Aertes raised his hands in apology. "Forgive me, I did not mean to imply that I believe you to possess these attributes, but hearsay certainly suggests they are among your characteristics. Having started out with the intention of risking death to interview women such as yourself in the hope of discovering witches and monsters, I found an entirely different phenomenon."

"Oh? How different?" I had taken another grape and found, to my consternation, that it was sour.

"I wonder why you, and other women, have been deified in this dark way," Aertes said.

"Perhaps because we are the witches and monsters we're supposed to be!"

Aertes shook his head. "Sadly, I disagree. For example, I came here looking for an evil enchantress and what I find appears to be only an isolated and perhaps disillusioned woman, someone whose sole crime could be said to have appreciated freedom in a world where the freedom of daughters was denied. You are not a compassionate creature, exactly, and I suspect never have been, but as I said, it is men – your father's chroniclers and lyricists perhaps – who have created your legend."

"Your theory is interesting," I said. "Personally, I believe that

I was not created by men's fascinated fear, but by their insensitive and brutish self-interest."

"You are bitter." He smiled at me sheepishly. Well, bitterness was certainly what I had intended to portray that night. Perhaps my mask hadn't slipped as much as I'd thought.

I shrugged. "Some wounds take their time to heal."

He nodded thoughtfully. At that moment, Baucis scurried in with a retinue of hags to serve us our repast. Despite appearances, her coven are accomplished cooks. Denying me stimulation of more intriguing kinds, my father saw to it that my palate, at least, was satisfied.

"So, tell me," I said as I neatly removed the legs and wings of my small, roasted bird, "what of these other fascinating goddesses you have investigated?"

He laughed in a vaguely apologetic manner. "You want stories? Well, I have plenty!" He rested his elbows on the table, one hand waving the leg of a bird like a baton to emphasise his speech. "Have you heard of the Siren Sisters of Anthemusa?"

I shook my head.

"These ladies are priestesses of the river god Achelus, who are reputedly monsters; half woman and half bird. Their temple stands at the place where the river exudes its waters into the sea. Their vows to the god insist on chastity and it is said that, embittered by this restriction, they vent their frustrated wrath upon the male species by crouching on the rocks outside their temple at sunfall. Here, they play upon lyres and double flutes, singing songs of lust and desire; their voices are reputed to be most enchanting. Men on passing ships overhear the songs and, espying the limpid maidens draped over the rocks, believe them to be hierodules offering their services to the worshippers of Aphrodite. Naturally, the men hurry towards land in order to take advantage of the situation and inflict their advances upon the priestesses. Whereupon, male priests, espying what they believe to be severe violation of the sacred virgins, rush out of the temple and slay the importunate wooers immediately. The Siren sisters continue to sing while this slaughter is under way, and some say there is a note of triumph in their warblings."

"A pretty story," I said, thinking I could do with such company myself to draw some entertainment to my rock. "And you have met these bloody ladies?"

Aertes grinned. "Yes. They were, as priestesses should be, retiring and modest creatures."

"And which half of them was avian?" I inquired.

He shook his head. "Neither. They wore sumptuous cloaks made entirely of the feathers of swans which, when they made their evening devotions, they raised about them with their arms. The cloaks did resemble wings, I suppose, but the ladies' limbs were entirely human and not one of them had a tail!"

"How grossly disappointing!" I said. "So none of it was true?"

Aertes shrugged. "Well, one of the priestesses did tell me that another of her sisterhood had indeed once sat upon the rocks beyond the temple and sung pretty songs into the sea breeze. A stray fisherman had been attracted by the lovely voice and had come to investigate." He sighed. "Human nature being what it is, the two unfortunates fell in love. When their alliance became news to the priests – which was inevitable, given that the girl's sisters must have envied her relationship – they killed the fisherman. And that gave rise to the legend."

I pulled a sad face. "Is that all? How lamentable!"

Aertes gestured with open hands. "You see? But perhaps you have more in common with the lady Atalanta, daughter of the King of Arcadia. Her father apparently never forgave the fact that she was born female, and sent his hunters to expose the babe on Mount Parthenius. Luckily, one of the men's wives had recently lost a child and was fretful and milk-bound because of it. He took the girl home and the couple raised her as theirs. As a young woman, Atalanta sorely resented the treatment meted out to her by her parent and took solace in hiding among the rocks and trees of the mountain so that she could fire arrows at passing courtiers. Legend has it that she was an accomplished murderer of men. Despite these unfriendly tendencies, her father eventually recognised her as his heir and wanted to marry her off. It is said Atalanta would only submit to marrying the man who could beat her in a race and, being a fleet athlete, was never beaten. Apparently, all the failed suitors were despatched by her in a grisly manner. At length, a man came to Arcadia equipped with golden apples, supposedly given to him by a goddess. By dropping these glittering fruits in Atalanta's path, he tempted her to pause in her running, thereby winning the race and claiming her hand in marriage!"

"What a shame!" I said, hoping she went on to murder the cunning beast.

Aertes shrugged. "Recently, I went to Arcadia and met the lady. She now rules there, a stately matron, with her husband. I asked her about the murders – especially those of prospective suitors – at which she laughed. She admitted having once caused a superficial cut on the head of one of her father's courtiers, however. As to her husband's deception, she confessed that she found him attractive from the start and merely used the apples as an excuse to lose the race. I found her a very kind and sweet-natured creature. She reminisces wistfully of being rather boyish in her youth..."

He leaned back in his chair, blinking languidly into the soft lamplight. "I have a host of stories such as these, and have found that every one of them has a fairly mundane explanation. It seems that an attractive woman of noble birth only has to have a small tantrum, or a fit of pique, to be elevated to the status of goddess. I suppose fabulists need these legends, and people find their tales more interesting if they are based on fact, but in reality, there is never much truth in them."

I grimaced. "So now you hope to deflate my legend, do you? It might be difficult. I did kill a man."

Aertes raised a finger and stared at me smugly. "Yet you yourself denied ever having turned men into beasts! That's one rumour cankered already!"

Anger was building up within me. Not just for myself, but for all these other women whom Aertes was determined to reveal as ordinary and dull, destroying their magic, which was theirs by right. How dare he! Resolve settled within me; I made a vow to veiled Hecate that this insulting little scrap of humanity would not leave my island in the same frame of mind as he approached it! Let him take on the might of female mystery. He thought to find a whinnying criminal, racked by shame and misery. What he had found was the very thing he thought could not exist. Only he did not know it yet.

The following day, Aertes set off, as he had promised, to explore the island. I paced up and down my chambers, trying to think of a way to penetrate his armour of protection, his scornful disbelief. All my attempts to attract him seemed to have no effect, and I knew, having heard his disrespectful "stories", that any mask I fashioned to wear in his presence, no matter how mysterious and alluring, would fail to impress him in the manner I desired. His smug confidence infuriated me immensely. Before he left, I inspected his retinue from behind my chamber drapes. What I saw resembled nothing more than a tumble of young pups; boys of impoverished noble families, no doubt, that could not afford to send their sons on expeditions with a more prestigious figure. It seemed incontrovertible to me that, having this giggling troupe of Ganymedes about him, he was impervious to feminine wiles. Perhaps a fatal dish of local banes served to his puppies might discommode him in a satisfying manner, but that plan was distressingly crude and ultimately did not directly affect the man himself.

Depressed by a heavy, black humour, I whistled to Ishti and set off for my favourite haunt among the sea rocks. It is a place where I always formulate my most effective schemes.

As usual, Mad Helen was sitting on the rocks, humming to herself and stirring a pool full of weed with her toes. "Good day, my lady," she said, smiling at me widely, with genuine welcome. A little warmth came into my frozen heart at the sight of it. I sighed and sat down beside her.

"Not a good day, Helen, my dear," I said.

The girl frowned. "Oh, my lady, what ails you?"

"The ship that sailed into our landing bay two days ago..."

"The *Persephone!*" Helen interrupted. "Yes, the beautiful man who owns her came to the village yesterday. He told us funny stories and sang a few songs. What a lovely voice he has! And what a gorgeous face! He sang of distant lands, where ladies clad in the feathers of swans..."

"Vile beast!" I cried, interrupting her recitation of Aertes' impertinent story, which I simply could not endure to hear again.

At my outburst, Helen's smiled hovered uncertainly around her lips. I realised she must be quite taken with Aertes. I laid a gentle hand upon her arm. "You do trust me, my dear, don't you?" I asked.

She nodded. "Without question, my lady."

I closed my eyes and sighed. "I am relieved to hear that. Listen to me: the poet Aertes is a cruel and dangerous man. Do not be deceived by his pretty little tales and gauche cavortings."

"Dangerous in what way, my lady?" Her eyes were round.

I leaned close to her ear. "He ruins women!" I hissed. "He has come here to destroy me!"

"No!" Helen gasped. "How awful! What will you do?"

I shrugged. "As yet, the appropriate stratagem eludes me..."

"Could you not attract the attention of one of your father's sea patrols?" she asked. "And let them deal with the scoundrel in the proper manner?"

I shook my head. "You do not understand, my dear. The destruction he wreaks is that of severing a lady's cord with her goddess, leaving her alone and soulless in the world. And I suspect there are few men of my acquaintance who would willingly interfere with such a plan. A woman without her goddess is a tractable creature, easily controlled. This is a woman's matter, and only women may take action against him."

Helen's eyes had now become quite dark with passion. I saw an underground light in their velvet depths which reminded me of a spear of starlight falling through a cavern roof into a still pool. Goddess light. She was thinking deeply, I could tell, and for that reason, I kept my silence to facilitate her musings.

"Last evening, before he returned to your palace for supper, he performed for the entire village," she said. I nodded encouragingly, aware that some deep intuition was struggling up through Helen's mind into the light. She looked at me with earnest eyes. "He spoke with such ardour! He strode about in the dust, throwing out his arms, grimacing, mimicking a weeping woman, talking in a voice like a child. These were all characters in his epic. Had I given that performance, it would have been absurd, and made people laugh. Aertes has a gift. He can make you believe you really are listening to a woman, or a child. And the truth is, it really is vital to him that his audience become enthralled by his performance. When he wants to make them laugh, he can, but laughter intruding into one of his tragedies would be, for him..." – she smiled – "... a tragedy!"

I squeezed her arm. "I feel that your instincts have just spoken to me, and that they carry a message from my goddess, Shadowy Hecate!"

She screwed up her nose. "It was just an impression of mine. Perhaps of use, perhaps not."

I mulled over her words in the privacy of my chambers. My intuition told me that within them lay the seed of a promising plan. Aertes was due back at the palace in a couple of days. I called my steward to me – a withered, half-crippled veteran of my father's army – and instructed him to deck the palace with garlands, to sweep out the enormous yard behind the building, where empty stables gaped and chickens ran about without restraint. "Scatter some sweet straw, for which I give you leave to barter with the local herders," I said. "String lanterns round the walls, and transform this place into an area fit for theatrical displays."

The steward bowed. "Certainly, my lady. Might I ask whether you intend to entertain here at the palace?"

"Indeed, Loxos! We have a poet among us, whose performances, I understand, are superb. My staff, and the gentle people of the village, lead a life bereft of whimsical distractions. I have a mind to host a celebration for their benefit. Have your menials convey my tidings to all upon the island. Upon his return, I shall implore the gallant Aertes to indulge my whim. I will suggest that three nights hence, he should perform his most rigorous tragedy, which perhaps he might be civil enough to follow with a few conceits of a lighter nature." Warming to the idea, I arose from my couch, and paraded around in front of the stunned Loxos, throwing out my arms, my robe aswirl. "We shall have music and dancing! Wine shall be drunk in quantity beneath Selene's light! Have the shrine of Dionysus cleared of

170

rubbish, light the votive lamps therein, and adorn the god's image in garlands of the vine!"

Loxos appeared to be quite overwhelmed by my enthusiasm. A hectic flush bloomed along his ancient, raddled cheeks, and he bobbed out of the room in an unprecedented lively manner. I was unsure how the spirit of the god Dionysus might react to my reanimating his rather neglected icon. His little shrine had once been regularly frequented by the family who used to live upon the island but now, it was no longer visited, never filled with the songs of adoration and sacrificial offerings so essential to divine well-being. At home, I had once been an avid devotee but, devoid of Dionysian delights as my existence now was, I had little occasion and even less desire to confront this particular god. Contemplation of his attributes would only serve to remind me of the paucity of my social activities. Hence, shunned in favour of the charcoaled walls of Hecate's fane, the shrine had been untended and left open to the elements. The nose of the statue inside had been broken off by a flying tree-branch during a winter storm, and its fingers were badly crumbled, but I hoped the god would forgive me this delinquency. An attempt to invoke his ecstatic influence could only prove beneficial to the coming event.

Aertes returned in the afternoon, his advent heralded by a great deal of noise emitted by his bouncing followers. Spring seemed to have fallen in a soft, sweet haze over the palace while he'd been away. Already the air was scented with blossom and the heady fragrance of Dionysus' incense – crushed ivy, pine resin and fennel seeds – floated through the chambers of my abode in a silvery mist. My servants had begun unaccountably to sing during their daily labours, and the ancients with which my father had equipped me had adopted an almost jaunty gait. Baucis' crones were already engaged in preparing a splendid feast for the coming celebration and the odours of their efforts mingled pleasingly with the offertory fumes.

Aertes found me on the sea terrace, where I sat with a loom, engaged in what he would see to be a proper womanly pursuit. The loom had been left behind by one of the palace's previous occupants. Scant hours before, I had had Baucis lug it out of one of the attics. A quick dusting down and a brief rub with beeswax had restored its wooden frame, and Baucis had appropriated some yarns for me to tangle on it. Aertes came marching towards me, his hair tied back, his head crowned with a garland of twisted ivy leaves – a sad omen, perhaps – which his puppies had obviously woven for him.

"The palace is decked as if for a wedding!" he exclaimed. "To what happy occasion have I returned?"

I smiled at him graciously. "That, my Lord Aertes, rests entirely with you. I have heard talk of your bewitching performances in the village and wondered whether you would indulge us with a major recital here at the palace."

He appeared rather surprised. "I cannot say this was expected, my lady," he said.

"I hope that doesn't mean you cannot comply." I stood up and approached him, even dared to place light fingers on his arm. "It is not for myself but for my people here on the island," I said in a confidential tone. "I have a retinue of thirty staff, all of whom are, through no fault of their own, in exile as I am. All I wish is to provide for them an evening's entertainment. We shall invite the local people, and have a lively celebration of your visit."

Aertes sighed. "Well, you certainly exhibit the caprices of the female spirit, Lady Circe. Before I left the palace, I could have sworn that you'd strike me dead before you'd show interest in my work. I seem to recall that you had little sympathy with my themes."

I raised my arms, turned away from him, shrugged, looked over my shoulder. "I was impressed by what I heard of your performances in the village, as I said." Crossing to the pale stone wall, I sat down, supporting myself on straight arms in a girlish manner. "Aertes, at home, I drowned in entertainment, music, dance and song. Here... I am shrivelling up into a sour and joyless hag. Indulge me; bring a little life to these empty, sorrowing walls."

Aertes gave me a sidelong glance, and my breath was stilled in my chest. Would he give in to my demand? I hoped his egotistic desire to posture and display himself might silence his

172

perplexity at my apparent change of heart. He looked around himself, at the ropes of spring flowers draping the terrace walls, the dishes of crushed herbs smouldering beside the door. "Well, you seem confident of my cooperation, having already done all this work; I can hardly refuse, can I?"

I exhaled gratefully. "Thank you. I've arranged everything for tomorrow night. Will that provide adequate time for preparation?"

"I know all my work intimately; there is no need for rehearsal," he said.

"Excellent!" I said, standing up. "Would you take a little wine, Lord Aertes?"

He nodded and sat down upon the wall, while I busied myself filling a goblet from the flagon Baucis had left me.

"One thing has always puzzled me," I said, as I handed him the wine. "Would you appease my curiosity and enlighten me?"

He took a mouthful of the drink. "By all means."

I sat down beside him. "Well, having seen many poets, actors and musicians perform, I have often wondered what it must be like standing up there before so many people."

"What do you mean, Lady Circe? It is our way of life, our daily office."

"I mean, how does it really feel to have all those eyes centred upon you, hanging onto your every word, your every gesture? What do you think about? As you utter those words you know so intimately, what passes through your mind? Do you recall some menial uncompleted task half forgotten through the day? Do you think about how your feet are aching? Do you wonder whether anyone has fed your animals, or paid court to your charming followers? Please tell me, I am fascinated to know."

A strange thing happened to Aertes' face. As I spoke, I watched it darken, until he was scowling openly. He put down the goblet quickly. "Lady Circe, I don't think you realise that, when I perform, I am held in the spirit of my art. I transcend the mundane world, swept aloft into the realms where the gods walk. My mind soars in beatific bliss, as the words fall like gems from my lips! There is no consideration of inconsequential, petty issues!"

"Forgive me; I only wondered," I said, pleased at his irritation.

"Then I hope I have dispelled your silly ideas! When I perform here for your people, take a look at their faces! Pay attention to their rapt contemplation of my words! Will they be thinking of trivial things, of animals and unwashed dishes and aching feet? No, I think not! They will be transported upon the wings of my oratory."

"It sounds enchanting," I said. "Indeed, from this moment forth, I shall regard each performer I meet with a new and deferential eye. I had no idea such lofty elements were involved in the act of reciting poetry, or lines of plays. Indeed, I feel inordinately educated! Thank you, Lord Aertes."

He flexed his shoulders, attempting to calm himself down. I really had not expected so fiery a response. How gratifying. "One thing I shall pray for," I said, steepling my fingers against my lips, and gazing at him with apparent reverence.

"And what is that?" he asked.

"That you do not recall this conversation in the midst of your performance."

He smiled a little, tightly. "That is hardly likely."

"Good. I would hate it if, from the rapturous depths of your transportation, you were abruptly brought down from the realms of the gods. It might mar the performance."

"Lady Circe," he said, "I am a seasoned professional. There is no danger of my being distracted during a performance."

Before the recital, I made my way to Hecate's fane, my place of private devotion. It is a short walk's distance from the palace, nestling in a grove of cypress trees, one of Her sacred plants. It was not Her time, because the moon was waxing full, but I still sought to invoke Her distant presence, burning a dish of sandalwood chips and dried mint, lubricated by the resin of the cypress. Prostrating myself before Her cruel countenance, I called Her presence into me. "Dark Lady, occupy my flesh this night," I implored. "Lend to me Your shady powers!"

The fane was silent, but for the spitting of the cypress resin as it burned. It seemed that a black wing was cast over every-

174

thing, eclipsing all but the eager hearts of the flames of the charcoal-powdered candles burning beside the statue. I felt Her there, hanging in the shadows, and among the thick spiders' webs of the blackened rafters above. Perhaps She was affronted I had made devotions to fair Dionysus these past few days, but I hoped She understood my intention, which was ultimately of Her design. "The man seeks to disempower Your handmaidens," I whispered. "I would avenge this abuse!"

At these words, I felt Her approach me. If I opened my eyes, I would have been able to see Her dark hand extended to touch me. A black flame ignited in my heart, and it seemed, behind my closed eyelids, as if the whole fane was suddenly alight with deep red flames. The candles roared and spat above me, the incense filled my body with a potent, earthy scent. For a few moments, I too was transported to the realm of gods but my performance was yet to come.

The winding path up from the village was filled with people making their way to my palace. Torches flickered and sizzled through the night, voices were raised in cheery anticipation of the celebration ahead. Muffled and disguised by a heavy black cloak, I entered the building through a rear entrance as if I were a servant, and hurried to the rooms on an upper storey that overlooked the bedecked yard. Already it was teeming with noisy peasants; herders who had been drawn down from the higher slopes by the promise of free wine, villagers in their colourful best clothes, vintners from further round the coast. It seemed that Loxos had spread the word efficiently and nearly every occupant of my little isle had converged on the palace that night. Lamb carcases were turning on spits over a fire near to the gates, beside trestles laden with Baucis' delicious fare. Crones in clean robes were stationed behind the tables, ready to serve the gathering with food. Huge pitchers of wine sweated in ranks along the wall, and through the open shutters I could see that my balcony was festooned with flowers, the couch upon it spread with fleeces for my comfort. In the centre of the yard, a raised platform had been constructed, from where Aertes would present his entertainment.

Loxos was already distributing cups of wine to the crowd, so that everybody would be in a relaxed and cheerful mood by the time the performance began. A few of Aertes' creatures were posturing beside the fire, although I knew the majority of them were presently engaged in preparing their lord's costume for the evening, fawning over him in that singularly tedious, grovelling manner employed solely by youthful males in the service of a man they admire. Soon, the gathering would expect me to present myself above them, but I wanted Aertes out before them first.

Loxos had been instructed to assume the role of Master of Ceremonies and, after a suitable time, when it seemed that everyone who had decided to attend had arrived, he hopped up on to the raised platform in the centre of the yard. Everyone turned towards him expectantly, and the tiresome old goat spent several minutes exchanging jocular repartee with them, before he sensed my critical scrutiny and sobered himself up enough to make a dignified yet flowery introduction of Aertes. At that point, I flung off my cloak and made haste to the room which led to the balcony. I hid among the drapes before venturing outside and watched Aertes emerge from a doorway opposite.

He looked magnificent; his hair plaited with glossy ropes of ivy, his robe of snowy white, edged with a discreet yet stylish border design of heavy gold thread. One shoulder was bare and his skin glowed tawny in the torchlight, fitting his frame with svelte and supple tension. I half expected his retinue to come after him, licking the ground where his feet had trod. It gratified me to notice that he flicked a quick, nervous glance at the balcony and seemed a trifle surprised to find it empty. As he climbed on to the platform, the crowd – many of whom were already familiar with his work because of his recent local performances – all began to cheer and clap their hands together over their heads. Aertes puffed up with arrogant vanity like a sail full of wind and bowed to them, holding out his arms, his hair falling forward like ropes of dark gold. Someone besotted with the man might have regarded him as an incarnation of Apollo. I, thankfully free of such fancies, saw only the monstrous love which Aertes reserved for himself. He glowed with it, and the feeling

176

was merely intensified by the adoration of his audience.

Sensing the moment right, I glided through the drapes and stood against the balcony. Picking up a spray of blossom, I tossed it down to land at Aertes' feet, thankful that my propensity for injuring servants' brats with hurled stones while I was a child had bequeathed me such an accurate aim. Aertes, seemingly already engrossed in performance, picked up the blossom with a misty eye and held it to his nose, gazing at me in apparent veneration. The crowd all made nauseating cooing noises, so that I had to gesture abruptly for Aertes to begin his recital.

I have to admit that he was really rather accomplished. To prepare himself, he walked with bowed head up and down the platform, while a few of his followers strummed on lyres to invoke the correct atmosphere. One of the boys began to sing sweetly and the entire crowd was transported to some distant field, where asphodels bloomed beneath the moon, and shadowy, rustling trees moved restlessly at the corners of vision.

As the voice died down to a whisper and the lyres insinuated a plaintive threnody into the night air, Aertes began to speak. His voice rang out into the scented darkness, his body swayed like that of a rearing serpent. He leaned towards the crowd, arms extended, his fingers clawing their hearts to his. He spoke of love among the asphodels, the forbidden love of a young priestess for a wild hunter. His voice invoked the trembling nuances of timid obsession, the heavy scent of the flowers, the still, humid presence of the night. The words effortlessly conjured up those precious, sacred feelings of a young girl's first love, when all is a terrible yet fascinating secret. A woman could not have composed the piece with more accuracy. In my heart, a wistful poignancy reanimated forgotten feelings; the breathless expectancy of youth.

I closed my eyes and lay back among the fleeces, listening to this intoxicating syrup of words that Morpheus himself could not have drooled more convincingly. The relationship he described was doomed, of course, and as Aertes' voice rolled ever more loudly over the crowd, he invoked the agony of grief, anxiety and guilt. I felt the angry, confused frustration of the

177

nubile priestess, as her older guardians discovered the illicit affair. I clenched my fists and raged with her as she argued with their passionless resolve. I wept with her as the order was given for soldiers to be sent out to hunt down the importunate hunter and slay him.

I could have lived it all, lying there among my fleeces. I could have let Aertes finish his performance and leapt to my feet as the crowd applauded. I could have showered him with blossoms, my adulation, my respect. But Dark Hecate was in my soul. As I gasped upon my couch, she prodded me from within with a stiff and icy finger. "What is this girlish fluttering of the heart?" she demanded. "Wake up, Circe, and go about your business, or I'll see to it you're punished sorely! Let another man into your soul and you risk the true destruction. Wake up! Get on with it!"

I felt as if someone had doused me with a pitcherful of cold water. I emerged, almost spluttering, from my delirium. Below, Aertes continued to exhort the crowd, and they, hypnotised by his story, stood around with mouths agape. The performance was reaching its climax, redolent with agonising grief, lost love, blood and death. All was silent save for Aertes' hypnotic voice, which was descending in timbre, unravelling the black threads of his tale. And I, reclining, extended my long legs to rest my feet upon the balcony. With one sandalled foot, I furiously scratched at the other, until the thin, soft leather gave way. The sandal fell over the edge of the balcony and, because of the hush, made quite a satisfying slap as it hit the ground. Aertes' eyes jerked briefly upwards and, using the moment wisely, for I knew it would be brief, I leaned forward and rubbed my feet as if they pained me. Aertes caught my eye. I smiled, and steepled my fingers beneath my lips.

"I hope you do not recall this conversation..." He could not help it. My gesture reminded him of what I'd said, and his voice faltered. I rested my elbows on the balcony, and directed the full force of Hecate's malignancy in his direction.

Do not continue, I urged him; lose the thread; forget the words.

The expression he sent back to me was one of anguish, even of disappointment and regret. I knew that a host of images were tumbling through his mind; images of aching feet, unwashed dishes, animals and faithless boys. His mouth worked on silence. He could not speak. The crowd began to murmur.

Fortunately for Aertes, one of his catamites had the wit to strike up a doleful song, and after a few moments, the poet recomposed himself and ended the recitation. But the magic had bled from it, and the applause, though loud, lacked the real emotion I knew Aertes expected as his fee. I had seen enough. Standing up, I arranged my robes, and went back into the palace. If Aertes glanced at the balcony again, he would find it empty.

At midnight, he came to my chamber. I was waiting for him. The incense was lit, the room full of the scent of the cypress. He flung open the door and stood facing me at the threshold. "I saw you," he said, in a low, hoarse voice, pointing at me like some vengeful spirit. "I saw you crouched there on your balcony like a serpent drenched in blood!"

I laughed in a low, musical tone. "Blood? I think not. Tears, maybe."

Aertes made an ugly snorting sound and gestured stiffly with his hands. "I know your kind! She-dogs! The first requisite of your nightborn breed is a complete lack of any natural feeling! You are scarcely human! Like a ghoul feasting on the flesh of the dead, you suck the very substance from men's souls, seeking to bloat yourself with those finer attributes which you lack. You mock life! I despise you!"

"An impassioned speech, Lord Aertes, perhaps more so than the conclusion of your recital tonight!"

He pressed his fingers against his brow. "I curse my foolishness! To think I felt sympathy for your circumstances!" He lowered his hands and stared at me steadily. His eyes were almost golden in the dim light. "I realise that I have been an unwitting component in some malignant scheme of yours," he said. "I hope it gave you pleasure, Lady Circe."

"It did," I said, quite simply. I had ruined him, taken from him the soul of his art. I knew he would never perform again without fear. And yet, his arrogance demanded he should seek to retain some dignity.

179

"I pity you," he said pompously. "You lead a desolate life. You have suffered at the hands of men, perhaps, and I had hoped we could be friends. When I saw you step out from your balcony curtains tonight, I had resolved to take you away from this island, take you with me when I leave."

"Pah!" I spat. "You dare to imagine I would fall in with such a plan? I do not need rescuing by a poet, and certainly not by you! What conceit!"

Aertes continued to stare and I was uncomfortably reminded of black Ishti's eyes as he meditated upon the secret arcana all cats are privy to. Then, he shook his head. "I was wrong about you. I believed you to be an intelligent yet restricted soul, someone whose sourness was caused by lonely pain. I know now that this is not so. As you sought to trivialise my performance tonight, I realised that your whole existence consists of petty spite and paltry malevolence. You are like an evil little girl, pulling the tails of her pets to hear them yelp with pain, to see how they wriggle. How ignorant you are! Don't you realise that I am beyond the reach of your sick iniquities?"

"So far beyond them that you felt moved to come and scream upon my threshold!" I smiled calmly, although my heart had begun to race unaccountably. There was a disturbing tremble in my limbs. I needed a weapon, oh how sorely I needed a weapon, and yet my sharpest darts, my words, all seemed to have fallen from my tongue, leaving me an empty quiver filled only with the vanished prospect of injury.

Aertes drew in his breath, folding his arms. His skin had the soft velvet bloom of fur. I sniffed and turned away. "Aertes, you are misguided. Stripping a woman of her magic, whatever her character, is no charitable or friendly act."

There was a brief silence, then his voice came, merely a whisper. "I cannot forgive you," he said. "I live for my art. It is my soul."

"Then the feeling is mutual. Yours is not the only art! You are a smug braggart!" Did he also think he was the only one capable of hurling insult?

Sadly, just as I seemed to be given a new quiver full of darts, he deprived me of continuing the assault. "We will be leaving with the tide," he said. "I thank you, my lady. You have given me much material for the major epic I am composing, although the manner in which I acquired it brings me sorrow."

"Good speed, then. May your journey be... safe," I said, refusing to look at him, although I felt him hovering at the door. He did not want to leave, I am sure. "Please, do not linger, Aertes. After all, you must be wanted elsewhere..."

"Of that, you can be sure!" he said. "I realise that I was wrong to dismiss the gorgons of legend as being entirely fictional, Lady Circe. You have taught me that much, because they live, at least, in you. Long may your royal father keep you chained to this rock. You deserve no other accommodation!"

With that, the door slammed. He left me.

And now I stand beside the waves, Helen pressed against me, and together we throw the vial of blood into the water. Aertes sailed away last night, but even so, I know his spirit, his grovelling dog-like spirit, haunts the curtains of my chambers. He will linger there for eternity, whining and snuffling. His vain words did not fool me; I know he lied. He'll never perform again. He won't! He can't! My magic is too potent. He is a dog now, craven and whipped into submission. Didn't he say himself I turned men into beasts? Let him think that distance weakens my influence if he likes. Time will prove that I'm right.

One evening, in the exotic city of a distant land, beneath the light of a softer moon, among the moth-dusted blooms of summer-flowering trees, he will attempt to perform for an audience again. I can see him now: his proud beauty, his gleaming skin, his hair...but at the climax of his recital, my face will come to him, and his pretty words will blow right away from his mouth like scented petals on the wind. Like a dog, he will court the praise he no longer deserves; tail wagging sheepishly, dog-eyes blinking in a humiliating search for love and adoration. My face will come before him. He will remember.

Men are all fools. I have proved them so. I have power, here on my island.

SALOMÉ
by
Brian Stableford

When Salomé the enchantress danced, she was beloved by all those who watched; she made them drunken captives of her art. Her silken costumes were sewn with crystal shards, which glittered in the light of ruddy lanterns like the scales of many-coloured serpents, and the gliding movements of her body were like the swaying of an asp in thrall. When she leapt up high with her white arms thrown wide, she was like a creature in flight: a lamia with frail wings, or a delicate dragon's child.

When Salomé the enchantress danced, she stirred the fires of Hell in the hearts of those who watched; she made them willing slaves of her passion.

Salomé was never taught to dance; hers was a spontaneous art born of inspiration and nurtured by an altogether natural process of growth. She danced because dancing was the most precious aspect of her nature, and she began to express herself in the rhythms of dance as soon as she began to know who she was.

Her earliest dances were witnessed only by the female slaves into whose charge she had been delivered when her mother died in bearing her. She first danced for her father, who was Herod the Magician King, when she was seven years old. He immediately commanded that the tongues of her slaves should be cut out, so that they could not speak of it, and that their eyes should be scored with thorns, so that they would never again see anything clearly.

In the seven years which followed, only Herod and his brothers in blood were permitted to watch Salomé dance, and to watch the magic grow within her as her art grew to perfection. She obeyed her father's command to reserve her gifts for his own delight, and for the seduction of his noble friends.

Herod used the spell which Salomé's dancing cast to increase his power over his brothers in blood. He took advantage of the state of intoxication into which she delivered them to bind them to his will, and paid them for their servitude by granting them the privilege of watching Salomé dance. The greater privilege, of slaking the lusts which Salomé's dancing excited, Herod reserved to himself.

Herod believed that in taking carnal possession of Salomé's unripened body he was protecting himself from the kind of sottishness which she inspired in her other admirers, but he was wrong. Although his eyes had never been scored with thorns he saw unclearly, and although he was a Master of Magicians and not a slave, he was captive without knowing it to the magic of his daughter-wife.

When the mother of Salomé had died in bearing her, Herod had used his magic to procure the death of his brother Philip. He did this in order to make a widow of Philip's wife Herodias, so that she would become his property under the law of his people. Herodias was very beautiful then, and well pleased with what Herod had done in order to possess her, for she knew the worth of a Master of Magicians, and was ambitious to be his mistress in every possible way.

Inevitably, with the passing of time, Herod became bored with Herodias, and left her alone in her apartments for months on end. There she played perpetually with her magic mirrors and her cards of fortune, by which means she sought – hopelessly – to discover a way to rescue her ambitions. Herodias never saw Salomé dance, nor heard any trustworthy report of the artistry of her dancing, but she divined in the end that it was Herod's infatuation with Salomé which had obliterated any trace of affection for herself which had ever lodged in his heart.

For this reason, Herodias grew to hate Salomé with a very violent passion. She tried to hurt her niece with curses and maledictions, but her own magic was not powerful enough to prevail against Herod's protectiveness and the armour of Salomé's maturing art. She was therefore forced by circumstance to be patient, although she could barely contain her rage against the irresistible pressure of time which leached away her glamour.

Herodias was chafed and teased by her frustration for seven long years, but she never despaired. She knew that there would come a day when Salomé ceased to be a child and became a woman, and she knew that when the day came, Salomé would be ready to be made captive in her turn by the savage grip of infatuation.

As the fourteenth year of Salomé's life drew to its culmination, there appeared in the borderlands of King Herod's petty empire a man named John the Prophet, who preached to the common people whenever and wherever they could be induced to listen to him.

John the Prophet told his hearers that those whose mastery of men was achieved by command of magic, wealth and privilege were doomed to burn in Hell for all eternity, but that the common people might acquire a kingdom of their own beyond the grave, if only they were virtuous and humble and hopeful. This kingdom beyond the grave was named by John the Prophet *Heaven*; he told his hearers that there was no suffering there, and that no man had power over another, because all were equal in the eyes of God.

Herod was glad when news of John the Prophet's teachings reached his ears. He was a clever statesman, and knew that it was always to the advantage of rulers when prophets appeared to promise the common people fabulous reparation for their current misery. Such notions helped to make his subjects content with their subjection, by deferring the promised settlement of all their grievances to an imaginary life beyond death, and deflecting their ambitions away from rebellion and revolution.

Like all petty emperors, King Herod loved to see his subjects confirmed in a determination to be virtuous, humble, and hopeful.

Although Herod was very pleased to have John the Prophet wandering in his kingdom, he knew that he would eventually have to destroy the preacher. It was in his interest to make it seem that he feared such men, and that he did not want their message to be heard. For this reason, he followed the methods of all wise rulers, making it his habit to imprison, torture and ultimately martyr all the prophets who came to his attention.

This way of dealing with prophets invariably brought

rewards to all who used it. It lent careful emphasis to the sermons which they preached, and made their teachings all the more precious to those foolish and unlucky persons who had found hope in them.

In his dealings with John the Prophet, King Herod was as careful and methodical as he usually was. His first move was to have his quarry hunted for a while without actually being caught. He sent out instructions for the arrest of the prophet, but made sure that rumours flew ahead of his instructions, so that John would always be one step ahead of the officers who came to take him. Then, at his leisure, Herod closed in. He issued a public proclamation banning John the Prophet from entering the gates of his Capital City, thus making sure that the preacher would be all the more enthusiastic to carry his message within the walls. Finally, he had the man seized as publicly and as violently as possible, and brought before his fully-assembled court to be mocked, scorned and condemned.

When John the Prophet was brought to stand before him, Herod deemed it desirable that as many people as possible should be looking on, so as to create a proper sense of occasion. He had summoned all his brothers in blood, and he had invited Herodias to descend from her apartments in order to appear at his left hand. At his right hand he set his beautiful daughter Salomé.

When everything was ready, Herod asked John the Prophet to repeat all his heresies, in order that they might be debated by the wise men of the kingdom.

John the Prophet stood up bravely, in spite of the bruises which had been inflicted upon him at the time of his arrest, and stated the items of his faith. All magic, he said, was evil; those who owned and used it were impure and ungodly, and would be condemned to the flames of Hell for all eternity. All men who exercised power over others, whether by right of birth or wealth or strength of arms, would likewise be punished for the abuse of their power. Only the meek, the virtuous and the pure in heart would be rewarded after death; they would be taken into the kingdom of Heaven, where they would dwell eternally in peace and harmony, without want or pain.

Herod's brothers in blood then stood, one by one, to ridicule the preacher. With clever sophistry and cunning logic they demonstrated the fatuity of his claim that there would be a further life beyond death for anyone save those gifted in magic, whose souls were immunized against extinction. Then they charged him with sedition, saying that his ideas were an insult to the honour and station of King Herod. Then they proceeded, each in his turn, to offer suggestions as to the particular way in which the false prophet might best be put to death.

While all this was going on, John the Prophet stood as straight as he was able, apparently quite unafraid. He was a young man, not more than twenty years of age, and very handsome. He had fine dark eyes of an unusual clarity, and neatly-shaped eyebrows. He never looked at his would-be tormentors or answered their gibes; instead, he alternated his gaze between the two women seated on either side of the Magician King who sat in judgment upon him. He looked long and hard at Herodias, and he looked longer and harder at Salomé; to them and to them alone did he present the argument of his eyes.

Although it might not have been his intention, what John the Prophet's eyes said to Salomé was: *I am a better man than any you have ever seen before, and were you to dance with me, we might discover a sweeter rhythm than any you have ever felt before.*

And although it certainly was not his intention, what John the Prophet's eyes said to Herodias was: *Here is an opportunity to serve your own ends, by persuading Salomé to loathe her father-husband.*

When the great debate drew to its close, Herod promised to think upon the matters brought to his attention, and to deliver his verdict the next day. The purpose of this delay was to allow the rumour of what had occurred to spread to every nook and cranny of the city streets, and to take wing even beyond its walls. Thus, everyone who cared to do so might have the leisure to discuss the justice of the case and the deliciously particular cruelties of all the methods of execution which had been proposed.

During the night, however, Herodias tricked one of Salomé's

half-blind slave-girls into carrying a letter to her, representing it as a message from John the Prophet.

The substance of the message was this: *You are the most beautiful woman in the world. It is not permitted to me to love you, nor can I recant a single word of what I have preached. I am doomed to die for what I believe, but the hours of life which remain to me would be immeasurably enriched by one more sight of your wondrous face. My one regret is that I will never see you dance.*

Herodias was careful to express these sentiments as artlessly as she could, in the cause of authenticity. She trusted to the logic of the situation to ensure that Salomé, in spite of her own extraordinary artistry, would not see through the deception.

Salomé was not allowed to leave her chambers unsupervised, but it was an easy matter for one of her abilities to dupe her half-blind guardians and the soldiers who stood watch over the prison where John the Prophet was held. She entered his cell without difficulty, and woke him up.

"I can save you," she said to him. "Only do as I instruct, and you will win free of the castle, the city and the nation."

"The truth dare not flee from persecution," John the Prophet told her, "else men would know it for falsehood."

"Do you prefer to die?" she asked him.

"I do," he told her. "Only by dying for his beliefs can a man hope to persuade others that they are worth dying for."

"You can say that," Salomé marvelled, "even though you have looked upon my face, and found it the most beautiful in the world? Can you really refuse to love me, now that I am with you?"

"Certainly," said John the Prophet. "I am a virtuous man, and must remain so if I am to persuade others that the highest rewards of all are reserved for the virtuous."

"You will not think so highly of virtue," Salomé promised, lewdly, "when you have seen me dance."

There and then, she danced for him.

She danced upon the floor of his cell, despite that it was moist with stinking excrement. The cell was narrow, with walls of filthy stone, and it was illuminated only by the light of a single tallow candle, but Salomé did not need a huge space or a polished floor or a bright light in order to display her art. She was full to overflowing with enchantment, and magic radiated from her body as soon as she began to move.

She lost herself in her dance, and was carried away by the tide of its bewitchment; she was as much its captive as she intended him to be, and it held her in perfect thrall as its rhythms thundered in her eager blood.

When it was over, she said to John the Prophet: "Will you refuse to love me now?"

"I cannot refuse to love you," he admitted, not entirely unhappily. "But still I must die, for the sake of what I preach. Even though my soul has been sullied by affection for a witch, I must be a martyr to my cause. My flesh has betrayed my heart, but my lips cannot betray the truth."

During the hour that she danced for John the Prophet, Salomé had ceased to be a child, but she was no *wiser* now than she had been before. She did not know the real reason why Herod was determined to kill John the Prophet, and could not tell him that the acceptance of his "truth" by the common people was what Herod most devoutly desired.

Even if she had been able to tell him, it might not have changed his mind; he was, after his own silly fashion, an extra-ordinarily sincere and virtuous man.

"You are a fool," Salomé told him, "but that will not prevent my loving you, as you love me."

On the next day, with all his court assembled before a crowd equal to that of the previous day, Herod pronounced judgment upon John the Prophet. He found him guilty of sedition, and announced the following plan for his execution: first, his tongue was to be cut out and he was to be castrated with shears; then, he was to be trussed from shoulder to ankle and placed breast-deep in a great urn full of oil, which would be slowly heated to boiling point; then, his head was to be struck from his neck and placed on a spike atop the city gate, so that passers-by might judge from the expression on his face whether or not he had really gone to a more pleasant place.

"Better to be boiled alive," John the Prophet said, before they cut out his tongue, "than to burn in Hell for all eternity."

Salomé watched while her lover was ungently castrated, knowing that what he was sacrificing was nothing that he needed. She watched slaves wind the ropes tightly about his body, and lower him into the huge bronze urn whose broad belly was filled with cooking-oil. Only his beautiful head projected from the narrow neck. She listened to the macabre music of his attempted screams, which rose to an ecstatic pitch as the oil, warmed by a roaring fire set beneath the urn, came gradually to its boiling-point. She watched them detach his head from his body, carefully studying the unspeakably horrid expression which agony had graven upon his features. Then she rose from her place, and went down to take the head from the man who held it; he was too astonished to refuse to part with it.

Herod was also taken by surprise, but when he saw Salomé take the head of John the Prophet from the soldier he came swiftly to his feet and ordered her to return to her place.

She ignored him.

Instead of obeying, she began to dance.

Whenever Salomé the enchantress danced, she enraptured all those who watched; it made no difference that thousands watched her now instead of a few. She made them instantly drunk with the sight of her; each and every one – man or woman – was captive to her art.

Her courtly attire was modest enough, though sewn from silken and golden threads, but as she whirled and cavorted across the arena, passing the head of John the Prophet from one hand to the other and back again, she shed her cloak to reveal a filmy chemise decorated with a thousand crystal shards, which glittered in the light of the morning sun like the scales of many-coloured serpents.

Her flowing movements held the whole vast crowd in thrall. No one moved once the dance had begun; only the expressions on the watchers' faces changed.

In the beginning, Herod's eyes were wide with alarm and

wrath, and his mouth was wide open in protest; but as the dance continued the alarm and the wrath faded from his eyes and his lips came together in a curiously wistful smile.

In the beginning, Herodias bared her teeth as she permitted herself a mockingly triumphant laugh, and leaned forward in anticipation of satisfaction; but as the dance progressed her lips came together, pursed with anxiety, and she tried unsuccessfully to draw back.

In the beginning, the dead prophet's eyes bulged out of their sockets, bloated by the pain which he had suffered, and the bloodied stump of his tongue was visible inside his mouth; but as the dance went on the eyes softened into an expression of adoration and the mouth relaxed into a curiously ironic yet loving smile.

When she leapt high into the air with her slender arms thrown wide, Salomé was like a creature in flight: a lamia with frail wings, or some delicate dragon's child. As she tumbled and soared, she stirred the fires of Hell in the hearts of those who watched; she made them willing slaves of her unleashed passion.

At first, only poor dead John danced with her, but as the dance became wilder and more insistent she drew Herod from his throne and Herodias from her lesser seat, and they moved as though to join her in the paces of a tarantella, partners to one another as John the Prophet was partner to Salomé.

Herod and Herodias now opened their mouths again, as though to cry out the gladness of their ecstasy, but their tongues were unkindly ripped out of their mouths and hurled – writhing like earthworms cut by a spade – to the ground.

Then the King and his former mistress reached out to one another as though to embrace in the heat of passion – but their clothes caught fire, and the skin came away from their flesh as if it were no more than a kind of clothing itself, and the flesh melted from their bones.

Still they danced. Even when there was nothing left of either of them beneath the neck but a wrack of bone and sinew they danced on, avid with excitement, fervent with the furious ecstasy of Salomé's magic.

Meanwhile, Salomé drew the head of John the Prophet tenderly to her breast and cradled it there, protectively. She continued to dance, but her arms were no longer flung wide and she slowed in her paces for a little while.

The severed head seemed to melt into her breast and become part of her; it was lost amid the shimmer of tiny sequins. Then the dance grew wild again, and wilder and wilder....

In the end, all three of the dancers came together, in a riotous tangle of bleached bones and many-coloured scales, and vanished into a whirlwind from beyond the world, which carried them away.

All the people who had watched the dance were freed from the spell which had been put upon them.

The commoners went swiftly away, to spread the news of the miracle which they had witnessed. They were convinced that Herod, Herodias and Salomé had all been carried away to Hell, but that John the Prophet was in Heaven.

Herod's brothers in blood fell to fighting among themselves to determine who might take his place, and eventually settled the matter. The Magician King who came after the one who had been taken was every bit as cunning and cruel as his predecessor had been, and there was no perceptible change in the condition of the kingdom.

In time, the new king's wife bore him a daughter, whom he loved very dearly. The careful disposal of her favours helped him to extend his power over his brothers in blood.

In time, another prophet came to the kingdom, to preach to any who would condescend to hear him. This prophet, inspired by the glorious example of his predecessor, told his hearers to be humble and virtuous, to love one another, and to wait with patience for their reward in the Kingdom of Heaven.

The new king was suitably grateful for this gift of circumstance. The new prophet was eventually crucified.

Meanwhile, in Hell, Salomé danced.

While the daughter of Herod danced in her peculiarly demonic fashion, before the courtly host of Hell, she delighted all those who watched her. She excited them almost beyond endurance with the magic of her art. Her silky skin was covered now with a million crystal shards, which glistened beneath the fiery sky like the scales of many-coloured serpents. Whenever she leapt up with her lovely arms thrown wide in rapture, she was like a creature in flight: a lamia with frail wings, or a delicate dragon's child.

When Salomé the enchantress danced in Hell, she stirred the fires which breathed life in the hearts of all those who watched; she made them willing slaves of her passion. But one and one alone was privileged to dance *with* her, and share the burning heat of her inmost soul, and that was John the Prophet.

Once, and once only, Salomé asked her lover whether he would rather have enjoyed the cool pastures of Heaven, from which he had been excluded by his love for her.

"Only the meek and virtuous and pure in heart," he told her then, "could ever believe that the flames of passion are naught but pain and punishment. Those who know the ecstasy of true enchantment could not possibly endure eternity, were they not perpetually bathed by such fire as ours."

SINGING UNDERWATER
by
Robert Irwin

Something new happened a few weeks ago (but so much has happened since that I can't remember exactly when). A few weeks ago the Palace Fool was brought to the edge of the water. Two of the Presidential Guards had him by the shoulders and they forced his head under the surface. I was curious, of course, so I did my fish-like wriggle and shimmied that way to look up at what was going on. The Guards were trying to drown him and he was holding his breath, so that the bulging of his cheeks was distending his clown's make-up. But then he saw me and his mouth opened in a great O of surprise. The water rushed into his lungs, the Guards let him slide into the pool and I took him into my arms, but by then, alas, there was no air in him.

I had seen the Fool many times before, entertaining at the President's parties, but, since he never swam, I was not expecting him to join me down here. He used to shadow the guests, mocking and mimicking them. I used to lie back and enjoy his antics and the rest of the goings-on at these parties, all of it spread out for me in a wavering trellis above and around the water. Along the pool's edges, artificial palm trees of coloured cement soar upwards and their vast green fronds, edged in gold paint, have been artfully designed to interlace and form the ceiling that I look up on every evening. Floating trays, carrying drinks and candles, obscure my vision and cast odd shadows on the blue and white mosaic which covers the bottom of the pool. The mosaic shows white-bearded Tritons lewdly sporting with full-blossomed nereids around a fleet of naval patrol boats and submarines. At night the underwater lights are switched on to create brilliant yellow highways through the murk. The parties are silent. The guests – diplomats, pistol-packing officers and tarty girls – dart among the cement trees, saying nothing, but they open and close their mouths and move their arms about, as if they were conversing, and it is easy for me to imagine that they are indeed having conversations with one another.

I drift from edge to edge and I idly comb the rippling underside of the water's surface. I lie in wait for a drunken man who may look down, expecting to see his reflection in the water. What he will see is me. He will gaze into my depths and I into his. Very likely, he will look down with a faint air of concern, as if he were contemplating an accident victim. Will he come to me? Or will he shake his head and wander off to rejoin his fantastic friends? These flickery men, who pace about the pool, making sharp, stabbing motions with their arms and legs, when they do finally come down to join me, move with a slow grace as if they had at last found their reality. Sometimes I have thought that these stick-like men in stiff suits and everything they do up there constitutes some sort of coded message. On the whole, though, I am inclined to regard them as mere entertainment, yet, if they are my playthings, they are oddly obstinate playthings. In time, some will come to rest in my damp embrace, but others will walk away, never to be seen by me again. Usually, when the party is over, I propel myself downwards into tunnels of green silence, brooding on what I have witnessed. If one idea could talk to another idea...

Lulled by the rock and slap of the water, I drift off to sleep entertaining such ideas.

In the daytime, the pool welcomes exercise swimmers, men who generally plough up and down length after length without looking where they are going or considering what lies beneath them. I lie beneath them, well below the surface, watching to see what sort of man it is who will enter my waters. I pick my swimmer as he dives in or descends by the steps at the deep end. Then I skull myself along the length of the pool, doing a kind of inverted breast stroke, lying on my back and using the pressure of my extended palms to keep myself close to the bottom of the pool. In this way I eventually find myself swimming underneath my chosen one and keeping pace with him. It may be that he refuses to look down, but, if so, I reach up for his pouched and gleaming crotch. Then he must look down and see me. I smile up. He smiles back and dips down to find me and, as I spread my legs, he is caught between my knees. I open my mouth to his and

194

drain his lungs of air. Then I lay him out in a corner of the deep end, where little cloud clusters of chlorine will gather and eat at his eyeballs.

The President does not enter the water when he is giving an official party. Perhaps he does not want his guests to know that he cannot swim. But on quieter occasions, the President leads his family into the pool.

"Come on in! The water's lovely!" he seems to be shouting to the little ones who are hanging back, and, if they still do not dare to follow him in, he scrambles out to catch them and throw them into the water. Then the children lie on their backs and their chubby little legs pump vigorously as they have splashing fights with one another. The President waddles about in the shallow end, exchanging jokes with his wife and bodyguards. I float by and allow my fingers to slide over his ankles, but he never looks down. He goes flailing about after his children and, when he catches up with them, he hurls them up to rise and descend in great spraying parabolas. Then he carries them piggy-back for a while before plunging them under. Sometimes the children catch sight of me darting between the President's legs and they look at me thoughtfully before they race up for air. The President's legs, white and hairy, are real and solid, but everything above the waist is weirdly insubstantial and shakes as he thrashes about.

I have not seen the President for a while and there has not been a party for a long time now. I have played with the notion that this might be my failure, that the absence of parties might be a product of the drying up of my imagination. Most of man is water. In fact, ninety per cent of a man is water; the rest is imagination. I scud about on my back, squinting out of the corner of my eye, in the faint hope of catching a half glimpse of a bunch of men in dinner jackets. Men are like ideas that one cannot quite grasp, walking about just beyond the edge of the pool, but, if I can catch at the fleeting thing, then I find that it, or he, ends up dead in the water.

The parties are over and the men in dinner jackets are gone, but the pool is crowded. Although the Fool was the first man to join me here who had no breath left for my kiss, soon after that three men in dark lounge suits were brought to the pool and pushed under – all three in one afternoon. About a week later, I noticed a hole in the lattice of palm fronds that form the roof and since then real leaves have drifted down through that hole to float on the water, before disintegrating into scum. The pool is no longer cleaned and fat black flies lie trapped on the silvery web that dances on the water's surface. For the first time in many years I have found myself thinking of my sisters. Where are they? Once there were many of us. I think that I should like to go back and join the sea people. I wish I could remember what they told me when we all lived together under the curl of the wave...

My every move disturbs black clouds of mud and algae, as I claw my way through the gathering darkness. Hundreds more corpses have joined those of the Fool and the three politicians and now the charred bodies are propped in ranks against the sides and more come sliding down to join them, so that one man's foot descends on another's head. In this waterlogged ossuary, I find it increasingly difficult to find my path and I ask myself what has happened to my girlish dreams.

DOCTOR PINTER IN THE MYTHOLOGY ISLES
by
Barrington J. Bayley

Doctor Pinter started back reflexively as a great briny gout of spume sprayed across the plexiglass protecting the hydrofoil's deck. The hydrofoil swayed and shifted, the engine revving. Had he not known better he would have thought the pilot was having trouble finding his way through the reef. The pink coral seemed to turn the normally placid ocean into a passionate and dangerous creature, which could wreck vessels far sturdier than this.

His companion on deck seemed unperturbed by the turmoil. He was watching three young women emerge from the lounge. Two of them wore flouncy flowered skirts which billowed up prettily in the stiff salty breeze from the ventilator. The third was clad in a loose yellow smock, which was blown like a second skin against her ample form.

"If you're interested, Doctor, there's a surplus of females in the Mythology Isles. Mostly tourists, looking for adventure."

"I am not interested in the slightest," Pinter said drily. "When I was a young man I decided to have nothing to do with women, in the romantic sense. I regard them as frivolous, emotionally unreliable, not worthy of the affection of a man of substance." He gave the briefest and coldest of glances at the three females who giggled their way down the deck, reminding himself of the tenet that had guided him through his life of celibacy.

Women change their minds too easily.

"Ah, so you are a misogynist. But what of...er...physical desire?"

"That can always be dealt with, by medication if necessary. Luckily, I do not need artificial aid. I am blessed with a controllable libido."

"A great blessing indeed."

The hydrofoil was now within the lagoon and approaching its docking at the island of Felicity.

"Are you to be here long?" the other asked.

"A day or two only," Doctor Pinter replied. "I have been

asked to collect a sample box of local ores from the Office of Administration. Speaking of industrial matters, I hear Intelligent Molecular have some facilities in these islands?"

"Intelligent Molecular Industries owns the whole island group," the other said with surprise. "Did you not know?"

"No, I didn't. My visit to this planet is fleeting. I am really on my way somewhere else. Anyway I don't know too much of molecular science. I work for Interstellar Metals."

"Indeed? I should introduce myself. I am Girish Catheny, an InMol employee. May I wish you a pleasant stay." Catheny held out his hand.

Pinter shook the proffered hand absent-mindedly. The hydrofoil surged alongside the wharf, and sank onto its hull. A gangway craned out, hooking itself onto the dockside. Pinter looked to make sure his luggage was sliding down the nearby chute, then joined his companion in the queue to disembark.

Catheny watched thoughtfully as the girls he had spotted went hurrying ashore with much chatter.

"Um, did anyone tell you what sort of work InMol is doing here?"

"Why, no."

"Perhaps I should mention..." Catheny hesitated and bit his lip before continuing. "Never mind – it's not important. A bit complicated to explain, really. Enjoy your stay."

Doctor Pinter blinked as Catheny left him and stepped briskly down the ramp. What an odd fellow, he thought. He had heard that these biochemical chaps were inclined to be temperamental. Lacking the hard-edged contact with reality enjoyed by metallurgists such as himself.

He dismissed the incident from his mind. The sky over Felicity was a dazzling deep blue, and the sound of the sea was in his ears. Felicity had the air of a coastal holiday town, the plazas thronging with gaudily clad people. The buildings, constructed from a light yellow stone which sparkled in the sun, were spaciously laid out. Pinter hailed a sky-blue taxi, collected his luggage and rode to his hotel. Once installed in the delicately decorated room, which had a view of the lagoon, he considered how to spend the next few hours. His appointment was not till the next day. An evening of relaxation seemed in order.

A look at the room's information screen helped him make his plans. He was surprised to see how numerous Intelligent Molecular Industries' facilities were – about one half of the structures mapped were company installations. But there were inviting promenades along beaches and clifftops, and not only that, a delightful feature for a small island – a fresh-water lake, the shores of which were a general recreation area, complete with restaurants, open-air bars, music pavilions, parks and gardens. What better than to saunter there for a while?

A walk inland through serene boulevards brought him to where evening sunlight sparkled on shimmering lake water. Music could be heard, carried by this natural sound reflector from a central island. Doctor Pinter enjoyed the conceit: an island with an island! He entered a bower, where he was served a refreshing drink of light rum and gene-cultured pineapple juice.

Sitting nearby was a somewhat older man who got into conversation with him. Pinter asked if he was a resident of the island, and was told it was so. "It must be a pleasant place to live," he allowed. "Are you in the employ of InMol?"

"Yes."

"Ah. A microbiologist?"

"Well, no. I'm on the administrative side."

Pinter was wondering whether he might tease from his new acquaintance the nature of InMol's work in the Mythology Isles, when suddenly the man became uneasy. He was looking towards the entrance to the bower. Someone had entered, though as the setting sun was in his eyes Pinter saw the figure only indistinctly.

The other rose to his feet.

"Nice to speak to you – I must be getting along now."

He spoke breathlessly, and turned to walk quickly to the exit at the rear of the garden, leaving his drink unfinished. Pinter peered to see what had caused him such consternation.

It was a woman who had entered. She was fairly tall, large-boned, clad in a simple white gown, moving with a kind of loose-limbed grace. She fell just short of being plump; her skin was honey-coloured and firm. Her thighs pushed forward the cloth of her gown as she strode in his direction, glancing this way and that. Her eyes fell on him. And to Doctor Pinter there came, quite unexpectedly, a totally new experience: his glance met hers, and a shock went right through him. It was as though he had touched a live electric cable.

He sat mesmerised as she continued to approach. As though she still had not noticed him, she took the seat recently vacated on the other side of the table. Doctor Pinter's heart began to beat loudly, so much so that he began to fear it was audible to others. He tried not to stare at her, to pretend that he was not totally absorbed by her presence. She seemed to glow, emanating an aura in whose radiance he was saturated. Her eyes were hazel, at once lively and restrained. Her face had that look of self-composure which women everywhere tried to emulate, with all their grooming and face-painting; but with her it was innate, and he noted that she wore no cosmetics.

All his fright vanished once conversation commenced between them. He was enchanted by the naturalness of her manner, by the ease of her companionship, even as he found himself privately dwelling on the fullness of her bosom and the soft curve of her belly, which the garment she wore so artlessly accentuated. They had talked for no more than five minutes when he asked for her name.

"I'm Felicity."

"Oh? The same as this island!"

"Yes. I was born here."

This surprised him. "Forgive me...you do not seem like someone who has spent all her life in an out-of-the-way place like this."

She inclined her head and smiled. "Oh, we aren't without culture here in the Mythology Isles."

On and on they talked, with never a moment of awkwardness, never a searching for something to say. The sun slipped away, bringing dusk to the island, and Doctor Pinter realized that a miracle had taken place.

He had fallen in love.

He recognised that he was in the presence of a superior type of human being. From her glances, from her lingering looks, from the secret understanding of their remarks to one another, from her readiness to spend the rest of the evening with him even though they had never met before, from the *unspoken* communication between them which seemed to be a direct contact of souls – he knew that she felt the same about him.

They rose and walked together to the lakeside, two people enthralled to be near one another. It was late when at last she announced that she had to depart. When they turned to look at one another in fond farewell, it was as if something moved them. They stepped closer. Their arms went around one another.

She was half a head taller than he, and she bent down, with a graciousness that was quite ravishing, as their lips met in a kiss of blissful union. How exquisite to feel that angelic body pressing warmly against him!

Gasping, he drew apart from her. Their arms dropped, and they clasped hands tenderly. "Where shall I meet you tomorrow?" he asked, eagerly.

Her answer was soft, and thoughtful, given after a suggestive pause. "Midday will find me in the Ulysses Esplanade."

Then she was walking away from him, swinging her ample rump rhythmically. Doctor Pinter watched her until she had faded from sight. Even then it was an effort to bestir himself. The strains of Duke Ellington's *Black and Tan Fantasy* drifted across the lake as he set off in a daze, strolling through the cool of the night back to his hotel.

Back in his room he inspected himself in the wall mirror. He was, of course, about twice Felicity's age, and not even particularly attractive to women – or so he had always assumed. And what of his so recently reiterated aversion to the female psyche? The answer to that seemed straightforward enough. Felicity evidently did not share the general deficiencies of her sex. She was that rarest of beings: a woman with depth of mind.

He understood that she, too, must have been frustrated by the lack of a suitable soul-mate among the opposite sex. Like him, she had doubtless preserved a life-long celibacy. With her natural dignity, her gentle gravity, it was inconceivable that she would defile herself with anyone not her psychological equal.

Studying his noble features, Doctor Pinter could not avoid congratulating her for having seen at a glance that he and he alone was a superior individual who could make her complete. How else could one explain the immediacy of their coming together, the instantaneity of their mutual recognition? It was as if they had secretly known one another all their lives, and had only been waiting for the moment when they would first meet.

The fateful transformation of their fortunes had now taken place. Theirs was a love story of legendary proportions. It deserved to be described in some great work of literature!

Doctor Pinter hardly slept that night. The enchanting face of Felicity haunted his thoughts and filled his mind with the febrile energy of anticipation.

He rose early in the morning and ate a large breakfast, determined to fortify himself for the crucial day that lay ahead. During the morning he visited the Office of Administration and collected the box of ore samples which was the purpose of his stopover, depositing it at the hotel. He could have taken the hydrofoil to the planet's spaceport there and then, had such a course not become unthinkable. The power of Love demanded that he extend his stay. When the time *did* eventually come for him to leave, he would surely be taking Felicity with him.

Ulysses Esplanade was quite near the hotel, fronting a stretch of shoreline, beyond which the sea shimmered and swirled within the protected haven of the lagoon.

A certain degree of nervousness attacked Pinter as midday approached. He bought a little spray of local flowers to present to Felicity, white with coral-red hearts, combed his breeze-tossed hair, and waited in one corner of the plaza, near to an elegant restaurant where, he thought, it would be pleasant for them to have lunch together.

His wait was not a short one. Nearly an hour passed, while he grew increasingly fretful. Then, at last, he spotted her, crossing the esplanade from the seaward side. She wore a gown quite similar to the one she had worn the previous evening, but this one yellow in colour, accentuating the golden glow of her skin.

Doctor Pinter's heart accelerated and he started forward. His steps faltered, however, as he saw that she was not alone. Walking by her side was a man. He was about her height, and the conversation between them was animated. He was sleek and expensively dressed, very handsome, confidently suave. Pinter suddenly became painfully aware of how nondescript he must seem by contrast, but he bravely put aside all negative thoughts and pressed forward, smiling in welcome.

"Felicity!"

Bewilderingly, he could not at first attract her attention. It was not until the two were about to turn into the entrance of the restaurant that she stopped, gazing mildly at him as he offered the spray of flowers.

"For you," he said.

"Why," she said, "it's Doctor Pinter!"

With her left hand she took the spray. Then she leaned forward and pinched his cheek between her thumb and forefinger.

"You dear, sweet little man!"

At once she turned and was gone. Her arm was linked with that of her escort, and they disappeared into the cool interior of the restaurant. Within, visible through the darkened glass panel of the door, were dozens of serene men and women dining in pairs, attended by courteous waiters. The food as undoubtedly sumptuous. The walls were tastefully decorated. But Pinter remained outside, without his flowers, and without Felicity. He stood there blinking, and was only roused by hearing his name spoken behind him, in a low voice.

"Doctor Pinter, may I have a word with you?"

It was Girish Catheny, the man he had met on the hydrofoil. Almost without a will of his own, the disoriented Pinter allowed himself to be ushered to one of the tables which were set out on the esplanade for passers-by. Catheny bit his lip and looked uncomfortable, but came straight to the point.

"Doctor Pinter, I can see that something unfortunate has happened. Perhaps it will help if I acquaint you with Intelligent Molecular's work here in the islands. It has been kept pretty much under wraps until now, though it's not exactly secret.

"InMol's biologists have been concerned to modify the human genome in various specific ways. It may have struck you that the average human being is a pretty mediocre individual, although there is, buried in the collective human psyche, a well-defined set of heroic archetypes – mythological figures with superhuman or near-superhuman qualities. InMol's forward planners regard these archetypes as the expression of an evolutionary urge, a challenge to the species and to their skill. What they have been doing here is to create these mythological heroes genetically. The idea is that such individuals will be the appropriate persons to continue mankind's adventures across the stars. They would be so much more suitable than you or I, you see. They would represent the leading edge of the species, if you follow my meaning."

Pinter stared at him, mutely.

Catheny went on, "A different archetype has been developed on each island of the group. On Felicity InMol's scientists have been trying to produce the archetype of femininity – the kind of being known throughout history as the Goddess of Love."

Pinter frowned in puzzlement. "Is that why these atolls are called the Mythology Isles? I had assumed that their discoverer gave them the name – a reference to the voyages of Odysseus. Because of the navigational hazards surrounding them."

"A serendipitous coincidence," admitted Catheny. "The Project itself is less than forty years old. But did you hear what I said? Felicity Island was allotted the task of incarnating the Goddess of Love."

"Felicity...?"

Catheny nodded. "An early prototype. The first of her kind to be grown to full maturity. She can no more help being seductive than a bird can help learning to fly. It's her nature and her *raison d' être* to evoke the most intense feelings of love in every man she encounters. It's safe to say that no ordinary male can resist her charms. The trouble is – I don't know how much you know about mythology? – that Love-Goddesses tend to be bitches and heartbreakers. Relationships with beings like her usually have the most devastating emotional consequences. The condition is generally represented as something akin to insanity." He shrugged his shoulders apologetically. "I was going to warn you as we disembarked, but I thought the chances of your actually meeting were remote. Most of the male residents have learned to avoid or ignore her. I'm sorry."

"This is all nonsense," Pinter ground out, when he had recovered his voice. "Absolute nonsense. Felicity and I were destined to meet. No force in the universe can prevent us from becoming man and wife. What you are telling me is some evil and ridiculous tale that you have made up to keep us apart, probably because you are jealous." He jumped up and rushed from the table. His first thought was to enter the restaurant and confront Felicity with the fact of their love; but once at the entrance he restrained himself. It was not the right place.

He needed to see her alone.

Pinter hurried back to his hotel room. It was the work of a few moments to find her residential address on the service monitor. Only one person forenamed Felicity was listed. He stared with incredulity at the full name which came up on the screen: Felicity Astarte.

Astarte. Love-goddess of the Babylonian pantheon.

There was nothing he could do for the time being. Doctor Pinter sagged in the grip of an emotional anguish which swiftly exhausted him. He lay down on his bed and fell asleep for several hours.

When he awoke again, it was early evening. He quickly freshened himself up and set out, giving the address to an automatic taxi.

Felicity's home, which was on Ishtar Boulevard, turned out to be a spacious villa having almost the dimensions of a mansion. An inconspicuous plaque set near one corner of the building announced it to be the property of Intelligent Molecular Industries. At the portico he looked for a microphone or call signaller, but found none. The sliding door, however, was withdrawn, inviting entry.

Taking his courage in both hands, he stepped into an airy entrance hall. He looked with fascination at the tastefully erotic statuary adorning the lobby, trying to assimilate it into his knowledge of Felicity's personality.

The house was silent; perhaps she was not at home.

He called out her name twice, but got no reply. He opened doors to the right and the left, discovering cushioned and padded lounges. They were bright, but without flowers.

He was reluctant to leave this hearth of her existence now he was in it. A semicircular stairway led to the upper floor. He took it, to find himself in a corridor with four doors leading off it.

"Felicity?" he called out softly. "Felicity?"

A sound came from behind one of the doors, a shifting noise accompanied by a faint murmur resembling her voice.

Made impetuous by the thought that she was near, Doctor Pinter opened the door and stood on the threshold.

He looked into a lace-curtained boudoir. Felicity was naked, and lay upon a great wide bed. Her weight was balanced on her shoulders; her body was raised up by the naked man who loomed over her, her legs around his waist, her feet hovering above as though she would plant them on the ceiling. Suspended from the ceiling was a tilted mirror, by means of which Pinter gained an alternative view of the event. He noted how her face, although suffused with pleasure, had not lost that dignity and self-possession which was her essential, endearing quality.

In that same mirror, she saw him. Her eyes met his in a fleeting glance of recognition, then turned dismissively aside.

Her partner, who drove so vigorously into her, must also have been aware of a stranger's presence, but he seemed equally unconcerned. This was not the man who had earlier gone into the restaurant with her. This was no tourist. This was a muscled Adonis, an Odysseus, an Apollo. He was blond and blue-eyed, his face was god-like. It was a face which spoke of supreme courage and great intelligence.

The rhythm to which they moved as they made love seemed to Doctor Pinter to be the rhythm of nature itself. He saw her grasp her lover's biceps, adding her own thrusting energy to his.

This magnificent male, Pinter realised, could only be one of InMol's genetically engineered heroes, visiting from one of the other islands. Never in his life had he felt so utterly small and insignificant.

They did not care at all that he was witness to their coupling. He might as well have been an insect clinging to the wall. For a minute or two he stood where he was, transfixed. There was no sound save for their deliberate, slickly noisy pelvic thrusts.

Then, feeling that he might be about to faint, Doctor Pinter fled.

On the next morning, haggard from distress and lack of sleep, Pinter left his hotel. He sent his luggage ahead and walked the distance to the wharf, carrying the sample case which he would not entrust to anyone else.

On the quay, while he waited to embark, he was surprised to see Girish Catheny again. The InMol employee approached slowly, cautiously, with some awkwardness.

"Er...Doctor Pinter. I thought I might find you here. I wanted to...wish you farewell."

Pinter gazed at him coldly. He wondered whether Catheny could see the dark shadows under his eyes, and guess what they might signify.

"I *do* hope you will see a physician, Doctor," Catheny said sympathetically. "As you said yourself, there are medicines effective against love-sickness."

Pinter's stare was unblinking. His tone, when he replied, was clipped. "If *I* were to be allotted the task of re-designing the human race," he said, "I would eliminate all sexual involvement from the process of reproduction. That would be the way, in my opinion, to produce a better human race."

"Wise words," Catheny admitted, sadly. "Very wise indeed."

Neither of them said anything further. Catheny acceded to Pinter's evident wish to be rid of him. He walked away, with a surprisingly dispirited step.

Pinter mounted the ramp to the waiting hydrofoil. Once, as he settled himself under the deck's plexiglass cover, he felt a panicky sense of nostalgia, but he suppressed it with practised determination and efficiency.

The hydrofoil swung away from the wharf, moving into the lagoon. As it picked up speed, it rose up on its foils very gracefully, racing towards the reef.

Doctor Pinter stood on the aft deck, watching Felicity Island recede. Spray flecked the glass like tears, reminding him that last night he had wept for the first time since he was a child.

The hydrofoil swayed, the water becoming turbulent as pink coral approached. Suddenly, his self control – which he had maintained, with difficulty, since he saw the light of dawn – faltered. He beat his fists on the plexiglass, staring longingly towards the island, calling out in a strangled voice.

"Felicity, my darling! I will return! I will return!"

The hydrofoil lurched violently. For a moment it looked as though the pilot might have made a fatal mistake in steering through the gap in the reef. The vessel seemed about to wreck itself on a huge pink and crimson outcrop.

Then, with a sudden surge of power, it turned aside; the skilful pilot pulled it away from the looming danger.

Soon they had gained the safety of the open sea.

THE WOMAN IN THE MIRROR
by
Brian Craig

The department store where Martin worked was closed on Mondays; by coincidence, the auction rooms a hundred yards down the road from the flat where he lived held the first of its two weekly sales on that day.

At first, his visits to the auction rooms were purely functional. He had to render the flat habitable as quickly as he could, and his wages as an assistant manager in menswear were inadequate to allow him to buy everything new, even with the advantages of his staff discount and special credit terms. The Monday auctions, where the detritus of houses cleared by reason of death or destitution were sold off for next to nothing, were a godsend. The better quality pieces were invariably knocked down to dealers, but there were always odds and ends of flimsy modern furniture which could be had for a pound or two, and there were ancient household appliances, in reasonable working order despite their age, which could be picked up for less.

By the time he had everything he needed, Martin was virtually an auction junkie. He enjoyed sitting anonymously in the middle of the crowd, on some old settee that would eventually be brought under the hammer, watching the ebb and flow of the bidding. He soon cultivated a certain skill in judging the prices which items ought to fetch, but he rarely bought anything even when he saw something going for a bargain price. He would have admitted, if asked, that his regular attendance was damning evidence of the fact that he had nothing better to do with his time, but nobody ever asked him. There was no one to ask; he was quite alone in the world.

Following his single mother's suicide when he was ten years old, Martin had spent the latter part of his childhood in care. He had conscientiously refused to make any friends among his new peers, whom his mother would have considered no-hopers and apprentices in crime. Thanks to the memory of his mother's good advice, he had always known that he could do better than they, provided that he minded his manners, and so it had proved.

He had a good, respectable job, and a place of his own.

The only thing to dislike about his job was that it involved him in constant contact with other people, but he had schooled himself not to mind that; his mask of earnest politeness never cracked, even under the strain of the most difficult customer.

Martin had no other hobby save for his regular attendance at the auction rooms. He spent all his evenings at home, watching TV or reading paperback books. On Sundays in summer he would sometimes go walking in the park, but even in good weather he preferred to be in his own private place, surrounded by things he owned. Although he was by no means agoraphobic he didn't much like open spaces or crowds. The bed-sitting room of his little flat was the only space which he inhabited with any degree of comfort. He felt as safe there as he had in the long-lost days of his early childhood.

Sometimes, as he sat in the saleroom, watching the physical remains of someone else's life pass fleetingly beneath the auctioneer's hammer, Martin wondered whether his mother's few effects had gone the same way, a decade before. Sometimes, he wondered whether a worn carpet or a dark mahogany cabinet might have ended up here because its former owner, tired of the endless tribulations of life and its relationships, had decided that the game was no longer worth the candle. Mostly, though, he just watched, possessed by that special kind of calm which attends activities which are interesting enough to hold the attention without being exciting enough to trouble the mind.

He had long thought that he had everything he needed for the flat, and had not made a purchase of any kind for more than three months, when his attention was suddenly and inexplicably caught by a mirror. It was a very ordinary oval mirror in a plain wooden frame, and he knew that he must have seen dozens like it come under the hammer in previous weeks, but as he looked at this *particular* mirror while the porter brought it up to the auctioneer's podium, it suddenly struck him that he had no mirror in his living-room. It was a peculiar thought, and he knew it; it had never before occurred to him that he – or anyone – needed a mirror in any room except for the bathroom, but once formed, it would not be put aside. Martin was quite overcome by the notion that he had no mirror in his living-room.

There was no contest for the mirror, which was not nearly ornate enough for the dealers to pass it off as an antique. He bought it with a single bid of twenty pence, and carried it home with him when the sale was ended.

He positioned the mirror over the closed-up fireplace, suspended by its loose-linked chain from a picture-hook. It hung at a slight angle, so he had to place its centre a little higher than eye-level. When he looked into it, with his head very slightly tilted back, he could see arrayed behind him the low, narrow bed and the chest of drawers which were set against the far wall, with the couch and the coffee-table in front of them, in the middle of the room. He saw that unless he deliberately moved to one side, he couldn't see the door which opened into the corridor or the doors which led to the tiny kitchen and the tinier bathroom, but while he was squarely positioned in front of the mirror, almost everything that he owned was visible, gathered together in a space without limits and borders.

Somehow, the mirror's image seemed to improve and dignify the room, and he was grateful for the impulse which had made him buy it.

Martin was not a narcissistic person. Indeed, he scarcely knew what he looked like, although he always took care to make his appearance neat. He looked into the bathroom mirror every morning while he shaved, and while he adjusted the knot in his tie, but he never studied his features or met his own eyes. If the mirror which now hung on his living-room wall began to seduce him, drawing him forward to look into it, it was not because he desired to look at his own face, but only because he wanted to study the room which contained him – the space which he had made his own. Once the mirror was in place he began to do that regularly, night after night, sometimes for as much as five minutes at a time. He soon became aware of the absurdity of it, but nevertheless found it increasingly hard to tear himself away from his rapt contemplation.

When two weeks had passed, Martin ceased to worry about the ritual of staring into the mirror. He accepted it as something

211

which simply gave him pleasure. After all, he told himself, what a man chose to do in the privacy of his own home was no one's business but his own, and needed no explanations. He surrendered to his fascination, and allowed himself to be drawn to the mirror whenever the mood took him.

Two more weeks had passed when a most curious thing happened. Martin was looking into the mirror, perfectly relaxed, having almost lapsed into a kind of trance, when it suddenly occurred to him that he could not see himself. The room was still there, filled with all its familiar furniture, but he was not. The mirror-image room was quite empty. Absurdly enough, he had the conviction that the image had been that way for some time, not just on this occasion but many others – that he, in fact, had been absent from the looking-glass world for some considerable time, without realising the fact.

Martin blinked, and moved his head slightly, but the image in the mirror didn't change. His face didn't reappear. He looked around, at the real room, and then looked back at the mirror, but nothing had changed. The room was present in every detail, with nothing out of place, but he was nowhere to be seen.

With infinite patience, Martin looked down at his arms and legs, to make sure that his real self was perfectly visible. Then he used his hands to check the solidity of his face. There was no doubt that he was physically present – and yet, the mirror stubbornly refused to reflect him. He had been casually eliminated from the looking-glass version of his room, callously excluded from the improved, dignified version of his personal space.

Deliberately, he turned away. He walked into the bathroom, and looked at himself in his shaving-mirror, which dutifully reflected every detail of his features, just as it had always done. He picked up a comb from the shelf and ran it lightly through his hair. Then he went back into the living-room and approached the mirror above the hearth, not without trepidation.

He knew even before he reached it that it was still adamant in its refusal to admit him to the imaginary space which it enclosed, but he was no longer astonished by that fact. Nor did he feel in any way threatened or endangered by it. He was intrigued, to be sure, but the sciences had remained completely

212

mysterious to him during the years of his inadequate schooling, with the result that he had no overweening faith in the laws of optics, and was easily able to remain undisturbed by their local suspension. The mere fact that a mirror had ceased to contain him was by no means sufficient to make him think that all reality was out of joint.

Martin felt no impulse to run from the flat in search of a witness to the startling event. He simply stood and stared into the mirror, patiently bearing witness to a trivial private miracle, wondering when or if the marvellous interlude would come to an end.

Because he had firmly set aside the surprise which he had initially felt at discovering himself absent from the mirror image, it did not surprise him overmuch when someone else entered the looking-glass room. He did not see her actually come in, because he could not see the door from where he stood, but he did not doubt for a moment that she had entered the reflected room in a perfectly normal fashion.

The woman threw her handbag on the bed, and slipped off her coat, which she draped over the back of the couch. Then she walked all the way across the field of view, and disappeared, presumably into the bathroom. A few minutes later she re-appeared, but only fleetingly, as she went from one invisible doorway to another, into the kitchen. Martin waited patiently for her to come out again, which she eventually did, with a cup of coffee in her hand.

It was not until she sat down on the settee, with the cup before her on the table, that Martin really had an opportunity to study her face and figure. The face might have been prettier had it seemed less tired and drawn. She had make-up on, but clearly had not renewed it since first applying it that morning. The figure was by no means voluptuous, but it was attractively slender rather than merely thin. Her clothes were inexpensive but they hung well; she wore a white blouse and grey skirt very like those favoured – with the unsubtle encouragement of the managers – by the salesgirls at the department store. The entire effect was somewhat let down, though, by her posture, which was so relaxed as to be almost a slouch.

Martin realised, with a slight start of guilt, that he had caught the woman off guard. She thought that she was quite alone and unobserved, and even the most elementary aspect of performance was gone from her behaviour. Had there been anyone else in the room with her – had she even suspected that someone might be able to see her – she would have held herself differently, controlling both the expression on her face and the attitude of her body. As things were, she had let herself relax into a state of private innocence.

While Martin watched her, though, she pulled herself together, took a sip of coffee, got to her feet, and walked unhurriedly over to the fireplace.

He knew immediately that she intended to look into the mirror, and felt a sudden stab of alarm lest she catch him standing there, a peeping Tom in *her* looking-glass world, who had no conceivable right to be there. Despite the stab of alarm, though, he didn't move. Nor did he need to, for as she fixed her eyes upon him, it was quite obvious that she saw nothing but her own familiar reflection.

At close range, he watched her touch her hands experimentally to her face, as though examining herself for signs of aging. Her incipient frown suggested that she found some, but Martin couldn't imagine how. She was a little older than he was, but only three or four years – he judged that she couldn't possibly be more than twenty-five – and there was not a wrinkle to be seen. Her height was apparently identical to his own, because her eyes, presumably fixed upon their own reflection, seemed to be looking directly into his. The general cast of her face was similar, too – he had always had effeminately delicate cheekbones and neat, full-lobed ears – and her eyes were as grey-blue as his own, but there the resemblance ended. Her shoulder-length tresses were a deep nut-brown, several shades darker than his abruptly-shorn hair, and rather more lustrous. Her teeth were more even than his, and whiter. Her nose was very different too, being narrower and far more elegant than his own, which had been broken by a schoolyard bully when he was thirteen and set rather crookedly.

The woman turned away from the mirror, and went back to

her coffee. Martin found himself letting out a deep breath, which he had not been consciously aware of holding, and then he shuddered inexplicably. He shut his eyes for a fraction of a second, and when he opened them, he found himself looking into his own eyes.

His reflection had returned, and the woman was gone.

His first impulse was to forget the whole episode, and to tell himself sternly that it hadn't really happened at all, but the intention faded as soon as it was born. He knew, and could not doubt, that what he had experienced was no mere hallucination, nor some inconceivably rare freak of chance that would never be repeated.

He knew that he would see the woman again – and again, and again – if only he were patient.

In the early days, Martin caught only brief glimpses of the strange alternative world where his flat was inhabited by a woman. For a while, they seemed to happen no more than twice or three times a week, and rarely lasted for longer than a few minutes – although he could never be certain that there were not other occasions which he failed to notice because his attention was elsewhere. As the weeks went by, however, the frequency and duration of the episodes increased steadily.

He soon found out how easy it would be to spend the whole time that he was in the flat watching the mirror, and he flatly refused to allow himself to become obsessed. He made something of a fetish out of going about his business as usual, making and eating his meals as he always had, watching all the TV programmes it was his habit to view. But he knew better than to take this calculated avoidance to ridiculous extremes; he forgave himself for his frequent glances at the mirror, and remained always ready to go immediately to the hearth if he caught the slightest glimpse of anything which suggested that the glass was no longer reflecting him.

Even the brief visions of the early weeks allowed him to build an impressionistic picture of the life which the woman lived, which was not by any means a mirror-image of his own.

The woman was evidently far more sociable than he, despite

the fact that she never invited her friends – male or female – back to the flat. She went out far more than he did, and he often discovered her coming home after eleven. Unlike him, she did not seem to be at all relaxed and at home in the flat; more than once he saw her looking round in frank distaste, and although she sometimes seemed to be deeply relieved to have escaped from the world at large when she came in and let herself down on the couch or the bed, she seemed quite unable to luxuriate in her surroundings or her own company.

Martin quickly became convinced that the woman was not a happy person. It was not so much that he never saw her smile – why should she smile when she was alone? – or even the fact that he saw her crying quiet tears on one or two occasions; what convinced him was the way she sometimes sat on the couch, wrapping her arms around her body as though to hug herself. As time went by, he was able to observe that she kept a bottle of pills on the little table beside the bedhead, and took one every night. That disturbed him more than anything else, because there was no such bottle on his identical table. He flatly refused to use any kind of tranquilliser or sleeping pill, even though he sometimes suffered from insomnia.

He often caught glimpses of the woman as she dressed or undressed, though he rarely saw her naked for more than a few fleeting seconds, en route to or from the bathroom, or before she switched off the light and plunged her mirror-world into darkness. Such glimpses excited him, but in a curiously asexual fashion. They brought a yearning ache to his heart, but left his loins as impotently numb as ever. He fell profoundly in love with her without any measurable delay, but he did not lust after her, or long to touch her. He was always fully conscious of the fact that she was in another, unreachable world.

As Martin's visions gradually became more frequent and longer-lasting, sometimes extending for as much as ten or twelve minutes, he was able to hazard a guess that the woman must work in an office of some kind. She often flexed her fingers and massaged her wrists, as though those were the parts of her body which took the strain of her daily labour. She did not make herself up as carefully or as completely as the sales staff in his department store, and she worked on Mondays but not on Saturdays. Sometimes she came in late, having apparently worked overtime.

He tried to pick up further clues to the kind of life she led from the small items which she left lying about on the coffee-table, but she was usually quick to tidy them away; oddly enough, the impression he gained from this was not that she was a habitually tidy person, but rather that she felt so little at home in the flat that she felt guilty about leaving it in a state of disorder, and could not bring herself to treat it entirely as her own.

It took some little time for Martin to realise that he might be partly responsible for this reluctance. The room in which the woman lived was, after all, a reflection of his own. Although the chest of drawers and the free-standing wardrobe had very different contents, they were the same items of furniture which he had bought for next to nothing at the auction rooms. The couch, the coffee-table, the bed and the carpet were all of his choosing, and he had chosen them with little regard for their appearance. He could not see, of course, whether she had his ancient fridge-freezer and electric cooker, because they were permanently hidden from view by the kitchen door even when it yawned wide open, but somehow he felt sure that she had.

No sooner had it dawned on him that some small part, at least, of the woman's discomfort might be due to the choices he had made than the corollary possibility occurred to him that he might be able to ameliorate her discomfort: *that he might have the power to affect the contents – and hence, in some measure, the course of events – of the world beyond the mirror.*

It was a realisation which changed his life.

The following Monday found Martin, as usual, in the auction rooms. He was, however, possessed by an unprecedented determination to purchase some significant item of furniture, paying less attention to function than to appearance. He wanted something that would look elegant, and he was prepared to pay – as he knew that he would have to – for the added aesthetic value. He was not unduly worried about matters of price. His rent and regular outgoings amounted to no more than two-thirds of his

217

weekly wage; since he had finished furnishing the flat he had been saving money regularly in the building society.

He enjoyed the sale more than he ever had before. He was briefly tempted by a new settee, but in the end he settled for a handsome glass-topped coffee-table.

When he had carried the coffee-table home Martin immediately set out for the auction rooms again, entering his old one to be sold at the next auction. Then he returned and waited, anxiously, to see whether the replacement would be reflected in the woman's world. As soon as he saw that it was, he was overtaken by a most peculiar feeling: a sensation of infinite opportunity.

The woman, when she came home from work that evening, made no evident reaction to the new coffee-table, and certainly showed no particular surprise or pleasure in consequence of its presence. Nevertheless, Martin felt that he had taken an important first step in the work of making her feel more at home.

He began to make plans almost immediately. Most of the replacement items which he would have to acquire, he decided, ought not to be bought second-hand. Fortunately, his staff discount, and the special low-interest credit terms which were available to employees of the store where he worked, would ease his burden considerably.

A little elementary research carried out during his lunch-hours soon familiarised him with the prices of beds and bed-linen, fitted carpets and made-to-measure curtains, patterned wallpaper and light-fittings. His calculative abilities, honed by long experience at the till-point, were easily adequate to designing a budget and a plan of campaign.

The transformation of the flat took three months to complete – and a further six months to pay for – but it was from the very first moment a labour of love. The fact that he had no real evidence of the woman's aesthetic preferences worried him a little at first, but he knew that he had no option but to trust to his intuitions, and he did so. He set out to make the room brighter, more cheerful, more feminine, and as each piece of the environmental jigsaw was slotted into place he became increasingly confident that his decisions were good.

As the woman's world was gradually transformed, she too seemed to become brighter and more cheerful. She took all the changes which he instituted completely for granted, as though every one had been her own purchase, according to her own plan, but Martin did not mind that in the least. It was enough that she seemed more approving of her surroundings, and that she eventually became comfortable enough to mingle a measure of delight with the relief which she so often showed when arriving home late after an evening out.

Even before the transformation of the room was complete – before he had replaced the chest of drawers or the curtains (which could not actually be seen in the mirror, no matter where one stood) – Martin began to buy small presents for the woman in the mirror.

He was not sure, initially, that he would be able to transmit small and trivial objects into the other world, because there were always minor differences between his room and hers, in terms of the everyday objects which were routinely strewn about. He knew from experience that a coffee-mug or a paperback or a can of coca-cola left on his table or his mantelpiece would not be reflected on hers, although he would usually be able to see a handbag or a magazine or an emery board in its place. There was, it seemed, an alchemy of alternativity which transmuted the minutiae of his life into the minutiae of hers, while faithfully reproducing more massive objects. Nevertheless, he was convinced that if only he could find appropriate objects – objects which would seem more at home in her life than his own – he might be able to transmit them across the divide by reflection. Having failed with flowers, boxes of chocolates and a few ornaments, he finally achieved success with an unequivocally-feminine item of jewellery: a pair of earrings.

Further experiments quickly demonstrated that items of feminine apparel were equally easy to intrude into the woman's life, and from then on he decided to concentrate his attention on jewellery and clothing. At first, it caused him considerable embarrassment to purchase such items, but it seemed to him that the end justified the means, and he soon steeled himself to the business of shopping for exactly those items which he most desired to see the woman wearing. He knew that the steady stream of purchases would generate prurient gossip at the store, but he didn't mind that; he had no friends there, and didn't care what might be said about him behind his back.

It would have been more convenient, in a way, had the little gifts which he bought for the woman been materially transmitted, disappearing from his world as they appeared in hers. As things were, however, he felt duty bound to keep and carefully preserve the originals once he was certain that they had been reflected. He knew perfectly well that the woman's closet and chest of drawers contained many items which were independent of anything in his – and vice versa – but he remained convinced that if he ever removed from his own flat any of the items which he had imported by design into hers, they would likewise be lost from the flat in the mirror-world, like the redundant furniture which he had sent back to the auction rooms as quickly as he could replace it.

For six months, while he remade her habitat and supplied her steadily with gifts, Martin did not doubt for a moment that the quality of the woman's life was steadily improving. It was true that she continued occasionally to hold herself as though comforting herself with a second-rate embrace, but she no longer seemed quite so desperate in so doing. It was true, too, that he would once in a while catch a glimpse of her while she was weeping miserably to herself, but he told himself that these were exceptional moments of weakness, each one caused by some momentary tragedy of the particular day. She still kept the bottle of sleeping-pills beside her bed, using them assiduously, but he convinced himself that this was mere habit, or – at worst – a harmless psychological dependence. He wished that she would smile more, but recognised that she was, after all, always alone when he saw her.

Eventually, though, Martin admitted to himself that whatever improvement he had wrought in her condition, it had not made her as happy as he would have liked to see her. Although she was far more at home in her new surroundings, still there was something lacking in her life – something that all his efforts and gifts could not provide. It took him a long time to begin to wonder whether she might be lonely, because loneliness was not something that bothered *him* at all, but in the end he had to face up to the fact that filling her room with desirable possessions was not quite the same thing as filling her life with worthwhile experiences. Nor could he avoid noticing that, so far as he could tell from his fragmented observation of her life, she never invited anyone else into the flat, not even for a cup of coffee. She still went out a good deal, but whatever it was that she was searching for in the mysterious world which lay beyond the doors of her flat seemed to be evading her.

Martin often wondered – how could he help it? – what it would be like to see her shopping in the store where he worked, or even to see her across a crowded street, walking in company with a girl-friend or a boy-friend, with her public face wreathed in smiles; but he always *knew* that such ideas were mere fantasy. He knew that he would never meet her in the flesh; that his world and hers could not and did not materially overlap. Nevertheless, he felt in his heart that one kind of contact between them *might* be possible. He felt, and even dared to hope, that he and she might one day make eye-contact. He had not the slightest doubt that he would never touch her, never kiss her, never hear her voice; but he believed that there was just a remote possibility that one day she might look into her oval mirror, and instead of seeing her own sad face, see his instead.

He began, almost in spite of himself, to yearn for that moment, even though he had at first no idea at all how he might help to bring it about.

Martin honestly did not know how or why it first occurred to him to put on some of the clothes which he had bought as presents for the woman in the mirror. He had no purpose in mind; it was simply that the idea popped into his head, in exactly the same way that the idea of purchasing the mirror had come into his head. After all, he thought, the items were *there*, cluttering up his drawers. It seemed somehow unfair that the originals should be scorned and neglected while their reflected images were used with evident satisfaction.

His first experiment in transvestism was rapidly concluded; it was simply too embarrassing, and the mirror – which was in its ordinary mode at the time – assured him that he looked ridiculous. But the feel of the undergarments against his skin was unexpectedly pleasant, and he was soon tempted to make a more concerted effort.

It was not until he had donned an entire set of clothes, and overcome the initial horror at what he had dared to do, that he was able to study himself carefully in the mirror, wondering at his temerity. For several minutes – perhaps as much as half an hour – the thrill he felt was quite self-contained. It was a purely sensual matter, without apparent connection or consequence. It was not until he had experimented extensively with movement and posture – walking, sitting, lying down, posing – that he looked again at the mirror, and saw himself as if from an entirely new angle.

It was then that he experienced his crucial moment of blazing enlightenment. He saw – quite literally *saw*, in his own reflection – that with careful effort, he might transform his own image into something very like the image of the woman who lived in the other world. He took it for granted, of course, that absolute similarity would be impossible to achieve, but the idea seized hold of him that if only he could make himself similar *enough*, then the awful gulf which separated her world from his might be bridged, if only for a moment, in such a way as to let *her* see *him*.

While he pondered this remarkable notion, with his eyes steadfastly fixed upon an image which for once refused stubbornly to disappear from the wayward looking-glass, the idea grew in his head with the force of an explosion. He felt that his moment of enlightenment was expanding, that the power of the thought was taking on a transcendental magnitude, that he was drunk with inspiration.

He suddenly saw, and wondered how he could have been so blind as not to have seen it before, that all the presents which he had bought for her had really been gifts for himself. More than that, he understood with unreasonable clarity that there had been an unsuspected pattern in all his purchases, directed to the end that they might be stored up as instruments which would one day enable him to make her one further and most precious gift: the gift of himself.

Everything that had happened to him, Martin now realised – beginning long before his purchase of the magic mirror – had been a matter of laying the groundwork for the project which he now conceived. Previously, his self-appointed task in life had been merely to live, to exist in a kind of limbo, perfectly safe and isolated; now, for the first time, he had a real goal.

His one ambition was to be seen by the woman in the mirror: to become *worthy* to be seen by her, and hence to make himself visible. The scheme by which he would accomplish this end was already forming in his mind.

Martin now began to watch the mirror very assiduously in the mornings, in order to see what the woman put on before going to work. When he came home each evening, he would try to match her dress as accurately as he could, so that when she came home from work, if she should chance to go to the mirror while he was able to watch her, he could stand before her similarly attired.

It was the most expectantly exciting time of his life – but it did not take him long to realise that his expectations were ludicrously over-ambitious. The first time she failed to see him, though he was dressed almost exactly as she was, he told himself that it was a mere misfortune. The second time, he assured himself that he had come within a moment of success. The third time, his tottering edifice of hope collapsed entirely, and he accepted that his imitation was so woefully inadequate as to be an insult.

Before the second week of his great experiment was out, he had acquired a wig which approximated as closely as he could contrive to the colour and style of her hair. He had become desperately avid to catch sight of the apparatus which she used in making herself up, and he was impatiently anxious about the fact that she always made up her face in the bathroom, out of sight. He improvised as best he could, but it quickly became apparent to him that anything he might achieve by these crude means would be a travesty. The wig stubbornly remained a wig, and obviously so; his unskilfully applied make-up was a clownish mask, and he knew that his crooked nose and discoloured teeth would ensure that it would always remain so. His refurbished hope that his imitation of her features might become close enough, given adequate opportunities for practice, dwindled away to nothing.

Martin's first reaction, on being forced to confront the ugly hopelessness of his new-found ambition, was to write off the whole episode as a moment of madness. He put the woman's clothes away, and hid the wig and the half-assembled collection of cosmetics in a box which he placed in a dark corner of the wardrobe. He became himself again – or tried to.

He found, though, that it was now *he* that was uncomfortable in his own lair. He no longer felt at home in the flat, and could not settle to his customary pastimes. He began to suffer very badly from insomnia, though not so badly that he relented in his hatred of medication, and for the first time he felt that he was becoming acutely, painfully and unhealthily obsessed with the mirror.

He had previously been able to believe that his interest in the mirror was an understandable fascination, and nothing to be feared. Now, he began to find it appalling and terrifying, an obvious sign of mental illness. No matter how hard he tried to relinquish his addiction, though, he simply could not keep his eyes off the dreadful object, and every minute that passed while it stubbornly showed him his own flat and his own person was a bitter torment. Once he had seen the way forward, it seemed, there could be no going back.

Martin was no fool, and he knew full well what kind of commitment would be demanded if he were to resume the project which he had begun so half-heartedly and botched so badly. From the depths of his despair he could see everything which lay before him. He understood now how stupidly foolish he had been to think that any mere caricature could serve his purpose, and was well aware of the extreme to which he would surely have to go, if he were to bring his new dream to authentic fruition. He knew well enough that any plan which he now made would require years to be brought to its conclusion, and would necessitate the cultivation of true courage.

The prospect was too appalling, and he did what he could to refuse to think of it; but he had not the power to sustain his refusal.

He had always been a coward, and was not unduly ashamed of the fact even now. He had always been small and thin, quite unequipped for the kind of adolescence which he had been forced by circumstance to experience. He had never fought back against those who had continually sought to hurt and humiliate him, always sustaining himself with the thought that time would give him his freedom, if only he could survive. Having won his measure of freedom, he had been content to continue to survive; it had been enough for him to have his own space, an adequate income, and peace. He had never dared to entertain any material ambitions, or ventured to desire any intimate relationship with another person; he knew only too well where such quests led. He had always been horridly afraid of falling ill, of being hurt, of having to go to hospital.

Now, though, he found his protective cowardice ripped away. He found that he simply *could not refuse* to contemplate a pathway of events which would mean long and stubborn defiance of the contempt of others, and a whole series of surgical interventions. He begin to imagine where he might discover the courage even to think of such things, and yet he *could not stop himself*.

The paradoxicality of it all was perfectly clear to him. The sheer insanity of it was as plain to him as the crooked nose on his all-too-plain face. He, who had never even contemplated owning a car, or getting married, or doing anything whatsoever to distinguish himself, had been possessed and overcome by the notion of recreating himself in the image of a woman who did not and could not exist, in order that he might become – just *might*, perhaps only for the merest instant – that which she saw while she peered unhappily into the imaginary mirror which hung above the imaginary hearth of her imaginary room in her imaginary world.

Martin knew that no one else in all the world could have seriously contemplated such an absurd project, even for a moment. He also knew, however, that no one else in all the world could have asked himself the question which sprung so readily to his own mind, and failed to find a ready answer.

The question was: *What alternative do I have?*

And the most horrifying thing of all was that he seemed to have none. No matter how long the task might take, and no matter what courage he would have to find, he could not imagine any other course of action; he could not see any other way.

The police had sealed the flat after the burglary – which had been reported, probably two or three days after the fact, by a neighbour. The police, or perhaps the neighbour, had made some slight attempt to tidy up before nailing the door shut, but they had not been able to do much to improve its appearance. The burglars, having had the leisure to do whatever they pleased, had taken care to wreck everything that they had not cared to steal. They had smashed the furniture and the light-fittings, fouled the carpet, slashed to ribbons the clothes in the chest of drawers and the linen on the bed, and daubed the papered walls with obscene graffiti.

Martine, discharged from the hospital only that morning, stood in the doorway with the policewoman, silently surveying the wreckage of her private world. Her gaze moved steadily back and forth, taking in everything, before coming to rest on the mirror above the hearth. The thieves had not taken it, because it was so evidently worthless, but they had taken the trouble to smash it. The wooden frame was still intact, but the thin backing had been splintered, and the silvered glass lay in smithereens, scattered about the marbled platform which still remained in front of the blocked-up grate.

"It's a terrible mess, I'm afraid," said the policewoman, awkwardly.

"Yes," said Martine, "it certainly is."

"If you could put together a list of missing items...for us, and for the insurers. Anything identifiable....well, you never know. I'm sorry it had to happen while you were in the hospital. Not much of a homecoming."

The policewoman was obviously highly embarrassed;

clearly, she knew what kind of an operation Martine had undergone.

"You needn't stay," Martine told her. "There's a lot to do. I can cope."

She waited patiently until the policewoman had exhausted her capacity for polite procrastination, and departed. She contrived to close the door, and to wedge it shut. Then she threw her overnight bag on to the bed, and took off her coat, draping it over the back of the ruined settee.

She went unhurriedly to the fireplace, and lifted the mirror-frame down from the wall. She carefully laid it down on a part of the crazed surface of the coffee-table which was still flat. Then she began to pick up the larger shards of the mirror from the hearth, placing them one by one within the frame.

She made no attempt to fit the pieces together as they had been before the mirror was broken; she simply assembled them as best she could into a patchwork of sufficient dimensions to hold the image of a human face. She deliberately held back until she had enough pieces in place, and hesitated even then for a moment before she leaned forward, to look down at her reflection as though she were looking down into a pool of water dappled by shadows.

Her reflection met her eyes, frankly and openly.

She saw, somewhat to her surprise, that she was weeping. It took her a few moments to recall that it was entirely appropriate that she should weep, because she was mourning the dead. She remembered, not without difficulty, that there had been another room contained in that mirror, once upon a time: a dingy, second-hand room, inhabited by a sad, frightened and incomplete young man. But he had been killed: cut up and destroyed, too evidently worthless to be carried away into the world.

When an empty minute had passed, she wiped her eyes. She knew that she had little enough time for mourning. First, there was the door to fix, and a new lock to be fitted. Then, there were very many purchases to be made. It all had to be planned, in order of necessity. It would not be easy, because her resources were strictly limited, but it could be done, in time. Everything which needed to be done could be accomplished, given time and resolution.

She knew that she had the time; she had learned the art of patience.

She knew that she had the resolution; she had learned how not to give up.

She knew that she could rebuild the apparatus of her life, if that was what had to be done.

As she carefully separated the shards of the mirror, breaking up her reflected image, Martine remembered that it was Monday. There would be an auction that afternoon in the saleroom down the road. There, where the detritus of lives obliterated by death or destitution was recycled into the lives of the living, she would be able to find everything she needed to furnish a new and better life.

BLUE ALICE
by
Steve Rasnic Tem

In Johnsonville, when you were born, more than likely you landed in Blue Alice's pale, beautiful hands. More than likely, too, she had a big say in your naming, and what was the first solid food they gave you, maybe even how they cut your hair or what clothes you wore your first day of school. When you were sick it would be Blue Alice standing by your bed with her homemade remedies. When you were looking for a mate or an opportunity she was always waiting there to be consulted, bribed, or begged.

And when you died, your body stretched out and exposed on a table, it was probably Blue Alice who washed your body, making sure you were clean enough of the world's dirt and pain to make that final journey.

People spoke in hushed tones around Blue Alice, and they didn't call her Blue Alice to her face, either. To her face it was always "ma'am" or "Mizz Wallace". The story was it was somebody's grandmother who, terrified to see Mizz Wallace approaching the house like Death himself coming, and taking note of the bluish halo around her mouth and eyes (like ordinary folks' air just wasn't good enough for her), she'd cried out, "Don't let Blue Alice in the house! Oh Lord, I'm not ready yet!" And the name had stuck.

Brian Thomas was only ten years old, but he had seen Blue Alice in all her forms. She was the midwife who'd guided him into this world (and his momma swore he screamed twice as loud once he saw Blue Alice's face). She was also the one who found his big sister Jennie a husband (he beat her half to death a year ago) and found his daddy a good piece of land to buy with a brand new barn already standing on it (the barn burned to the ground a week after the sale). She'd been the one to treat his daddy with her herbs and liquids and mud packs and leeches when he'd first caught the fever.

And now Blue Alice was on her way to their house once more, this time to bathe the body of Brian's daddy resting lifeless in there on the dining room table.

Brian hid in his bedroom with a box of crackers and a comic book. He wasn't about to come out until Blue Alice had left. He was looking around his room for the best places to hide if she forced her way through his door. Then he heard the porch boards creaking.

He crawled over to his window and pulled aside an edge of curtain. And watched as Blue Alice did her little dance out in front of the door.

Dip and twist and shuffle shuffle shuffle. Slow as a dream, stiff as a machine. Blue Alice made her way several times up and down the porch. Brian would have laughed, but he just couldn't bring himself to laugh at anything Blue Alice did. She did her dance several more times before finally stopping before the door again and striking it once, twice with the palm of her massive left hand. He could hear his mother scurrying through the front room to answer the summons.

"Mizz Wallace, I'm so grateful you could come." The fear in his mother's voice made Brian slightly ill. "He's...he's in the dining room. On the table." Brian got a funny picture in his head of his daddy all laid out on the table like he was dinner, mashed potatoes piled around his face and a big cooked tomato stuffed in his mouth. And Blue Alice, looking so hungry, picking up a fork and the table knife. Then he could hear his mother's footsteps padding softly away to the bedroom she had shared with Brian's father for more than twelve years.

Brian tried to imagine what Blue Alice was doing now, what her face looked like, what she would be thinking, but couldn't, any more than he could know what a tree or a mountain might be thinking.

He'd seen Blue Alice with other people, though, and knew that pretty much everybody in Johnsonville had the same problems where she was concerned. Once old lady Smythe had had some kind of argument with her. Something about a calf Blue Alice had delivered for her, born with something terrible wrong with it, but Mrs Smythe never exactly specified what, at least not in public.

Usually people delivered their own livestock – it had to have been a pretty sticky situation for them to call Blue Alice in like that.

"You done somethin' to it!" he remembered Mrs Smythe yelling. "It just ain't right! And that price you charged me ain't right neither!"

"I charge what I charge," Blue Alice had said, low and hard, and Brian remembered how glad he had been that Blue Alice wasn't looking at him the way she was looking at Mrs Smythe.

Mrs Smythe never did have another good calf, or lamb, or foal born on her farm after that. Brian heard that she even had trouble paying people enough money to help bury the things that came squirming out of those poor animal's wombs.

But for all that, Brian guessed that most men would think Blue Alice a beautiful woman, from the little he knew about such things. Her hair was long and looked like fine silk thread, and her skin so pale and soft he could imagine falling right into it, getting lost there, never coming out. The rest of her seemed equally soft, and full, and brought Brian secret stirrings when he looked at her too long. What's worse, he always felt that Blue Alice knew he was looking at her, and why.

So it wasn't too surprising that Blue Alice had her suitors, new fellas in town who didn't know that much about her, who followed her around town for a time like lonely pups.

He remembered one such fellow by the name of Jacobs, who came into town selling kitchen gadgets. It wasn't long before he was bringing Blue Alice all kinds of presents.

"Damn fool," Brian's father had said, one day when they saw the two of them together in town. "He'll be lucky if he still has his hide when she's done with him. Once she's picked you there ain't no escape." Then his daddy made this funny little grimace, like he wasn't joking, like he had seen it all before.

Dip and twist and shuffle shuffle shuffle.

Mr. Jacobs had looked real funny to Brian that day, his face all scrubbed and scraped till he was pink as a baby's bottom, his hair brushed back so hard Brian was sure it must hurt something awful. Jacobs had a dazed expression on his face, and moved in a stagger, his steps following Blue Alice's steps down the street,

231

his movements a perfect match to hers. At first Brian wondered if maybe he was making fun of her, but that would have been really crazy. Then he thought maybe the man was hypnotised, like that magician had done when he visited the school that time. But Brian somehow knew it was much more than that, something he didn't even want to think about.

He never saw Mr. Jacobs again after that day, and relatives came through town looking but with no luck, but once he was standing by Blue Alice at the grocery store – he didn't want to, but it was so crowded it was the only place to stand – and he was looking at her shawl, and in the busy pattern that ran around its edge he saw the brushed back hair, the bewildered eyes, and the long awkward legs, and then he knew what Blue Alice had done with Mr. Jacobs.

There was a loud sniffing on the other side of Brian's door, like a cat sniffing out a mouse. He started to hide but then the voice came from underneath: "Come on out, boy. I'm gonna need your help with your daddy." Then Brian knew it wasn't going to do any good to hide – once she's picked you there's no escape – and he opened the door to face her.

Blue Alice sniffed and coughed into her hand. "Do you ever bathe, boy?"

Brian nodded mutely.

"Well, there's not much indication of it." She took a deep breath like she was swelling up. "But nothing to be done about it now, I suppose. Come along with me."

His daddy was lying on the dining room table. Blue Alice pulled the sheet away to show his daddy's naked body. Brian gasped. His daddy was thinner than he remembered, a lot thinner. Like something had eaten him up from the inside. His daddy's ribs were showing, and they'd never showed before, and it looked like somebody had stolen the insides out of him.

"You look at him good, boy," Blue Alice said behind him. "That's what death looks like. Don't you ever forget it."

Brian wanted to cry but he couldn't. His crying had oozed down into the bottom of his throat and made a big knot there. He tried to swallow it away but he couldn't swallow at all. He heard familiar noises behind him and turned.

Dip and twist and shuffle shuffle shuffle.

Blue Alice's preparation of the body seemed to go on for hours. She kept Brian busy hauling in buckets of warm water from the kitchen stove. She explained that the water had to be a certain temperature in order to cleanse the body properly and because of the time it took her to wash down each section of skin (rubbing lightly, in tiny circles, she seemed to have a system but Brian couldn't tell what it was, but every now and then she would stop, rise to her full height, sigh, and dip and twist and shuffle shuffle shuffle) and because of the coldness of their house, the water quickly lost its ideal heat and had to be replaced. What was left in the rag after she washed his daddy's dead flesh she squeezed out into another large basin. Soon the liquid in that basin was pink and soupy, with little clouds of white floating here and there. Brian offered to empty it for her but she just looked at him and said, "Now don't you go doing that. Don't you know that that soup is all that's left of your daddy now?"

Pretty soon she was yelling at him to move faster and so he was splashing water all over the floor and he could hear his mother sobbing behind the closed door of his parents' bedroom.

He saw Blue Alice gazing at the door where his mother's crying made a low, broken music and then she looked at him and nodded. "Sometimes a grief like that will make you dead," she said. "She dies, you come live with me. Okay, boy?"

Then she looked at his parent's door again, as if she were considering things, then she went back to her crazy, careful washing of his daddy's dead body, and her dip and twist and shuffle shuffle shuffle.

Brian didn't let her out of his sight after that, keeping his head turned her way even as he trotted back and forth to the kitchen. He didn't care how much water he spilled, or how much Blue Alice cursed him for doing it.

His daddy's body seemed to get paler and paler as Blue Alice washed it, and the stuff squeezed off into the basin thicker and thicker, until in some parts you could practically see through his daddy's skin. And the paler it got the less it seemed to weigh – on one of his trips Brian barely brushed his father's thigh and

233

the whole body seemed to lift. Any second now Brian half expected his daddy's body to float up off the table and join the cobwebs on the ceiling.

A ragged-looking, emaciated silver squirrel came to the open kitchen window. Brian started to chase it away.

"Stop that, boy," Blue Alice said low, but firm. "I know that one, I do." And the squirrel bounded in and crouched under the dining room table, waiting.

Brian went for some more water and heard the shuffling begin again. Dip and twist. He edged around the doorway and saw Blue Alice remove a tiny tomato – red and juicy as blood – from his daddy's mouth and offer it to the squirrel. The squirrel backed away and Blue Alice pocketed the tomato, chuckling.

Later she had Brian put down some milk and cut apples for the horrible-looking thing. The squirrel staggered over to the food like an old man on his last legs, then pounced on the meal suddenly, greedily.

Late into the evening Brian thought he could see the dark lump that was his daddy's heart through the pale window his skin had become. Dip and twist and shuffle shuffle shuffle.

Blue Alice removed two more tiny tomatoes from his daddy's throat.

The raggedy silver squirrel squealed crazily, racing back and forth under the table that held his daddy's body.

Blue Alice sent Brian out into the icy woods behind the house to gather some pine cones and boughs. He didn't want to go, but he didn't know how to avoid it. On his way back with an armful he stopped outside the dining room window and peeked inside.

Blue Alice stood at the head of the body, her arms stretched out like a huge dark bird's wings. She took a deep breath and rose up on the tips of her toes. Her head started to warp and expand, her chest flowing out of the front of her gown and across the floor. Brian didn't know what she was, except maybe a bundle of furious shadows, and a huge mouth, which now had the biggest and reddest tongue he could imagine dropping down over his daddy's face, the tip of it pushing his daddy's lips aside and entering his mouth, turning and turning like a bloody whirlwind as it twisted its way deep into his daddy's throat. And finally came out again wrapped around four more small, slimy red tomatoes.

Then she stepped back, shrinking rapidly back down to normal. She waved to the squirrel, who immediately raced up on his daddy's body and down his throat, coming back out seconds later red and wet and with his daddy's heart locked tight in the squirrel's narrow jaws. The squirrel ran back out the kitchen window with the heart and Brian came back into the house trying hard to act like nothing had happened.

Blue Alice was waiting for him, looking usual enough, a bowl of the small shiny tomatoes in her hand.

"You give these to your ma," she said. "They're real good in salads." Brian just nodded and put the bowl on the kitchen counter. "Now you just give me that greenery and wait in the kitchen. This looks like enough." She paused and looked down at the large basin of squeezings. She stooped and dipped her hand in it. "Getting cold. Why don't you take it and put it up on top that old stove of your mother's? Don't let it boil, mind you. Just let it simmer awhile."

Brian did as he was told, but couldn't resist peeking around the door frame to watch Blue Alice stuff bough after bough down his daddy's throat until his daddy started looking full again. Blue Alice never looked directly up at him, but he knew she knew he was watching her the whole time.

Brian turned back to the stove and started to stir the thick pale pink mess in the basin. He looked over at the counter. Taking up a sharp knife he chopped up the bowl of tomatoes Blue Alice had given him and dropped them into the stew.

Dip and twist and shuffle shuffle shuffle.

"All done in here," she called. "Your daddy sure looks pretty! And smells just like the green forest in springtime, he does. Now bring me in that basin!"

A few minutes later, while Blue Alice was drinking the stew in one gulp, Brian moved back and forth behind her, singing a monotonous tune to himself as he moved: dip and twist, dip and twist, shuffle shuffle, shuffle shuffle shuffle.

235

SELF-SACRIFICE
by
Francis Amery

There is a ritual element to matters of this kind, which must be carefully observed. It is important that you make the correct selection, most particularly on this occasion, and the search – however uncomfortable it may be – must not be hurried.

It does no good to drive slowly along the usual streets, scanning the dim-lit ranks of careerist whores; authentic professionals are no use at all, however fresh and lean and tender they may appear to be. Girls of the right kind are never to be found on the usual pitches. The regulars will not tolerate them, not because they consider them to be competition (although they may be had cut price) but because they worry about the reputation of their streets, and do not wish them to become known as places where addicts ply their trade. In the civilized heartland of whoredom there is no worse strategy than to take one's stand in an area which is moving downmarket; the honest tradeswomen who take a pride in being service sector professionals, who believe and hope that they are clean and wish to advertise their cleanliness – honestly or not – must at all costs steer clear of the dead-enders who are past caring about what they pick up or what they pass on, or anything at all except the magic powder which sets them free.

To find what you need, you must go where the derelicts go, into the Underworld beyond and beneath the enterprise culture, and there you must search with infinite care for your Eurydice. You must go deeper, into the innermost circles of Hell, in search of the derelict and the desperate, to find a girl who is not merely child-like but so exclusively dependent on her regular fix that she has utterly abandoned all self-regard.

There is no functional necessity in this, of course – she will undoubtedly be positive, as you are, and that may be taken for granted – but in matters of this kind aesthetic priorities are paramount and it is aesthetic necessity which governs your choice.

You are duty bound to celebrate each anniversary as though

it were the last – as indeed it might be.

When you do find her, she will be initially reluctant to go with you; that is inevitable. She is in Hell, but she is with the devils she knows, and you are a devil she does not. It is not that she fears what you might do to her; if she fits your requirements she will not be afraid of any kind of imaginable physical abuse, or being killed. What she fears is losing her connection. Her worst nightmare is that she might find herself in a place she does not know, where she does not know how to score. What she wants to do is to get into the front seat of your car and suck you off as fast as she possibly can, so that she can run with her wrinkled ten pound note to some pit of shadow where the Candy Demon always waits, ever-ready to do business. When you tell her that you want something very different, she is certain to hesitate. Even if you showed her five notes instead of one she would hesitate. So you show her something else: something white.

It wouldn't have to be genuine, if all you needed was to draw her into the car. If the quantity were right, the mere possibility would be promise enough; even here, hope has power enough to conquer cynicism. But in ritual matters of this kind, authenticity is of paramount importance. When you show her the heroin, it must be real.

Everything must be *real*.

Ideally, the girl should be intelligent. She would listen to you anyway, and her attentiveness will be mere performance in either case – it would be far too much to hope that she might *care* – but if she is intelligent, she will more fully understand what you say, and that is good. It does not matter what her reaction is – she will probably think you are mad, even if she does not say so aloud – but in this day and age almost everyone holds the opinion that almost everyone else is mad; that is always the last defiant claim of an imagination which can no longer cope with the enormity and ugliness of the world.

After all, there is a strong case to support the claim that everyone is mad, or at least deluded. We think that we're in charge of ourselves and our lives, but we aren't. Those few who try to do their best for their loved ones, and for mankind, never do what needs to be done, and never even permit themselves to recognise what needs to be done. We can't control our fundamental urges and impulses well enough to render them harmless. If the world is moving, at last, in the direction of sanity, it is no thanks to Everyman; he is simply a fool and a madman, fiddling while the Human Empire burns. Nor, in spite of everything you have done, may you count yourself a shining exception. You can't avoid your share of the guilt, your share of the sin, your share of the madness. You must remember that, today of all days. You're no better than anyone else.

Once she has been lured into the back seat of the car she immediately becomes a prisoner of the child-proof locks. It doesn't matter whether she is aware of it or not. She is in any case a prisoner of evil circumstance. The plush seats of the BMW have merely brought a poignant hint of luxury into the cold rigour of her meagre existence.

You study her carefully in the rear-view mirror. Such are the boundless benefits of modern-day technology and the scientific perspective. Orpheus did not know what was happening behind him, and could not resist the temptation to look around as soon as he thought – wrongly – that it was safe to do so. You have a better understanding of the limits of possibility than he had, and your journeys into Hell always achieve their purpose.

This time, she is blonde, although it is not easy to tell because her hair is so dirty and hangs so raggedly about her face. The face is obviously good, though: thin and gaunt, with watery, haunted eyes. She wears an anorak and blue jeans, which hide her figure, but she is evidently half-starved. She has become accustomed to feeding her spirit rather than her body, and evidently knows well enough how superstitious conventional ideas about a heathy diet really are.

She is only five feet tall, possibly four-eleven. It is hard to tell how old she really is – perhaps as much as eighteen, or even twenty – but she *looks* fifteen. She will certainly pass for a child when she strips down, if only by virtue of her emaciation. Authenticity matters in this instance as in all others, but on this particular point authenticity is compromised by ambivalent circumstance. This is Sally's twenty-first birthday, and the ninth anniversary of her death. Her image in memory is both twelve and twenty-one, at one and the same time; she is child and woman both, just as she is dead and also – by virtue of her reflection in the rear-view mirror – still alive.

When you stop in the underground car park and let her out she looks warily around.

"Here?" she asks, wearily, as though it makes no difference at all to her.

"Upstairs," you say. "The thirteenth floor."

She follows you to the lift – after all, you have the plastic bag full of powder in your briefcase: the bread of Heaven, the staff which supports her precarious life. You have become, in her eyes, the Candy Demon, the deliverer of sweet oblivion. You are her Grim Reaper, her Father Time, bearing a cup instead of a scythe.

If only she knew what a Reaper you are! But she will know, later, when the time comes for the most sacred part of the ritual. Then, she will hear your confession and know what you are. She will not grant you absolution, and probably will not believe a word that you say, but she will hear the truth.

There is no gratitude in her eyes as she looks around the flat, no sense of wonder at all. If there is any speculation in her gaze it is a pathetic attempt to guess whether anything easily portable would be worth the effort of stealing it should the opportunity arise. Alas for her ambitions, there is a marked dearth of ornamentation, and nothing to be seen which is made of gold or silver. Your tastes and inclinations have become increasingly Spartan since you became a widower.

When you lead her into the bathroom she is resigned but faintly resentful; she has no notion of ritual cleansing, but she must know that her face will be fairer, and her hair silkier, and her body more pleasant to the touch, once the stain of the streets has been removed. Perhaps that is what she resents: the obligation to provide sensual pleasure. She ought to be grateful for the chance to take a bath, but she shows no sign of it as you run the water. She should be alert to the possibility that your purposes might coincide in some respect with her own desires, but her attention is so narrowly focused on the magic powder that

239

it has no scope for any other satisfaction.

She does not undress until you instruct her to do so, but she makes no complaint. She is not unduly ashamed or uncomfortable to be seen naked, nor to be soaped and scrubbed by your gentle hands. When you give her the clothes which you have set aside for her to wear she puts them on indifferently. She is not the kind of whore who plays parts like this as a matter of course, but she has heard her share of stories about the crazier kind of client and she is incapable of surprise. Perhaps she believes that she is acting out some stereotyped and vulgar cliché.

"I really need the stuff," she says, when it dawns on her that this may take some time, but she does not expect to obtain her reward so easily. You open the bathroom cabinet and show her the hypodermic, still in its sterile wrapping, and the rest of the apparatus, all ready for her. She has already seen the drug itself. For the first time some fugitive relic of her former curiosity urges her to say: "You a user?"

You shake your head. "It's all for you," you tell her. "You can take it all."

That makes her anxious; she has gauged the quantity and its value, and reckons this too generous a promise. She knows that she is not worth a tenth as much, on the open market, and wonders if she has been taken for a ride.

"Where'd you get it?" she asks, suspiciously.

"I'm a doctor," you tell her. "It's easy for me. I can get hold of any quantity without having to account for it. I cut it myself. It's perfectly safe."

Her fears are not altogether quieted. It is in her mind that she might, after all, have been brought here to suffer some hideous ill-treatment, perhaps cruel enough to break down the sturdy wall of her indifference to harm. But she knows that it is too late to pay attention to such possibilities. She allows herself to be shepherded back into the sitting-room, squirming as she tries to make herself comfortable in the party dress which was made for a little girl.

Then you bring out the birthday cake, and light the candle, and display yourself for the harmless eccentric that you really are.

There are twenty-one candles: twelve white, nine black. You hesitate before explaining, hoping that she might be clever enough to deduce what is happening, to provide the beginning of the story herself. Perhaps she is – might that be a flicker of comprehension in her weak, red-rimmed eye? – but if she is, she will not voice her conclusions.

"My daughter," you say, as tenderly as you can, "would have been twenty-one today, if she had not died. I always have a party."

She nods. She thinks she understands. She knows how small and thin she is, and what kind of clothes she has been given to put on – although she does not know as yet precisely what she might be asked to do, if anything, when she takes them off again.

"Your name," you say, "is Sally."

She has sufficient sense of occasion not to contradict you. In fact, she reveals a certain flair for the dramatic by asking: "What did I die of?"

She is probably thinking of something like leukaemia. It is tragically romantic when children die of leukaemia. She is probably hoping that the answer is tragically romantic, because that will reassure her about the nature of the pantomime in which she has been invited to play a leading part.

"You were murdered," you say, staring at her face to catch her reaction. Because she has relaxed her guard a little, she does react, but the shock is subdued; her emotions are still anaesthetised, although she certainly needs her fix.

"You were knocked off your bicycle by a drunken driver," you explain. "You fractured your skull, broke your pelvis and ruptured your spleen, in addition to various minor injuries. It was a Sunday afternoon. The driver was a childless housewife aged 39, who had nothing better to do with her time than commit the occasional desultory adultery and drink herself stupid. She was banned from driving for four years but the judge thought that a custodial sentence would be inappropriate, presumably because she was middle class."

"Oh," she says.

"It was your birthday," you add, bleakly. "You died on your birthday."

241

"Oh," she says, again.

"It destroyed your mother. She wouldn't have caved in so soon, if it hadn't been for that. She'd have been stronger."

This time, she doesn't even bother to say "oh".

You sit down beside her. You have to blow out the candles yourself, before you cut the cake. You offer her a neatly-cut slice whose size is judged to perfection, and she looks down at it suspiciously. It is a sponge cake, dyed in pastel shades, with thick, soft, white icing and glutinous synthetic cream.

"You don't have eat it if you don't want to," you say, amicably. "I didn't bring you all the way up here just to eat cake. In a little while I'm going to fuck you, and then I'll give you the stuff. But it won't hurt to eat. Please."

This confirmation of the game plan helps her to relax. Perhaps she sighs with relief, thinking that it all makes more sense now, and that the ritual is crazy in an altogether commonplace sort of way. She thinks about saying: "Did you used to fuck your daughter?" but she doesn't. She isn't as impudent as some of her predecessors, although her thoughts run along the same lines.

"No," you say, as though she *had* asked. "I didn't ever fuck you while you were alive. I wanted to, very much, but I never did. I thought that it would constitute child abuse, and might cause you to have psychological problems in later life. If I could have been confident that you would continue to love me, I might have taken the risk, but I wasn't. Incest and child molestation get such a bad press, you see, and I wasn't able to assess the accuracy of the common opinion that girls fucked by their fathers always hate the experience. I didn't want you to hate me, so I never took my opportunities while you were alive. Now that you're dead, it's much easier. I don't have to feel guilty about the fucking – only about the fact that it gives me a reason, however small, to be grateful that you were killed. If you were still alive, I probably never would have fucked you, unless you had gone out of your way to seduce me. I'm sure that happens, sometimes, but it may be just wistful thinking."

If she notices the play on words she doesn't react.

"Aren't you having any?" she asks, before taking the first bite out of her slice of cake.

242

You shake your head. "I never do," you say. "It's for you."

She is still suspicious, but she eats the slice of cake. She disposes of it rapidly, but not avidly; it is not greed which moves her but a desire to get on with things. Her attention is fixed on the moment when she will be given the superabundant supply of heroin, with which she gratefully will hammer one more figurative nail into her coffin.

The sugar in the icing and the cream conceals the bitter taste of the muscle relaxant. The dose is precisely calculated, as it invariably is, thanks to your long experience and profound respect for ritual. It will gradually rob her of the power of movement, but it will do no real damage, and she will remain fully conscious. It is necessary that she lies still, not in order that you might fuck her – she would, of course, lie still for that anyway – but in order that she will not become restive afterwards, when she must listen to what you have to say. She will be impatient for her overdue fix, but a vital part of the price will still remain to be paid, and it is necessary that everything should run smoothly.

"I loved you, Sally," you tell her, while the drug takes effect. "I loved you with a devotion and a passion which you probably cannot imagine. The sexual component of that love was only a tiny part of it – a belated extension of something much vaster and more profound. I loved you even before you were born, when you were merely an unformed idea. I am elderly, as you can see; I had long planned to have a child, in spite of the terrible state of the world, but I felt – deeply and sincerely – that I was not entitled to do so unless and until I had first accomplished something that would make the world a better place. I took my duties as a father seriously, you see. I still do. Everything I did in those distant days I did for love: for love of the wife I had and the daughter I intended to have, for love of all the wives and daughters which good men and true would have. I could never care as much for my fellow men; I could not help but feel that they were the ones who had made Hell on Earth, while women and girls were merely their victims. I have always loved women – the *idea* of womanhood."

She opens her mouth to reply. It is bound to be something

sarcastic; a person like her is incapable of understanding what you have just said, and incapable of sympathising with it even if she did. Persons of her kind have no sentimentality left in them – but that is not her fault. She too was a child once: an *authentic* child. It is the world which has made her into what she is, obliterating all the potential beauty with which her mind and heart once overflowed. She is, after all, the victim on whose behalf you have laboured all your life. She is the reason, the daughter, the idea.

She finds it unexpectedly difficult to speak. She hasn't yet lost her voice entirely, but she can't quite formulate the mocking words she intended to use.

You stand, and pick her up. She weighs very little; you have no difficulty in lifting her and cradling her in your arms. Just for an instant, anxiety makes her cling to you, as if you were indeed her father, come at last to rescue her from sore distress, come to repair her anguish with the protective embrace of your arms. But she cannot sustain the effort, physically or spiritually.

You take her into the bedroom and you lay her out on the bed. You undress her, one precious garment at a time, lovingly and reverently. Then you undress yourself, looking down at her all the while.

She is not entirely devoid of a sense of duty. When she realises that you mean to fuck her without any protection, her eyes widen slightly, and the ghost of a frown creases her forehead. If she were able to mobilise her paralysed vocal cords she would warn you. In spite of what she thinks you are, she would warn you. She does not wish you dead.

"It doesn't matter," you say, soothingly, while stroking her pale cheek. "I'm positive. I've been positive for years. We belong, you and I, to the same legion of the damned."

And then, for a while, you say no more. Actions speak louder than words.

The purpose of ritual is to dignify a mere event and thus transform it into something more significant, something more meaningful. The purpose of ritual is to magnify thought and action, to elevate them to a higher plane, where the particular may become general and one lonely act of love may symbolise the love that all mankind has – or ought to have – for the world which gave them birth and gives them sustenance. Through ritual, the tawdry becomes noble, the ordinary becomes extraordinary, and the mundane becomes supernatural.

Because this intercourse is a ritual, mere appearance becomes irrelevant. This is not a drug-addicted whore at all; it is your daughter. It is the idea of your daughter, the ideal of your daughter, the idol of your daughter. What you are doing is no mere obscene performance, and what you will achieve is no mere release of libidinous frustration. This is the perfect act of love, the ultimate celebration, made glorious by its very impossibility.

The flesh which you touch is *her* flesh. It has *her* texture, *her* odour, *her* vivacity. The rapture which you feel is the rapture of communion with *her*.

This is no illusion, no pretence; this is *real*.

This is, in fact, the *only* reality; all else is false. The entire world in which you live and labour, save only for this, is but a delusion laid before your eyes by a mad and spiteful demon. You are in Hell, even here and even now, but for this one extended, infinite moment in time you have the ecstatic power to transform that Hell, to redeem the world from its desolation.

You delay the culmination of the process and the inevitable decay of ecstasy as long as possible, but you cannot delay it for long. The experience is too powerful; it is too great a gift to have your daughter released, if only for a few precious moments, from the world beyond the grave. You close your eyes, hoping against hope that if you obey the cunning injunction of the Prince of Hell you might keep what has been covenanted to you, but in the end it is impossible.

You, as a scientist, must respect that. The impossible remains, and always will remain, beyond your reach.

Afterwards, you make your confession. While she is still present and conscious – though lost and probably frightened, in the strange, lumpen, useless body which you have helped her to borrow for a little while – you tell her what you were never able to tell her while she was alive. You explain to her why you did what you did, for her and for the world.

"Long before you were born, Sally," you say, patiently, "it had become obvious to the enlightened few that the world was in deadly danger – that the Great Mother of us All was sick, and that her children had become her unwitting enemies. There were those who said that it was the machinery which had run out of control, that it was all to do with automation and the polluting excrement of factories, but men of my kind – the doctors, the biologists – knew that was false. We knew that men did not require heavy machinery to poison rivers and make deserts, that subsistence farmers cutting wood for cooking fires could devastate ecosystems as efficiently as the makers of motorways and diggers for oil. We knew that the real, underlying problem was simply a matter of numbers. We knew that the sole solution, however unpalatable it might be, was to reduce the size of the human population. We also knew, though, that the only people who would voluntarily accept the necessity of having fewer children, or none at all, were people like us, and that we were too few to make any material difference.

"You must understand, my darling, that this was a matter of inevitability. Those of us who understood were a tiny minority – perhaps one in every million – but there was no doubt about what we saw. The world was descending into ecocatastrophe, like a huge lorry careering down a steep slope, unstoppably. People were complacent, because the effects they saw around them seemed to be no more than a series of minor nuisances, but that is what a man thinks when a mosquito bites him, unaware that the malarial parasite is now in his blood, and that the havoc it will wreak, destroying his health and strength, is inevitable. The great majority of men have always been blind to the future, Sally. Even among those who can see, the majority feel themselves to be helpless, incapable of any constructive action save complaint.

"Only a few of us truly understood, and only a few within the few were prepared to act. Only a tiny, infinitely precious few, were prepared to take responsibility, to take upon themselves the burden of mankind's sins of omission and commission, to swallow the bitter pill of necessity. We had the means, in our laboratories; we had the will, because we loved the world, and loved our daughters; we had the courage, because we saw and understood that if we did not act, Mother Earth herself was lost.

"What was needed, my love, was a single vital move in the great game of life, which could save the world. We knew that no such salvation could be achieved overnight, or even in our lifetime, but we also knew that great oaks from little acorns grow, and that if only we could plant the right seed we might set in motion a train of events every bit as unstoppable as the juggernaut of world population. We had known for centuries what the three significant checks of population were: war, famine and plague. We were not the kind of men who could start wars, and famine was by then too blunt and powerless an instrument, but we were the kind of men who could engineer plagues. We were doctors, men who understood the elementary chemistry of genetics and disease. We had the knowledge and the technology required to devise and manufacture a new plague, and we had the intelligence to calculate exactly what kind of plague would do the job required of it.

"Our plague had to be the kind of disease which was immune to ordinary chemical defences; it had to be a virus rather than a bacterium. It had to be the kind of disease which would kill all but a tiny fraction of those who contracted it, but not quickly; the cleverest parasite is the one which does not destroy its hosts but carefully preserves its capacity to spread. It had, therefore, to be the kind of disease which could lie dormant for a long time, spreading through the population insidiously. It had to be the kind of disease which could evade the body's own natural defences, so that people would not easily acquire immunity to it, with or without the aid of inoculations to stimulate antibody production. We knew that however deadly our plague might be there would be *some* who would not die, because some would eventually reach a biochemical accommodation with the virus, but we knew that we had to ensure that only the strongest and the best were likely to survive to become the parents of a better, wiser, less prolific race.

"A group of a dozen men designed and created exactly such

a disease. We worked in secret, under no one's orders. No government was involved in what we did; we and we alone were responsible for what we did. We knew exactly what we were doing, and why. We did it for entirely selfless reasons – for the sake of our children and our children's children. We decided in advance that none of us should profit from what we had done, or try to evade its consequences. As soon as we were certain that we had engineered a virus which met all our specifications, we inoculated ourselves with it. We moved quickly to create other, far more efficient, centres of infection, but we did not shirk our own responsibilities. We could only justify inflicting what we had made upon our fellow men if we were willing to sacrifice ourselves, and that is what we did. We destroyed all the evidence of what we had done, including ourselves. We accepted destruction, to prove that what we had done we had done for the benefit of others and the salvation of our Mother, the Earth.

"All the members of that tiny regiment of unsung heroes are dead, save for me. I am the last. There is a reason for this, although I cannot deny that pure chance has played a large part in ensuring my survival. Once a person has been infected by the virus we invented, you see, it lies dormant for some time – perhaps two years, perhaps ten, and in rare cases indefinitely. All victims of the virus become participants in a great lottery, waiting for their turn to sicken and die, but the lottery is biased. People who are weak with hunger, or very young or very old, or who suffer from some other disease or genetic deficiency, are more vulnerable than those in the prime of life and the pink of condition. Psychological factors play a part too: those who are under stress, or chronically depressed, or emotionally unstable, are more vulnerable than those whose lives are on an even keel, who are calm of mind and buoyed up by a sense of purpose, and are not eaten away by guilt or remorse or bitterness.

"It was not obvious to me in the beginning that I would be the last survivor of the initial group, but I have proved to myself that I am a stronger man than I ever thought possible. When you died, I might have followed you into the grave, but I did not. I fought back against the vicious whim of fate. I reminded myself that I am a solver of problems, a man of achievement, a man who had taken it upon himself to save the world by obliterating the human surplus and preserving only the essential, only the best. I knew that I could undo the fact of your death, and its effect on me, if only I had the strength and the skill – *and I did*. I have brought you back from the Land of the Dead, from the deepest pit of Hell to its outskirts, its earthly borderlands. Year after year, I bring you back – and as long as you can return, I may stay.

"I was never able to tell you this while you were alive – I was never able to confess what I had done to *anyone*, because I had sworn a solemn oath. But the oath cannot apply to conversations with the dead, and so I have the opportunity to explain what I have done, to ease my conscience, to justify my decision. I wish with all my heart that you were not dead, my darling – I would far rather that you had taken your chance among the ranks of the living, perhaps to become the mother of a daughter yourself – but I cannot change places with you. This is the only way in which you can continue to live, and in order that you may have this, I too must continue to live. I *will* continue, as long as I can.

"I will see you next year, my darling girl."

When it's all over, you let her use the bathroom to shoot up. She is entitled to her reward and her privacy. She does not know that she was drugged; she believes that her sudden incapacity was mere exhaustion, a weakness of her own, simply one more arbitrary manifestation of the inexorable deterioration of her body and her mind. She is even grateful for it, because it made the fucking less burdensome for her, and postponed the clawing agony of her dependence.

She shows no sign of remembering anything which you said, although she was conscious throughout. Her memory has discarded it as though it were a dream. That is understandable, and appropriate; it wasn't, after all, this shabby, skinny prostitute to whom you were speaking.

As you finally show her to the door she looks down, hesitantly, at the plastic bag full of white powder which she is trying to conceal about her person. There is such an abundance of magic there, such a cornucopia of promises.

She looks up at you, not afraid now that she is high to take a risk. Her caution is thrown to the winds on which she soars.

"I could stay," she said. "As long as you like. I'd *be* your daughter. I'd be anything and everything you wanted. You said you could get the stuff – that it was easy."

"It wouldn't work," you say, softly and paternally, as you open the door to let her out. "It couldn't work. You see, *you're dead*."

She curls her lip, abruptly transforming her impression from innocent, pleading temptation to malevolent, contemptuous wrath, and says: "You and me both, motherfucker."

And she is right: positively, inevitably, decisively right. But thanks to you, the world will one day be saved.

THE GLAMOUR
by
Thomas Ligotti

It had long been my practice to wander late at night and often
to attend movie theatres at this time. But something else was
involved on the night I went to that theatre in a part of town I had
never visited before. A new tendency, a mood or penchant formerly unknown to me, seemed to lead the way. It is difficult to
say anything precise about this mood that overcame me,
because it seemed to belong to my surroundings as much as to
myself. As I advanced further into the part of town I had never
visited before, my attention was drawn to a certain aspect of
things – a fine aura of fantasy radiating from the most common
sights, places and objects that were both blurred and brightened
as they projected themselves into my vision.

Despite the lateness of the hour, there was an active glow cast
through so many of the shop windows in that part of town. Along
one particular avenue, the starless evening was glazed by these
lights, these diamonds of plate glass set within old buildings of
dark brick. I paused before the display window of a toy store and
was entranced by a chaotic tableau of preposterous excitation.
My eyes followed several things at once: the fated antics of
mechanized monkeys that clapped tiny cymbals or somersaul-
ted uncontrollably; the destined pirouettes of a music box bal-
lerina; the grotesque wobbling of a newly sprung jack-in-the-
box. The inside of the store was a Christmas-tree clutter of
merchandise receding into a background that looked shadowed
and empty. An old man with a smooth pate and angular eyebrows stepped forward to the front window and began rewind-
ing some of the toys to keep them in ceaseless gyration. While
performing this task he suddenly looked up at me, his face
expressionless.

I moved down the street, where other windows framed little
worlds so strangely picturesque and so dreamily illuminated in
the shabby darkness of that part of town. One of them was a
bakery whose window display was a gallery of sculptured
frosting, a winter landscape of swirling, drifting whiteness, of

251

snowy rosettes and layers of icy glitter. At the centre of the glacial kingdom was a pair of miniature people frozen atop a many-tiered wedding cake, but beyond the brilliant arctic scene I saw only the deep blackness of an establishment that kept short hours. Standing outside another window nearby, I was uncertain if the place was open for business or not. A few figures were positioned here and there within faded lighting reminiscent of an old photograph, though it seemed they were beings of the same kind as the window dummies of this store, which apparently trafficked in dated styles of clothing. Even the faces of the mannikins, as a glossy light fell upon them, wore the placidly enigmatic expressions of a different time.

Actually, there were several places doing business at that hour of the night and in that part of town, however scarce potential customers appeared to be on this particular street. I saw no one enter or exit the many doors along the sidewalk; a canvass awning that some proprietor had neglected to roll up for the night was flapping in the wind. Nevertheless, I did sense a certain vitality around me and felt the kind of acute anticipation that a child might experience at a carnival, where each lurid attraction incites fantastic speculations, while unexpected desires arise for something which has no specific qualities in the imagination yet seems to be only a few steps away. My mood had not abandoned me but only grew stronger, a possessing impulse without object.

Then I saw the marquis for a movie theatre. It was something I might easily have passed by, for the letters spelling out the name of the theatre were broken and unreadable. The title on the marquis was similarly damaged, as though stones had been thrown at it and a series of attempts made to efface the words that I finally deciphered.

The feature being advertised that night was called "The Glamour."

When I reached the front of the theatre I found that the row of doors forming the entrance had been barricaded by crosswise planks with notices posted upon them warning that the building had been condemned. This action had apparently been taken some time ago, judging by the weathered condition of the boards

252

that blocked my way and the dated appearance of the notices stuck upon them. In any case, the marquis was still illuminated, albeit rather poorly, so I was not surprised to see a double-faced sign propped up on the sidewalk, an inconspicuous little board that read: ENTRANCE TO THE THEATRE. Beneath these words was an arrow pointing into an alleyway which separated the theatre from the remaining buildings on the block. Peeking into the otherwise solid facade of that particular street, I saw only a long, narrow corridor with a single light set far into its depths. The light shone with a strange shade of purple, like that of a freshly exposed heart, and appeared to be positioned over a doorway leading into the theatre.

It had long been my practice to attend movie theatres late at night, and I reminded myself of this. Whatever reservations I felt at the time were easily overcome by a new surge of the mood I was experiencing that night in a part of town I had never visited before.

The purple lamp did indeed mark a way into the theatre, casting a kind of arterial light upon a door that reiterated the word "entrance." Stepping inside, I entered a tight hallway where the walls glowed a deep pink, very similar in shade to that little beacon in the alley but reminding me more of a richly blooded brain than a beating heart. At the end of the hallway I could see my reflection in a ticket window, and on approaching it I noticed that those walls so close to me were veiled from floor to ceiling with what appeared to be cobwebs. Similar cobwebs were strewn upon the carpet leading to the ticket window: wispy shrouds that did not scatter as I walked over them. It was as if they had securely bound themselves to the carpet's worn and shallow fibre, or were growing out of it like postmortem hairs on a corpse.

There was no one behind the ticket window, no one I could see in that small space of darkness beyond the blur of purple-tinted glass in which my reflection was held. Nevertheless, a ticket was protruding from a slot beneath the semi-circular cutaway at the bottom of the window, sticking out like a paper tongue. A few hairs lay beside it.

"Admission is free," said a man who was now standing in the

253

doorway beside the ticket booth. His suit was well-fitted and neat, but his face appeared somehow in a mess, bristled over all its contours. His tone was polite, even passive, when he said, "The theatre is under new ownership."

"Are you the manager?" I asked.

"I was just on my way to the rest room."

Without further comment he drifted off into the darkness of the theatre. For a moment something floated in the empty space he left in the doorway – a swarm of filaments like dust that scattered or settled before I stepped through. And in those first few seconds inside, the only thing I could see were the words "rest room" glowing above a door as it slowly closed.

I manoeuvred with caution until my sight became sufficient to the dark and allowed me to find a door leading to the auditorium of the movie theatre. But once inside, as I stood at the summit of a sloping aisle, all previous orientation to my surroundings underwent a setback. The room was illuminated by an elaborate chandelier centered high above the floor, as well as a series of light fixtures along either of the side walls. I was not surprised by the dimness of the lighting, nor by its hue, which made shadows appear faintly bloodshot – a sickly, liverish shade that might be witnessed in an operating room where a torso lies open on the table, its entrails a palette of pinks and reds and purples...diseased viscera imitating all the shades of sunset.

However, my perception of the theatre auditorium remained problematic – not because of any oddities of illumination but for another reason. I experienced no difficulty in mentally registering the elements around me – the separate aisles and rows of seats, the curtain-flanked movie screen, the well-noted chandelier and wall lights – but it seemed impossible to gain a sense of these objects, and the larger scene they comprised, in simple accord with their appearances. I saw nothing that I have not described, yet...the round-backed seats were at the same time rows of headstones in a graveyard; the aisles were endless filthy alleys, long desolate corridors in an old asylum, or the dripping passages of a sewer receding into the distance; the pale movie screen was a dust-blinded window in a dark unvisited cellar, a mirror gone rheumy with age in an abandoned house; the chandelier and smaller fixtures were the facets of murky crystals embedded in the sticky walls of an unknown cavern. In other words, this movie theatre was merely a virtual image, a veil upon a complex collage of other places, all of which shared certain qualities that were projected into my vision, as though the things I saw were possessed by something I could not see.

But as I lingered in the theatre auditorium, settling in a seat toward the back wall, I realised that even on the level of plain appearances there was a peculiar phenomenon I had not formerly observed, or at least had yet to perceive to its fullest extent. I am speaking of the cobwebs.

When I first entered the theatre I saw them clinging to the walls and carpeting. Now I saw how much they were a part of the theatre and how I had mistaken the nature of these long pale threads. Even in the hazy purple light, I could discern that they had penetrated into the fabric of the seats in the theatre, altering the weave in its depths and giving it a slight quality of movement, the slow curling of thin smoke. It seemed the same with the movie screen, which might have been a great rectangular web, tightly woven and faintly in motion, vibrating at the touch of some unseen force. I thought: "Perhaps this subtle and pervasive *wriggling* within the theatre may clarify the tendency of its elements to suggest other things and other places utterly unlike a simple theatre auditorium – a process parallel to the ever-mutating images of dense clouds." All textures in the theatre appeared similarly affected, without control over their own nature, but I could not clearly see as high as the chandelier. Even some of the others in the audience, which was small and widely scattered about the auditorium, were practically invisible to my eyes.

Furthermore, there may have been something in my mood that night, given my sojourn in a part of town I had never been, that influenced what I was able to see. And this mood had become steadily enhanced since I first stepped into the theatre, and indeed from the moment I first looked upon the marquis advertising a feature entitled "The Glamour." Having at last found a place among the quietly expectant audience, I began to suffer an exacerbation of this mood. Specifically, I sensed a greater proximity to the point of focus for my mood that night, a tingling closeness to something quite literally *behind the scene*. Increasingly I became unconcerned with anything except the consummation or terminus of this abject and enchanting adventure. Consequences were evermore difficult to regard from my tainted perspective.

For these reasons, I was not hesitant when this focal point for my mood suddenly felt near at hand, as close as the seat directly behind my own. I was quite sure this seat had been empty when I selected mine, that all the seats for several rows around me were unoccupied, and I would have been aware if someone had arrived to fill this seat directly behind me. Nevertheless, like a sudden chill announcing bad weather, there was now a definite presence I could feel at my back, a force of sorts that pressed itself upon me and inspired a surge of dark elation. But when I looked around, not quickly yet fully determined, I saw no occupant in the seat behind me, nor in any seat between me and the back wall of the theatre.

I continued to stare at the empty seat, because my sensation of a vibrant presence there was unrelieved. And while staring, I perceived that the fabric of the seat, the inner webbing of swirling fibres, had composed a pattern in the image of a face: an old woman's face with an expression of avid malignance, floating amidst wild shocks of twisting hair. The face itself was a portrait of atrocity, a grinning image of lust for sites and ceremonies of disfigurement. It was formed of those hairs stitching themselves together.

All the stringy, writhing cobwebs of that theatre, as I now discovered, were the reaching tendrils of a vast netting of hairs. By virtue of this discovery, my mood of the evening – which had delivered me to a part of the town I had never been and to that very theatre – became yet more expansive and defined, taking in scenes of graveyards and alleyways, reeking sewers and wretched corridors of insanity, as well as the immediate vision of an old theatre that now, as I had been told, was under new ownership. But my mood abruptly faded, along with the face in the fabric of the theatre seat, when a voice spoke to me.

"You must have seen her, by the looks of you."

A man sat down one seat away from mine. It was not the same person I had met earlier; this one's face was nearly unblemished, although his suit was littered with hair that was not his own.

"So did you see her?"

"I'm not sure what I saw."

He seemed almost to burst out giggling, his voice trembling on the edge of a joyous hysteria. "You would be sure enough if there had been a private encounter, I can tell you."

"Something was happening, then you sat down."

"Sorry," he said. "Did you know that the theatre has just come under new ownership?"

"I didn't notice what the showtimes are."

"Showtimes?"

"For the feature."

"Oh, there isn't any feature. Not as such."

"But there must be...something," I insisted.

"Yes, there's something," he replied excitedly, his fingers stroking his cheek.

"What, exactly? And these cobwebs..."

But the lights were going down into darkness. "Quiet now," he whispered. "It's about to begin."

The screen before us was glowing a pale purple in the blackness, although I heard no sounds from the machinery of a movie projector. Neither were there any sounds connected with the images which were beginning to take form on the screen, as if a lens were being focused on a microscopic world. In some mysterious way, the movie screen might have been a great glass slide which magnified to gigantic proportions a realm of organisms normally hidden from our sight – but as these visions coalesced and clarified, I recognised them as something I had already seen, or more accurately *sensed*, in that theatre. The images were appearing on the screen as if a pair of disembodied eyes were moving within venues of profound morbidity and degeneration. Here were the reflections of those places I had felt were superimposing themselves on the genuinely tangible aspects of the theatre: those graveyards, alleys, decayed corri-

257

dors, and subterranean passages whose spirit had intruded on another locale and altered it. Yet the places now revealed on the movie screen were without an identity I could name: they were the fundament of these sinister and seamy regions which cast their spectral ambience on the reality of the theatre but which were themselves merely the shadows, the superficial counterparts of deeper, more obscure regions. Farther and farther into it we were being taken.

The all-pervasive purple colouration could now be seen to be emanating from the labyrinth of a living anatomy: a compound of the reddish, bluish, palest pink structures, all of them morbidly inflamed and lesioned to release a purple light. We were being guided through a catacombs of putrid chambers and cloisters, the most secreted ways and waysides of an infernal land. Whatever the condition of these spaces may once have been, they were now habitations for ceremonies of a private sabbath. The hollows in their fleshy, gelatinous integuments streamed with something like moss, or a fungus extended in thin strands that were threading themselves into translucent tissue and quivering beneath it like veins. It was the sabbath ground, secret and unconsecrated, but it was also the theatre of an insane surgery. The hairlike sutures stitched among the yielding entrails, unseen hands designing unnatural shapes and systems, weaving a nest in which the possession would take place, a web wherein the bits and pieces of the anatomy could be consumed at leisure. There seemed to be no one in sight, yet everything was viewed from an intimate perspective, the viewpoint of that invisible surgeon, the weaver and webmaker, the old puppetmaster who was setting the helpless creature with new strings and placing him under the control of a new owner. And through her eyes, entranced, we witnessed the work being done.

Then those eyes began to withdraw, and the purple world of the organism receded into purple shadows. When the eyes finally emerged from where they had been, the movie screen was filled with the face and naked chest of a man. His posture was rigid, betraying a state of paralysis, and his eyes were fixed, yet strikingly alive.

"She's showing us," whispered the man who was sitting

nearby me. "She has taken him. He cannot feel who he is any longer, only her presence within him."

This, at first sight of the possessed, seemed to be an accurate statement of the case. Certainly, such a view of the situation provided a terrific stimulus to my own mood of the evening, urging it toward culmination in a type of degraded rapture, a seizure of panic oblivion. Nonetheless, as I stared at the face of the man on the screen, he became known to me as the one I encountered in the vestibule of the theatre. Recognition was difficult because his flesh was now even more obscured by the webs of hair woven through it, thick as a full beard in spots. His eyes were also quite changed, and glared out at the audience with a ferocity which suggested that he did indeed serve as the host of great evil. All the same, there was something in those eyes that belied the fact of a complete transformation – an awareness of the bewitchment and an appeal for deliverance.

Within the next few moments, this observation assumed a degree of substance, for the man on the movie screen regained himself, although briefly and in limited measure. His effort of will was evident in the subtle contortions of his face, and his ultimate accomplishment was modest enough: he managed to open his mouth in order to scream. No sound was projected from the movie screen, of course; it only played a music of images for eyes that would see what should not be seen. Thus, a disorienting effect was created: a sensory dissonance which resulted in my being roused from the mood of the evening. The spell that it had cast over me echoed to nothingness.

The scream that resonated in the auditorium originated in another part of the theatre: a place beyond the auditorium's towering black wall.

Consulting the man who was sitting near me, I found him oblivious to my comments about the scream within the theatre. He seemed neither to hear nor see what was happening around him and what was happening to the members of the audience. Long wiry hairs were sprouting from the fabric of the seats, snaking low along their arms and along every part of them. The hairs had also penetrated into the cloth of the man's suit, but I could not make him aware of what was happening.

Finally, I rose to leave, because I could feel the hairs tugging to keep me in position. As I stood up they ripped away from me like stray threads pulled from a sleeve or pocket.

No one else in the auditorium turned away from the man on the movie screen, who had now lost the ability to scream and had relapsed into a paralytic silence.

While proceeding up the aisle I glanced up towards a rectangular opening high in the back wall of the theatre: the window-like slot from which images are projected on to the movie screen. Framed within this aperture was the silhouette of what looked like an old woman with long and wildly tangled hair. I could see her eyes gazing fiercely and malignantly at the purple glow of the movie screen, and these eyes sent forth two shafts of the purest purple light, which shot through the darkness of the auditorium.

While exiting the theatre the way I had come in, it was impossible to ignore the sign that said "rest room," so brightly was it now shining. But the lamp over the side door in the alley was dead; the sign reading ENTRANCE TO THE THEATRE was gone. Even the letters spelling out the name of that evening's feature had been taken down.

So this had been the last performance; henceforth the theatre would be closed to the public.

Also closed, if only for the night, were all the other businesses along that particular street in the part of town I had never before visited. The hour was late, the shop windows were dark – but how sure I was that in every one of those dark windows I passed there was the even darker silhouette of an old woman with glowing eyes and a great head of monstrous hair.

MRS VAIL
by
Kim Newman

You have asked me for a story to add to your collection. A *ghost* story. I confess that I am unsure whether the following – shall we say *anecdote* – qualifies as such. You must make up your minds as to whether the case of Martin Vail is fit for referral to Mr Carnacki of Cheyne Walk or to Dr Freud of Vienna.

Martin Vail has not lately been much in our society, but you must all have cause to remember him. It is scarcely a secret that Mrs Twemlow, celebrated authoress of *Love's Sundered Shadows* and other popular fictions, drew heavily upon Martin Vail in creating the character of Lord Rurik Davenant, the degenerate who is much given to importuning the heroine of her currently notorious volume *Perfume and Poison*.

Since his marriage, Martin has lived a somewhat reclusive life – certainly by comparison with his former habits. The reason for this withdrawal from his old circles will, I hope, become evident. Uniquely among our crowd, I have had some acquaintance with Mrs Martin Vail, the former Miss Louisa Sorrell. A deaf mute since childhood, Mrs Vail is nevertheless one of the most charming and pleasant ladies of my acquaintance. I shall brook no unkind remarks to the effect that Mrs Vail's pre-eminence among her sex is a result of her inability to talk.

Some days ago, I had cause to be in the vicinity of the Vail residence on business – something tedious about an old lady's much-altered will, with which I have no intention of burdening you. Naturally, I took the opportunity to call on Martin. I have to admit that I found him in a sorry state: unshaven, ill-dressed, pale of complexion, nervous of manner. The transformation was complete.

"You must forgive my appearance," Martin beseeched me. "Three weeks ago, I found it necessary to put an end to my marriage...."

I made as if to protest. Mrs Vail had herself ushered me, with every courtesy, into her husband's study. Within the bounds of her infirmity she seemed to be in the best of health, and her behaviour in no way betrayed any breach in the household.

"I have killed my poor Louisa, and now she haunts me night and day. Her ghost walks the house. See..."

At this point Mrs Vail did indeed enter the room. However, far from appearing as a discarnate spirit, she displayed a most pleasing physical form, and was carrying with her a very welcome tray of comestibles.

"Look!" whispered Martin in a dreadful tone. "The tray! See how it floats as if supported by untenanted air. It is she, Louisa, invisibly reproaching me for my crime."

Mrs Vail smiled prettily at me, indicating no more than a mild social embarrassment. She placed the tray on a low table between her husband and myself.

"See how the teapot rises, as if on phantom wings! Behold, it pours!"

Mrs Vail poured out two cups of excellent Darjeeling. I quite enjoyed mine – but Martin's, I fear, went cold from neglect. He quaked in his armchair, paralysed by inexplicable horrors, while his wife performed the customary niceties. When she withdrew from the room Martin stared in her direction, but his eyes seemed not to focus.

"She's there. *There*, I tell you!"

"Quite," I responded. "I can see her for myself. I must compliment your wife on her complexion. Married life obviously suits her. Now what is all this nonsense about a murder?"

"I drowned her in the bath, and cast her weighted corpse into the Serpentine. The body is irretrievably lost, but her spirit haunts me perpetually."

My tolerant humour was, as you may suppose, wearing thin. "Surely," I said, determined to take a sarcastic view, "the usual arrangement is that the ghost of the murdered wife is visible *only* to the guilty husband. Here, the situation seems to be the reverse."

"That's it!" he cried. "That's it, exactly. You have no conception of the torments I suffer. Objects carried as if by transparent hands move through the corridors of my own house. Food and drink disappear into an absolute vacuum at my table. And

– I hardly dare tell it! – in my bed there is a displacement of the clothes, as if they were heaped about a form which simply isn't there!"

Mrs. Vail returned, bearing a plateful of buttered scones augmented with strawberry jam. Martin cringed, and waved a ragged hand ineffectually. I ate most of the scones. They were delicious – and, I assure you, bore no trace of any supernatural agency. Evidently, Mrs Vail had become quite accustomed to her husband's monomania. While he cried out in terror and writhed in a fashion that would do Henry Irving credit in the last act of *The Bells*, she serenely doled out her fine scones, and shrugged in knowing tolerance at his antics.

"I killed her," he said, when she had departed again with the empty plate. "I killed her because – you must believe me – because she *talked*. Not with her lips, but by means of some strange power that enabled her to form the words *inside my head*....incessantly, in a meaningless babble...a language without order. Ever since our wedding night she has plagued me with this infernal chatter – and even now, though she is dead, her unnatural voice is with me still...."

No amount of scones could have persuaded me to endure much longer that sort of rot. I made my excuses and left, bidding a polite farewell to Martin and a sympathetic one to his wife.

"Louisa," I said to her as she handed me my hat, "as you know, I am a member of the legal profession. I believe that I could, without any blame being attached to your person, secure an annulment of your marriage. Take my card – and please, I beg you, consider my offer...."

Mrs Vail smiled sweetly at me, and, after the merest glance at my card, returned it. She shook her head gently, the very image of the archetypal angel in the home.

"Ma'am," I told her, "I admire you greatly."

With that, I left the house. At the end of the street, I happened to turn and look back. Mrs Vail was upon her doorstep still, taking delivery of a package from the butcher's boy. Plainly, the lad had no more difficulty than I in perceiving Louisa Vail's materiality. I waved to her, and my wave was cheerfully returned.

263

I thought then, as to some extent I still do now, that Martin Vail had gone quite mad. But this morning's events have perforce changed my mind.

You must all know the story of the actress who misplaced her valuable necklace while boating in Hyde Park with a certain royal personage – and you must also know what came to light when he arranged for the Serpentine to be dragged....

BRODY LOVED THE MASAI WOMAN
by
Ian McDonald

In half a century a man inevitably draws a mantle of legend about him. Indeed, for a white man in Africa, it is almost mandatory. No matter that you have planned for yourself a peaceful retirement observing the passing world in all its exponential craziness from the cool of your verandah, punctuated by the occasional pause for contemplation of the ocean on the reef; rest assured that your legends, more so than your sins, will find you out. Among a people whose major form of recreation is gossip – ever the way with expatriate communities, which is why you will not find *me* down in those discreet bars and cafés far away from the tourist circuit – the yearning for a quiet life is no excuse: if you have no legends, they are more than content to make them up for you. With or without your consent.

Not that I am complaining; if it so happens that a few of those legends find their way into Berlitz, so much the better for the Inn, even if I must endlessly recount them at my table on the verandah to fat, peeling German *haufraus* in ghastly peach-melba micro-dresses, or barely post-teen share-brokers smelling of wetsuit and Piz Buin who cannot wait for the Old Fart to stop his Endless Rambling so they can tell everyone about the Really Important Things they do. If they think they are buying a piece of Real Africa – a thing I grow less and less certain exists as the years pass, or that, if it does exist, cannot be found in the pages of any Kuoni World-Wide Klub-Afrika brochure – I am content to please. The first rule of hospitality; the pleasure of one's guests. At my prices, they deserve it. The truth, as ever, is less glamorous.

I did not kill the leopard with my bare hands. I found him rooting around the back among the bins and, after promptly soiling my vestments, (one thing the Great White Hunters never tell you is that Big Game is Big – bloody Big), blew the bugger to glory with the old Mauser that hangs up behind the bar now. The old Syrian taxidermist down in the Old Port most successfully patched up the bullet hole, and a legend was born.

I did not singlehandedly drag Ernest Hemingway out of the bar, along the jetty and throw him into the harbour. Certainly, he was grossly drunk, utterly obnoxious and quite astonishingly boring, but it was Jack Patience, the then District Commissioner who, when the bum threatened me with violence if I did not serve him another whiskey-soda, had his faithful askaris hand-cuff the slob to the big baobab until he dried out. I subsequently read every word the man ever wrote and was disappointed to find the episode sadly omitted.

I was not held hostage while the Inn was taken over by the crew of a German U-Boat and used like some kind of submariner's Port-Royal until Kapitan Goestler and his merry crew were sent to the bottom of the Gulf of Aden by Sunderlands operating out of Oman. During the war I played host to Dr. Schrenk, an Ophthalmic Missionary for the Lutheran church, who was placed under my custody mainly to protect him from people who might think he was a spy, which he almost certainly was not. Dr. Schrenk was a man of such angelic ingenuousness that had he indeed been a spy, he would have had 'Occupation: Spy' written in his passport.

The one legend that has never found its way into Berlitz is the best of the lot, but you will not find me telling it to the tourists over G & quinine in the cocktail hour. You can never do the true ones justice.

As Hamid, my *maitre d'* back in those days in '38, would have said, "Necessity, she is the great mother of strange bedfellows". If only he had mixed his cocktails as well. There never was a stranger bedfellow than Angus Brody. Now, there was a man fitted by nature to bear the mantle of 'legend'. And legend was what he became – though not, I would think, in any way he could have imagined.

Under any other circumstances, in any other country, Brody and I would not even have crossed courses, much less become business partners. If the genteel Dr. Schrenk would have tra-velled the world under the title 'spy', then Brody's passport would have had entered under 'occupation' the word 'cad', which might have been invented for the man. He was the only son of some decaying clan of Anglo-Irish nobility, and had been sent down from Cambridge on a conspiracy of such complexity that no matter how often he explained it – which he did, frequently, and with much relish – I still could not unravel it. He had been a radio-navigator on the big Imperial flying-boats from Southampton down to the Cape until, after a by-all-accounts-memorable disagreement with his Captain – they were an autocratic bunch of Blighs, those Imperial Captains – he walked out and left them high and dry on Lake Baringo until a replacement could be flown out from Khartoum. Immediately thereafter he took Lord Delamere and his Happy Valley bunch for a truly obscene sum in cards and, with a fine instinct for survival, fled to the coast before they closed ranks and arranged some small but mortal hunting accident for him.

I first met Brody the day he took delivery of a brand new Grumann Goose seaplane. Of course, it was memorable. Woken from my siesta by an ungodly roar of engines, I was hailed by this red-haired figure clad only in khaki shorts and flying goggles looming from the cockpit of a seaplane and asking would I mind awfully grabbing hold of the end of this rope, he'd been tootling up and down between those bloody dhows for the best part of an hour now trying to find somewhere to tie up. The sea-plane mail-service he ran up and down the coast was, on paper, perhaps the most spectacularly flagrant enterprise since the Tower of Babel, yet he still found himself with enough of a surplus to sink into some West Country bumpkin's daft notion of an Inn on the north mainland of Mombasa.

Money stuck to Brody like shit to a blanket. He spent profligately, he earned even more prodigiously. When I proposed we name the Inn after its major partner he said, "For God's sake don't, I have no desire to be associated with it when the damn thing starts to make pots of money." Which of course it did; far more than even he could absorb with his gloriously unprofitable airline. In those last couple of years before the War it became quite the fashionable thing to do; pop down on the overnighter from Nairobi, spend a day or two acclimatising at Hedley's Inn and then fly up to Malindi, Lamu and points north with Brody Marine Airways.

Once the Inn was firmly established as *the* place to swill your

Gordon's of an afternoon, I found myself propelled from the anonymity of an impecunious English teacher at the Foreign Nationals' School through the ivory doors of Coast Society, which suddenly opened before me. Truth be told – and tonight we tell the truth, the whole truth, the dark truths, the painful truths – I suspect that I rode into the consular parties and dickie-bow and stiff-little-finger cocktail receptions on Brody's coat-tails. Though it was my name on the shingle, it seemed to be the one they could never quite remember. A salutary experience was overhearing some plump – no, we are to tell the truth, so the truth shall be told: *fat* – heiress asking her equally fat companion just who was that one?...yes, that one standing there?...the little mousey, school-mastery one?

Brody of course was as attractive to women as to the pound sterling. All credit to him, he always felt it meet, right and his bounden duty when at the centre of some circle of bedazzled admirers to summon me to join him with an imperious wave of the hand – "Ladies, you really must meet my very good friend Mr. Neville Hedley" – before gravitating toward the champagne, leaving me trying vainly to keep hold of the reins of social nicety as, one by one, the dainty things made their apologies with ill-concealed boredom and slipped away.

Perhaps if I had not gone to the coming-out party at the Henderson place, it might never have happened. But then again, this is Africa where what will happen will happen. Here, God's ways are not easily frustrated by human free will. I would have declined but for the prospect of an evening behind an empty bar with only the enigmatic silences and occasional surreal pronouncements of Hamid for amusement. Not even a frock flown in from London could disguise *La Bella* Henderson's inherent lumpishness as she fluttered and twittered through her social *debut*, striking paroxysms of embarrassment into all with whom she came into contact. The horse-riding; that is what I blame. Some kind of transfer of atoms takes place through the saddle between arse and ass.

"How about we quietly tip our champagne into the pot palms and vanish into the night?" I suggested. "We could be in Zanzibar by midnight. The smell of cloves on the wind from the shore, the soft caress of white surf on the reef, muted saxophones under the banyan trees..."

Brody was staring with the pietistic fervour of a contemporary Catholic saint at the door where a small, toad-like gentleman in a preposterous evening cloak and hat like a collapsing stovepipe was handing gloves and cane to the house-boy.

"My God, what kind of creature is that?"

"Sergio Schiavoni, the Italian Honorary Consul. I'm surprised you haven't met him before. Loves to scandalise. Something to do with being virtually socially ostracized over the Abyssinian affair."

"No no no, not him, not that tedious little tit. I know him. That. With him."

By any standards, she was quite staggering. As she drew the hood of her gown away from her face I will swear to this day that a gasp ran through the Henderson's ballroom, a thing I have only ever thought to be a writer's literary fancy. Sergio Schiavoni's Mr. Toad features were creased in unabashed smugness.

Somali, perhaps, or Galla. Masai even. She wore her Nilo-Hamitic poise and nobility with the sensuous grace that a panther wears its pelt. Her skin was of that texture that you know you must touch to feel if it is as powdery-smooth as you imagine it: Earth-coloured, the red ochre Earth of Africa: it will not be so bad, you think, to be buried in the earth if it is like her. She was dressed in white silk, Italian silk; a sheer, clinging sheathe of fabric that amplified her essential *primality* into something almost god-like.

After the lightning, the thunder. As the rumbles and grumbles followed in the wake of the shock – *too much, too far, far too far this time, that damn Eyetie has gone too far this time, I tell you, bringing a black, look at Hettie, she's distraught, quite distraught, the dear thing* – a light gleamed in Brody's eye, a look of steely resolve I had not seen in him before.

"Mind this." He thrust his cocktail glass into my safekeeping. "I've got to talk to her. I will die if I do not talk to her." He moved through the mutterers and nodders like an elegant snake while I attempted to console Hettie Henderson, spectacularly eclipsed and weeping long mascara tears down the front of her London party frock.

"Masai, actually."

If the Empire Upon Which the Sun Never Sets has a soft underbelly it is the Slump; that half hour, forty-five minutes in early afternoon during which luncheon presses heavily on the duodenum inducing a most un-English torpor and lassitude. Should it be let slip to assorted fuzzie-wuzzies, mahdis, dervishes, wallahs and sepoys that around two-thirty, three o'clock the way to Buckingham Palace lies flung wide, belts slackened, collars undone, waistcoats unbuttoned, we would be swept from the face of the earth between Gin and Its and afternoon tea.

"I know. Lake Natron Masai, to be precise."

We sat in wicker chairs at a wicker table with a bottle of Bushmills watching the white triangles of the dhows set out upon the trade winds for Arabia and India. A tramp steamer lay long and ugly and incongruous in the offing.

"What's more," I said, "I also know that she's a Mission widow." The primly dressed doctrinally sound missionaries have it all wrong. The universe is not monotheistic. The universe is governed by an essential dualism that balances evil with good and good with evil. Africans are born understanding this. We call it African Fatalism; they call it common sense. Why, even the *wazungu* missionaries prove it every time they morally blackmail some young Masai *moran* into taking a dip in the river: oh yes, you may sing with the saints and the saved, but it is Written that a man shall leave his parents and cleave to a woman and only unto her. Meaning, one woman only. Meaning, Solomon and his six hundred wives notwithstanding, no true washed-in-the-blood Christian can enjoy polygamy. Meaning, on the principle of last in, first out, you, you and *you* are divorced and *you* will be my one and only.

It is not even that easy in Islam.

And so the poor cows end up drifting into the towns and petty prostitution or witchcraft or semi-slavery on some smug Gikuyu's shamba or a shadowy existence as concubines to fat, balding Great White Hunters, riddled with halitosis and impotent with gin and masturbation. Because sure as when an elephant shits it shits, no Masai worth his cattle is going to take a used wife; one careful owner.

"Story is some railway surveyor found her half-dead by the side of the Lake Magadi Branch line, took pity on her and brought her down to Mombasa. He already had a Giriama woman but he kept her anyway – a little taste for the exotic, never suspected in the Uganda railway employee. Anyway, before long the Giriama woman is accusing this Masai of being a vampire – you know, one of those women who turn in the dead of night into leopards, or spiders, and do whatever scary things it is vampire leopards or spiders do. Superstitious people, the Giriama, almost as bad as ex-pats – they may have Allah on their side but they still have to say a prayer every time they turn on the tap or flush the toilet in case the *djinn* that lives down the *choo* drags them to perdition. The upshot is the Masai woman ups and leaves, the surveyor and his Giriama are posted to Eldoret and the next thing we know Schiavoni is parading around all the best places to be seen with her on his arm. Took her back to Italy, you know. Met *Il Duce*."

"How the hell did you find this out, Hedley?" Brody poured two gushing measures from the banks of the far river Bush.

"People tell me things. You may find it hard to believe, but they do. It's because I stay quiet long enough to listen to them."

"Pretty much squares with what I learned from her. Didn't know about the Giriama bit." He studied the five fingers worth in the tumbler. "Well Nev, here's cheers: up the King and down the queers." He threw down the liquid in one swift, golden motion. "I am going to have her, you know."

"It will be over Schiavoni's dead body."

"That can be arranged."

He was gone three days, up coast on a mail run and engaging in what he cautiously referred to as his 'shameful secret', which seemed to involve Amharic coffin ornaments and forged bills of lading from Mogadishu. On his return, I had news.

"It seems Allah smiles favourably upon you. Your wish is to be granted."

271

"How now, *petit* Neville?"

"Schiavoni is sick."

He actually grinned, the rogue.

"Nothing trivial, I hope."

"Dr. Coupar's bluffing and blowing but he doesn't have a clue. Word is they might as well measure the poor bastard now."

"Italy's adversity is Ireland's opportunity."

"You appal me."

Schiavoni was dead within a month. Dr. Coupar, chief consultant of the big mission hospital across the pontoon bridge and a regular at the Inn, where I kept a bottle of sacramental single malt under the bar for his personal abuse (savvy Hamid? you no good Muslim, there are more ways than one of marking a bottle), attributed the cause of death to Tropical Pneumonic Fever which he, and we, and everyone in the ex-pat community with the possible exception of equine-arsed Hettie Henderson, knew meant Sweet F.A.

"Place'll be a lot quieter without him." The nearest the dour Coupar ever came to a eulogy.

"When's the funeral?" Only when you have known Angus Brody at the constant close-range our partnership entailed can you distinguish the malevolent gleam in his smile of opportunism from a trick of dentistry. To the practised eye, it is the exact shape and colour of an Arab riyal.

Such a pity we never get to laugh at our own funerals. Schiavoni would have been delighted. As he lay in state hoping for a few fond farewells and perhaps forgivenesses from those he had so magnificently affronted, one of the bearers accidentally kicked out a trestle and sent Sergio tumbling from his coffin, smirking mordantly, to fall at the feet of the dowager Lady Amehurst who never quite recovered and was shipped back to Cheshunt on the first passing P & O. Then the Archbishop of Afars and Issas, apparently an old University friend, turned up in full arch-episcopal purple and was stoned by the local tenement children who later claimed he was an *afrit* but in all probability had heard of his reputation as a celebrated pederast. Then, as Schiavoni, at last eternally reunited with his box, was lowered into the earth, a sudden squall blowing up from God knows where reduced the dignified ensemble to a fleeing shambles of sagging feathers, dripping parasols and drenched mourning suits.

"Tremendous fun," declared Brody. "I wish I'd known the chap better now. You noticed her, of course."

I had to admit that I had not. Brody waved in the direction of the Holy Ghost Church. A patch of darkness detached itself from the general shade beneath the trees that surrounded the tin-roofed church and moved away, as if ashamed to have been caught privy to some complex, secret white ritual.

"Excuse me old son if I dash, but the lady seems to be in need of a chaperone."

"For God's sake, the man isn't even cold yet."

"I know. Dreadful, aren't I?"

And off he went, loping across the still-wet grass with that silly, affected half-run they only teach at public schools.

For Brody to absent himself for a week at a time was quite characteristic. Ten days was nothing unusual. When a fortnight passed without his breezing in and skimming his hat in the general direction of Hamid I became concerned, but not unduly. When three weeks passed and the Goose was still tied up at her landing stage, I put the word out.

The very next evening, as I was preparing for the cocktail hour rush across the Nyali bridge – a flotilla of Baby Austins crunching to a halt on Hamid's neatly-raked gravel – in he sauntered, fresh as the proverbial daisy. Damnably nonchalant, insufferably Brody. He slipped in behind the bar and helped himself to a brace of Guinness Exports.

"Really, Neville, there was no need to have your Baker Street Irregulars out after me. We're not married, you know."

"Where the hell were you?" Though I knew, and Brody knew that I knew, and I was angry at myself and angry at him and angry at all the subtle, feminine little psychological intrigues that such knowledge forced us to play with each other. He had been out and about. With her. All over town, into every club and restaurant that would admit them, making scenes at those that would not, up to Nairobi, down to Dar, showing her off

273

everywhere and to everyone. And now, last of all, he had brought her home to show me. It was that that angered me most.

She was casually dressed, European style, in a sleeveless collared blouse and wide-legged cotton lounging pants. The heeled sandals seemed uncomfortable and confining to her, as though she had been born to go barefoot upon the earth. But neither casual nor formal, European nor African, dress could add to nor detract from her. She commanded attention, drew every eye in the room to her and would not release them.

"Isn't she a stunner, Nev?" His matey slap on the back felt heavy and treacherous as a wooden cross. He tossed her a Guinness bottle; with one swift, elegant pounce she caught it and uncapped it with her teeth. "My God, look at that? What can you say Nev? What can you say?" He beckoned her over. She moved like the long rains. "N'Delé, Neville Hedley; Nev, N'Delé. Actually, Nev," (he leaned across the bar in best ham conspiratorial fashion) "I have a bit of a favour to ask you."

You can always tell the big ones. They are always 'little'. Or 'a bit'.

"Seems, old chap, that what with Schiavoni kicking the bucket, passing on, buying the farm, and going to join the choir invisible we have a bit of an accommodation problem. In that the house, old chap, has now passed into the hands of some aged Aunt, the ertswhile Terror of Salerno, and latterly Djibouti, who has made it manifestly clear in a broadside of truly blistering telegrams that under no circumstances, no circumstances, Nev my son, will she tolerate the presence of *that woman* on the premises. So, Nev, old comrade, we find ourselves with a little bit of, shall we say, a housing crisis? Which could be speedily and satisfactorily resolved by the simple application of the words *'Yes Brody I'd be delighted'* to the request *'Might N'Delé and I move into the Inn for a while?'* Old chap? Nev, old comrade? Nev, you've gone uncharacteristically quiet, even for you."

Quiet, Brody old bean? You could hear the ice melting in the glasses. Every head was attentively turned elsewhere in that grotesquely stilted *me? listening?* attitude.

"No Brody, I would not be delighted."

And the long bar room of Hedley's Inn came to life again.

He wheedled. He pleaded. He bantered and charmed and fawned. He blustered. He blew. He threatened, he bribed. Through it all I kept shaking my head and saying "No Brody, no, not this time", and the Masai woman sat on the edge of a glass-topped bamboo table and took long, luxurious swigs from her triple-X Guinness.

As with everything to do with Brody, his departure from the Inn was spectacular. He could make an exit, I'll give him that. He lifted a heavy glass ashtray from the bar and hurled it with all his considerable strength (he had bowled for Cambridge, he claimed) into the bottles racked behind the bar.

It was not racism. Nothing as simple as that great late Twentieth Century panacea that always seems to be levelled at the white race and no other. I did not mind if Brody humped his Masai woman six times a night and crowed like a cock from the balcony each time. I did mind him doing it under my roof, in my rooms, at my bar; I did mind seeing my regular patrons that I had built up over the months drifting away one by one, with polite, but final apologies, to someplace with a more conducive atmosphere, you know, with a better class of clientele. You know.

It was a simple business decision.

The hell it was. Now I must come to the heart of my honesty. Half a century of life as a bachelor gay (cannot even say that any more: no piracy on the high seas as dreadful as the piracy of the words on your lips) gives one a certain perspective, if not exactly breadth of vision, upon one's own self – one has little else to do than contemplate and cultivate the inner man when one *gets on* – and I know now that what really prompted me to say 'no' was jealousy. Good Old Testament green-eyed bugger-you jealousy.

One thing. I remembered it after he had gone, she following three steps behind, a subtle, mask-like smile on her face. One does remember things, afterwards, one replays those painful scenes in the mind trying to make them come out right after all. But they never do. I remembered that throughout our conversation, Brody had picked incessantly at a long, narrow scab on his left forearm. Picked and picked and picked until it bled.

Of course it was the talk of the city. Damned perversity – just when I did not care if I never saw that freckled, grinning, *Boy's-Own-Paper* face again, I was bombarded by daily itineraries of their goings and doings, recorded and reported in such microscope detail that I could have retraced every step they took from the hotel where Brody rented a suite to the café where they took breakfast to Mackinnons market where the Masai woman bought the food she prepared so lovingly for her Brody. Biltong, papaya and beer; I even had detailed breakdowns of their daily menu whispered to me across the bar.

All things pass. But by the time I was filled with repentance and remorse (and, truth be told, fed up to the back teeth with tedious old farts creaking in their wicker chairs all day and mumbling for whiskey-soda and longing for a bit of Brodian mirth and japes) – they were gone. Malindi, Lamu; or south, Pemba, Zanzibar. Rumours circulated that the Grumann Goose had been sighted as far down-coast as Isla da Moçambique.

It is not an illusion. It is true. Time is speeding up. For everyone, not just for old fascists like me. Three months is like an evening gone, as the hymn says; then, it was like a thousand ages. Three months, fed on nothing more substantial than rumours. I was upcountry when the telegram came, some safari with the Earl of Rutland – more an excuse for an epic piss-up than any serious shooting; if an elephant had blundered into our tents we would not even have been capable of hitting it. Hamid was waiting for me at the compound gate, driven by concern into hitherto unheard of unintelligibilities.

The telegram was eloquent enough. While attempting a take-off run from Pemba to meet up with a safari group at lake Eyasi, Brody had lost control and crashed the Grumann. I later heard he had ploughed straight through a fleet of fishing boats – not killing anyone purely by Anglo-Irish luck – hit a jetty and ripped off a float and the tail section. He was alive – more Celtic luck – and relatively uninjured, but on medical recommendation had been flown up on the first Imperial to Mombasa. The telegram was dated five days previous. I knew the schedule of the Imperials like the Lord's Prayer.

"Hamid, where is he?"

"The CMS Hospital, Mr. Hedley." I have never permitted Hamid any of the *bwana m'kuba* nonsense. "Ludwig Krapf Ward. I have taken the diabolical liberty of summoning a taxi-cab."

Pity he never could mix cocktails worth a damn.

Coupar was waiting for me at the inquiries desk. Prim Protestant missionary nurses from Halifax and Pontypridd rustled hither-thither, in crisply starched white linen.

"God, he's not dead is he?" What else could one's reaction be, on being greeted by the Chief Consultant.

"A little less free with the Fourth Commandment, Hedley. This is a Mission Hospital. Brody? Dead? Not a chance. However, he is a very sick man."

"The crash. But I'd heard he'd sustained only minor injuries."

"Mostly cuts and bruises. He walked away from it, up the beach, into the village, found a Catholic mission and asked the sisters if they could contact his insurance broker for him. Then he collapsed. The sisters took one look at him and flew him up here.

"He seems to be suffering from some kind of pernicious anaemia of a kind quite unfamiliar to the sisters, and, I must confess, to me." He looked at me askance in that parsimonious, Scots-covenanting way that does not apportion blame, but does not exonerate either. "Has he been in any fights recently?"

"Apart from ours? No. Brody has no shame. He is impossible to insult. He would walk away from any potentially violent situation."

"I was hoping you wouldn't say that. It's just that he has a number of scars, old lesions that do not seem to have been caused by the crash. A large number, in fact. Both forearms are very heavily scarred, calves likewise; upper arms and thighs are more lightly marked. Some are several months old, others barely scabbed over. If I did not know better, I would say they were knife wounds."

While we had been talking, Coupar had been leading me along the gloss-painted, antiseptic-perfumed corridors and stairs to the small private ward where Brody was being kept.

277

"See if you can get anything out of him," were Coupar's parting words to me as he opened the door and showed me in.

Someone, perhaps Brody himself, had filled the room with flowers, more as a defence against the all-pervasive and deeply-dreadful smell of *hospital* than to cheer the room, which was brilliantly lit by a large latticed window with a splendid view of Port Tudor and the North Mainland. The sea was that pure ultramarine you only find in tropical waters, which seems deep and blue enough to invite you to drown there.

"If you open the window and hang out with one hand, you can see the old place," said Angus Brody. "So I'm told. Haven't been able to try it yet. Good of you to come Nev. Got anything to drink?"

The brilliance of the room only emphasised the more his ghastliness. He was a ghost of himself. Gaunt. Drained. Exhausted and devoured. Skin a tight-stretched translucent drumskin behind which the life but barely beat. He sat propped up against pillows like a disconsolate marionette, dressed in smoking jacket and old Harrovian tie.

"Best bloody view in Mombasa. Pity you have to be here to enjoy it."

She sat at his side on a tall, straight backed chair, like carved ebony, perfect, absolute, moving only to light cigarettes for her Brody. She did not even acknowledge my arrival. Her expressionless face remained fixed on Brody, like an icon, as she slipped the cigarettes between her lips, drew flame.

"Seem to have had a bit of a prang, as the saying goes. In fact, I would go so far as to say, a bona fide, *wizard* prang. Be a long time before I can look my insurers in the face again. Sure you've got nothing to drink?"

"Sorry."

"And you running a pub. N'Delé, love, do us a favour. Slip out the back way so Coupar doesn't see you down to the Falfarino and get me a bottle of Bush on the account?"

She looked from him to me and I saw suspicion flicker in her eyes. It is like a widening of the pupils, the look of suspicion, just wide enough for you to be able to see a little into the soul.

When she was gone Brody seemed to relax. It was a painful relaxing, like a bag of bones settling onto the earth, but he seemed at ease.

"Coupar told you?"

"About what?"

"About my membership of a bizarre Thuggee self-mutililation cult? He's right, you know, but for all the wrong reasons, hah hah you bloody little Scot."

He drew up the sleeves of his smoking jacket. Both forearms were a raw, cross-hatched mess of scars, scabs and still-oozing wounds.

"God Almighty, Brody..."

"She was right, you see."

"Who was right?"

"The Giriama woman."

I thought for a moment that he had succumbed to some malarial ranting madness, then remembered. Our conversation, at the table, over the bottle, in the Slump. "The railway surveyor's Giriama."

"Well done Neville. The one who drove N'Delé out because she maintained she was a vampire." He lit a cigarette. It seemed a relief to him. The ashtray was full to overflowing. "She was right. All along. She is a vampire.

"Oh, none of that swirling capes and turning into bats and aversion to sunlight and garlic, not even changing into a leopard or spider at the full of the moon. Nothing remotely Bram Stokerian about it. She's a real vampire. A true vampire. She is a creature that feeds on blood.

"It's their way, you see. It's always been their way, the Masai. Blood and milk. From the cattle, usually. They'll open an artery in the leg or the neck, run off a quart or so – the cow can spare it – mix it in a gourd with milk and drink it freshly curdled.

"It's in the Old Testament, isn't it? I've been looking it up in the Gideon. Everything is in the Old Testament; here all human vice and wickedness are writ. The blood ye shall not touch, it is sacred to me, for in the blood is the life and the life is mine, saith Jehovah. Or words to that effect."

He exhaled slowly, luxuriously into the bright, flower-filled room. The scars on his forearms were livid.

"They were a nomadic people, the Jews, when the Ten Commandments were handed down to them. Like the Masai. Jehovah was right. The life is in the blood. Life, for her. She can't live without it. I don't understand the biology, maybe Coupar could give some explanation about cells and haemoglobin and vitamins and that stuff; all I know is that if she does not have blood, she will die.

"When she first suggested it, I must confess, I was horrified. Terrified. Something totally outside my experience, totally outside my imagining; dammit man, all I wanted was a little bit of snatch, not to have my wrists slit. Even though it seemed like the vilest perversion imaginable to me, I did not hate her. Can you understand that, Nev? I could not hate her. I love her—I think it is her nature that it is impossible for men not to love her – but I did refuse her. And she faded. Faded, Nev. Day by day, she faded before my sight. She grew listless, irritable, sensitive to the light. She was prone to bouts of dizziness, to fainting, vomiting up blood. What could I do? What else could I do? No hell worse, Neville, than being caught between two hells."

His fingers traced a pale, puckered laceration almost invisible beneath the festering slashes of new wounds.

"It was there she opened me that first time, that first night, with the edge of her Masai knife. In the end, I could not refuse her. But Neville, I learned a terrible thing that first time, that night in Schiavoni's house, in Schiavoni's room with the plaster cherubs on the ceiling, in Schiavoni's bed, something about myself. Neville: I have never known a love as deep, as thrilling, as totally consuming, as lying there in the hot, sweating dark having my blood lovingly, adoringly sucked from my veins."

"Christ, Brody!"

"She's here, Nev."

But I did not hear anything.

"You'll have to go. You must go. No, I know what you're thinking. I wouldn't even dream of leaving her. I love her. She loves me, after her fashion. Blood seals the bond. She needs me in a way no one else has ever needed me; for once in my goddam spendthrift useless life, I am important to someone."

280

The door opened. The Masai woman entered with a bottle wrapped in a copy of the *Times* several months out of date. She flickered her eyes toward me, studied me suspiciously. It was the most regard I had ever received from her.

"Nev's just leaving, darling. Pour us one, would you?"

One of the manifold curses of age is that imagination becomes too easily confused with memory. In my mind I see still the glitter concealed within the curve of the fingers of her right hand – but is it imagination, or the real, bright gleam of the knife's edge?

The Viking funeral was Jack Patience the D-C's idea. He was a Manxman, the Norse blood ran thick and frothing in his veins – and anyway, we had been drinking. When you drink, and reminisce, when you sit on the verandah with a bottle and a few friends and the moon rising out of the distant edge of the monsoon , when you commemorate all the many infuriations and excesses and eccentricities and dazzling triumphs of a life like Angus Brody's, you pass beyond mere drunkenness into a clear-sighted, rational insanity where a notion as mad as the hero's farewell seems utterly reasonable, even desirable.

"What did the cause of death read?" I asked Coupar as the edge of dawn lit the oceanward horizon. "Tropical Pneumonic Fever?"

"A pneumonic fever caused by unknown infection. Did he ever tell you, Hedley? What the hell caused those scars? What the woman had to do with it?"

I shook my head. We were all – myself, Jack Patience, Coupar, and the mechanics who had had the Grumann towed up from Pemba by dhow – too drunk to see what a bad lie it was.

"I don't know. I'd like to say I'd never seen anything like it before, but I had," Coupar said.

"Schiavoni," I murmured into my glass, but no-one heard.

Coupar signed the release forms that morning – the prim Protestant nurses regarded him queerly, sniffing as they rustled past – and we had Scobie the Harbour Master tow the seaplane out beyond the reef. It was a nightmarish voyage; with the exception of Scobie we were all dreadfully hung-over. One of the mechanics set the engines to idle, the other liberally soused the plane with fuel. Scobie's Harbour Commission launch kept a respectful station as the Grumann headed east, toward China across the ocean. Jack Patience assumed the mantle of responsibility. He was the best shot of any of us, but what with the tossing boat and the brilliant noon-day sun and our general malaise, it took him three attempts before he hit the Grumann with a flare from the Very pistol. As flames engulfed the speeding seaplane, he pronounced the epitaph: "Fare thee well Angus Brody, we salute you."

We bobbed on the tossing sea, watching, each much occupied with our own thoughts. Then a bright blossom of flame lit the ocean, and seconds later the thump of an explosion shook the boat and we all thought it was the bloody best funeral we had ever been to.

So that is the legend: the legend of the man who died from the love of the Masai woman. But legend is not life. Life goes on beyond the end of the story. Life is not conveniently tied to literary devices and contrivances. Despite Coupar's suspicions, which he carried with him until he died a few years back, I never told a living soul the secret of the Masai woman. She disappeared soon after Brody's death; the fool had left her a colossal whack of his fortune, but all the money in the world, for her, would not have balanced a single drop of blood. The remainder passed to me, with it I was able to expand the Inn into a small hotel and restaurant. Brody was right, it did make pots of money. Flying in the face of all economic trends, it still does.

I never saw the Masai woman again. Rumours of her still abound up and down the East coast, from Cairo to the Cape, though by now she must be very old, unless, like the vampires of legend, she possesses eternal youth and beauty; doubtless she has found new prey for her appetites. But I do not think she does it callously, I believe she did love Brody, as best she could; and that each man she takes, she loves as deeply, and truly. The blood is the bond, the sign and seal of the covenant of souls.

Why did Brody die? Why did Schiavoni die? The Masai are careful of their herds, they count their wealth in cattle; they would not bleed one of their cows to death.

The answer lies, I think, with the new, powerful mythologies by which we explain the world. We know so much more now. We have our own, unique Twentieth Century legends: physics, biology, biochemistry.

It is said that we very seldom invent a new sin. Also true, I think, is that we very seldom invent a new plague. They have all been waiting for us since man first walked in the valley of Ol Duvai. Some we defeat: the more blatant, immediate ones, the ones that once ravaged entire populations, and the old ones, the slow ones; but the subtle ones move up to take their place. New plagues, old plagues. I read an article in a magazine recently. It was by a French scientist. He said that it has always been with us. All those laws handed down from Sinai on the morality of sex were to keep it out of the household of the Chosen. It kills primarily by sex, but also by blood. I see the photographs of today's victims in the newspapers and my mind is cast back inescapably to Brody, pale and luminous in his bed in the bright room. The only difference is half a century.

Those nightly subjections to the tender knife, the slow, sensuous swallowing down of his blood, must have weakened him until he had no resistance. Then it swept through him and within two months killed him.

Rationalisations. Explanations. Mythologies. Legends. We do not like to think that there are such things as monsters prowling the edges of our comfortable human societies. When we banish them with our incantations – physical, chemical, biological, psychological – are we any different from the Giriama woman who mutters a prayer to the *djinn* in the toilet and sees the beast in a beautiful woman?

No new plagues.

No new sins.

No new truths?

How I wish I could take comfort from that.

NOTES ON THE CONTRIBUTORS

FRANCIS AMERY has translated numerous texts from the French for *Black Feast: The Second Dedalus Book of Decadence* (1991) and is working on a collection of stories by Remy de Gourmont, *Angels of Perversity*, which will be published by Dedalus in 1992.

CHARLES BAUDELAIRE (1821-1867) was the most influential French poet of his generation, largely through the medium of his classic collection *Les Fleurs du Mal* (1857), from which "Metamorphoses of the Vampire" is taken. He was the father figure of the Decadent movement, and his work is extensively featured in *The Dedalus Book of Decadence (Moral Ruins)* (1990) and *Black Feast: The Second Dedalus Book of Decadence* (1992).

BARRINGTON J. BAYLEY is the author of numerous novels, including *The Fall of Chronopolis* (1974), *Soul of the Robot* (1974), *Star Winds* (1978), *The Pillars of Eternity* (1982) and *The Zen Gun* (1983). His short stories are collected in *The Knights of the Limits* (1978) and *The Seed of Evil* (1979). He is a contributor to the Dedalus anthology *Tales of the Wandering Jew* (1991).

STORM CONSTANTINE's novels include the Wraeththu trilogy, which comprises *The Enchantments of Flesh and Spirit* (1987), *The Bewitchments of Love and Hate* (1988) and *The Fulfilments of Fate and Desire* (1989); *The Monstrous Regiment* (1990) and its sequel *Aleph* (1991); and *Hermetech* (1991).

BRIAN CRAIG is the author of four novels: *Zaragoz* (1989), *Plague Daemon* (1990), *Storm Warriors* (1991) and *Ghost Dancers* (1991). His short stories can be found in a number of anthologies edited by David Pringle, including *Ignorant Armies* (1989), *Wolf Riders* (1989) and *Route 666* (1990).

THÉOPHILE GAUTIER (1811-1872) was one of the leading writers of the French Romantic movement, producing abundant poetry and numerous essays as well as prose fiction. His novels include *Mademoiselle de Maupin* (1835), *Fortunio* (1837), *Avatar* (1856), *Jettatura* (1857) and *Spirite* (1866); collections of his short fiction include *One of Cleopatra's Nights and Other Fantastic Romances* (translated by Lafcadio Hearn, 1882), from which "One of Cleopatra's Nights" (1845) is taken, and *My Fantoms* (1976).

ROBERT IRWIN is the author of *The Arabian Nightmare* (1983; first published by Dedalus), *The Limits of Vision* (1986) and *The Mysteries of Algiers* (1988). He was a contributor to the Dedalus anthology *Tales of the Wandering Jew* (1991).

JOHN KEATS (1795-1821) was one of the leading poets of the British Romantic movement. His unhappy infatuation with Fanny Brawne provided the emotional impetus for much of his best work, including "La Belle Dame Sans Merci" and many of the other items in his *Poems* (1820).

VERNON LEE was the pseudonym of Violet Paget (1856-1935), whose various works include three volumes of supernatural fiction: *Hauntings* (1890), from which "Amour Dure" is taken; *Pope Jacynth and Other Fantastic Tales* (1907) and *For Maurice; Five Unlikely Stories* (1927).

THOMAS LIGOTTI is the author of numerous short stories of a highly distinctive kind, many of which were published in small press magazines before being collected in *Songs of a Dead Dreamer* (1990) and *Grimscribe* (1991).

IAN McDONALD's novels include *Desolation Road* (1988), *Out on Blue Six* (1989) and *King of Morning, Queen of Day* (1991). Some of his short stories are collected in *Empire Dreams* (1988). He is a contributor to the Dedalus anthology *Tales of the Wandering Jew* (1991).

KIM NEWMAN is the author of *Nightmare Movies: A Critical History of the Horror Film Since 1968* and numerous novels; the ones which bear his own name are *The Night Mayor* (1989), *Bad Dreams* (1990) and *Jago* (1991). He has written several stories in collaboration with Eugene Byrne, including one which appeared in the Dedalus anthology *Tales of the Wandering Jew* (1991).

ARTHUR W. O'SHAUGHNESSY (1844-1881) spent the greater part of his working life at the Natural History Museum, where he specialised in reptiles and fish. His first book of poems, from which "The Daughter of Herodias" is taken, was *An Epic of Women* (1870); his later work was more closely akin to the poetry of the Pre-Raphaelite Brotherhood, of which he was a fringe member.

EDGAR ALLAN POE (1809-1849) published several volumes of poetry before he began to write morbid and macabre short stories in the hope of winning cash prizes offered by newspapers. Many of these, including "Morella", were collected under the entirely appropriate title *Tales of the Grotesque and Arabesque* (1840). His work, translated into French by Baudelaire, became a major influence on French writers, including those associated with the Decadent movement.

MARCEL SCHWOB (1867-1905) was the author of two short story collections: *Coeur Double* (1891), from which "Arachne" is taken; and *Le Roi au masque d'or* (1892). He also wrote a collection of speculative biographical sketches, *Vies imaginaires* (1896). A selection of his work in English translation may be found in *The King in the Golden Mask and Other Stories* (1982), and two stories not in that volume are included in *Black Feast: The Second Dedalus Book of Decadence* (1992)

BRIAN STABLEFORD is the author of numerous novels, including *The Empire of Fear* (1988), *The Werewolves of London* (1990) and *The Angel of Pain* (1991). Some of his short stories are collected in *Sexual Chemistry: Sardonic Tales of the*

Genetic Revolution (1991). This is the fifth anthology which he has edited for Dedalus; the others are: *The Dedalus Book of Decadence (Moral Ruins)* (1990), *Tales of the Wandering Jew* (1991), *The Dedalus Book of British Fantasy* (1991) and *Black Feast: The Second Dedalus Book of Decadence* (1992).

ALGERNON CHARLES SWINBURNE (1837-1909) lived to a ripe old age despite being a career invalid; his output of poetry remained prolific. "Dolores" is taken from the first volume of *Poems and Ballads* (1866; the other two volumes were issued in 1878 and 1889).

STEVE RASNIC TEM is a prolific writer of short stories for horror anthologies and American small press magazines. His one novel to date is *Excavation* (1987). He is a contributor to the Dedalus anthology *Tales of the Wandering Jew* (1991).